# Refracted

## The Celadon Circle
## Book Two

# Nicole Storey

*Even Angels Cast Shadows...*

*Refracted* (The Celadon Circle Book Two)
Copyright © 2015 by Nicole Storey

SACRED OWL
PUBLISHING

This book, and original publication, was registered with the United States Library of Congress Copyright Office.

Cover Design by DARK IMAGINARIUM Art and Design
www.darkimaginarium.com

Model: Alexandre Cukovic
https://www.facebook.com/AlexandreCukovic

Formatting by Rich Meyer of Quantum Formatting
http://quantumformatting.weebly.com/

# Refracted

## The Celadon Circle
## Book Two

**S**uffocating.

Quinn's lungs, constricted and burning from constant exertion, screamed for air. Legs as weak as matchsticks, he stumbled around another piece of machinery he couldn't name. His fingers trailed along the corrugated surface. Toxic snowflakes of burnt-orange rust peeled away and drifted to the floor.

The vacant factory had seen better days. It was a labyrinth of dark passages, tipped catwalks, and fetid air. The cloying scents of diesel fuel, damp concrete, and urine clung to him. It seeped into his clothes and the pores of his exposed skin. Quinn imagined how horrible the smell would be if it were August instead of October. He swallowed hard against the bile that crept up his throat.

Rounding a corner, he tripped over a nest of moldy blankets and something squeaked. A rat the size of a Chihuahua scampered from the pile. Quinn halted his labored progress until the rodent's fat, leathery tail disappeared beneath a scarred desk. He shivered. Rats were the least of his problems but he still hated them. He nudged the makeshift den with the toe of his boot and prayed no more critters were home. Quinn speculated on the number of derelicts who took refuge in the dreary, crippled building, and hoped none of them squatted there right now. To be anywhere in his general vicinity meant death.

*Death.*

It was coming for him.

The sun climbed higher in the sky to burn away the fog that lingered around the scattered buildings of this abandoned industrial park. As the wet foundations dried, their lighter color hinted at subtle purity.

Illyria was also searching for someone to purify. Quinn wondered if he'd feel clean after she scorched him from the inside out with the touch of her hand or ran him through with her sword. Maybe, once his ashes mingled with her maniacal laughter and the wind carried them ever upward toward Heaven, he would be whole again.

Vengeance and guilt, with their voracious appetites, had gnawed at his soul for years: the victims he couldn't save, the family he left behind, the sister he tormented...nothing suppressed their cravings for long.

Once Illyria took his life, perhaps their hunger would be sated.

Unable to go any farther, Quinn's legs buckled. He crawled to a nearby wall and leaned against it. Moisture from the floor seeped into his torn jeans, adding to his misery. His lungs whistled as they sucked in air. Legs, splayed like a broken marionette, seized, and then cramped. Too tired to massage them, he clenched his jaws to keep from crying out.

In the silent, drafty room, the sound of a door shattering was akin to ringside seats at a car crash.

The angel had arrived.

# I Gabriel

Gabriel's footsteps reverberated off sleek marble walls and echoed throughout the antechamber. He winced, and felt he was committing a sin by disturbing the solitude of this pretentious palace. God forbid he scuff the diamond-inlaid floor.

Oh well, it couldn't be helped. He wasn't going to leave his vessel and transform to his natural state for a twenty-minute meeting with Michael. The archangel would get over it.

Or not.

As he took in the expansive staircase, Gabriel sighed and then began to climb. Why couldn't Michael's heaven be less demanding? The need to stretch his wings and fly was an itch he desperately wanted to scratch, but it was not allowed here. Neither were displays of power. Just a few of the ridiculous rules Michael had set to emphasize his position in the third Triad – as if they didn't know.

Legs pumping, his pace providing a pulse to the otherwise lifeless climate, Gabriel reflected upon his brother.

He wasn't sure how he felt about Michael. For as long as he could remember, the archangel had been a constant in his life. God knew Lucifer, His first son, would fall. He also knew Evil would be let into the Garden and the first sin would be committed. He created Michael to lead His army. Gabriel was created to be a messenger – a courier between humans, angels, and God.

And there were others: Raphael the Healer, Uriel the Light of God, Salaphiel the Patron of Prayer, and more. Gabriel rarely got the chance to interact with his brothers and sisters of the First Chosen, save Michael. They were all too busy with their tasks.

A mere decade before, Gabriel considered his older brother the image of a perfect seraph. Michael was humble, holy, and guarded their Father's children as if they were his own creations. Poor Raphael couldn't keep up with the number of healings their eldest sibling demanded of him. The ones who couldn't be saved were met at Heaven's gate by Michael himself, guided inside with words of comfort and love. Gabriel's only wish was to be as earnest and devoted as his mentor.

But something changed.

Gabriel paused in his ascent to admire the view through one of many impressive stained-glass windows that adorned the palace. He wasn't tired. He was worried.

Before him, the calm waters of a green sea stretched in a never-ending pattern of hypnotic rolls and crests. Its gentle waves embraced a shore in hues of purple and blue, smoothing the sands as a mother might smooth the brow of her child. In the distance, a whale breached the surface and slowly descended to the depths again.

The vitreous sea was tranquil today, nourishing. But Gabriel knew it could turn stormy and threatening without notice…just like Michael.

To his left, far upon rocky crags, a statue of an angel guarded his brother's domain. Wings spread wide and poised for flight, a dress rippled and billowed around her bare feet in pretend gales. Arms open, a serene smile softened the hard lines of her face. Through this particular piece of stained glass, she was painted in red.

*Perspective.*

Life was all about perspective. Through his eyes, the angel appeared covered in blood. To someone else, she might glow like the sun. He shook his head; his thoughts drifting back to the archangel.

Was it stress? Is that why Michael had become so callous? It was as if the brother he once knew no longer existed.

Gabriel pushed the thought away. It was a sin to question the actions of a superior, especially a First

Chosen. It was much worse to feel the way he did about his own brother – one who had been there for him many times in the past.

He ran a hand through the soft, brown curls on his head – a human gesture Michael would frown upon. Gabriel couldn't help it. Guardians had more interaction with humans and often picked up some of their mannerisms. Though discouraged, this flaw was tolerated. Developing strong attachments to humans was not.

Gabriel cleared the final step of the staircase, surprised to find himself at the top. He made a right turn and entered a passageway created of glass. Outside these walls grew a lush garden with every flower and tree imaginable. It was a favorite part of Michael's heaven that ended much too soon.

Gabriel pulled the cord that hung outside the elaborately carved door of Michael's office, and told himself he felt no strong attachment to his charges. Jordan, Casen, and the twins meant no more to him than other humans he had contact with.

From inside, a bell rang, signaling his arrival.

Gabriel wondered if it was a sin to lie to one's self.

## II Quinn

The screwdriver slipped, gouging a sizeable chunk out of Quinn's hand.

"Dammit!"

He hurled the offending tool across the yard while his brother snickered. Quinn shot Nathan a warning look, which only succeeded in making his twin laugh harder.

Quinn sighed and reflected on the past three months. They were frustrating nightmares strung together, measured in crawling hours, cheap whiskey, blood, and scalding tears he only allowed freedom when he was alone.

Nathan's laughter faded; his expression grew as somber as the day. Quinn wondered if his brother sensed his anxiety in the crisp October air. With the bond they shared, it wouldn't surprise him. Nathan was always quick to read his emotions, absorbing them like a sponge, sharing the burden. The connection was useful, especially on hunts. Being able to anticipate each other's moves is what made them such successful Slayers.

Now, Quinn found it embarrassing.

Although more open with his feelings around Nathan, he didn't like to appear vulnerable – out of control. Like graffiti on a wall that eventually bled through no matter how many times you painted over it, so were his insecurities. The stress of losing Jordan had caused him to become reckless, make stupid mistakes. Losing control could have devastating consequences.

Nathan grabbed two beers from a nearby cooler while Quinn wrapped his injured hand in a grease-covered rag. With a grunt and some popping of the knees, the two lowered themselves to the front porch steps.

For a while, the only sounds were an occasional call of a bird and the wind rattling the skeletal branches of the giant oak in the yard. No words were needed.

Snow would fall soon. Casen was out in the fields, preparing the cattle for the long winter ahead, making sure the barns that dotted their acreage were secure against the bitter cold. Quinn took another pull from his longneck bottle and wondered if Nathan had seen to Archer, Jordan's beloved quarter horse.

"Yes," his brother answered the unspoken question. "I gave him oats, fresh hay and water, and a good brushing." Nathan picked at the label on his bottle. "We're gonna have to do something with him soon. That horse is miserable, and neither of us rides."

Quinn stared into the distance, remembering how Jordan's face had lit up like a borealis the first time she'd laid eyes on Archer. She'd shared a bond with that horse almost as strong as the one he shared with Nathan. To give the animal away would be admitting defeat, giving up on the sister who needed them.

But Nathan was right. Archer was used to more interaction and exercise, and Jordan's absence affected him deeply.

Closing his eyes, a flood of images washed over him – happier times when he watched from a distance as Jordan raced through the pasture on the back of the magnificent animal, red hair rippling behind her like a cape, a smile of pure joy on her face. Her moments with Archer were probably the happiest in her life.

Reluctantly, Quinn nodded.

"Maybe we can loan him to The Good Shepherd Riding Academy for a while," Nathan said, referring to a local ranch that paired special-needs children with horses to help them gain confidence, learn to trust, and believe in themselves.

Jordan thought a lot of the program. The idea of Archer helping children while receiving some much-needed exercise and attention wasn't a bad idea.

"But only as a loan, though," he stressed. "Jordan won't be gone forever."

Standing, Nathan took Quinn's empty bottle and placed it upside down in the cooler with his own. Quinn was tempted to ask for another but drowning himself in alcohol would only result in a hangover the next morning and a headache that would linger for days.

Nathan retrieved another screwdriver from the tool chest and went back to work on the mangled Charger. Just looking at his baby made Quinn's heart ache and his blood boil. The car was a mess.

Three days before, on yet another tedious hunt, a Jersey Devil used the car as a trampoline...after Quinn ran into it. The results were a busted radiator, fan, and a hood that looked like Pegasus performed *Riverdance* on it. It would take many months and a lot of cash to make the repairs.

The angels had finally coughed up the dough, but still denied them time off. They barely slept. He and Nathan were sent on one assignment after another, to all corners of the country, leaving their uncle to manage the ranch alone.

Since that fateful hunt for the *Kongamato* in Tennessee, everything was different. The fabric holding their dysfunctional family together had unraveled, with one important thread lost in the fray. How were they going to pull their sister from the pits of Hell, which may very well be where she was right now? After all, she had left with demons.

So much needed to be done.

There were mountains of ancient lore on Cambions – half-demons – they needed to dig through. Quinn had no idea if there was anything specific on how to banish the demon part, and he no longer cared. Jordan was his sister. That's all that mattered.

The hardest part would be keeping her safe from angels once they found her. Word in the Celadon Circle was that the Powers That Be were still actively searching for her. For reasons unknown, Michael saw Jordan as a threat. Quinn wanted to know why.

For the past two months, their orders came from the Hornblowers, and never the same wings twice. Gabriel hadn't shown his face (or wings) since the day Jordan left with her demon father, Aamon. Of course, Casen shoving the business end of a pistol in Gabe's face might have something to do with their Guardian's absence.

It was obvious the angels were keeping them busy to thwart any attempt to save their sister. Well, that was going to stop.

The approaching rumble of Casen's John Deere signaled he'd finished for the day. Quinn helped Nathan put away the tools and cover the Charger with a tarp. They finished just as their uncle rounded the corner of the house.

With a curt nod to his nephews, Casen stripped off his leather work gloves and fished the remaining beer from the cooler. Staring toward the sky, he finished half the brew before pulling the bottle from his lips. Shoulders pushed back, jaw set – Quinn knew that look. It was the same stance, the same expression his uncle got on hunts when he tired of playing by the rules. Uncle Case was ready to make up his own.

"Come on inside," he ordered, eyes as dark as the coming dusk. "We've got work to do."

# III Jordan

She pulled her fingers through the wolf's thick fur in an attempt to calm down. If this tactic didn't work, she would more than likely strangle Gina.

*That bitch!*

As if echoing her sentiments, Koda, the wolf who'd adopted her, chuffed and licked his chops.

Jordan laughed. "I tell ya what," she said, scratching behind his ears. "If she pops off one more time, you can eat her."

Pulling her coat tight, she snuggled next to the wolf. In the Huron Mountains, snow was falling, and Jordan was homesick.

She missed flat pastures and open spaces. The mountains, though not very tall, were beautiful with their multitudes of fauna and wildlife. But the closeness of the forest paired with the ever shortening days felt stifling. She needed more sunlight.

Jordan craved the feel of grass under her feet and

the smell of hay. She missed her horse. She *ached* for her family. She'd give anything to look up some ancient lore, clean a gun, or cook dinner for Uncle Case and her brothers. Until they'd been taken away, Jordan had no idea how much the tasks she used to loathe meant to her – *defined* her.

She wanted to feel normal again.

The storm door leading to the enormous front porch, attached to an equally colossal cabin, slid open like a well-oiled machine. Jordan's heart gave a little pang as she remembered the storm door of her humble home in Wyoming that always stuck.

*God, if you're up there, please, get me the hell home!*

Ivy crossed the porch, zigzagging through rocking chairs and porch swings that swayed to and fro in the frigid breeze. When she reached Jordan, she handed her a mug of hot coffee, sank gracefully to the thick blanket Jordan and Koda shared, and took a sip from her own cup. Ivy had a thing for humorous coffee mugs. Hers had a picture of Darth Vader's face with the words "Who's Your Daddy?" The one she handed Jordan had a smiling stick figure stating, "I procrastinate and that's okay because I am ten times less likely to become a serial killer."

Jordan nodded her thanks as her half-sister leaned over to wipe a wayward tear from her cheek.

"Why do you let Gina get to you?" Ivy asked after a few minutes. "Rattling your cage is her favorite pastime – well, that, and spreading her legs for anyone who has more hair on their body than she does."

Forgetting her sadness for the moment, Jordan spit her coffee out, choking as she laughed.

It was no secret that Gina was into extracurricular activities, and she had the hairiest arms Jordan had ever seen outside of a zoo. Considering how bad things could be, Jordan should thank her lucky silver knife that her biggest problem right now was a psychotic Heinz 57 with "Daddy issues."

Looking at Ivy, Jordan found cool gray eyes staring back.

"Thanks," she said.

Ivy shrugged. "It only takes a few minutes to make a cup of octane with that fancy brewer Dad's got."

*Octane* was Ivy's pet word for their favorite brand of brew.

"I wasn't talking about the coffee."

"I know."

The two sipped in silence while Koda napped between them. Jordan couldn't believe it was only three months ago that her world went to hell in a sidecar with no brakes, no handlebars, and no GPS. She had no control on this downhill run. She was barely hanging on.

Back in July when the sun shined brightly, the

days were long, and children chased each other around an Arcadian lake, Jordan lost her family – lost herself. What should have been a routine snag and bag at a seedy campground in Tennessee had resulted in windswept revelations…and her death. Her demise had been temporary. Too bad she couldn't say the same about the predicament she found herself in now.

Death had been better.

"Have you seen Aamon today?"

Ivy's nostrils flared. Jordan knew she hated it when she referred to their parental figure by name. Ivy had no trouble calling him "Dad," but then again, Aamon was the only father she'd ever known.

Technically, Aamon was Jordan's father, too (just thinking about it left a nasty vomit taste in her mouth) – her *demon* father. His satanic duty was procreating with the common folk, also known as humans, to keep the demon population off the endangered species list. He'd possessed Richard Bailey, the man Jordan had grown up thinking was her real dad, the man Aamon had killed.

To be fair, Aamon hadn't mistreated her. For a demon, he was oddly…*human*. A handful of his children lived here at the cabin they called home, and he acted no differently than any other parent as far as she knew. He scolded, enforced rules, bestowed hugs, praised, and even provided tutors for schooling. It confused Jordan. Demons weren't supposed to act that way.

According to Ivy, Aamon's children stayed with him until they were old enough to be on their own. Some went out into the world to live normal lives with jobs and families. Others were given assignments within the demonic regime. Many were placed in government positions. Some were even sent to different countries.

The kids at the cabin ranged in age from twelve to nineteen. When she first saw the gigantic home, Jordan expected to find an orphanage full of Aamon's offspring. She'd been shocked to learn that only ten resided here, including herself. When she asked Ivy about the numbers, she'd only told her Aamon didn't like to talk about it.

Most of Jordan's half-siblings were nice. A few of the younger ones irritated her at times but that was to be expected. Only Gina gave her grief. From day one, the platinum Barbie-lookalike treated Jordan like a nuisance – a pimple on her otherwise unblemished face that she just couldn't get rid of. When Aamon was around, sugar wouldn't melt in her mouth but the moment his back was turned, she transformed into the hateful, sneaky cur she really was.

Cambions had latent supernatural powers that were not awakened until Aamon touched his children. Gina was a Dream Walker. Her gift (or curse, depending on how you looked at it) was the ability to enter and manipulate people's dreams. She could make sleepers see anything she conjured. She could also kill them.

Jordan hadn't had a decent night's sleep since she arrived. Gina entered her dreams every night and turned them into nightmares. Jordan had seen her brothers and uncle die countless times. She'd been attacked by Koda and endured the pain of having him eat her alive. The latest one found her strapped to some sort of sacrificial stone table while hideous creatures carved symbols into her flesh with wicked, curved knives. As soon as one symbol was carved, another would heal and disappear and the process started all over again. The first cut was always the deepest. Jordan screamed each time, and hated herself for it. In the background, Gina's laughter bounced off the cave walls.

Her hands shook. Jordan balled them into fists and took a deep breath. Ivy touched her knee.

Besides being able to harness enough electricity to stop a mortal's heart with a touch of her finger or fry them from the inside out, Ivy was also an empath. She could sense the feelings of others.

"Dad will be home later. Will you tell him about Gina? She's not supposed to use her power on anyone in the house."

"No."

Ivy pursed her lips. "Jordan, you're not sleeping! She has you wound tight 24/7. Why won't you say something?"

Necessity.

She refused to ask for help. It wasn't so much that she was the new kid here at Camp Demon. Jordan could handle that. She could handle Gina, too, and would – soon. The problem was that she couldn't risk depending on anyone. Things happened. People or circumstances changed. The ones you count on today may not be there tomorrow.

No. It was better that she take care of Gina herself. Her true family was miles away. Her Guardian chose obedience over loyalty. If she wanted to get back to the ones she loved, she would have to do it alone.

Gabe's golden eyes and familiar smile flashed in her mind. Jordan bit her lip and shoved his face out of her thoughts. Above everything else, the fact that the one being she could always depend on had lost faith in her – walked away and left her to this fate – hurt the most. Had he known she was a Cambion? If so, why hadn't he told her? Why hadn't he helped instead of abandoning her when she needed him the most?

"You need to tell Dad."

Ivy continued to flog the dead horse. Jordan appreciated her concern, but still couldn't be sure of her half-sister's true feelings toward her. Did she really care or was she bluffing to keep the situation under control – to keep Jordan from leaving. She wouldn't be surprised if Aamon had ordered Ivy to keep tabs on her.

17

"Tell Dad what?"

*Speak of the demon...*

Jordan hadn't heard the storm door open so Aamon probably transported to the porch from wherever he'd been. He looked handsome in a cranberry-red sweater, khaki pants, and Timberland boots. Not a strand of his salt and pepper hair (mostly pepper) was out of place. His blue eyes looked kind, but Jordan reminded herself that this stylish, middle-aged man was not Aamon. *This* was a puppet – some poor soul he possessed. The real Aamon probably looked like something born of nightmares.

That thought had her reaching for the silver knife in its sheath on her side, but she caught herself and faked scratching her leg instead. Ivy gave her a dirty look, probably sensing Jordan's disgust of the man who had impregnated her mother.

"It's nothing," Jordan mumbled.

Aamon sighed, a very human reaction. He was a good actor. Most demons were, though.

"Jordan, if you're having a problem you know you can tell me–"

"*I'm not.*"

Beside her, Koda growled, baring long, sharp canines. For the most part, the wolf got along with everyone in the house but had bonded with her, sort of like a familiar. If Jordan was unhappy, Koda sensed it.

The demon looked at Ivy, who shook her head as

if telling him to let it go.

He shrugged. "Very well."

Jordan hoped he would go inside and leave them alone. Instead, he pulled one of the rocking chairs closer and perched on the edge. Fingers steepled, he cleared his throat.

"I've just come from a meeting. Tomorrow, we have an appointment."

This was new. The entire time she'd been here, Aamon had not gone a day without reminding Jordan that she was on the celestials' most wanted list. The cabin and surrounding forest were protected against angels. To leave the area would mean certain capture.

Now, Aamon planned to take her from the safety of the wards.

"Where?" she demanded. "With who?"

Aamon looked away, not meeting her eyes.

"My boss."

*His boss*? Who the hell was Aamon's boss?

Ivy cursed under her breath.

*Aw, crap.*

# IV Gabriel

**M**ichael's office was ornate in the extreme. Marble columns, gold frames on the walls, statues, silk draperies, and the calming trickle of a stone water wall played on Gabriel's senses when he walked in.

The most remarkable adornment was the archangel himself.

In their true form, angels were pure energy derived from the planets, moons, stars, and all they encompassed. In Heaven, that energy had no boundaries, so angels took any form they wished. The only constant was their wings. In Heaven, those were always present.

Michael stood in the middle of the room. The sun shining through the large windows behind him provided a spotlight which illuminated his blond hair and licked at the edges of his deep-red wings like flame. A crisp white T-shirt stretched against his sculpted form. Khakis and boots completed the look.

Gabriel had never seen his brother in such casual attire – a middle-aged Ralph Lauren model going through an identity crisis standing in Donald Trump's office. He looked ridiculous.

"Michael," Gabriel acknowledged his brother with a nod. "You called for me?"

For a moment, Michael only stared. His eyes, sparkling with power, never blinked and seemed to pierce his very soul. Nervous, Gabriel spread his own impressive wings. The *whoosh* of displaced air as they unfurled was comforting – a familiar sound in the oppressive silence.

Finally, Michael returned his nod and spoke.

"Gabriel, I appreciate your response to my message, but do wish you had been more observant of the time."

Comprehension settled like a favorite blanket, and Gabriel relaxed by a degree. Michael was only upset because he was five minutes late.

*As if my tardiness is significant in the grand scheme of things.*

Evil multiplied on Earth at a rate they never anticipated. Demons collected human souls like old ladies collected cats. Jordan, a member of the Celadon Circle, was half demon, and they were no closer to solving her problem than three months ago.

*And Michael is obsessing over five minutes.*

Gabriel wished he could make him *see,* make Michael behave like the brother he had looked up to for so long.

Instead, he bowed his head. "Forgive me. I've been…distracted. I promise to do better."

The words coated his tongue like saccharin. They started out sweet but left a bitter aftertaste. Gabriel hated his weakness but couldn't help himself. Loyalty was wired into his very being.

As he waited for reprieve, Gabriel's emotions churned and thrashed like a monstrous squall. He questioned whether his subservience to Michael was design or self-inflicted. He hoped the former. Humiliation was easier to swallow if he could believe he had no choice.

"Very well, Gabriel."

The archangel turned away. Gabriel felt his strength return with every step his brother put between them. Before he could fully appreciate the passing of the storm, Michael stopped and looked back.

"Never forget, Gabriel; obedience must begin at home. We cannot request it from our Father's children if we refuse to embrace and exemplify it ourselves."

Was this why Michael paged him? Did he plan to scold him about rules he already knew?

Gabriel fumed. He wasn't a *malakhim* – a common angel. He didn't have time for a power trip.

Hoping to expedite Michael's time upon his soapbox, Gabriel didn't argue.

"Yes, brother, I will remember."

After another long look at Gabriel, Michael stretched his wings, giving them a little shake before folding them against his broad back.

"Sit down." He gestured to one of two leather-padded chairs across from the handsome cherry wood desk. "We need to talk."

*Finally.*

Gabriel lowered himself onto the seat, folding his large wings across the back.

Michael settled behind the desk. His gaze took in the entire room. Gabriel wondered if he was stalling and if so, why? By the time those silver-blue eyes met his, he felt as if he would explode – from nerves or impatience he wasn't sure. Michael's expression was unreadable.

"I've made a decision," he began.

Gabriel almost cheered. At last, his brother had come to his senses.

After discovering Jordan's Cambion status, Michael had suspended Gabriel's duties to her family, refusing to let him search for her or contact Casen and the boys. The archangel was convinced that she presented a threat, though he never disclosed his reasons.

Gabriel had spent the entire month after the fiasco in Tennessee pleading with Michael to see the situation as it really was. Jordan, like her brothers and uncle, remained a loyal member of the Celadon

Circle. God had given her the rare gift of Seeking. Surely their Father would not bestow such a crucial and strenuous ability to someone unworthy – someone evil. There must be a way to help her.

Michael disagreed.

"Gabriel," he'd snapped. "You know as well as I that there is no way to cure a Cambion! She isn't possessed – it's in her blood, part of her DNA." The archangel had clenched his fists, eyes glowing. "There. Is. No. Help."

Undeterred, Gabriel argued that perhaps God had a greater purpose for Jordan's condition, one their Father had yet to explain. He begged for permission to speak with the Virtues – angels whose responsibilities were to ensure God's intentions were executed. At this request, energy had flown from Michael's palms, blasting Gabriel halfway across the lobby of The Focus. Other angels gathered at the central meeting place had looked on, alarmed, but quickly turned away. Gabriel had lain on the cloud-covered floor, seized by spasms of incredible pain, and watched through tendrils of mist as his brother took to the air and disappeared. That had been his last encounter with Michael…until today. Gabriel secretly rejoiced over the archangel's amended decision.

But his euphoria proved short-lived. Anticipation often builds us up before words tear us down.

"I have decided to terminate Guardianship for the

Bailey family. You may be assigned to another family if the need arises. For now, I would like you to assist the Hosts with their duties at The Focus."

Michael's words scattered about in Gabriel's mind like fallen leaves caught in the wind. He couldn't put them in an order that made sense. Why take away Guardianship for Casen and the boys? With Jordan in the hands of demons, now was when they needed a Guardian most! If Jordan refused to adhere to Aamon's rules or rocked the boat in any way, the demons would threaten the lives of those closest to her. They would crush her resolve and make her submit to their demands.

Unconsciously, Gabriel shook his head. Jordan had a problem with powerhouse-types who made demands instead of requests.

*Knowing her like I do, she won't just rock the boat – she'll capsize the darn thing.*

He could only imagine the torture Casen and the twins would be subjected to…the look on Jordan's face as she begged for their lives. It was too much.

Gabriel stood up. Panic pulled at his wings and flooded him with power, the force of which sent his chair flying into the stone water wall.

"No."

Michael's eyebrows inched toward his hairline. "No?"

Ignoring the warning tone in his brother's voice, Gabriel pressed on. "Michael, this is insane. Why would you take away their Guardianship *now*? Casen and the boys are members of the Circle. Their sister is being held by demons. Who do you think they'll go after when Jordan tells them to take a flying leap?"

Gabriel's golden eyes flinted blue as Michael lounged behind his desk, seemingly untouched by his outburst.

"Save your words, Gabriel. My decision is made."

With the snap of his fingers, Michael repaired the broken chair. It slid across the plush carpet and came to rest behind Gabriel's legs.

Michael's steely gaze bore into him, demanding obedience. Waves of pain, like fire and ice, washed over Gabriel's soul. The intense heat seared to the point of permanent damage and was then assuaged by a frigid blast, only to be replaced by flames again.

The message was clear. Gabriel could sit down and accept Michael's authority or, well…he didn't want to think about the alternative. This torture was enough.

His legs trembled, but Gabriel managed to keep his expression blank as he lowered himself onto the chair with dignity.

A muscle twitched in Michael's face, his thin, bloodless lips the only physical manifestation of the archangel's annoyance, and maybe surprise, at his younger brother's resiliency.

Slowly (too slowly for Gabriel's liking) the pain

diminished. He returned Michael's harsh stare, never flinching. Part of him wanted to lash out, to inflict a little pain of his own, but there was no point. It wouldn't improve the status quo. No, he would have to appeal to the elder's compassionate side – if he still had one. Gabriel was beginning to wonder.

"I'm s-sorry."

He had trouble pushing the words past the fury he felt, but the stutter worked to his advantage. Michael's shoulders relaxed slightly.

"I've been their Guardian for a long time. I can't help but care for their well-being."

Something – a tenderness of sorts – flashed in Michael's eyes like a shooting star and died just as quickly. For a moment, Gabriel saw the angel he used to be.

"I know you do, Gabriel, and that's the problem," Michael stared down at his hands. "You care too much."

Gabriel shifted in his chair.

Michael looked up and smiled, but the gesture didn't reach his eyes.

"Did you think I hadn't noticed? I see how attached you've become to them." The archangel's voice was discordant, like a piano slightly off key. "Of all the angels I know, you are the one who loves the strongest."

Gabriel said nothing. Was Michael upset or envious?

"Perhaps that is the way our Father made you, but it can't be allowed to continue."

"Why?" Gabriel dared to whisper. "Aren't we supposed to love them?"

Michael sighed. "Yes, of course, but we are also supposed to keep Evil at bay. When you become too enamored with certain humans, it clouds your judgment, prevents you from doing what is right instead of what is *easy*."

"I don't understand."

Michael was quiet. Gabriel waited.

"Sometimes, the responsibilities of one duty take precedence over another. Our primary task is to keep Evil in check. If we grow lax in that responsibility, there will be no human race to care for. On occasion, sacrifices must be made for the greater good."

"*Sacrifices*? That's what Casen, Nathan, and Quinn are to you now?!" Gabriel slammed his fist on his brother's elegant desk, cracking the surface. "A few months ago you called them the best Slayers in the Circle. How did they go from receiving your praise to lambs tied to the stake waiting for slaughter?"

Gabriel stood, too furious to sit still. His hands shook, eager to wrap themselves around Michael's neck and squeeze until his head popped off.

"They are people, Michael, *our people*! They've given everything to the Circle. You want to talk about sacrifice? They go days without sleep. They risk their lives to help us keep humanity safe. They obey without question and never ask for anything in return." Gabriel leaned down into his brother's face, daring him to move – to challenge him now. "They have done nothing wrong. For you to abandon them goes against everything we are."

Michael gripped the arms of his chair, his knuckles white. His dilated, manic eyes darted around the room as if looking for an escape.

"How can I make you understand?" Michael huffed and crossed his arms. "The Baileys are in a delicate situation. One of their own has been revealed as half-demon. Will they continue to abide by the rules of the Circle or stand with Jordan? I need to know where their loyalties lie."

He stood and came around the desk. "I'm not abandoning them, brother, and I am hurt that you jumped to that conclusion. You are too close to this situation. I need someone objective – someone who cannot be manipulated to act in a way that could endanger lives."

"Who?"

As if on cue, a door, partially hidden by a hanging plant with trailing vines, opened across the room. Gabriel and Michael turned at the same time to see a beautiful angel enter the office.

The innocent white dress she wore did not weaken her strong, purposeful strides. The lush, sweeping hair could not soften the stern expression.

She came to a clipped halt beside Michael, carriage straight, arms held stiffly at her sides. She wore her vessel like the soldier she was. Gabriel's spirit fell like an axe, cleaving a huge split somewhere deep inside.

*Illyria.*

# V Quinn

The abrasive, raw temperature inside the house had nothing to do with the weather. As the three men shambled to the kitchen, Quinn noticed how dejected and empty the rooms they passed appeared. It wasn't that they were dirty, not really. There was a bit more dust than usual, a few more cobwebs clinging in the corners, but with him and Nathan on hunts for days at a time and Uncle Case left to rattle around like the last bean in a coffee can, the house stayed fairly clean.

Quinn's eyes fell on the coffee table. Normally cluttered with books and at least one coffee cup, the blank surface looked too clean, sterile. The plaid afghan that had belonged to their mother always rested on the back of the couch when it wasn't keeping Jordan's feet toasty-warm. It now lay folded and forgotten on a chair in the corner. Shadows that were once held at bay by the bright candle she kept burning in the window crept eagerly across the walls and floor. Soon, they would swallow the room completely.

Quinn remembered how he had yelled at Jordan for that candle, claiming her habit of leaving it lit when she went to bed would one day result in an inferno. His words, wickedly sharp and hurled with precision, had left her a sobbing mess on the floor. She'd been fourteen. It was the last time she had ever shed a tear in front of him. A few days later, Uncle Case told him Jordan kept a candle burning to serve as a beacon so they could always find their way home, as a symbol to hold onto while they were away, as a reminder that someone who loved them kept their names close to her heart and in her prayers.

Quinn bit back a sob.

Standing at the faded laminate counter, Casen put on a pot of coffee while Nathan rummaged inside the refrigerator for sandwich fixings. Almost every room in the house suffered from Jordan's absence, but this room seemed especially forlorn. The kitchen had been her domain.

From the time she was old enough to follow a recipe, Jordan had kept them all fed. There were quite a few failures during those first years. The men had choked down burnt biscuits, dry meatloaves, gluey mashed potatoes, and lopsided cakes. Gradually, her cooking had improved. By the time she was thirteen, Jordan could take the most meager ingredients and turn them into a delicious meal.

*And I never thanked her – not even once.*

An old vase filled with wildflowers sat in the middle of the kitchen table. Jordan had picked them a day or so before they left for Tennessee. Now, there was nothing left but shriveled brown stems, the water long used up. Scattered around the vase, dried petals lay where they'd fallen, memories of more normal times.

Uncle Case forbade them to touch the pitiful remains, as if throwing them away would be equivalent to tossing any chance they had of getting Jordan back. So the dead flora remained on the table – a shrine of sorts – and waited with the rest of them for her return.

They sat down to eat. Quinn attacked his sandwich with gusto, his hardy appetite rarely affected by anything. But his hunger waned when Nathan pushed his food away after two bites. His brother had lost weight. Quinn watched him lift the coffee mug with shaking hands. The dark brew sloshed over the side. Nathan's eyes, partially hidden behind wisps of hair in desperate need of a trim, were lifeless and far away. He seemed unaware of his trembling hands, the spilled coffee, or anything else. He'd taken to falling into these trance-like states far too often.

Quinn and Casen's chairs moved at the same time and still, Nathan didn't notice. They met on either side of his chair, Quinn with a dishtowel and

Casen with a bottle of Black Bush.

"Nathan."

No reaction. Uncle Case set the bottle of Irish whiskey down and placed a calloused hand over the top of Nathan's mug to steady it while using the other to gently pry his fingers away.

"Nathan," Casen said a bit louder. "Let go of the cup, son."

Quinn busied himself with the spilled coffee.

For as long as he could remember, Nathan had been the rock he'd clung to. At 6'4" and 225 lbs. of pure muscle, his brother was a formidable Slayer. He could snap necks, plunge knives through thick bone. He never backed down from an adversary, often going hand-to-hand against creatures with extraordinary strength, distracting them so Quinn could sidle up and deliver the fatal blow.

Brute force and powerhouse techniques were just a few of Nathan's talents. As easily as he could take life, he could also give it. Hands that broke ribs and crushed skulls had delivered baby calves and mended tiny bird wings. He had a brilliant mind that could find answers where none seemed to exist and a heart as big as the Chrysler building. Nathan was the one they all came to for answers…for hope.

*My brother's falling apart and I'm cleaning up coffee. Damn, I'm such a douche.*

Quinn straightened and tossed the dishtowel on the counter. Casen reached for the whiskey the same way Chinese people reached for tea. It was his preferred brand of medicine. If it didn't cure what ailed you, it sure as hell could make you forget about it for a while.

Nathan rubbed his weary eyes with the heels of his hands and then pulled them down his face, as if hoping to wipe away the months of confusion.

"I phased out again, didn't I?"

Quinn placed a hand on his brother's shoulder. God help him, he didn't know what to say. Their positions were usually reversed with Quinn, always quick to anger, pissed off about something trivial like a scratch on his car, and Nathan soothing his twisted ego with words of comfort. The one time Nathan needed him to be the strong one, the one with the right words to ease his pain, and Quinn felt about as useful as a condom machine in the Vatican.

In a choked voice Nathan said, "I have no idea what's wrong with me."

Casen slid his coffee cup toward him, now spiked with a generous glug of whiskey. "Sip this," he instructed, and moved back to his seat. "I know exactly what's wrong."

*Uncle Case to the rescue*. Relieved, Quinn took a calming breath.

Nathan drank his coffee and waited for the explanation. Casen spiked his own brew before passing the bottle to Quinn.

*Guess we all need medicating tonight.* Quinn

took his seat and followed suit.

Uncle Case cleared his throat and pointed at Nathan. "You're exhausted, son. You ain't getting more than an hour or two of sleep a night."

Nathan opened his mouth, perhaps to protest, but Casen held up a calloused hand and stopped him before any words escaped. "Those bible thumpers upstairs work you boys like dogs, and the few nights you have free are spent rambling around the house like a ghost with no one to haunt."

Casen slid the paper plate with Nathan's sandwich in front of him and grabbed their empty coffee cups for refills at the pot. "Eat," he ordered, his tone leaving no question for argument. He crossed to the counter like a man with a mission.

Quinn was relieved to see a spring in his uncle's step again. Nathan must have felt the same. He picked up the remainder of his turkey sandwich and took a bite, chewing and swallowing like a prisoner condemned to a life of hard service.

After cups of spiked coffee were back in front of their respective owners, Casen sat down and placed his feet firmly on the old linoleum, hands on his knees – gestures that were usually followed by serious conversation. Both boys paid attention.

"While Nathan finishes his food, we're gonna do some talkin'. Afterward, Quinn and I will check our weapons supply and you–" he looked pointedly at Nathan, still taking rabbit bites of his sandwich, "–are going to bed."

Nathan slammed his hand on the table – a sign of how tired he really was. He was hard to rile.

Quinn studied the dark smudges under his eyes and wondered how he'd missed them before. Then again, his bedroom was on the other side of the house from his brother's. He wasn't aware of Nathan's nocturnal wanderings and sleep deprivation.

"I'm not a fucking kid!"

Nathan was cursing. Yep, he was definitely frazzled. Quinn could curse like a sailor on a three-day bender when the mood struck him. Nathan's language was usually as clean as the Pope's.

Uncle Case blew a deep breath out through his nose, sounding a lot like Jordan's horse when he got impatient while waiting for his oats. "Son, calm down."

"Don't tell me to calm down," Nathan growled. "I'm not your son."

The room went silent. Even the ancient refrigerator stopped wheezing. Quinn closed his eyes and wished he could push his brother back over the imaginary line he'd just crossed.

Uncle Case had taken over as patriarch of the family after his brother – their father – was killed by a demon. In many ways, he was a better parent than their dad. Though he loved his children, Richard Bailey lived a lukewarm existence at best. For the most part, he'd been apathetic, numb. The life of a

Slayer fed on his emotions like a parasite, leaving a shell behind.

Casen, on the other hand, made sure to remind them there was more to life than the Circle. He encouraged hobbies outside of killing monsters and ancient lore. He'd bought Quinn the first clunker he'd ever fixed up.

Quinn smiled, remembering how he'd balked when Case dragged him out to one of his seldom-used outbuildings and rolled open the doors. The hull of that rusted Mustang resting on concrete blocks was the ugliest sight he'd ever seen. Quinn had restored many cars since then, including his own '66 Charger and Nathan's '69 Camaro. Some he sold for extra cash, but he could never part with that Mustang. He'd passed it on to Jordan when she turned sixteen.

Uncle Case had bargained for Jordan's horse. He'd scrounged up money for the internet, used laptop, and shelves of books since Nathan was kind of a nerd. His brother loved reading, researching anything to do with history or science, and had (in Quinn's opinion) an unhealthy passion for epic fantasy books. It didn't matter if the fads they pursued were temporary or not – from karate lessons to stamp collecting (God, Nathan really was a nerd) – Casen was there, cheering them on while Richard had kept to the shadows.

Still, Quinn couldn't imagine the guilt and stress his father had lived with, every breath spent protecting a child who wasn't his. The only person to share that secret was his wife, and she had died giving birth to Jordan. There were so many unanswered questions. Why had his mother gone through with the birth if she knew a demon had impregnated her? Why had his father died to keep Jordan away from demons when the angels were just as hell-bent on taking her away?

Quinn took a quick peek through half-closed lashes. A vein bulged in Case's forehead. His uncle flexed his fingers before uncapping the whiskey. Instead of spiking his coffee, he tipped the bottle to his lips and downed the remainder in three deep swallows.

"I'm sorry," Nathan whispered. "I didn't mean it."

His eyes were those of someone tortured. Swollen and bloodshot, the red veins magnified by unshed tears.

Casen took a deep breath. "I know."

"Please…"

Nathan held out his hand, as if needing something. Quinn wondered if he had any idea what.

Casen grasped his nephew's hand in both of his.

"I didn't mean it," Nathan repeated. "I don't know why I said it. I don't feel that way. I've never felt that way."

Casen nodded. "You needed to vent, to let the poison out. It's about damn time."

"Huh?"

"You keep it all inside – always have."

Uncle Case pointed at the sandwich. Nathan picked it up the way one would a heavy bag of rocks.

"You've got to have an outlet. Lord knows I don't agree with how your brother releases stress. He probably has several rug rats he doesn't know about, and every demon within the first three pits of Hell wants a piece of him, but–"

"Hey!" Quinn interrupted.

"–But," Casen continued, speaking over Quinn's grumbling, "he doesn't keep it *all* inside. Nathan, you can't always be the anchor for this family. Everyone has a breaking point. If you don't create some sort of outlet to release all that worry and tension, it'll end up killing you."

Nathan rose on unstable legs. Quinn jumped up, happy to be the one providing support for once, and wrapped an arm around his twin's waist.

"I don't know what to do – how to help her." His words, slurred from lack of sleep and alcohol, were barely discernible. "It's hopeless," he mumbled.

Casen got up and pulled Nathan's free arm around his shoulders. Together, they managed to half-walk half-drag him to his room. Once there, Casen pulled the quilt down on Nathan's bed and Quinn helped him to sit.

"What are we gonna do, huh?"

His brother continued to talk even though his

eyes were closed. Quinn unlaced his boots and pulled them off.

When Casen slipped the T-shirt over his nephew's head, a black leather necklace with a Crescents Rising protection amulet swayed back and forth from his neck. Jordan had given it to Nathan the same day she'd gifted Quinn the Celtic Warrior ring he wore. As he worked a knot loose in his brother's boot laces, Quinn wondered if Nathan ever bought Jordan anything. His chest tightened and he swallowed several times. He never had.

They got Nathan stripped to his boxers and tucked under the covers. It probably would have been easier shoving a wild boar into a burlap sack. Nathan complained that he wasn't sleepy, that they needed to plan. He flailed around and fell off the bed twice, once landing on top of Quinn.

"What the hell, Nathan?!"

His brother didn't drink much but wasn't a teetotaler, either.

*How much of that whiskey did Uncle Case give him?*

"Get off me, you oaf!"

Nathan patted Quinn's cheek.

By the time they got him settled, Quinn felt like he'd gone ten rounds with a sumo wrestler. Uncle Case, on the other hand, still had some juice – either that or he was a good actor.

He sat on the edge of Nathan's bed and spoke

softly. "Don't worry, son. Get some rest while Quinn and I do some research. In the morning, I'll fix us a good breakfast and we'll fill you in."

His brother was snoring before they left the room.

Back in the kitchen, Quinn cleared off the table while Casen fixed a fresh pot of coffee. "I think you gave him too much whiskey."

The coffee pot gurgled as if in agreement.

His uncle picked up a brown pill bottle off the counter and gave it a shake. "Nah, just slipped him a few of my Ambien. We won't see Nathan again until after lunch tomorrow."

Quinn frowned. "Are you supposed to take more than one?"

Casen shrugged and took his Stetson off. "He's a big boy."

In the study, they pored over research books: some modern religious texts written by professors of theology, others tomes so ancient the paper nearly crumbled in their hands. They needed spells, information, protection wards – and a miracle.

Hours later, Quinn placed another book on the growing pile balanced precariously on the long refectory table. He closed his eyes, pinching the bridge of his nose to try and ease the headache he'd acquired sometime during the night.

"Anything?" Casen asked.

His uncle leaned back in his desk chair before another tall stack of books. Quinn heard his back pop.

With a sigh, he said, "I found plenty of information on *Cambions* and *Nephilim,* but nothing we don't already know. I did run across another word associated with the two: *Paladin*."

Casen tapped his pen on a notepad. "Hmm…that sounds Latin. Does it give a translation?"

Quinn's eyes followed his finger across the yellowed page. He stopped at a phrase and snorted. "Yeah, if you can call it that." He cleared his throat. "'*Paladins* are warriors for the cause.'"

"Cause? What cause?"

"It doesn't say." Quinn drained the rest of the coffee from his cup and slammed it on the table. "As a matter of fact, it doesn't say anything else about *Paladins* other than the fact that they are rare, powerful, and 'hybrids of Light and Dark.'"

Casen groaned and stood up. He walked to the refectory table and flipped to the cover of a book in front of his nephew. The tome was huge – the largest anthology in the study, the brown cover bare except for a gold-colored symbol in the lower right corner. Although old, it was obvious by the preserved condition of the soft leather and the crisp lines on the symbol that the book had been well-cared for. Hand-written pages were filled with religious references, maps, stories, definitions, and runes – none of which Quinn had ever seen. Research wasn't his thing, though. He preferred hunting.

"Where did you find this book?" Casen slowly turned the pages.

Quinn pointed to one of the numerous bookcases in the room. "There, next to the last shelf."

His uncle turned another page and paused, hand hovering over the book. Quinn glanced down and his stomach rolled. A burning, sour taste climbed his esophagus and nested in the back of his throat.

"Case, what is this book?"

The language on the page had changed – the words as ambiguous as tea leaves in a swami's cup.

Casen flipped the book closed. "I've no idea. I know this study like the scars on my body. Most of these books have been passed down through generations of family – the others I secured myself. I have never seen this book before."

"Maybe Nathan bought it."

"I don't think so. Nathan would have said something if he purchased a book that constantly changes." He pointed to the cover.

Quinn leaned closer, sure his eyes were playing tricks on him. The symbol on the cover had been a golden bird in flight. Now, there was a pentacle with a cross in the middle, both in a majestic purple.

He looked at his uncle, who nodded. "The book's grown at least two inches in thickness since I've been standing here."

As members of the Circle, not much surprised them anymore. Quinn thought they'd seen everything but this book was altogether different.

"What do we do with it?"

Mesmerized, he watched as the symbol on the cover slowly faded and a new one – this time in black – emerged in degrees, growing darker and more defined – a pair of wings.

Casen picked the book up. "I'm gonna keep it in my safe when we're not studying it." He ran his hand lightly over the cover. "Something tells me it's more powerful than anything we've ever seen. We don't need it falling into the wrong hands."

Quinn opened his mouth to agree and yawned instead. The hands on the grandfather clock inched toward 3 a.m. They had been at it for almost six hours.

Casen guided him to the door. "Let's get some sleep and take another look in the morning."

Quinn nodded and moved to the stairs.

"Quinn."

He turned back around.

"I just want you to know that the changes you've made haven't gone unnoticed. I'm proud of you. I know it hasn't been easy."

Overwhelmed, Quinn's eyes dropped to the floor. Casen was right, it hadn't been easy. He was a damned good Slayer but a piss-poor brother and nephew.

In Tennessee, Quinn had realized he put the best of himself into the hunts. The scraps left for the ones who mattered most were no more than dregs – cold and unappealing. He'd always given more to the Circle than his family because it was *safe*. There were no attachments, no anxiety if he failed. The people whose lives depended on him were strangers. Quinn did his best, but never lost sleep if a mark managed to slip the noose. The fact that everyone couldn't be saved was a truth every Slayer accepted. If they didn't, the job would drive them mad.

After losing his parents, Quinn couldn't bear to suffer that deep, piercing ache again. If that made him a selfish bastard, so be it. He'd rather live with the stigma than stand at another grave and wonder why it hadn't been him instead.

Circumstances were different now. Quinn understood that hiding behind the Circle wouldn't change a future he couldn't control. His family needed him. Maybe they'd have a better chance of surviving the storms to come if they did it together.

He wasn't quite there yet. Sometimes the urge to rebuild the thick walls he'd surrounded himself with for so long was overwhelming. Quinn had no idea the most difficult battle he'd ever endure would be with himself.

Halfway up the stairs, he paused and whispered g'night to his uncle who watched from below.

# VI Jordan

Jordan tossed and turned in bed, worried about the meeting to come. Aamon assured her it was routine – that all of his children eventually met with his boss. Ivy agreed, but was uncharacteristically quiet the remainder of the evening.

After counting sheep, meditation, and a Daughtry CD failed to lull her to sleep, Jordan sat up and patted the space beside her. Koda sprang onto the bed, turned three times, and then curled up with a contented sigh. Jordan normally didn't allow him to sleep with her. The wolf was a bed-hog and he snored, but she needed his comfort tonight.

She lay down and ran her fingers through his sable-colored fur. If someone told her a few months before that she'd end up living in a house full of Cambions with a pet wolf, she would have reached for a weapon. It was amazing how contrary her life had become.

"Koda, what am I gonna do?" she whispered.

The wolf snored in reply and she smiled.

◇◇◇

He was a strange one, that's for sure. Not that she had much experience with wolves. They sometimes roamed the pastures back home looking for an easy meal. The donkeys did a good job of keeping them at bay. When they didn't, a blast in the air from a shotgun did the trick.

The day she came across Koda, Jordan was walking a deer trail in the woods that surrounded the cabin. While animal tracks were everywhere: rabbit, deer, raccoon, wolf…the trail itself was clear of pine straw and obviously well-used.

She rounded a corner where the brush grew thick on both sides of the path, and a growl interrupted her woolgathering. Jordan's head snapped up and a headache bloomed. The unknown threat woke the demon inside. She knew her eyes were glowing. Power erupted from her core and flowed to her extremities like water, making her hands tingle. She had no idea what she could do with that power but wasn't above finding out if it meant saving her life.

The wolf lay a few feet in front of her; its dark-brown coat meshed perfectly with the trees and brush. If not for its eyes, which were two different colors – one blue and the other yellowish-green – she would have stumbled right into it.

Jordan slowly retreated, backing away with tiny steps, when something rattled and the wolf cried out. It was then that she noticed the mangled, bloody leg and the trap that held it fast in razor-sharp, spring-loaded jaws.

*Fucking hunters.*

Due to the false complaints of a disgruntled farmer and a lying politician, Michigan's Department of Natural Resources legalized the first wolf hunt in fifty years, set to begin in a month. Some drunken hunter with an I.Q of two must've jumped the gun.

The wolf looked pitiful. She couldn't leave it. The ass who'd set the trap could return any time. Jordan fumed at the placement of the steel death-device. Any animal running around this densely-packed curve in the trail would never see it until it was too late. Even if they did, they wouldn't have room to veer off the path to avoid it.

Hunting for food when one couldn't afford another option to feed their family was one thing, but killing because you got your rocks off on it was sick and cruel.

The wolf whimpered and her heart broke. Looking around, Jordan searched for a way to free the animal or a flaw in the trap's design. There neither. The chain attached to an O-ring on the trap was wrapped around a thick tree and padlocked.

*Oh, God, what can I do?*

She'd gotten fairly good at suppressing the

demonic power when it flared unexpectedly. She'd watched, repulsed yet undeniably interested, when other kids at the house practiced their abilities without a second thought as to what the consequences might be. Aamon had offered to help her explore her own skills but Jordan had refused.

"I don't want to."

The evil passed to her from Aamon was not her choice. What she did with it was. She would never willingly call on that power, much less use it. Tapping into energy derived from demons had to leave a stain on your soul. She might be a Cambion but she was going to try like hell to keep her soul untarnished.

"Jordan, those powers could save your life. You need to know how to use them."

She shook her head.

Aamon threw his hands up. "Why can't you trust me? The demon is all you see, isn't it? If you could look past that, you'd see there's a father inside," he pointed to his chest, "one who wants to help you. But dammit, Jordan, you've got to give a little."

His words sounded sincere. Part of her – the exhausted, heartbroken part – wanted to believe him. She was tired of fighting a battle she didn't even understand. It would be easier to accept the situation and make the best of it. The problem was she didn't know how. She had not been raised to give up or take the easy path. She wouldn't even know how to look for it.

But, God, she was tired.

"I don't *want* to be evil."

Aamon stared, lips parted slightly. Jordan could almost pinpoint the moment when comprehension knocked him over the head.

"Oh, hon…" He swallowed hard and Jordan watched his Adam's apple rise and fall. "Is that what you think – that you're evil?"

She shrugged, not wanting to admit it out loud. Giving it a voice might make it true.

"Listen to me. Being a Cambion does not make you a bad person. Being a Nephilim does not make you a *better* person. You are still you, Jordan, just…more. The powers you inherited from me and the grace you took from Sariel can both be strengths or handicaps. It depends on how you use them."

The wolf whined again and Jordan thought about what Aamon said. The capacity for evil was there and always would be. She could feel it inside – sometimes alert and pacing the length of its cell, other times resting in the corner. But the girl who risked her life to save others was there, too – and she was stronger.

The realization caused her eyes to glow but the pain that usually accompanied the manifestation did not come. It gave her hope. With caution, she approached the wolf.

"Look here, boy, I only want to help," she said

softly, inching closer.

She wished she could make her eyes go back to normal but anxiety kept them brightly lit. The wolf watched every step she took. Sweet Jesus and Mary, what was she doing?

Jordan was so intent on gauging the wolf's reaction, she forgot to watch where she placed her feet. An exposed root was her undoing. She waved her arms wildly trying to regain her balance but momentum carried her forward. She stumbled, rolled, and the wolf was there to meet her.

The first thing to register when she lifted her head was a pair of beautiful eyes and how the two different colors, though odd, looked right on the wolf. The second was a pair of ridiculously long canines that dripped warm saliva on her arm, and just how close she lay to those teeth.

She waited for her pulse to race and adrenalin to flood her body in preparation for the slaughter. Neither happened. Jordan realized she wasn't afraid. She should have bowed her head, avoided eye contact, and shown submission. Instead, she stared at the wolf in awe. He cocked his head to the side as if listening to secrets.

It was unreal, but Jordan didn't question the wolf's trust, which she wasn't sure she'd earned. There wasn't time. She crawled over to the tree the trap was anchored to and grasped the lock.

*Damn.*

If she had her pick set, she could pop this baby in a minute flat. Unfortunately, it was at home, her *real* home, where she should be instead of tramping about in the woods rescuing a wild wolf which would probably eat her as soon as she set it free.

"Stupid, stupid girl," she mumbled.

She could go back to the cabin for help. Jordan imagined the look Gina would sport when she begged Aamon for help. Ugh. She'd rather be eaten by the wolf. No matter what happened, she would never ask him for help. Ever.

So, she did the only thing she could. Her soul would be damned or it wouldn't. She couldn't leave the wolf to die.

Concentrating on what she needed to do, Jordan tried to harness the power that swirled inside like smoke. She focused on the chain and imagined it thin and brittle, easy to break. Jordan pulled power into her hands. They vibrated with energy. She sent up a silent prayer.

The chain didn't break. Instead, several of the links closest to her fingers grew hot and then turned soft, gooey. Jordan pulled them apart like taffy.

*Okay. Not exactly what I had planned but it works.*

Later, she would reflect on the fact that she melted a steel chain with her bare hands and freak out about it. Right now, the wolf still had the worst part of the trap wrapped around its leg. How in the happy crap was she going to get it off?

Kneeling beside the butchered limb, Jordan's mouth flooded with saliva and she fought the urge to hurl. The leg was broken, the bone exposed.

Her breath came in shallow gasps and she broke out in a sweat. Panic bubbled like noxious fluid in a test tube. "How do I fix this, huh? I'm not a friggin' vet!"

The surrounding wood was silent in reply.

The forest slipped into an opaque evening gown. Sharp lines grew softer as shadows prepared for bed. The sun fought hard to hang onto its position in the sky but could not compete with the high mountains. Fall and winter would always belong to darkness in the Hurons.

The wolf nudged her hand. She felt sure it was his way of asking for help, to finish what she'd started. A tear rolled down Jordan's cheek. She couldn't do this. Her body might contain all the power of a nuclear reactor but a fat lot of good it would do her if she had no idea how to use it.

"I'm sorry," she whispered, gently rubbing the wolf's head, letting the tears she hid from everyone else fall freely. "I'm so fucking sorry. I'd save you if I could. I wouldn't care if my soul turned as black as smut. Your life is worth more than mine." Helpless, she waved her hands above the trap. "Get off, dammit! Release!"

And to her surprise, it did. The trap sprang apart

with such force, it startled them both. Jordan fell back on her ass and the wolf jumped, snapping his jaws.

Without hesitation, Jordan waved her hand again, this time over the busted leg. *Heal*, she pleaded, drawing more energy from her core and mentally pushing it down her arm. *Heal!*

Pulsing blue light emanated from her chest. It traveled down to her hand, flashing in time with her heartbeat. In radiant waves, it flowed from her fingertips and surrounded the injury. Jordan held on, even though her body shook from the strain and she felt faint. When she finally let the power go, the backwash of energy hit her like a tidal wave. She collapsed, but managed to flip to her back. A shooting star was the last thing to cross her field of vision before her eyes rolled back into her skull.

She came to with the wolf lying beside her and Aamon calling her name. She opened her eyes to find him kneeling on her other side, a flashlight in his hand. Immediately, her teeth began to chatter. The moon had just broken the tops of the trees. She'd been lying on the frigid ground for...how long?

"Let me help you sit up," he said.

The forest swam in her vision and Jordan closed her eyes again until the dizziness passed. Aamon threw a coat around her, helping to get her arms through the holes and zipped up, then gave her a bottle of water. Jordan swallowed it eagerly, not realizing how dehydrated she was.

"How long have I been out here? What time is it?" Her voice was raspy.

"It's close to 8:00," he answered, looking on as she poured some water in her cupped hand for the wolf. His gaze traveled to the busted trap. "You did a good job on his leg. How did you heal him?"

Jordan shrugged. "I just did. I...I don't know how."

"You could have come for me," he said. "I would have helped."

She didn't reply. The truth was, she didn't want his help.

Aamon shook his head. "So, did the pulsing white light scare you? If you could spare five minutes out of your busy schedule, I could explain–"

"The lights didn't scare me, and they weren't white – they were blue."

In the glare of the flashlight's strong beam, she saw him frown. "Blue?" he asked.

"Yes. Why? Is that wrong?"

As if anything about her plane-crash of a life was *right*. She pressed her lips together to keep from screaming.

"I wish I knew the answer, Jordan, but the truth is, I don't...not for certain." Aamon shrugged and looked up at the sky, as if searching for guidance in stars or somewhere beyond.

Jordan rolled her eyes. He was looking in the wrong direction.

"This is uncharted territory for me," he continued. "I've never had a child who was part demon, human, and angel. I am fairly sure the blue color that surfaced is an inheritance from Sariel. Angels' eyes glow blue with power and so do those of their offspring – Nephilim."

"But you don't know." It wasn't a question.

He shook his head.

Jordan's heart pounded in her ears. Her father, the one who *made* her, the one she was supposed to rely on and trust, had no clue what she was. If he didn't know what powers she might possess or how she was supposed to adjust to this life, then who the hell did?

The answer, of course, was *no one*.

Angry tears blurred her vision but not so much that she couldn't identify the expression Aamon wore – pity…*for her*. Well, she didn't want his pity.

She wanted his head.

Until that moment, she'd managed to hang onto a flicker of hope. It hadn't been much – just enough to protect the small flame she'd thus far kept from going out. To Jordan, that light represented information, which she desperately needed in order to get back to her family. Though she never actually acknowledged it, the desire of not having to ride this crazy train alone had also been fed by the flame. She'd kept it burning through tears of frustration, homesickness, torture from Gina – and her transplant into a world she'd only glimpsed from the outside – usually right before she stabbed it with something pointed and coated in silver.

With the shrug of his shoulders and a confession of incompetence, Aamon not only dimmed the light, he smothered it. Jordan knew she'd never have the courage to try and revive the tiny spark, even if it were possible.

And she hated him for it.

The laughter that forced its way from somewhere dark and deep inside her had a maniacal edge. It ended in a scream that was both hair-raising and sad, like a banshee's wail.

Afterward, Jordan felt empty, yet somewhat better. She had purged herself of the toxins for the time being.

Aamon wasn't surprised by her PG-13 meltdown. He'd obviously been expecting it. Jordan didn't care. What her fiendish father did *not* know was that his admission of ignorance rendered him insignificant. He didn't have any information that could help her. She didn't need him. That realization was a double-edged sword. It was a kind of relief to know she was truly on her own. She didn't have to wait on others to make decisions. She could do research on the internet, use the books in Aamon's study – hell, she would even contact Gabe if it got her closer to her goal of reuniting with her family, of going home.

She was scared, though. Being on her own meant no one would have her back. Eventually, she would have to leave the warded safety of the Hurons. When that happened, she would not only have angels circling overhead but demons nipping on her heels. She could use a trusted friend.

*Oh well, no sense wasting time wishing for things I can't have.*

Jordan got to her feet and the wolf followed. The hair on the leg she mended was missing but there was no sign of the horrible injury. She reached over and scratched behind his ear. The wolf made a sound almost like a purr.

"Tell me one thing," she said. "That is, you know, *if you can.*"

Aamon ignored her jab. "What?"

"Why didn't the wolf attack? He's wild, yet never showed any aggression."

Aamon took hold of her elbow and, using the flashlight, began to guide her down the path to the cabin. The wolf walked on her other side as if he'd known her all his life.

"Did your eyes reflect your status as a Cambion?"

Jordan thought back. "Yes. I thought it would scare him but I couldn't change them back. I still have trouble controlling that part."

*Every part*, she added silently.

Aamon nodded. "That's how they identify us –

our eyes. God may have created the animals but the wolves have always belonged to us."

"You mean demons?"

Her father looked thoughtful but his voice was flat, barely above a whisper. "No. I mean those of us who are *misunderstood*. The wolves can relate. It's why they trust us above all others." He gave her a sad smile. "Maybe he can teach you."

Before she could reply, he walked on ahead, leaving Jordan to her new companion.

The luminous green numbers on her alarm clock cheerfully displayed the time of 1:12 a.m. Jordan wanted to fling it out the window. Giving up on sleep, she flicked the lamp on and reached for her copy of Rachel Caine's latest release. Might as well pass the sleepless hours with the Morganville Vampires. It was one of her favorite series. Myrnin could always make her laugh. If only real vampires were as humorous.

A muffled sound interrupted an excellent fight filled with witty snark, wooden stakes, and crossbows (God, she really needed to get one of those). Jordan thought she'd imagined it, but Koda raised his burly head, signifying he'd heard it, too.

After a full minute of silence, the wolf relaxed. Jordan flipped back to her spot in the book, eager to continue the story. The sound came again, louder this time. The eerie chord – something between a moan and a sob – made her jump out of bed and reach for her knife. Koda leapt to the floor and stared at the opposite wall, hackles raised.

There were only three bedrooms on the third floor of the cabin. She and Ivy occupied two. The last belonged to twelve-year-old Mazie. The noise came from there.

Jordan's bare feet sank into plush carpet as she silently crossed the room and eased the door open. The hallway, dimly lit by a single nightlight, was empty. A television grumbled from Ivy's room. She always fell asleep with it on. Koda brushed past her and went to sniff at the dark crack beneath the door to her left. She followed him.

Characters from the X-Men movies stared from numerous posters that covered Mazie's walls. Jordan smiled, remembering the first time she'd visited the girl's room. Their eyes seemed to follow her as she moved about, examining different knick-knacks, and she'd commented on it.

Mazie's laugh, like her personality, was warm and happy. Her soft-brown eyes twinkled with innocent mischief. "Of course their eyes follow you! The X-Men are my heroes. They watch over me."

Now, the girl called out in her sleep. Her small form thrashed upon the bed as she struggled to escape some nightmare-induced terror. Jordan looked up at an oversized poster of Hugh Jackman as Wolverine. "Dropped the ball on this on, Big Guy," she mumbled.

Koda, confused by Mazie's distress, took it upon himself to search the room for hidden monsters while Jordan attempted to wake her. She gave the girl's small hand a gentle squeeze. "Honey, wake up."

With her free hand, Mazie clawed at her throat. "Gina, please...I'm sorry!" She gasped for air.

*Gina.*

Jordan's temper flared like dry timber during a drought. Her eyes glowed, stimulated by power, fueled by hate.

# VII Gabriel

The soldiers in Michael's army were known as Aeons, and Illyria was first in command under the archangel. Handpicked by Michael, they were drilled in discipline, combat, and kept isolated to inhibit distractions. Due to their lack of communication with anyone except each other, Aeons were not as familiar with the human condition. Their loyalty belonged to Michael and Heaven. Any protection they provided for mankind was based on orders and nothing more. A majority of the soldiers behaved this way because they knew nothing else. They weren't intentionally apathetic – most of them used to be human themselves. But centuries of strict instruction and explicit decrees of behavior rubbed at the soul like sandpaper, smoothing the rough spots and transforming it into something more polished, though not necessarily better.

Gabriel studied Illyria and was reminded that, while some soldiers were creatures of habit and could not be blamed for their indifference where humans were concerned, Michael chose others specifically for their lack of emotional capacity.

Standing at attention, she kept her face devoid of expression and her eyes focused on the wall. Michael circled, appraising her appearance like one would a thoroughbred horse. If his brother ran his hands down her leg and asked for her foot, Gabriel would not have been surprised.

Finished with his inspection, Michael stopped in front of his best soldier. He stared at her face for so long Gabriel felt uncomfortable for her. Illyria, however, never moved a muscle. If Michael intimidated her, she didn't show it.

Somewhat of a mercenary in her former life, Illyria had received training in the military. She'd proved proficient in combat and with weapons. When not on active duty, she took it upon herself to deliver justice to those she deemed unworthy to live. Rapists, child and animal abusers, murderers...it mattered not. There were even a few people on the F.B.I's Most Wanted list that would never be found.

Illyria rationalized the killings by calling herself God's sword, purging the world of the "unwashed." Torn to shreds by an IED during the Gulf War, she'd been surprised when the reaper who came to collect her soul quipped, "You'll be moving a little farther south. Kind of ironic, especially since you always thought Alabama was hell in the summertime."

Lucky for her, Michael interceded. He offered to save her soul under the condition that she serve in God's army. Illyria was happy to accept. The reaper, on the other hand, was having none of it.

"I've got my orders. Death doesn't give reprieves."

"This is a special case," Michael argued.

"Why?" The reaper fingered the onyx scythe pendant that hung around his neck, eager to finish his job and move onto the next, "because she's 'God's sword?' The last I heard, God didn't need help doing His job, Archangel. Humans aren't supposed to judge, and neither are you."

It was hard work convincing the reaper. Though angels themselves, reapers were a different breed and only answered to Death. The status of an archangel did not impress them. In the end, Michael got his way. He usually did. Illyria joined his Aeons and flourished under the extreme conditions he forced them to endure.

Gabriel believed the ex marine's real motive for killing 58 humans during her time on Earth was not as holy as she professed. The truth, he felt sure, was that she enjoyed it.

"That's an odd choice of attire, Illyria," Michael said.

Gabriel agreed. The flowing shift dress was pleasing with its lace and tiny straps. The white color and cut accentuated Illyria's perfect physique, honey-colored skin, and lush brown hair. If Gabriel had been in his natural form, he would not have noticed such things. The human soul he'd once shared his vessel with had departed long ago. Gabriel's soul sustained the body now, and his grace kept it from aging. This was vital in order to visit Earth undetected. The only flaw was that the longer his soul occupied a vessel, the more comfortable it became.

Right now, he felt anything but comfortable. Gabriel began to sweat – something he rarely did – and a strange sensation bloomed like a beautiful, virulent plant in the middle of his stomach.

Illyria gave him a wicked smile when Michael's attention was diverted. She returned to the model of subservience when the archangel turned back around.

"Forgive me, Commander. It was not my intention to displease you. You did not specify the attire for our meeting."

Her voice was strong, steady, with no hint of deceit. Michael nodded.

Gabriel wished he was someplace else. Illyria could add another talent to her resume – musician. He wondered how long she'd been playing Michael. It was embarrassing to see someone as powerful as his brother strung up and strummed like a harp.

"I do apologize for my oversight," Michael said.

"I should have explained this assembly would be brief and your uniform would suffice." When Illyria continued to stand at attention and did not reply, he added, "Repose."

She relaxed to a degree, switched one mask for another, but the soldier could be seen beneath the surface – a mirror that reflected the past and the present. She clung to it like a talisman. Gabriel wondered just how close she kept the killer.

"Gabriel," she acknowledged. "It's always a pleasure to see you."

Instead of answering, he whirled on Michael. "*Illyria* is going to replace me?"

She stepped aside as Michael came forward. "Yes, Gabriel. Illyria is now in charge of Jordan's situation. She will leave tomorrow and you will report to The Focus."

Behind the archangel, Illyria smiled sweetly. Gabriel managed to resist frying her soul and mailing what was left to demons for hellhound chow, but just barely.

"Michael, please tell me how this makes any sense. Illyria is an Aeon. How is she supposed to improve Jordan's circumstances?"

Head tilted, his brother's eyes bore into him. Gabriel didn't flinch or look away. He had a right to know.

Michael must have come to the same conclusion. He took a deep breath and blew it out loudly. "As

I've already explained, I need someone impartial – someone who can take in the status quo with fresh eyes. Illyria may be able to devise a solution, and with her special training, she will be able to keep Casen and his nephews safe."

"And you believe my time would be better spent helping the Hosts mediate and give advice at The Focus? I'm an archangel! I can help–"

"Gabriel, no." Michael pulled him into a tight embrace. "Please, trust me on this," he whispered. "I need you to stand down and let me handle it."

Gabriel was too shocked to answer. His brother was not one to display affection, which worried him. He wished he could take Michael's hug at face value, but his instincts screamed desperation. Love had nothing to do with it.

Michael started to pull away but Gabriel held him in the embrace a moment longer. "I know something is wrong," he said softly. "You are not yourself and haven't been for a long time." Michael went rigid in his arms. "Use caution, brother."

Gabriel let go and, ignoring Michael's flared nostrils and clenched jaw, continued in a voice loud enough for Illyria to hear, "Do you swear no harm will come to Jordan or her family?"

"I do," Michael replied. "My objective is to find a result that will work for everyone involved."

Gabriel nodded and made his way to the door. He turned the knob and looked back to see Michael and Illyria exchanging glances. He knew they were impatient for him to leave.

"I'll hold you to that." He spoke to Michael, but his eyes were on the soldier. "I know what Illyria's *specialty* is and it has nothing to do with keeping people safe."

As soon as he closed the door, Gabriel transported to his heaven. He didn't care if it upset Michael that he didn't use the stairs. The archangel would sense the excess energy from his departure and know he had truly left. That was all that mattered.

Gabriel took a moment to let his eyes roam the quaint cottage he called home. It wasn't large or handsomely decorated. The furniture was worn but comfortable. The rooms were small but inviting. A multitude of picture windows acted like magic portals to a fairytale forest and a whispering brook outside. Like Gabriel, it was simple, peaceful, nothing like Michael's heaven. He wanted to go outside, sit on the porch swing with the plump cushions, and let the sounds of nature ease his mind.

Instead, he lay on the couch, closed his eyes, and let a sliver of grace slip from his vessel. It wasn't much – just enough consciousness to possess something very small, something he could control safely from a distance. Carefully, Gabriel transported the tiny blue spark.

The next second, he had safely concealed it in the flourishing garden outside Michael's office. Soon, a curious black and yellow butterfly lighted nearby. Angels' grace drew creatures of all kinds. The innocence of it closely resembled their own.

Gently, Gabriel directed his grace inside the insect. He waited, letting the butterfly adjust to his consciousness, and then persuaded it to fly to the window ledge of his brother's office. A gold-colored lamp resting on a side table blocked Gabriel's view inside but that wasn't a problem. He didn't need to see – he needed to *hear*.

Butterflies can't see or hear like humans do. Instead, they sense vibrations through their antennae and wings. With a few adjustments Gabriel was able to transform those vibrations into words. He put his little insect buddy into a restful state and settled down to listen.

"Have the arrangements been made?"

Michael sounded preoccupied. Gabriel heard the shuffling of papers.

"Yes," Illyria answered. "Everyone has been given instructions. I will be made aware of any updates which, of course, will be passed to you."

Illyria paused before continuing. "You know, Michael, all of this worry may be exaggerated. The girl could be a Cambion and nothing more. You didn't sense anything unusual when you approached her in the barn the day she had the vision of the *Kongamato*."

What was Illyria talking about? What could Jordan be other than a Cambion? It didn't surprise Gabriel to learn there was more to the situation. Michael was expending way too much energy and time for a simple demon incident, *and he'd known*. He'd known Jordan was a Cambion .

He heard a crash, the sound of breaking glass. "That's just it, Illyria! I've been in close proximity of Jordan hundreds of times over the course of her life and never sensed the demon inside had grown more powerful."

"Perhaps her human essence is stronger – so strong it dilutes the demon genes."

"Or perhaps it's something else," Michael countered.

His tone was caustic, like ammonia. The usual controlled, infallible demeanor his brother presented like a badge of honor had burned away. What remained was raw panic and urgency. This was the real archangel, the part Michael kept hidden.

"I can understand why you didn't sense that her demon powers had grown – you're rarely around Cambions, not to mention that Aamon hadn't fully released them yet. But if Jordan is also part angel, I mean, wouldn't that be *easier* to detect?"

*Part angel?!*

Back in his Heaven, Gabriel's eyes flew open.

He sat up so fast he almost lost connection with the butterfly. Taking a few deep (unnecessary) breaths, he forced himself to relax and concentrate. He couldn't afford to miss a word they exchanged, but Illyria's insane gibberish echoed in his thoughts. She must be mistaken. To Gabriel's knowledge no such being existed. It was not possible.

"One would think so, especially for a more powerful angel like myself." Michael paused, perhaps to let the meaning of his words sink in.

Gabriel did not need to see his brother to know how he looked at that moment. Standing tall with fists clenched, his eyes would flicker with power – a warning for Illyria to remember her place. Michael did not like to have his authority questioned or challenged. Most angels in the Third Triad would never attempt it. Illyria, on the other hand, appeared to have no problem speaking her mind. Now that she was alone with her commander, the pretense of the obedient soldier – clearly another mask in her collection – had disappeared. Just like with Michael before, Gabriel felt sure this was the real Illyria, the brazen killer who did as she pleased with no fear of consequences.

"It would greatly benefit you to remember we are dealing with the unknown. If what I believe is true and Jordan absorbed Sariel's grace while in her mother's womb, her powers could be like none we've encountered before. She could very well have the ability to reduce your soul to a stain on the floor. Now is the time to exercise caution, especially since you have been charged with bringing her to me *alive.*"

The implication of Michael's words was the perfect plot for an outlandish, spectacular fiction story. Surely it couldn't be true, but what if...?

Gabriel needed to find out if such an occurrence was possible. He had an idea but Illyria's voice interrupted his train of thought.

"*Alive* I can guarantee," she replied. Her voice slowly migrated closer to where Gabriel had last heard Michael speak. "*Uninjured*, well, that's a check I can't sign just yet."

"You will not needlessly shed blood to satisfy your sick, twisted needs. I won't allow it. I need the girl whole if I am to determine her true nature." Michael's tone changed. He tried to sound threatening but came across slightly off, like a piece of classical music played on an electric guitar. The chords were there, but the song was not as powerful and moving. "Everyone's replaceable, Illyria."

She laughed long and hard. "Oh, dear commander, *aren't we all*? Remember, I know why Jordan's situation is so important to you. Do you honestly believe it has never crossed my mind how easy it would be to dismiss me from your service? Do you think I have not taken steps to insure myself a permanent place in Heaven? If I go missing, your dirty little secret will spread faster than a California wildfire. When your Father finds out, how long do you think it will take Him to strip you of that Archangel title you're so proud of or worse? I hear His wrath is the stuff legends are made of. After all, He sacrificed His own son for the sake of humanity. If He learned one of His most trusted children dressed up in His clothes and took it upon himself to play God with the very humans who were commended to his care…I can't imagine He'd be too pleased. As a matter of fact, I think He would be downright furious."

Gabriel was still. He pressed his fingers to his temples hard enough to leave marks and waited to hear what came next.

"Illyria," Michael began in his Let's-Be-Reasonable voice. "I need Jordan unscathed. I can't ascertain the strength of her powers if she is not able to function normally."

Illyria's voice now dominated. Gabriel wondered about the secret she dangled over his brother like a swinging ax. It must be powerful. The Aeon switched roles with the archangel as easily as politicians changed the minds of millions of people with a single, well-delivered sentence. It was all about patience and timing.

"Very well, Michael. I will make sure she is delivered without a scratch. How should I proceed if there is interference from the demons?"

"Kill them all."

"And if Jordan's family does not cooperate?"

Michael sounded sad, defeated. "Use your best judgment, but please remember I made a promise to my brother. Don't harm them unless you have no other choice. It would shatter Gabriel's soul into pieces too small to reconstruct. I've made mistakes I can never atone for. I have a long list of people I have wronged and it grows every day, all because of a single act of egoism. I'd like to keep Gabriel's name off of it as long as I can. He..." Michael's voice shook. "He has a pure spirit. My Father chose wisely when He made Gabriel a messenger between worlds. He cares about everyone. I think I could bear any punishment except having to look into his eyes if he ever finds out what I did."

"I'll keep that in mind, Michael. What you need to decide is how far you'll go to keep your secret. How many rules are you willing to break?"

Gabriel had heard enough. He directed the butterfly to a bright yellow flower nodding in the sweet breezes, released the creature, and retrieved his grace.

It was time to pay a visit to the Virtues.

## VIII Quinn

The gray Chevy pulling the horse trailer left a cloud of dust in its wake. Quinn watched it depart with mixed feelings – watched until it rounded the bend in the dirt and gravel drive. Sunlight winked on chrome and then it was gone.

He had no idea when he called The Good Shepherd Riding Academy that morning they would want to pick Archer up the same day.

"We would love the opportunity to have him, even if it is only temporary. We have more children than we do horses right now. Could we pick him up today?"

*So soon?*

Quinn suddenly had a hard time swallowing. Was he doing the right thing? Jordan loved that horse more than white bread. She wouldn't want him to be depressed. Archer was a sweet horse, a patient horse. He'd proven that these past few months when he fell into the care of two men who knew nothing about horses. The day they tried to saddle him with intent to ride was one he and Nathan both agreed to never breathe a word of. Through all their fumbling and half-assed attempts with buckles, bits, and bridles, Archer never moved, though Nathan swore he rolled his eyes several times.

"My sister is away…," Quinn racked his brain for words. "…on business, for an undetermined length of time. My brother and I don't ride and my uncle is busy with the cattle. We want to make sure Archer is taken care of until she gets back." He bit his lip. They already agreed to take him but still, Quinn had to ask. "What if he doesn't work well with the kids? I mean, I'm sure he will – Archer is a great horse. But, if by chance he doesn't, will you still board him? Make sure he gets exercise and attention? We'd be willing to pay–"

The nice lady on the other end cut him off. "Don't worry. If Archer is nervous around kids, we'll work something out. You're trying to do the right thing. Most wouldn't give his well-being a second thought. As someone who loves horses, I can appreciate that." Her voice, so soft and motherly, soothed and assured Quinn. "We'll take care of Archer. He won't go lacking for anything."

Quinn was still staring at the empty drive when Casen slapped him on the back. "I think Archer's gonna be just fine. Those people are real nice – Archer took right to 'em – and just think of the kids he'll help."

Quinn smiled, feeling torn. He was glad Archer would get the love and care he needed but wondered if his place at the riding academy would become permanent. Maybe the decision to let him go stemmed from some hidden suspicion that his sister was never coming back.

He turned on his heel and headed for the house. No, he wouldn't think like that. He might be a screwup, he might be a smart ass, but he was *not* a quitter.

Uncle Case kept up with his fast pace. "I sent word to The Powers That Be – told 'em to pawn their Circle assignments on someone else for a while. Told 'em we're gonna figure out this mess with Jordan, seeing as how they were too busy polishing halos and blowing trumpets to give a damn."

Quinn paused on the top porch step and looked up at the cloudless sky. There wouldn't be any snow today, but soon. "Think we'll have any trouble?"

Casen shrugged. "Who knows? We could worry about it, if you like. We could worry about swarms of locusts and wine turning to blood, too. If it happens, we can't do anything about it." He jerked open the storm door before it could stick and motioned for Quinn to go inside. "Let's focus on what we *can* do something about."

Nathan shuffled into the kitchen long after lunch. His

hair stuck up on one side of his head like a rooster's tail. His usually clean-shaven face was a day past a five o' clock shadow and he needed a shower. But his eyes were clear.

Quinn watched his brother dump that morning's coffee grounds into the trash and rinse the pot. Once Nathan had a fresh pot brewing he turned to Casen, who flipped through the mystery book Quinn found the night before.

"What did you give me?"

At least he didn't sound upset, which proved his brother was thinking clearly. Nathan could usually see the reasoning (if there was any) behind decisions made by the family. Quinn generally ranted first and reviewed later.

Uncle Case turned another page and squinted at the print. "Ambien," he answered without looking up.

Nathan plucked a pair of reading glasses from the counter and passed them to Quinn, who slid them across the table to Casen.

"One Ambien knocked me out for...how long was I asleep?"

"About seventeen hours," Case said, staring at the book. "And I never said how many I slipped you."

Nathan rolled his eyes and lifted the lid of a cast iron pot on the stove. The entire kitchen filled with the heavenly aroma of their uncle's famous chili.

"I could eat the ass end of a rhino," he said.

"Well, before you go on safari, how about a dip in the watering hole?" Quinn waved his hand in front of his face. "You smell worse than a Skunk Ape and you're starting to attract flies."

Nathan flipped him off and headed for the stairs, coffee in hand.

Quinn smiled. It felt good to have Nathan back on even ground. He remembered the weeks leading up to the night before. His brother had good days and bad days, but the bad ones kept multiplying. He and Uncle Case should have done something before but Nathan rarely needed help – or so it seemed.

*Maybe there were times he needed me and I was too busy being a selfish prick to notice. Too busy running away from my own fears and pretending I didn't care.*

Quinn brought a hand down over his face. He was trying, he really was. He didn't know if he'd ever be able to allow anyone all the way into his heart. He was too good at barring the way once they got a foot in the door.

After Nathan showered and wolfed down two bowls of chili (Quinn didn't think he chewed at all, just swallowed it by heaping spoonfuls), Casen showed him The Book, as they had taken to calling the strange tome of anthologies, definitions, spells, and instructions.

"This is incredible."

Nathan slowly turned pages. Some were written

in English, some in Latin, some in Hebrew, Aramaic, and Greek. Several chapters contained nothing but symbols that wavered on the yellowed pages before being replaced by others.

"What do you make of it, son?"

Case's eyes twinkled in the dim light of the old fixture hanging precariously from the kitchen ceiling. Ancient lore of any kind always excited him.

Nathan chewed on a hangnail and frowned. "As far as I can tell, the references are biblical – even the spells and symbols."

Quinn sputtered, nearly choking on his beer. "Excuse me? *Biblical spells?* Isn't that taboo or something? If those religious coots started chanting and throwing chicken blood, I'd think their robes would burst into flames."

"There are different kinds of spells, Quinn."

Nathan pointed to some lines on the page he studied. The words looked like a bunch of slanted T's and dots to Quinn.

"This one here uses stones, dirt from the Holy Land, and the feather of a dove." His finger trailed down the paper as he read to himself. "Every spell has ingredients based in nature, the elements, or animals, but only bits of their fur, feathers, or bones. The animals must have perished from natural causes and the bones exposed by decomposition."

"In other words, you can't take a rifle and blow Bambi away for the use of a rib."

"Not hardly."

Case got up and paced. "Nathan, you ever heard of a book like this?"

He shook his head. "No, but I've never researched anything like it, either."

"You might want to give it some thought. In the meantime, when we aren't studying The Book, it stays locked in the safe in my room." He grabbed a bowl and filled it with chili. "Something tells me it's mighty important."

Quinn had no doubt the book was important. What bothered him was the way it magically appeared on their bookcase. An intruder could never have breached their security – unless it was an angel.

"I think we need to research wards to keep angels out of the house."

Nathan and Casen looked at him like he'd just announced his plan to become a monk.

"It makes sense," Quinn continues. "That book didn't grow legs and walk into our study, someone put it there. A human would never make it through the front door and a demon would have been stuck in a Devil's trap until we dealt with it. That only leaves one suspect."

Quinn could almost see the gears turning in Nathan's head. His brother knew he was right. When they'd returned from Tennessee, they had completely demon-proofed the house. Aamon's visit to Jordan revealed how lax their security was. Before, their work never followed them home. Before, demons rarely gave them a second thought.

*But that was before…*

Nathan nodded. "I think you're right. It sure as hell can't hurt. If we can't work something out with the angels once Jordan returns, we'll have to secure the house against them anyway."

Casen chewed slowly, a faraway look in his eyes. A moment later, he shook his head as if to clear the thoughts that had collected there and dropped his spoon. The sound of metal clanging against the empty ceramic bowl made Quinn wince.

"There's so much to do," he said, pushing his chair back from the table.

Quinn looked on while his uncle appeared to struggle with the decision to get up or stay seated. For once, his customary Stetson was nowhere to be seen. Case looked vulnerable without it. The wrinkles around his eyes stood out against his tan skin. There was more gray in his hair than brown. Every one of his fifty-two years was on parade.

Nathan headed toward the hallway.

"Where are you going?" Quinn asked.

"Uncle Case is right; there's a lot to do." He kept walking, calling over his shoulder as he disappeared around the corner. "We can sit and mope about it or we can get started!"

"I ain't moping, boy!" Casen barked. He dropped his bowl and spoon in the sink and followed his nephew through the door, all the while mumbling about disrespectful children.

Quinn laughed aloud and then clamped his lips shut, looking around to make sure no one heard. It felt wrong to laugh in the middle of the shitstorm that was their lives right now. It felt wrong to feel *good*, even for a second, while his sister was trapped with Hades' finest.

*Jordan wouldn't want you to feel that way.*

The thought brought him up short and he squeezed too much dishwashing liquid into the running water from the tap, causing a mountain of suds to spill over onto the counter and the front of his shirt.

It was true. For years, the only sounds to fill the rooms of this broken-down farmhouse were raised voices, whispered secrets, and muffled tears. If nothing else positive came from all the pain they inflicted on themselves and each other, Jordan would be happy to know that healing was possible – that her home was capable of hearing and feeling more from its occupants than anger and discontent.

A familiar sight greeted him when Quinn entered the study with a full thermos of coffee, mugs, and a box of glazed donuts on a tray. Nathan and Case sat at the refectory table with The Book between them. The glare from his laptop screen illuminated Nathan's face and his fingers flew across the keyboard. A pile of books, notepad, and pen were Case's research materials of choice. His bespectacled eyes traversed from The Book to his notepad, where he occasionally scribbled a word or passage, and then to a different book opened on his other side. Every so often, information was passed between them in soft, conspiratorial murmurs...They were in their element.

Quinn set the tray down at the other end of the table. It was on the tip of his tongue to ask what he needed to start on when his phone rang. Muffled strains of BOC's "Don't Fear the Reaper" sounded from his back pocket.

"Needs more cowbell!" Nathan shouted.

Casen rolled his eyes and Quinn grinned. "Always."

He didn't recognize the number that flashed on the screen but answered it anyway.

"Hello?"

Quinn pressed the button to activate the speaker and lay the phone on the table.

"Yeah," a rough voice answered.

Both Uncle Case and Nathan paused in their reading and stared at the tiny black device. The man on the other end sounded familiar.

"Is this Quinn Bailey?"

"Who's asking?"

"Lucas Fane from Mississippi. Not sure if you remember but you and your brother worked with me and my boys on a hunt in Louisiana."

Quinn thought for a moment. Two years ago,

wasn't it? A memory of slogging through a swamp with a scrawny teen – one with a buzz cut and a birthmark that surrounded his left eye drifted by.

"A *Rougarou*, right?"

Nathan nodded.

It had been a particularly difficult hunt. *Rougarous* were one of the worst types of demons. They could posses both humans and animals. Any person attacked by the demon, regardless of form, took on violent tendencies, ensuring their soul went to Hell when they died. Not only did they have to hunt down the *Rougarou*, which swapped bodies at will and attacked with swift ferocity, they also had to perform a ritual on each victim (the ones who lived) before they could scar their soul by shedding the blood of others. It was one of the most complicated cases they'd ever worked and it had lasted for over a month.

"That's the one," Lucas replied. "I didn't think it would take much to jog your memory. Those *Rougarous* are hard to forget."

"Please don't tell me y'all have another one down that way."

Lucas laughed – a guttural sound, like chunks of stone and glass in an industrial grinder.

"Hell no! I told the cloud crouchers upstairs if they ever sent me and my boys after another one of those bastards, I'd set their robes on fire."

It was Quinn's turn to laugh. He didn't know

Lucas and his sons well – that long hunt was the one and only time he'd ever interacted with them – but he remembered now that Lucas' wife died in a home robbery while he and his eldest son were on an assignment. Two men, high on every substance they could smoke, drink, snort, or inject, stabbed her with a rusty kitchen knife. Thankfully, the youngest boy slept through the entire incident and was spared. When all was said and done, the thieves stole thirty-seven dollars, Mrs. Fane's wedding ring, and her life.

Lucas' son, the one who paired off with Quinn in the swamp, confessed that his father had lost all respect for the angels after that. He said his father felt that since they risked their lives and gave up so much for the Circle, the angels owed it to them to keep an eye on their loved ones while they were away. They decided to stay members of the Circle but worked for the angels on their own terms.

"I've got the phone on speaker, Lucas. Nathan and Casen are here with me. What can we do for you?" Quinn poured the coffee. Nathan gestured for the donuts.

"Well, it's more like what I can do for *you*."

Casen frowned. "What do you mean?"

Lucas cleared his throat, twice. Quinn thought he sounded nervous.

"Ah…" He sighed. "Look, it's not a secret in the Circle about what happened to Jordan. I hate it; I surely do. It's just another example of negligence on the angels' part. We take all the risks and they don't do a damn thing for us."

Nathan put his half-eaten donut down, his expression slack. Quinn wished with everything he had that they could avoid this subject.

Over the imaginary line, Lucas' voice was thin, pensive. "*Why do we do it? Why?*"

Quinn wondered if the man had momentarily forgotten them. He faked a cough in hopes of bringing the conversation back on point – whatever the point of this out-of-the-blue phone call was.

It worked.

"Anyway, I heard the angels aren't doing much to improve the situation. Matter of fact, word is they're actively looking for Jordan. Have any members of the Circle offered to help y'all out?"

"No," Quinn answered, "and we don't expect them to. After all, we know who holds the cards in this game and it isn't the ones with the scars and calluses."

"I heard that," Lucas said. "You know, folks would be a lot better off if they learned one simple fact: There's a bit of darkness in everyone – makes no difference who or what you are – and desperation reveals it every time."

Quinn had no idea how to respond. For the most part, it was true. Desperation often revealed other things, too. A girl who avoided confrontation and believed she could never perform an act of bravery found the courage to kill a boy she'd known her entire life to protect her mother and a friend she barely knew. An angel, who watched over Jordan and witnessed every significant moment of her life from the time she was born, confessed that loyalty had limits – and the greater part of his loyalty was given to his older brother. A group of people who spent most of their lives defending humanity from monsters and spitting in the face of Evil realized they were meek and inept when it came to assisting one of their own. Some lines can't be crossed.

"Me and my boys, we want to help."

Uncle Case scowled and scratched his head. "Lucas, while we appreciate the offer, I really don't see how you can."

"You and your boys will land yourselves on Michael's shit list right below us," Nathan added. "We don't want to be responsible for that."

"Now look here, me and my boys know what we'd be getting ourselves into. If we all end up in a holy jail cell somewhere, at least we'll have enough for a decent poker game. In the meantime, I have a plan on how we can locate Jordan."

Quinn rolled his eyes. If Lucas had a plan worth listening to he would trim Michael's toenails. The man was a decent Slayer but wasn't known for having a high I.Q.

"And just what plan is this?"

"I'd rather not say over the phone."

Lucas made a noise with his mouth and Quinn groaned. He'd forgotten the man's bad habit of sucking on his teeth like someone who had eaten a steak and saved half of it between his cogs for later.

"The decision is yours. We're in Arizona right now, 'bout a day and a half out."

"What's in Arizona? Why so far from home?"

Something didn't sit right about this. Nathan threw Quinn a look that said he could close the harbor anytime, but he ignored him. Why would a man they barely knew, who was also a member of the Celadon Circle, want to help rescue their sister, who just happened to be a Cambion? Why would they risk their position in the Circle, and possibly more, for a couple of eighty-sixers and a half-demon?

Lucas chuckled. "What's in A-Z? Not a damn thing. A couple of hikers go missing, a body turns up with some animal bites, grandma falls in the backyard…you know the song and dance. Any little thing happens outdoors and a hundred people swear they saw the Mogollon Monster somewhere in the vicinity. As for the *why*, I have no clue. Why were you sent all the way to Tennessee a few months back? Hell, some people in the group get assignments close to home and some of us have to haul ass all over the country. It's a good thing they pay for my gas and Slim Jims."

*So that's what he spends half the day sucking out of his teeth.* Quinn grimaced, wondering if Lucas would be offended if he sent him a case of dental floss.

Maybe because he sensed hesitation, Lucas hurried on. "Talk it over. If y'all decide not to go this alone, give me a call. If I haven't heard from you by noon tomorrow, we'll head on home – no hard feelings." He expelled a sigh so deep he must have fetched it from his boots. "I know this is personal. I know you're probably wondering who you can trust. Just remember, my wife was taken from me because those bastards upstairs were asleep at the switch. My boys lost their mother. You lost both your parents. Haven't we sacrificed enough?"

Later, Quinn tossed the book he was researching on his uncle's pile and, without a word, went to bed. He'd been outvoted on whether or not to include Lucas and his boys in their personal business. He tried to keep a leash on his anger while arguing his case. For the most part, he succeeded, but sheer aggravation prompted plenty of growls and barks. Quinn wasn't used to going against the grain.

His reaction was a surprise to Nathan and Case, too.

"Are you both stupid? We don't need Lucas' help. It's a miracle the man can tie his shoes much less devise a plan to find Jordan."

Casen took his glasses off and rubbed his eyes. "Son, we need help. Lucas is willing to provide some. His idea may be a good one or it could be a dud–"

"Or it could blow up in our faces!"

His uncle proceeded without a hitch. "But at least he's *willing*. Why does this upset you so much?"

Quinn tried to laugh but anger turned it into a sound that could accompany someone vomiting up their shoes. "Why? *Why?!* He doesn't know us. We don't know him. Doesn't it seem a bit psycho that a stranger calls from way out in left field, or in Lucas' case, *Arizona*, offers to put on the nice, white jacket that straps in the back, and jump on our kiddie-ride to Hell?"

Nathan turned another page of The Book, his confident, peaceful demeanor a welcome change to the spring-loaded zombie he was before, but now Quinn wanted to shake him.

"He told us why. The circumstances are different but he still lost someone because of the Circle. Well, more specifically, those *in charge* of the Circle."

Quinn shook his head. "Nate, it isn't the same. The angels weren't the cause of his wife's death. Unless your family has a Guardian – and only those with Seekers do – they don't tend to sit around and babysit when we go on hunts." Before Nathan could open his mouth and spew more unwanted insight, he said, "Hell, we had a Guardian and still got screwed. Not to mention Jordan spent plenty of time alone when the three of us were on assignments."

"Maybe he doesn't see it that way," Casen said.

Quinn yanked hard on the chain as his temper

lunged. "I'll tell you exactly how Lucas sees it: He doesn't want to help because it's the right thing to do or he feels he can relate to what we're going through. He doesn't give a two craps about our sister – he's just pissed at the angels and wants a little payback."

"Personally, I don't care what his reasons are. He and his boys are extra bodies and we need 'em."

Quinn sat on his bed and faced the window. He watched as the light outside faded from dusky-blue to the barest pink, and waited. Lucas' offer skipped over his mind with feather-light fingers, creating an itch he couldn't scratch. He knew Uncle Case was right. Help was help and the why's shouldn't matter so much, but he couldn't shake the feeling that there was more to it.

The itch grew worse and still he waited.

He wanted nothing more than to lie down and close his eyes. He wanted to drift into oblivion and let everyone else research and plan, waking him when it was time to act. He didn't have the patience for groundwork. He only felt useful when he was *moving*. His eyelids drooped as the weight of exhaustion grew heavier.

But he waited.

The faint pink color grew deeper in hue. Through the window, Quinn watched as the pasture became more distinct. Cows began to stir. The land was waking up. He directed his attention to a steep hill dotted with trees in the distance.

Slowly, the light grew more intense, changing in color once again. Dark pink became brilliant orange. Like a sentinel taking his turn to guard the world while the moon slept, the sun climbed the backside of the hill, his golden rays casting the trees in shadow with every step.

Quinn squinted against the glare. His eyes watered and burned. He ground his teeth against the discomfort and waited.

In a sudden burst of luminous splendor, the sun completed the journey and took his place in the heavens. Quinn waited for that moment every morning since returning from Tennessee. The significance of a new day meant they made it through another night and most monsters would be kept at bay for a while. It meant they had another chance to make amends for their mistakes, and maybe get it right this time. It meant that Jordan, wherever she was, still fought, still breathed, still had a heartbeat. The sun would cease to rise if she didn't.

# IX Jordan

*ina.*

How could that hateful hag justify using her powers on a child? Jordan reflected on all the hellish scenarios the Dream Walker forced on her and her stomach rolled at the thought of Mazie having to endure such torture.

With that in mind, Jordan gave the girl's shoulder a brusque shake. "Mazie!" she hissed. "Wake up!"

Her half-sister exploded out of sleep and would have tumbled out of bed if Jordan hadn't stopped her. Eyes wide, curly hair plastered to her head with sweat, she raised her hands in a defensive posture. Jordan took a step back to give her some space.

"Are you with me?" she asked.

Mazie blinked once, twice, and then lowered her hands. Slowly, she raised her head.

"Jordan?" she rasped.

After getting a damp cloth and a glass of water

from the bathroom, Jordan sponged her sister's face and told her to drink. She didn't like her color at all. Mazie's flawless mocha skin looked icy – pale.

"What happened?" Jordan took the glass and put it on the side table, then sat on the bed and pulled the girl close.

Mazie shivered and snuggled next to her. The Black Beast inside Jordan clawed at its cage, eager for revenge – for blood. Though she kept her distance from almost everyone in the house and they had no problem giving her space, Mazie somehow missed the memo. She hadn't been pushy or invasive but, unlike the others, she wasn't afraid to show her feelings. Jordan had never met someone with such a joyful spirit. Mazie regarded her Cambion status the same way she did her curly hair and biracial heritage. It was simply a part of who she was. Before Jordan knew it – despite how hard she fought against it – the tiny girl with the big heart had won her over.

"It's nothing," she whispered against Jordan's chest. "Just a nightmare is all."

Even through the blankets, Jordan could feel her sister's rawboned shoulder blades. Mazie was small for her age – short and all angles. She wasn't unhealthy and ate like a high-school football player, but there was not a spare inch of fat to be seen.

*I should be so lucky*, Jordan thought.

She gave the girl an encouraging squeeze. "You mentioned Gina's name in your sleep. Don't tell me it's nothing. I know better."

Mazie twirled a strand of hair around her finger; a sure sign that she was worried or thinking hard on something.

"You know you can tell me anything, right?"

Bottom lip trembling, she nodded.

A few silent minutes of staring at her heroes as they watched from their respective places on the wall and Mazie stopped shaking. She motioned for the water and drained the glass.

"I broke her iPod."

Jordan ran the sentence by her fatigued mind three times and it still failed to grasp the meaning.

"What?"

Her sister sighed. "Gina's iPod was on a table in the living room. Someone sat a glass of juice beside it. I accidentally bumped the table with my leg when I passed by and the glass tipped over." Mazie gripped the comforter like a lifeline, something to keep her grounded in the here and now while she relived the incident.

"I ran to the kitchen for some paper towels. When I got back, Gina was there, holding her iPod and looking around. She...she saw me with the paper towels and started yelling. I tried to tell her it was an accident but she wouldn't listen.

"Aamon showed up, told Gina he'd get her another iPod, and that she needed to calm down. He said accidents happen and it was no big deal. She nodded, told me she was sorry for yelling, then went upstairs. I cleaned up the juice and thought it was over."

"But it wasn't," Jordan assumed. She kissed the top of Mazie's head, knowing the worst was still to come.

"No," she whispered. "On my way to bed, I stopped by Gina's room to apologize again. She would barely speak to me, just told me it was fine and to leave her alone. When I walked away, I heard her mumble something about *sweet dreams.*"

Jordan took a deep breath and asked, "What was the nightmare, Mazie?"

She didn't want to hear it, not really. Speaking the words would only confirm that Gina had no heart, and would likely push Jordan over the edge.

"I was in my bedroom – the one at my old house. My mom and dad were there…"

Mazie's voice was soft, eerie. It pulled Jordan in like a haunted song.

"I was standing on a chair. There was a rope around my neck. It was thick, tight, and I couldn't get it off no matter how hard I tried. I asked Mom and Dad to help but they only stared with blank faces. They looked at me like I was a stranger."

Gulping air, letting it out in broken spurts, it sounded like something (her heart) was lodged in Mazie's throat. Jordan grasped her hand and held on tight.

"I heard whispering but couldn't tell where it was coming from. Most of the room was dark, which I thought was strange. A streetlight on the corner usually kept my room pretty bright at night."

"The whispers got louder and my parents smiled, only it wasn't the smiles I knew before. Their eyes were wild, popping out of their sockets; they looked crazy."

Jordan could have stopped her there, *wanted to*, but Mazie didn't need to keep it inside, to relive the horror over and over like Jordan did. The quiet moments were the worst, when the day ended and she had nothing to occupy her mind. That's when the nightmares came back. Instead of diminishing over time, they grew like a cancer. Jordan hoped talking about it would be therapeutic – a balm for the girl's aching heart, an elixir to shrink the malignancy before it spread and dominated every moment, awake or not.

"My dad walked to the chair I was standing on and, for a second, I thought he was going to help me. His face changed, became less creepy-looking. He looked like himself. He took my hand…" Mazie choked back a sob. "He took my hand and I could smell his aftershave. I just wanted him to help me down and hold me like he used to.

"He gave my hand a squeeze and said, 'This is going to hurt, baby, but won't we have fun?' I didn't know what he meant. Dad let go of my hand and then, like magic, he was holding the end of the rope instead.

"I heard whispering again just before Gina walked out of the shadows. She was smiling like she'd just won a beauty contest. Her mouth was moving. The whispers crawled over my skin like cockroaches but I couldn't understand what she said. My mother hadn't moved at all. Her face was still crazed and she swayed back and forth like Gina's words were music."

Mazie licked her dry lips. "The first time Dad pulled the rope, I was too shocked to do anything but hang there. It cut into my neck and closed my airway. I couldn't think, couldn't move my arms or legs. By the time it finally registered that *my father* – the man I thought walked on water and held the moon – was trying to kill me, he'd already set my feet back on the chair and I could breathe again."

Kicking off the covers, standing on shaky legs, her sister wobbled to the attached bathroom for more water. Jordan would have gotten up to help but knew her offer would be refused. Mazie needed to prove to herself that she was physically okay. She needed to take some deep breaths, to move, to *be*. Jordan knew the feeling. After waking from a nightmare devised by a sadistic headcase, it was almost impossible to believe you came through unscathed.

Mazie emerged from the bathroom. Other than the glass, which occasionally rattled against her teeth as she sipped, she seemed more in control. It broke Jordan's heart to see her try to be brave. Mazie was so small, all but lost in the baggy T-shirt she wore. Jordan wanted to hug her, to erase the fear from her eyes and reassure her – and she would, but not yet. To coddle her would peel away the newly formed scab covering the wound.

"That's pretty much it," she said, waving her hand as if dismissing the subject. "It happened over and over. Gina would whisper, my dad would pull the rope, and I'd hang a little longer each time he did." She wrapped her arms around her middle. Water sloshed from the glass onto the carpet but she didn't notice. "Each time my toes found the chair, I would gasp for breath and plead with Gina to stop, but she just laughed and whispered again."

Mazie's eyes met Jordan's, burning with shame. Her chest hitched. "I shouldn't have begged."

A sweet, delicious heat formed in Jordan's chest. It spread like napalm, searing away every rational thought, dissolving the inner-voice that tried to remind her she didn't want to go there, that self-control was the only way to keep the beast restrained.

"Jordan, are you okay?"

Mazie's voice sounded far away but Jordan forced herself to concentrate. The girl had been through enough tonight. Gina was downstairs and wasn't going anywhere. Her hands itched to get around the twatwaffle's throat.

"I'm fine, sweetie." Jordan pulled Mazie into a hug and put the brakes on her speeding heart. "How about you? Are you okay?"

She felt Mazie nod and then the girl yawned widely. She was exhausted.

"Let's get you to bed."

Jordan straightened the blankets but Mazie didn't move, stuck while the need to sleep wrestled with the likelihood of another traumatic dream.

"I swear; Gina won't bother you again." As soon as the words cleared her mouth, Jordan felt her eyes smart, her vision eclipsed by salty tears.

Mazie must have noticed, too. Her teeth worried the skin on her bottom lip while her fingers danced through her curls. "What are you gonna do?"

Reigning in her anger and lust for Gina's head on a platter, Jordan tried for a smile. It felt as phony as collagen injections. "I'm just going to talk to her."

"Yeah, and I'm gonna marry Wolverine one day."

Mazie may have wanted to argue the point more but fatigue won out. As she shuffled past, Jordan pulled one of her curls. "If you and Wolverine ever do hook up, watch out for those shanks of his. A surprise appearance could ruin the mood real fast."

Mazie mumbled, "Don't talk 'bout sex. It can cause psychological damage to a kid my age."

Jordan tucked her in and was surprised when Koda jumped on the bed. He spun three times and curled up next to Mazie.

"Traitor."

Koda snorted, and her sister threw an arm across her new sleeping companion. "He likes me better."

Jordan kissed her cheek. "Nah, he's just waiting for your skinny behind to fall into one of the creases in the blanket so he can have the entire bed to himself."

Smiling, Mazie turned on her side and drifted off.

"Stay," Jordan whispered to the wolf. Koda's eyes were closed but his ears twitched at the sound of her voice. Ever vigilant, he would protect the girl and keep watch over her dreams.

Jordan barely made it out of the room before tremors took her. She squeezed her eyes shut as a deluge of images battered her like freezing rain, temporarily cooling the fire inside. Mazie, struggling on the bed, beads of sweat along her upper lip. The faint tremble of her chin as she spoke. The longing in her eyes for her parents. Defeat in her voice when she said she shouldn't have begged.

*Oh, God! No one should feel that small, that…damaged.*

Jordan wanted to cry, to scream to the heavens. She wanted to let go of all the emotion, just lie down, let it pour out, and be absorbed by the expensive carpet.

Instead, she headed for the stairs and Gina.

There was only one door open on the second floor. Jordan heard the rise and fall of music. Soft light spilled from within and climbed the opposite wall. Inside, Gina sprawled across her bed, a magazine in her hands. On a desk in the corner, her blue iPod rested in a docking station with two small speakers. Strains from *The Phantom of the Opera* flowed from them like liquid silk.

Her iPod played just fine.

# X Gabriel

Yasen's heaven rested in the center of the Helix Nebula, surrounded by the constellation Aquarius. The Second Triad was spread out amongst the galaxies. Gabriel hoped he wasn't wasting precious time by coming here. Virtues never stayed in one place too long. Thankfully, Yasen was a creature of habit. He refused to move unless absolutely necessary. He had been in the same place the last three times Gabriel visited. He prayed that was still the case.

He teleported to the Helix, then used his powerful wings to propel him to the center. As Gabriel travelled through dust, different ionized material, gasses, stars, and planets, he often caught himself hovering to admire the view. The colors were breathtaking: spectacular oranges, lucid blues, vibrant greens, dazzling yellows and reds, deep purples...Gabriel could explore for eons and never grow tired of this particular masterpiece his Father had created.

A Throne guarded the entrance to Yasen's heaven. Beryl-colored wheels within wheels, these particular celestial beings were some of the strangest amongst the angels. Their 'rims' were covered with hundreds of eyes. Members of the third choir of the First Triad, Thrones were assistants to Cherubim, who guarded the Tree of Life and the Sacred Garden. Gabriel was not surprised to see one placed at Yasen's door. As the senior Virtue, the angel had access to many important scrolls and artifacts. He was also their Father's most trusted advisor.

*Hello, brother.* Gabriel addressed the Throne telepathically. *I was hoping to see Yasen. Is he available?*

The Throne's inner wheel spun continuously while the eyes around its rim took turns blinking against the lights and cosmic dust. The effect left Gabriel feeling woozy.

*He is, and quite eager for your company. He has instructed me to allow you entrance.*

A rent appeared in the fabric of space to the left of the Throne. It slowly opened wider, revealing a sky-blue tunnel.

*May our Creator continue to bless you, brother.*

Gabriel entered the mouth of the tunnel.

*God be with you and protect you*, the Throne replied.

*And also with you.*

Gabriel watched as the entrance closed behind him. He drifted in the blue light until he arrived at a plain wooden door with an iron knocker. Before he could grasp the ornate circle, the door flew open to reveal Yasen – spectacles askew, white hair standing on end, and a big smile on his face.

"Gabriel! Come in, come in!"

Yasen pulled him across the threshold and embraced him with strong arms swathed in green robes. Immediately, Gabriel felt at peace. Yasen exuded confidence and strength. He was smart, kind, and never wavered in his purpose to Heaven and God. No matter how bad things seemed, he didn't worry, knowing it was all part of their Father's plan.

Yasen pulled away and held Gabriel at arm's length. The Virtue's green eyes were bright, alive with joy. "It has been too long, my boy, much too long!" He put a fatherly arm around Gabriel's shoulders and led him into his heaven.

The rooms in Yasen's home were unlike any Gabriel had ever seen. The walls and ceilings were round and smooth, as were the windows that looked out upon the magnificent nebula. His den boasted a handsome fireplace, sturdy, comfortable chairs, and floor to ceiling bookcases full of beautiful tomes.

A tray with a steaming teapot, two cups, milk, sugar, and a plate of chocolate-chip cookies rested on a small table between the two armchairs. Yasen directed Gabriel to one of the chairs and took the other for himself. He immediately poured tea, a ritual the older angel performed every visit and one Gabriel knew better than to decline. Yasen enjoyed "playing house," as he called it.

With drinks poured, the obligatory cookie consumed, and pleasantries exchanged, Gabriel searched for a way to broach the subject of Jordan's status. But he had no idea how to bring it up without sounding like he'd drunk more than tea. Fortunately, Yasen was observant.

"You look troubled, brother. Is all well in the Third Triad?"

Gabriel set his teacup on the tray. His hand shook, making it rattle against the polished silver.

"What it is, Gabriel? What has happened?" Yasen set his own cup down and removed his spectacles, which he polished with a corner of his robes. "Before you answer, let me say that I am a Virtue, dear boy. I have heard...*rumors*."

Gabriel wasn't surprised by this admission. It was hard to keep things from Virtues. Still, he couldn't help but ask. "Such as?"

Yasen smiled. "I'd rather hear from you first."

Gabriel hesitated. Yasen was his only chance for answers but if Michael discovered he'd gone behind his back, disobeyed orders, he would be punished – severely. He no longer cared about the angel hierarchy or the fact that Michael was in charge. He did not fear the pain, incarceration, or exile. His only concern was for Jordan and her family, and what would happen to them if Michael suddenly made him disappear.

"Can you promise what we discuss will be kept between us?"

Yasen placed his spectacles back on his nose and pursed his lips. "That's a strange request."

"I have my reasons which I will explain, but I need your word first, Yasen."

The elder angel frowned, an expression that didn't sit well on someone who was normally jubilant and steadfast. Gabriel felt guilty for laying this burden at Yasen's feet but had no choice.

Finally, Yasen said, "I cannot make any promises other than to hear you out and, if I feel the problem is above my position in the Second Triad, to only discuss it with our Father and no one else."

Gabriel took a swallow of tea to moisten his dry mouth. Coming to Yasen was the right choice. For the first time since leaving Michael's office he felt some of the weight lift, making it easier to think, to breathe.

"That sounds fair, brother. Thank you."

Yasen reached over and placed a hand on his arm. "Then share your burden with me, Gabriel. I do not like seeing you this way. Please, let me help."

After telling his story to Yasen, starting with the events in the Bailey's barn when Jordan's eyes first changed and ending with the conversation he heard between Michael and Illyria, the angel beckoned for him to follow and they ended up…here. Gabriel was overwhelmed by the cavernous room.

It was infinite. As far as the eye could see, the walls went on and on, climbing to forever. Cylinders rested in cubbyholes carved into the walls every few inches. Each cylinder contained a scroll.

There was no particular index as far as Gabriel could determine. Each cubby and cylinder looked exactly like the next. Yasen flew around the room on grand silver wings, stopping every few feet to pull out a scroll and quickly scan it.

"And you are sure they said the Cambion was also part angel?" Yasen hollered down to Gabriel as he replaced a cylinder and reached for another.

"Yes," Gabriel called back. "Michael said Jordan may have absorbed Sariel's grace while she was in the womb." He sat down on a rolling stool in front of a large oak table. More to himself than to Yasen, he said, "I don't see how that is possible. Jordan's mother would have to agree in order for Sariel to possess her, and why would she unless Sariel gave her a valid reason?"

"Was Jana Bailey the type of person who would agree to possession?" Yasen flitted to another section of the room.

Gabriel lay his head down on the table. "I don't know; I never got the chance to meet her before she passed. I was appointed the Baileys' Guardian a few months later."

"And that," Yasen continued, "raises another question. Only families with Seekers are given Guardians. You were sent to Jordan's family a few months after she was born, yet she did not receive her first vision until the age of fourteen. At a few months old, Jordan's position in the Circle was still undetermined. There is no way for an angel to foretell who will be a Seeker. Why did Michael send you to them so soon?"

Gabriel grabbed a quill from the table and rolled it between his fingers. *Another question.* That was the problem – too many questions and not enough answers. He thought back to the day Michael had named him Guardian of Jordan and her family. Not once had he questioned why; he'd simply accepted the position, accepted another order from his older brother like he had for as long as he could remember.

*Maybe it was because he knew she was a Cambion.*

With a groan, he stood up and paced. The sound of Yasen's wings overhead were driving him crazy. "What are you looking for anyway?" he yelled.

Dear God, he had to get a grip. He'd just raised his voice to an *elder* – something he would have never done before. Maybe Michael was right; maybe he *was* too close to his charges.

"Found it!" Yasen called, waving a clear cylinder.

By the time his brother conjured another pot of tea and some raspberry scones (Yasen had a weakness for human desserts), Gabriel felt ready to explode. His patience had grown thin. Every minute was important. Jordan, Casen, and the boys were in danger – he could feel it.

"If in fact Jordan is part human, demon, and angel, then she is a *Paladin*. That is the name God assigned to them."

Gabriel tested the word on his tongue. It was foreign to him. "There are others? Impossible! More angels would have heard of them if there were."

Yasen blew on his tea and took a sip. "No, but not for lack of trying."

"What happened?"

Yasen looked thoughtful. "When Lucifer fell, he was angry – so angry with our Father. He could not accept His love for humans, much less love them himself. He thought the flawed race was beneath us, and swore to never pledge his allegiance to those who would eventually destroy all that our Father created."

Gabriel nodded patiently. He knew the story of his older brother's fall from grace but Yasen had to tell things in his own way.

"Many years later, Satan made our brother one of the seven princes of Hell. Lucifer and the other six overthrew the Dark Lord and took control for themselves. It was then that Lucifer had the idea of *Paladins*. He commanded his fellow fallen angels to lie with humans who were possessed by the Dark Lord's demons. Lucifer assumed the children of this unique coupling would be the most powerful in existence. He would have been correct, but he forgot one very important detail."

"What?" Gabriel sat on the edge of his seat.

Yasen pulled his spectacles down and looked at him over the rims, his eyes fierce. "What happens to an angel if he or she falls?"

Gabriel closed his eyes, remembering his one and only trip to The Vault. "They lose their grace."

He had been a young angel at the time. His Father, whom he rarely saw, had asked Gabriel to accompany Him on an errand. He was only too happy to oblige.

"I want to show you something important, my son."

They transported to a small island surrounded by blue-green sea. Gentle waves lapped upon the shore. A sandy trail cut a path through tall trees dotted with colorful birds. The ground shook as something large and powerful lumbered farther away. Gabriel couldn't see it, but heard its sonorous call, which was answered several times from different areas on the island.

"Where are we?" Gabriel asked. He hurried to catch up to his Father who had started up the trail.

"This," He explained, "is a planet I created a long time ago. It is quite small compared to most, but it does not need to be large to serve my purpose."

As they walked, Gabriel noticed a beautiful waterfall which fed into a magnificent pool. Lounging beside it was an animal that resembled a saber-tooth tiger. Farther along, he saw a herd of Sauropod dinosaurs.

They arrived at an entrance to a cave. It was sealed, but the massive stone rolled away with the wave of his Father's hand. Once inside, they were pulled through another dimension in space and spit out in front of a vaulted room.

His Father whispered words of an ancient language and then placed His hand upon the door. Slowly, it swung open.

The expansive room twinkled with lights that looked like opals. Power pulsated through Gabriel in currents. The walls were fitted with shelves that held hundreds of small bell jars with nameplates. He walked closer to examine them. Inside each one floated a substance that was neither solid nor liquid. It was the color of pearls streaked with blues, oranges, greens, yellows, reds, and purples – the grace of angels.

Every so often, a jar would break. The grace

inside would either rise and dissipate or travel to a clear cylindrical opening on the far side of the room. Even less often, a bell jar would repair itself, complete with a new nameplate, and magically fill with another angel's grace.

"Father, what is this place?"

Dread made Gabriel's voice quake.

"When angels sin, they fall to Earth. Their grace is taken and stored here in The Vault. They are then made to live as humans."

His Father moved to a section of jars separate from the others. He gently picked one up and held it close to His face. The glass magnified His misty eyes. Gabriel saw the name *Lucifer* engraved on the brass plate.

"Depending on the infractions committed and how they live their lives as humans, there is a possibility of grace being restored. If they repent for their sins and live honorably on Earth, their souls return here when they die and their grace finds its way back to them.

"If their sins are too great or if they refuse to repent while on Earth, their souls go to Hell when they pass and their grace returns to the cosmos from which it was derived." He placed the jar back on the shelf and turned to His son. "This is the vault that keeps their grace safe until your brothers' and sisters' lives are finished as mortals and judgment is made."

Gabriel shivered, even though the air was not

chilly. "And those?" he asked, nodding to the section of shelves where Lucifer's grace lay shimmering in its jar.

"These are fallen angels Lucifer brought into his fold – Watchers. They, like your brother, are now immortal; kept alive by the Evil they embrace. Their grace cannot be released until their souls pass. For now, it sits…and waits."

"And that," Yasen continued, bringing Gabriel back to the present, back to the problems at hand, "is where Lucifer's plan fell apart. He, as an immortal filled with Evil, forgot that his fellow brethren were powerless. Instead of creating *Paladins*, he only succeeded in creating Cambions."

Both were silent for a moment. Gabriel now had a name for Jordan's supposed condition, but still didn't know if a *Paladin* was possible. He asked Yasen for his opinion.

The elder nibbled on another scone, eyebrows furrowed. "Let's consider what we know to be true. Richard Bailey was possessed by the demon, Aamon, who then impregnated his wife. That would make Jordan a Cambion." He dusted his hands of crumbs and took a swallow from his cup. "Now, according to what you overheard between Michael and his Aeon, he believes Jordan may have absorbed the grace of the Bailey's first Guardian, Sariel. The angel must have been in possession of Jana's body at the time for that to be plausible.

"I do not know why Sariel would need to possess Jana or how an unborn child – even a Cambion – could take an angel's grace. It has been noted that some humans can retake their bodies from demons, but the percentage is minute…" Yasen scratched his head, mussing his unkempt hair even more. "Perhaps that is how Jordan's mother did it. Maybe, with assistance from her unborn Cambion, Jana was able to take control *back* from Sariel. If so, then just like with the demon cases we know of, the angel would have been trapped and momentarily powerless."

"But is *that* even possible?" Gabriel could not fathom such an occurrence.

Yasen smiled. "My brother, if there is one thing I have learned in all my many years, it is that *anything* is possible."

"What should I do?"

Gabriel could barely wrap his mind around the fact that his ward could be the most powerful being in existence second only to his Father; much less how to proceed.

"Isn't that obvious, dear boy? You need to locate Jordan. She and her family must be protected at all costs while I search for more information on *Paladins*."

Gabriel made a strangled noise in the back of his

throat as he ground the quill in his fist. "I can't! Michael relieved me of my duties as Guardian and ordered that I serve the Hosts at the Focus."

"So?"

Propelling himself off the stool with a huff, Gabriel faced his older brother. "Yasen, Michael is above me in the hierarchy. I must obey him. To refuse is a sin."

"Goodness, boy! Who told you that?" Yasen pulled at his beard while a twinge of a smile played on his lips. "Michael is commander of God's army and the Celadon Circle. Where those two factions are concerned, yes; you must obey your brother's wishes."

Gabriel raised his hands. "Exactly!"

"But Jordan is no longer a member of the Circle. Her Cambion status makes it so. I received word that Casen and his nephews have taken a sabbatical from their duties. They are no longer Michael's concern."

Yasen must have noticed Gabriel's discomfort. Discussing the subject of disobedience made him feel like a sinner. The elder placed a hand on his shoulder. "You and Michael are part of the same Triad and the same Choir. He cannot give you commands unless you are directly involved with his posts in Heaven."

Gabriel felt like an idiot. All this time he'd done Michael's bidding without question. Why had his brother lied to him?

*Never again*, Gabriel fumed inwardly. *Never*

*again will I be Michael's simpleton.*

He would go to Casen and the boys, explain why he deserted them in Tennessee, beg for forgiveness, and help them find Jordan. It sounded like a good plan, but if anyone could throw a monkey-wrench in the works and blow it up, it was Michael.

"What if he pulls me back by claiming my presence interferes with his army? He *is* sending them to Earth to look for Jordan and he put Illyria in charge of the mission."

At this, Yasen seemed to grow taller (if that was possible). His eyes sparked like flint on stone. "As a member of the highest Choir of the Second Triad *and* the senior Virtue, my position is much higher on Michael's beloved celestial ladder. It is *my* wish that you assist Casen and his nephews in locating Jordan. When you find her, please make sure she is put somewhere safe and then contact me – *only me*."

Gabriel frowned at Yasen's choice of words. Before he could ask, the elder added, "Something is wrong here, Gabriel. There is more to this than we know." He closed his eyes tight. "I remember the day our Father spoke of *Paladins*, but not everything that was said."

"Is there any way to find out?" Gabriel prayed there was.

Yasen opened his eyes and winked. "Of course!" He pointed to the walls where an endless number of scrolls rested in cylinders. "It will just take more tea, scones, and time."

# XI Quinn

They had just cleared away the remains of a thrown-together supper when a rattletrap Suburban pulled up the drive. Nathan and Casen went to the front porch to meet Lucas and his sons. Quinn stayed in the kitchen. He wanted to retreat to his room or maybe move to a bar (preferably one with strippers) until they left. He'd managed to keep his snide remarks and doubts about Lucas' incentive to jump head-first into their hallucinogenic horror story to a minimum. Nathan and Casen were optimistic now that there were more hands on deck to search for Jordan, and Quinn just didn't have the heart to keep stomping on their hope.

He'd put the last plate in the dish drainer when a pair of roach stompers the size of small boats appeared in the doorway to the kitchen. The boots were attached to skinny legs dressed in threadbare Wranglers. Quinn's eyes drifted up to a faded Molly Hatchet T-shirt, big grin, and a strawberry birthmark that covered half of a young man's face.

Lucas' son, Brody, had changed in the two years since Quinn seen him last. The 18-year-old he'd gone swamp-slogging with dressed in camo, wore a boonie hat over his buzz cut, and had Skoal-stained teeth. The 20-year-old who stood before him now looked a lot like…him. The boots, jeans, and T-shirt were similar to what Quinn wore. Brody's hair was also longer, and sported a style that mirrored his own. Jesus, the kid even had a bomber jacket, though Brody's was clean and in better shape than Quinn's.

*Creepy much?*

"Quinn! It's good to see you, man." Brody crossed the kitchen and pulled him into a one-armed bro hug.

Quinn hesitated. He wasn't the hugging type. When he saw Brody wasn't going to let go until he reciprocated, he gave him a few pats on the back.

"When Dad said we were gonna help you guys out, I was so relieved. If Nathan hadn't called, Dad had us set up to clean out a vamp nest in New York." He rolled his eyes. "I hate that city."

"So, who's working the vamp job?"

The question seemed to throw Brody. He broke eye contact with Quinn and looked over his shoulder instead. "Um, well, I think…that is, I'm pretty sure Dad uh…yeah, he passed it to another Slayer."

Quinn stepped into Brody's range of sight, forcing the man to look at him instead of the cabinets behind him. "You know," he drawled, taking his time, gauging the guy's reaction, "I've never knew Slayers were allowed to make calls like that. Lucas must be pretty tight with the angels to shed a job and fork it over to someone else."

"Nah," a gravelly voice replied from behind, "I just don't give a frog's ass what they think."

Quinn waited a beat before turning around to meet Lucas. His son's strawberry birthmark had gone darker – so dark it had a purplish hue. Everyone has certain tells that manifest when they're nervous...*or lying*. Quinn had found Brody's.

"Can I bother you for a cup of coffee?"

Quinn composed himself and faced Lucas. Uncle Case, standing behind their guest, wore a mind-your-manners frown.

"Sure thing, Lucas," Quinn poured it on thick. "Can I fix you a sandwich, too?"

Uncle Case cleared his throat – a warning. He ignored it.

"I mean, I can't be sure, seeing as how I've never done it, but I imagine that shucking a vamp job in New York and pawning it off on someone else just so you could drive a day and a half to help us locate our half-demon sister really works up an appetite."

"Quinn!"

Casen's shout brought Nathan and Lucas' other son, Caleb, running to the room. "Did we miss something?" Nathan asked.

"Nothing you haven't seen before," Casen growled as he pinned Quinn with an icy glare. "Now listen here, boy; if you can't act civilly to the only ones willing to stick their necks out and help us, then keep your yap shut and stay out of the way."

Quinn nodded and pushed past Lucas to the door. Nathan and Caleb parted as if he was Moses.

"We only came to help," Lucas called to his back.

Quinn paused in the doorway and spun on his heel. "Help who, Lucas? Help us? Help my sister? Or help yourself?" His heavy tread on the faded linoleum rattled glasses in the cupboard. "Why are you really here? I'm sure you understand my concern. You barely know us, yet you dropped everything – including a job – to come here." Quinn was close enough now to smell the funk wafting off the man's body, three days past its last shower. When Lucas sucked his teeth, it took every ounce of Quinn's willpower to keep his tongue in check. "I've lost too many people I love already. I'll be damned if another member of my family gets so much as a *scratch* because of someone's ulterior motives."

The wheezing of the ancient refrigerator was the only sound as Quinn left the room.

"We need to talk."

Nathan barged into Quinn's room about an hour after his tirade in the kitchen.

Quinn glanced up from his position on the bed,

The Book in his hands. "How about running to the kitchen and getting me a cup of that coffee I know Case brewed special for his *guests*."

"Quinn, I'm serious."

"I am, too. I need to research but damn, I'm so friggin' tired."

Nathan crossed his arms, his tone firm, yet quiet. "You're tired because you aren't getting enough sleep. Didn't you and Case perform an intervention on me a few days ago for the exact same thing?"

Quinn closed The Book and leaned back against the pillows, drained. It was half past eight and he felt like an old man who'd forgotten to take his Metamucil. He could get by on 2-3 hours of sleep a night, but the added stress of worrying about his family and the mountains of research were getting to him. Quinn longed to get outside and work on his car. He needed to go to a bar, get a buzz on, and pick up a woman (who was looking for a good time and nothing else) for some extracurricular activities. He needed a break.

Nathan pulled up a chair from the corner and sat down. "Do you think your overreaction to Lucas' offer of help may stem from the fact that you're burnt out?"

Quinn's yawn was so wide his jaws cracked. "I didn't overreact."

Nathan smirked. "*Really?* Do you have any idea how much damage control Uncle Case and I had to do after your performance?"

"Did you make sure to tell him how exhausted and *burnt out* I am?"

"Something like that."

"Good." Quinn smiled and closed his eyes, "then Lucas and his children of the corn won't suspect a thing while I'm checking out their good intentions."

Nathan rolled his eyes. "Why are you so sure they aren't legit? I mean, damn, Brody idolizes you. Do you really think they're under false pretenses?"

"Yeah, 'cause a guy showing up at my house dressed exactly like me with the same hair style – *the same jacket* – after only seeing me once for a few weeks two years ago isn't strange at all. If you came in here to tell me he has a '66 black Charger outside, I'm moving out."

Quinn sat up, swinging his legs over the side of the bed, suddenly serious.

"Nathan, why…" He stopped. Trying to pick thoughts from the sludge that was his worn-out brain was like picking pieces of sand out of taffy. His brother leaned back in the chair.

"Why would Lucas risk putting a target on his back – on his *sons'* backs – for us? Who are we to him? We're no one. He barely knows us."

Nathan nodded. "I know what you're saying but since his wife died, Lucas pretty much does as he pleases. He doesn't care if the angels get their robes in a bunch."

"So he says. We have no idea if he's telling the truth. We don't know him, and you can't tell me that spending a few weeks on a hunt where we were separated and scattered over three counties counts as quality time."

"Quinn–"

"I'm not just talking about the angels, either."

"Quinn, I think–" Nathan shook his head. "Wait, what do you mean?"

Quinn ran a hand through his hair and tried to sound like someone who wasn't deranged from exhaustion. Not an easy task.

"What I mean is that it isn't just the angels we have to worry about. Jordan isn't sipping Mai Tais in the Bahamas right now. She's with demons. I can't imagine they'll keep us on their Christmas card list after we get her back. If it was that easy, Aamon would have brought her to us himself, or at least let us see her.

"In other words," Quinn stood up and stretched, "not only is Lucas risking the angels' wrath, he and his boys may soon find themselves wishing for the days of messy *Rougarou* hunts and air conditioning."

He started to walk out of the room but Nathan jumped up and stood in his way.

"Just tell me one thing," he demanded.

Quinn gave a half-hearted shrug.

"Are you really having doubts about Lucas' motives or is this an excuse to push people away again?"

Nathan's words were like a shot of adrenalin. The desire to punch his brother in the mouth was hard to resist but Quinn remembered that, up until a few days ago, Nathan hadn't been running on full cylinders. It was more than possible that he hadn't noticed the changes in Quinn, subtle though they might be. So, he kept a check on his temper (he was too pooped anyway) and swallowed down the insult before it sprang off his tongue like an Olympic diver looking for no backsplash and a perfect ten – always easy for him.

The words he did manage to squeeze past his numb lips were much more difficult. "No, I don't...I don't do that anymore. I know I'm good at accusing people of things they aren't guilty of and I'm a pro at behaving like a douche if it keeps people out. I hurt Jordan for so long and where did it get me? In the end, I still got hurt and she's gone." He looked Nathan in the eye. "I know I'm not there yet – hell, I may never be like you. Even after losing Mom and Dad, you didn't let it harden you, but I did. I can't lie and say I don't sometimes feel the urge to slam the door, get in my car, and bolt. It's my security blanket. But I'm not pushing people away."

Nathan stared...and stared. It made Quinn uncomfortable.

"Damn; take a picture or something!"

Nathan shook his head. "Sorry. It's just that I

wasn't expecting that."

"What? You heard me confess to Jordan that night at the cabin before everything went to hell. I'm all about feelings now."

"Yeah, I knew you had broken fences. I never expected you to mend them." He rolled his eyes. "And the day you're all about feelings is the day I pay for sex."

"You've never paid for sex?" Quinn held up a hand. "Never mind, not important." He started for the door.

"Where are you going?" Nathan asked.

"To get some coffee."

"Grab some mattress. I'll get it for you."

Unexpectedly, Nathan pulled him into a hug. Quinn knew it was his way of saying he understood why he'd spilled his guts like some melodramatic teen-vamp pansy on T.V. and that he appreciated the confession.

The whole bonding moment lasted about four seconds. When Nathan moved away, Quinn said, "Promise you'll keep an eye on our 'saving graces.' I have a bad feeling, Nate."

Nathan nodded and left to get the coffee. When he returned, Quinn was asleep. He picked up The Book, which was splayed open across his brother's chest, and turned off the light. He closed the door softly when he left the room.

The farm was peaceful. An owl hooted from its perch in a nearby pine. Farther away, cows settled into barns for the evening while donkeys stood guard against predators. The moon stood out in the indigo sky – a vintage pearl in a field of diamonds. Her pure, vanilla light penetrated Quinn's windows and fell upon a photograph on his dresser. Casen, Jordan, and Nathan stood in front of a classic red Camaro, arms thrown around each other. The trio wore big smiles.

His entire world summed up on a single piece of printing paper. These people were Quinn's life and he would do anything – *anything* – to keep them safe. He would have to be watched carefully. The last thing they needed was a wild card to bring the entire house down.

The figure hovering outside the window landed silently on the ground. The resident owl watched as the strange being looked around, surveying different vantage points. With a flash of gleaming eyes, the shape smiled and disappeared.

The next morning, the sky was swollen and bruised. Thick clouds promised rain soon. Quinn mentally kicked himself all the way to the kitchen for falling asleep the night before and cursed Nathan under his breath for not waking him. At least he managed to see the sunrise.

Brody shambled into the room, rubbing sleep-crusted eyes, just as the coffee maker sputtered the last few drops into the carafe. Quinn grabbed a thermos, poured out the hot water he used to heat it with, and filled it with the rousing brew.

"That smells good." Brody fell into a kitchen chair. "Any left?"

Quinn purposely poured every drop into the thermos, giving it a shake for good measure, while Brody looked on.

"Nope."

"Can I make some more?"

A tic jumped under Brody's eye and Quinn smirked. "Help yourself."

Quinn had barely made it to the door when he heard, "Why are you being such a dick?"

He turned around. "It's just coffee, dude. What's the matter, don't know how to measure the water? Turn on the machine? Need me to hold your hand?"

Brody flipped him off.

Quinn laughed. "Oh my, such a rude gesture. I'm crushed, really." He walked to the table and slammed the thermos down. Quicker than fear, Quinn spun the boy's chair around and leaned over him. "Why don't you tell me why your daddy's really here?"

Swallowing hard, Adam's apple rising and falling like the Nasdaq, Brody said, "You know why. We want to help find your sister."

The birthmark flamed and changed color.

"That's a lie," Quinn's grip tightened on the chair by Brody's head. "Listen closely, *boy*. I just gave you a chance to come clean. I won't offer it again."

He stayed in Brody's face, not moving, not blinking, until the boy lowered his eyes. Quinn shoved away, nearly toppling the chair and grabbed his thermos.

"What the hell, man?! What's your problem?"

"My problem," Quinn answered, walking away, "is fucktards messing with my family."

It was mid-day by the time he finished tending to the cattle. Quinn drew the task out as long as possible and then cleaned the barns. Nathan helped roll his Charger onto the trailer and store it in Quinn's shed. He intended to grab a bite and work on it for the remainder of the evening.

A crack of thunder announced the arrival of the storm. It had positioned itself over the farm all day like a waiting assassin. Lightning sliced open the sky and rain fell in torrents. Quinn walked slowly to the porch, letting the cold water wash away the layers of dirt, sweat, and anxiety.

Casen met him on the porch. He was silent as Quinn kicked off his boots and stripped down to his boxers.

"Are you gonna help us find Jordan or not?"

Quinn laid his clothes over the porch swing. His anger, which had waned during the long hours of work, caught and flared once more.

"You help Jordan your way; I'll help her my way."

"And what way is that, Quinn? Did you receive a revelation while shoveling cow shit today?" His uncle tipped his hat back and regarded him like one would a four-year-old who'd gotten too big for his britches. "Admit it; you have no idea how to get your sister back...but Lucas does. Why don't you at least hear him out."

"No."

"Quinn–"

"No." He jiggled the storm door and then yanked it open when it stuck. "Lucas is going to screw you over, just wait and see. Someone has to come up with a plan – a real one – while he has you hunched over like Seattle Slew."

Casen looked out at the trees and Quinn immediately regretted his choice of words. "Uncle Case, I'm sorry. I shouldn't have said that. It's just that I can't understand how you – *you*, of all people – can't see that this is some sort of scam."

Casen calmly turned to his nephew and punched him in the face. Quinn's head rocked back and his eye burst in excruciating pain. Casen had hands as large as two by fours and twice as hard.

"You must have forgotten who you're talkin' to. Consider that a reminder."

Point taken, Quinn followed his uncle inside.

◇◇◇

The house was quiet. Quinn spent most of the evening underneath the hood of his car. He didn't get much work done with his one good eye (the one Casen punched was swollen like a plum and had the purple color to match), but at least it was peaceful. The rain hammering against the tin roof, Toad the Wet Sprocket playing in the background, and the familiar scents of motor oil, sanding dust, and rubber from the tires felt more like home to him than the farmhouse. The little barn was Quinn's safe place – a getaway where he could lose himself in normality and create something beautiful instead of destroying something ugly.

After grabbing a beer from the refrigerator, Quinn went in search of his brother. He checked Nathan's room and the study with no results. He didn't see anyone else, either. No cars were missing, so that only left the basement where they stored weapons.

From the concrete stairs, Quinn heard several voices. The basement was partitioned off into separate rooms, most padlocked and warded. Toward the back, underneath the kitchen, was the only open area. They normally used it to store extra household items like cleaners, paper towels, and spare light bulbs. Tonight, it was being used for a different purpose.

A Devil's trap, also known as The Key of Solomon, had been chalked on the floor in the middle of the room. Surrounding the crudely drawn circle, which enclosed a pentagram and several symbols, Nathan, Caleb, Brody, and Uncle Case all held shotguns. Lucas stood at the northern point of the pentagram with an open book in his hands.

A Devil's trap is used to capture and incapacitate demons. There are several types; some more complicated than others. The traps can be placed just about anywhere and drawn with mediums such as chalk, paint, marker…but one drawn in blood is the strongest. Once a demon steps inside the circle, they can't escape as long as the trap remains intact. It renders them powerless.

*What the hell is an empty Devil's trap doing on our basement floor?*

Quinn, hidden in the shadows, studied the group before him – guns at the ready, aimed at the center of the pentagram, Lucas with a leather-bound journal that looked familiar, an empty Devil's trap drawn in chalk and easily broken…and suddenly he knew. They weren't planning on trapping some random demon; they were going to *summon* one.

"Have you all lost your minds?"

He stepped into the light and took in their startled faces. Nathan looked as if he'd been caught playing with matches or looking at a dirty magazine. Lucas, however, didn't seem upset that Quinn caught him in the process of inviting a demon into his home. Casen's expression was wooden. As a matter of fact, he didn't acknowledge his nephew at all, choosing to study the rolls of Charmin instead.

"Tell me this is the result of too much Jack Daniels or an alien encounter."

Lucas marked his place in the journal Jordan had painstakingly copied with her own hands. Quinn's fists shook. This was the man who was supposed to help them – help his sister. Instead, he was planning to play host to the very body snatchers she was trapped with. Lucas had crossed a line.

Quinn's stride was a determined one. His steps were even paced and strong. He only had one thing on his mind and Brody must have sensed it. He moved to intercept, raising his shotgun to aim at Quinn's chest.

"Either shoot me or get the hell out of the way!"

Lucas moved to his son's side. "Quinn, let me explain before someone gets hurt."

Ignoring the elder man for the moment, Quinn pointed his finger at Brody. "Put the gun down before I spank your ass with it."

Brody laughed. "Big words coming from someone sporting a black eye. Looks like Casen got a good piece of you." His smile faded. "Now, *you* back off before I mess up the design on that bitchin' Metallica T-shirt."

Nathan moved to Quinn's flank. "You can't shoot a damn thing with the safety on."

Brody fell for the ruse. He took his eyes off of Quinn and turned the gun to check the safety on the side. Quinn plucked it from his grasp, broke it open across his arm, and removed the cartridges of silver shot. He then proceeded to knee Brody in the gut and, while the boy was bent over and gasping for air, smacked him across the rear with it a few times for good measure.

Unlike Nathan, who always had his back, Quinn noticed Caleb didn't attempt to defend his brother.

*Smart guy.*

"That's enough."

Though his words were spoken in a normal tone, everyone in the room stopped and looked at Casen.

"Quinn, turn him loose."

He let go of Brody's arm and shoved him towards Lucas, whose face twisted in anger.

"If you ever lay a hand on either of my sons again, I will–"

"Lucas, for the love of God, shut your mouth or risk having your ass whooped with that gun barrel, too." Casen propped his own weapon against the wall and folded his arms across his chest. "I'll deal with my nephew."

*Oh, really?* Quinn thought.

"You–" Casen pointed at him. "If you can't handle this then go back upstairs."

Quinn was floored. There were no words to describe how betrayed he felt. His own uncle was allowing a man he didn't know to summon a demon into his home. As it turned out, he didn't have to say anything. The look on his face must have been enough.

"We're doing this," Casen continued. "It's the only way to get information on Jordan's whereabouts and it's a good idea, too."

"A good idea?" Quinn managed. "Do you have any idea what all could go wrong? What if the demon gets pissed for being locked in your trap and calls some friends to help? What if it gets out and possesses one of you?" He wanted to scream. "Are the risks you're willing to take worth that? Hell, the demon probably won't tell you a damned thing!"

"She will."

Quinn spun to face Lucas. "How in happy crap do you know what it will or won't do?"

Lucas sucked on his teeth and Quinn's nostrils flared. "Because I've called on her before."

It took a second or two for the words to sink in. When they did, Quinn didn't know whether to beat the man to a bloody pulp or puke. He did what he always did when uncertain about his next move, which wasn't often. He looked to Nathan.

"Are you fucking hearing this?! He calls on *demons*!"

Before his brother could answer, Quinn asked

Lucas, "Why? Why do you call on demons? What kind of sick bastard are you?"

"First of all," he replied, "I don't call on demon*s*." He stressed the plural form of the word. "I call on one demon. As for why, well, she's handy at giving tips on how to deal with some of the things we hunt."

"For a fee, I'm sure." Quinn shook his head. "You are insane. What – you don't have the competence for research or are you just too lazy?"

The man didn't answer.

Quinn looked over at his brother. "Are you going to stand by and let this happen?"

"It wasn't my decision." Nathan's eyes cut to his uncle. "I'm just here to make sure everything stays cool."

"Are you in or out?" Casen asked.

"I'm out." Quinn swallowed the excess saliva that flooded his mouth as nausea threatened to overtake him. Once again, he focused on Nathan. "I'm going to pack a bag. I'll take Jordan's car." He pulled his twin into a hug and whispered, "Call me if you need me. I won't be far away."

Nathan nodded, understanding. Always understanding.

"You don't have to leave," Casen said.

"Yeah, I do."

"And here I thought you were back, son – really back."

Finally, he looked at his uncle. There was a hint of the old disappointment there. It read like the familiar lines of a road map – one Quinn had memorized.

"I did come back, Uncle Case." His smile was as tremulous as his decision to leave. "You're the one checking out this time."

The figure sat on the steps leading down to the basement door from the outside. He smiled at the information he'd overheard. So, they planned to summon a demon to try and locate Jordan – a demon who (according to the man, Lucas) had helped him before. His master would be very interested in learning who this demon was. He settled back to wait for her arrival.

## XII Jordan

*Her iPod was fine.*

Gina invaded Mazie's sleep, made her the star of a horror movie she directed for...what? Kicks? Because she could?

No, because she was sadistic and got off on it.

Surrounded in a haze of white-hot anger, Jordan crossed the room without realizing she had done so. She snatched the iPod from the docking station, silencing Sarah Brightman in mid song.

"What in the hell do you think you're doing?"

Gina's voice was barely audible over the roaring in her ears. Power surged, filling her up, flowing to every nook and cranny of her body. Exerting the tiniest amount of pressure, Jordan snapped the MP3 player in half. She squeezed the two parts of the device, ignoring the cuts it made, not feeling the pain. In a dream-like state, she tipped her hand. Mangled pieces and dripping blood showered the pale carpet. It was beautiful in a twisted kind of way.

"Hey, Psycho! I'm talking to you!"

A sharp crack and stinging pain on the left side of her face brought Jordan out of her rage-induced trance. It took a second for her to realize that Gina had slapped her.

"Do I have your attention now, Short-bus? If not, I'll be happy to try and knock some damn sense into you again."

The corrosive fury still whirled inside like a tornado, sucking up every negative feeling and thought Jordan had, adding to its power. The beast thumped harder on the bars of the cage. She relished the feeling. Never had she felt so *free*, so unbridled. For as long as she could remember, maintaining control had been a necessity, like breathing. On hunts, to keep the visions from driving her mad, with Quinn. Clamping down on her emotions was part of her morning routine, right after dressing and brushing her teeth. To let go, to just not give a damn…it was a dangerous high. She had to find a balance.

But now, with Gina snarling in her face, Jordan didn't have time. She pushed the hate aside so she could reply without ripping Gina's throat out.

"If you *ever* lay a hand on me again, I'll break it off and use it as a candle holder."

Gina threw her head back and laughed. "Well, well, well…where *did* this sudden burst of bravery come from? Did you eat Wheaties for breakfast this morning?"

"Why did you do it?"

Gina's eyes grew big and round. She placed a hand on her chest. "Do what?" she asked, voice high and sugar-sweet.

"You know damn well what I'm talking about! Why did you do that to Mazie? She's just a kid for Christ's sake."

Gina shrugged. "She broke my iPod. I had to teach her a lesson."

"But she didn't break your iPod, *I did*." Jordan kicked a piece of the broken device. Gina's eyes followed as it landed underneath her desk. "Anyway," she continued, smirking a little, "who made you queen demon of this psycho summer camp?"

Head cocked, Gina ran a perfectly manicured nail across her bottom lip. "Since you're the new kid on the block, I'll excuse your ignorance. Obviously, I am quite special to Aamon. Otherwise, why would I still be here? By the age of 18, his children are chosen for different positions and move on, yet he keeps me by his side. Why do you think that is?"

"Maybe because he feels you can't be on your own," Jordan replied, sizing her up. "After all, a Dream Walker isn't very powerful. I mean, what can you do, really? You have to wait until someone falls asleep to use your limited powers. There are kids in this house who have abilities much more useful than yours. I bet that really gets under your skin, huh?"

Gina's lips curled like a rabid dog on the verge of attacking. Jordan felt sure this was the first time anyone had stood up to her. She was being served a huge helping of humiliation and it clearly did not agree with her. Even worse was the fact that the truth had been exposed. All the time she spent crowing and using intimidation to mask her insecurities had been a waste of time. Jordan had called her bluff.

"The kids in this house respect me," she insisted as if not only trying to convince Jordan, but also herself.

"That's not respect, Gina, it's fear. There's a difference – learn it."

Jordan headed for the door. If she stayed any longer, she would lose the tiny amount of control she'd managed to hang on to. Regardless of how good it felt to let go, she couldn't lose who she was. If she surrendered to the rage, she'd lose herself to the demon.

"You bitch! How dare you walk into my room, break my belongings, and then climb up on a pedestal and preach to me about useless powers! Big talk coming from someone who doesn't have *any*."

A hard shove from behind sent Jordan careening into the hallway. She stumbled but caught herself against the opposite wall. She turned and watched as Gina slowly followed her out, the light from her room illuminating them both – predator and prey. The only question was, which one was she?

"What makes you so damned special, huh? What abilities do you have, Jordan, other than running your mouth?"

From the corner of her eye, Jordan saw barefoot bodies in different sleepwear slink into the hall and the open area by the second-floor banisters. They had attracted an audience. Gina noticed them, too, and smiled.

"Answer me, Miss 24-karat. Why did Dad go through such pains to bring you here? As far as I know, you haven't done anything extraordinary." Gina looked around, making sure all eyes were fixed on her. "Hell, you don't even possess the *basic* powers of a Cambion. For instance, can you do this?"

She raised her hand. Green light radiated from her palm. An invisible force threw Jordan back against the wall. She was frozen in place, not able to move so much as a finger.

Gina made a tsking noise and shook her head. "No? How about this?"

She moved her hand towards the ceiling and Jordan's body responded in turn. She slid higher up the wall. A scene from *The Exorcist* flashed across her mind.

"And, of course, we *all* know how to do this."

Helpless, Jordan watched as Gina slowly curled her hand into a fist. Her stomach clenched and began to ache. Nausea filled her. Sweat broke out along her hairline and the back of her neck. She wanted to heave, to rid herself of the intense pain, but Gina's power kept her motionless. She couldn't even open her mouth. Bile rose in her throat but had nowhere to go. Jordan choked. Just when she thought she'd die strangling on her own vomit, Gina released her and she fell to the floor.

Jordan pulled herself to a kneeling position and retched so violently it felt as if she were expelling her organs. Through her tangled, sweat-dampened hair, she saw Elliott – another half-sibling easily noticeable in the dimly lit hall because of his white hair – turn and make for the stairs.

Gina didn't see him, as busy as she was gloating over Jordan's reenactment of a scene from *E.R.* When she puked yet again (*God, how can anything be left inside to hurl?*) Jordan heard her say, "Who's useless now?" Gina's braying laughter rubbed her raw nerves. More acid churned in her stomach and Jordan fought it down.

She focused on the rage, still spinning inside like a mini cyclone. She remembered Aamon's words about drawing power from her core. Jordan closed her eyes. The hate she felt might be a manifestation of her power, but it wasn't the source of it. She pushed it from her and looked deeper, closing herself off to everything around her. Soon, she felt it, a calm but continuous energy. It was ancient, timeless. Images suddenly appeared in her mind. The ocean, deceptively serene from afar but teeming with life, busy beneath the surface. Tree limbs swaying, leaves dancing on a refreshing breeze. Air constantly moving, soothing. Tilled earth, rich brown rows waiting to provide life. A roaring fire, powerful enough to sustain or destroy. The night sky, winking with stars, blazing with comets, beautiful colors swirling around planets. Angel wings, pearl white and stunning, crashing to Earth.

Although it felt like hours had passed, it was only a minute or two later when Jordan opened her eyes. She could feel energy flowing through her like water, heating her chilled core like fire, lifting her up like air, nourishing her like the Earth, and it was endless, like the galaxies above. She knew this was where Sariel's grace came from just as her demon power was the result of Lucifer's fall.

Now that she was aware of it, Jordan realized how unnatural it felt. The two powers were never meant to be contained in the same vessel. There would never be any balance, not really. Like oil and water, no matter how much energy she exerted to combine them, separation was inevitable. It felt like three different beings shared her body, yet all of them were her.

*How in the hell did this happen?*

She got to her feet and circled around the pool of vomit. Gina wrinkled her nose and took a step back but Jordan barely noticed. Instead, she studied the kids standing around them.

They were all so different; short, tall, black, white, Asian, shy, funny, but each had a common bond – they were all Cambions. Jordan was the only one who didn't belong, and never would. She was human, angel, and demon, but not enough of either to be counted. It didn't matter where she called "home" – the bowels of Hell, the gardens of Heaven, or a farmhouse in Dixon's Bluff, WY. She would always be an outcast. For the first time in her life, Jordan looked for her future and couldn't see a damned thing.

"What's going on here?"

Aamon appeared in a pair of sweats and white T-shirt, hair rumpled from sleep, eyes squinting against the glare of the light. Jordan had never seen him so casual before. It made him look vulnerable, more human.

Elliott stood behind him, Ivy to his right. She met Jordan's gaze with raised eyebrows – an unspoken question, *Are you okay?*

Jordan nodded once.

When Ivy noticed the second party to the early-morning disturbance, her eyes took on the red hue of her inner demon. She took a step forward with obvious intent to do bodily harm. Mumbling words Jordan couldn't make out, Ivy pushed another kid aside, the only obstacle in her path, but Aamon grabbed a handful of her shirt and pulled her back.

Gina, delighted with Ivy's anger, gave her a little

wave.

Ivy lunged, but Aamon's grip was solid.

"Jordan, what's the problem here?"

Before she could open her mouth to answer her satanic sire, Gina whipped up some fake tears and beat her to the punch.

"Dad, she stormed into my room and broke my iPod!" She gestured to the open door. "Come look. It's in pieces all over my floor!"

Brow furrowed, Aamon ignored her request. "Gina, during the unfortunate accident earlier, you claimed that Mazie broke your iPod."

Jordan could see the tiny imps behind her eyes, working feverishly to devise an excuse. Aamon shook his head.

"Jordan, perhaps you can elaborate."

She sighed. Jesus, she was tired. All she wanted was her warm bed and eight hours of sleep. "Yeah, I broke her iPod. It was fine before that, though. She was listening to it when I came into her room."

Aamon massaged his temples. Jordan heard someone snicker.

"Why did you break it?"

"Because she's a bitch and she hates me," Gina wailed, running to his side.

He put an arm around her, shushing in soft, soothing tones. The internal fury Jordan had pushed to the back of her mind jumped to the forefront. In her frazzled state, she couldn't tell if she was angry because Gina was leaving out her part in this or because Aamon was consoling her. Surely she wasn't jealous.

Was she?

*Don't be ridiculous*, she scolded. *If Aamon's too stupid to see through her charade then that's his problem, but I'll be damned if I'll let her get away with what she did to Mazie.*

"I broke her iPod because she lied to you about Mazie, made her feel lower than dirt and wouldn't accept her apology no matter how many times she offered it, and then took a walk through her dreams and tortured her."

"You shut up!" Gina screamed. She turned to Aamon. "Dad, she's lying!"

"*The hell I am.*" Jordan advanced toward Gina, fists tight by her side. "You invaded her dreams. You gave Mazie back her parents and then made her father hang her with a rope over...and over." She stood toe to toe with Gina, her voice low and menacing – the sound of wrath. "You were there, watching, laughing, *while she begged you to stop.*"

Aamon blanched. He stared at Gina with his mouth half open. Jordan wanted to knock some sense into him. After what she just revealed, all he could do was gape like a fish out of water.

"How many more, huh?" Jordan raised her voice, addressing the other kids. "How many times has she abused her power? Who else has been a victim of

Gina's low self esteem and barbaric pastime?"

Whipping around, she glared at Aamon. "I know *I've* been visited by her several times in the dead of night. I've been eaten alive, maimed with knives, watched my family die in every way imaginable..." She swallowed hard. "And it happened on *your* watch, *Dad*."

Aamon scanned face after face. Most of the kids nodded before turning away to look at something else – anything else.

When his eyes sought Jordan, she wasn't swayed by the pain she saw. If anything, it made her despise him more.

"I didn't know," he whispered. "Why didn't you tell me?"

Her strangled laugh made him wince. *"Because we shouldn't have to! You* brought us here. *You* took us from our families. *You* claim to love us. *You* are our father. Act like one."

Aamon exhaled through trembling lips. He pulled one child after another into his arms and still, Jordan felt nothing.

"I promise," he murmured, "this will never happen again."

When he got to Jordan, she shrugged. His words meant nothing to her. She walked past him, intent on checking on Mazie and falling into bed.

A hand shot out and grabbed her hair, twisting it and yanking her backwards. Gina's scream was a mix of primal madness and injured animal. Unfortunately, she wasn't aware of Jordan's proficiency with hand-to-hand combat – or her newly discovered power.

Instead of trying to get away, Jordan stepped back into Gina, catching her off guard. Leaning forward slightly to protect her head, she used her body to slam the Cambion against the wall. The crash was deafening. Jordan felt sheetrock give beneath them.

Ivy and Aamon screamed in unison. Gina touched the back of her head and smiled like the devil himself at the blood that covered her fingers. Her voice cut through the din, stoking the fire that Jordan had barely gotten under control.

"Tell me, Jordan, who will protect Mazie after you're dead?"

Before she could react, Gina raised her hand, glowing bright, eager. Jordan only had enough time to connect with her own power before she was flung against the wall with the energy of a wrecking ball.

Her lungs struggled for oxygen. A rib snapped, and then another. Her chest ached, seeming to grow smaller with every small breath she managed. Gina was literally crushing her from the inside.

Panic dug in with long claws, scrambling for purchase as it made a slow climb to her throat. Jordan wanted to scream, to beg for mercy. Somehow, she managed to push the fear down before it manifested on her face. She needed to get control but dear God, the pain was excruciating!

All around her, chaos ensued. One girl named Becca, whose special ability was the element of fire, wound up like Sandy Koufax on the mound and threw a blazing slider. Unfortunately, there wasn't enough power behind the pitch. The fireball fell short, set the carpet on fire, and only succeeded in separating Gina and Jordan from everyone else. The light from the orange and yellow flames caressed Gina's face like a lover, highlighting her blue eyes, softening the harsh lines as she frowned. How could someone so beautiful be so ugly?

Jordan's vision grew dark around the edges. She could barely get air to her shrinking lungs. Panic began its ascent again, faster than before. A tear slipped from between her closed eyes and tracked furrows of pain on her face. The beast within cried silently with her, begging to be let out. Not knowing what else to do other than to give Gina the satisfaction of her death, Jordan opened the door and set it free.

Power pulled like a cresting wave. Jordan felt her soul rise as the swell grew. At the top, she waited, balanced on the precipice, as the whitecap formed.

The rush Jordan felt as the wave broke and surged through her body was almost more than she could take. She fell to the floor, landing on one knee. One hand dug into the piled carpet to keep from tipping over, the other curled tight against her chest.

She could breathe again! Once accepted, the power leveled out, surrounding her with warmth, healing her injuries, giving her strength Jordan never thought possible. The beast, she knew now, was nothing more than fear of the unknown. She was afraid of what she was, of changing into something evil. Well, she would find a way to cope with it. Gina's cloudburst was mild compared to the squalls a full demon could conjure.

The fire eating away at the carpet and licking the walls a few feet away suddenly disappeared as Jordan lifted her head and met Gina's wide-eyed stare.

"What the hell?"

Jordan rose to her feet, Jordan said, "Hell has nothing to do with this."

Slowly, she advanced, shoulders back, arms at her side. She thought about Mazie and the other kids Gina had hurt. It was hard enough being plucked from the only families they'd ever known and transplanted to a world full of demons and other creatures that shouldn't exist. The last thing they needed was a crackpot in head-to-toe Abercrombie and Fitch invading the only reprieve from madness they had. The daytime horrors were bad enough.

"Jordan, are you…okay?"

"Look at her eyes!"

"What's happening to her?"

Jordan ignored the whispers, the exclamations of shock. She couldn't worry about them now.

158

Gina raised her hand again. The green radiance pulsing from her palm hinted at what was to come. When she closed it into a tight fist, a mild throb – a ghost of the pain that had assaulted Jordan before – returned. She brushed it aside, but the fact that Gina was trying to hurt her, to *kill* her, was just as bad. What gave her the right to decide anyone's fate?

A whooshing noise made Jordan pause, but just like the headache, she shoved the noise aside. It reminded her of Gabe, and her heart lurched at the thought. No one was coming to help her, not ever again. The middle of her back, right between her shoulder blades itched and burned. She pushed that aside, too.

More excited whispers reached her ears. Aamon yelled for her to stop. *Too late*, she thought, and paused in front of Gina.

The Cambion's eyes were as large as hubcaps. Shaking her head, Gina dropped her hand and backed into the wall.

"What the fuck are you?"

"That," Jordan said, raising her own hand, "is the least of your worries."

Her fingers circled Gina's slim, sculpted neck before she slammed her against the wall.

"Get off me or I swear the next time you doze off I'll gut you like a deer. Your last breath will be spent watching Mazie feast on your steaming entrails!"

Gina knew what buttons to push. She used

Jordan's affection for the youngest child in the house like a tool, twisting the pain and desperation deeper.

But Jordan no longer felt desperate, at least not for Mazie's safety. Gina would soon find out why.

She squeezed Gina's neck harder, cutting off what little air she had allowed before. Gina's eyes bulged and she clawed at Jordan's arms and hands, scratching deep furrows with her acrylic nails. Blood instantly pooled in the ragged slits and splattered the floor like the beginning of a murder scene. It didn't go unnoticed by Jordan that this was the second room of carpet she'd ruined.

"Jordan, that's enough!" Aamon yelled. "Let her go!"

She bent close enough to Gina's face to smell her musky, spicy mélange of fear, sweat, and overpriced perfume. "Hear me good, Gina, because I won't say this again. You will never hurt another kid in this house or anywhere else. If you do, I swear on my brothers' lives I will kill you…slowly, and I'll enjoy every minute I make you suffer." She watched as the girl's face began to change from dark red to purple. Her eyes fluttered and she swayed on her feet. "Nod if you understand me."

Like a drunk at closing time, Gina managed a loose head bobble. Jordan let go and felt a small bit of satisfaction when the girl sank to the floor, staining her silk pajama bottoms in blood.

Gina panted, rubbing her neck, which would

sport bruises in the shape of Jordan's fingers soon. Using the wall for support, she clambered to her feet. In a raspy voice, she said, "You owe me a new pair of pajamas."

Jordan smiled sweetly. "Put it on my tab."

"Bite me, bitch." Gina spat in her face.

Something inside Jordan snapped. Instinct told her Gina would never stop. Not only had she lost her position in the house, she'd also been found out. The Cambion would retaliate with a vengeance.

Gina reached back, fist cocked and ready to fly. In her weakened condition, she still managed to put the force of a Brahman bull behind the punch. Even then, Jordan had no problem palming it, stopping her cold.

Her fingers tingled. Rage – raw and unfiltered – saturated every pore of her being. The rancorous black thorn tattooed upon her heart, dormant for months, quickened as bitter blood raced through her veins, baptized in tainted sap.

But there was something else inside, as well. Something pure and good. Something that said she was right for what she was about to do.

Just like when she healed Koda's wounds, blue pulses of light passed from her chest. They raced down her arms, underneath her skin, riding her veins. Jordan could feel friction as the energy searched for something to save…or kill.

When the throbbing flashes reached Gina's fist,

she began to scream. Aamon leapt into action. Jordan watched, unconcerned, as he raced towards her and slammed into an invisible barrier. Until it happened, she had no idea she was capable of such a thing. But on a deeper plane, in her subconscious, Jordan *knew* she had that ability. It was like remembering something from a long time ago, or perhaps sharing someone else's memories.

"Jordan, remember the dream!" Ivy pounded against the barrier. "Remember Gabriel and what happened to him – what you did to him? You have to stop!"

But this was right. Wasn't it? She was a Slayer. Gina was evil. Evil should be destroyed.

In her mind's eye, she saw her Guardian fall. Agony filled her once again as his ashes scattered in the wind. She'd killed him out of hate. Was she doing the same to Gina?

*My God.*

She let go of the girl's arm and fell to her knees beside her, checking for any signs of burns or damage. There was nothing, no marks to indicate she'd done anything permanent.

Aamon rushed over and began his own examination. Gina put her head between her bent knees and took deep breaths. Jordan stood up and backed away. Ivy was there to meet her, pulling her into a comforting hug.

"Are you okay?" she asked, squeezing harder.

Jordan nodded, unable to speak. The power was still there and always would be. She'd tapped into it, called it to her, and now it was hers whether she wanted it or not.

"Gone."

At first, Jordan thought Ivy mumbled the word, but realized it came from farther away.

*Gina.*

"It's gone." She held her hands up in front of her face, shaking them, clenching them into fists. "It's GONE!" She raised her eyes to Jordan. "You took it!"

"Took what, Gina? What are you talking about?"

Aamon looked at Jordan, but she didn't acknowledge him. She focused on Gina and waited to hear what she already knew.

"My powers. That bitch took my powers! I have nothing left – nothing!"

Everyone regarded Jordan with mixed expressions. Some seemed fascinated while others looked horrified. Only Ivy stood beside her, unflinching.

"I didn't take anything, Gina," Jordan informed her. "I burned them away. You abused what you were given. You didn't deserve them anymore."

"You psychotic freak, give them back! You're a Cambion just like me. You can't burn up someone else's powers."

Jordan cocked her head, hearing a different

personality – one hidden for so long but present for the moment – answer her half-sister. It was her, but felt alien.

"The Cambion part of me agrees. The angel part sees things differently."

# XIII Gabriel

It was good to be back on Earth again. Although he loved Heaven – his heaven in particular – Gabriel couldn't deny that Earth felt more like home. He'd never questioned why that was. Now, he couldn't help it.

After his meeting with Yasen, Gabriel had left Heaven as quickly as possible, not knowing if Michael was aware of his journey to the Helix Nebula. He hadn't stopped to speak to any of his brothers and sisters who called out as he hurried through the Gates. He'd left like a fugitive fleeing from his homeland.

*No one should ever feel that way*, Gabriel thought.

Some humans believed that, after they passed, a better place waited for them, a paradise with no sorrow, no disease, no war. There was a Father who loved them – loved them so much He gave his only son for their sins – and He would be awaiting their arrival with open arms. For the most part, this was true…for human souls. For angels, it was much more complicated.

Though Gabriel loved his brothers and sisters and the role assigned to him as an archangel and messenger between worlds, he did not like the politics. If every angel cared about Heaven, Earth, humans, eradicating Evil, and did their jobs, there would be no need for the hierarchy. They would all work toward the same goals. Unfortunately, some did not. Some, like Michael, focused on the wrong things.

Ironic. Humans were destroying one of his Father's most beautiful creations while His own angels were hell bent on destroying another. Heaven and Earth…Pretty soon, there would be no difference between them at all.

So why did he feel so drawn to Earth? Why did it feel more like home?

Gabriel smiled as different faces came to mind.

Casen, with his gentle ways, kind nature, and never-ending strength. Gabriel had watched the man struggle with the transformation from bachelor cowboy to surrogate father. It had been a difficult change. When Richard Bailey slowly descended into his own personal hell, neglecting his children while he obsessed over keeping Jordan out of Aamon's clutches, Casen had taken on a more paternal role. He'd pulled on Richard's boots and, though they were uncomfortable, he'd managed, not knowing if he'd ever be able to take them off again. Casen never complained. He did what had to be done for his niece and nephews and had come to love them as his own.

Nathan was a lot like Casen in many ways. He rarely complained, was easy to please, and had a big heart. He loved information and learning. He cared about others more than himself. He would make a wonderful angel some day. Nathan sacrificed so much – as a Slayer protecting others, and for his family, but it never even crossed his mind how much he gave up. He understood people, and they were drawn to him, listened to him. Nathan was the best kind of leader – one who had no idea that he was.

Quinn was everything Nathan was not. Gabriel had no idea how twins could be so different. Like opposite ends of a pole, Nathan kept a cool temper while Quinn's always ran hot. But where one was weak, the other was strong and in that, they complemented each other. Quinn was a fighter. When standing side by side, enemies always looked warily at Nathan because of his build, not realizing Quinn was the dangerous one. In combat, he was poetry in motion, wielding weapons like an artist wields a brush. He glided silently around his enemies. Every move was intricate, effortless. His battles were tantamount to a ballet and beautiful to behold.

One would think Jordan, the baby of the family, would be spoiled and perhaps a bit needy. She was anything but. Gabriel felt closest to her because he'd watched her grow up and been there for almost every milestone. Unlike Casen, who was already a grown man and set in his ways, Nathan, who was strong in mind and body and rarely needed to lean on others, or Quinn, who kept everyone at arms' length, Jordan was the only one who'd let him into her heart. She didn't see Gabriel as an angel, but as a friend and confidant. She had good qualities and some that made him want to scream, but she was his ward and he wouldn't change a thing about her.

Those four people were why he loved Earth so much. They were his family – more so than any angels in Heaven.

*And I left them when they needed me most.*

Gabriel picked up a rock and threw it toward the night sky. He'd been such an idiot. What if Casen, Nathan, and Quinn refused to let him back into their lives, even after explaining why he had left? He probably wouldn't get far, fairly certain one of them would finish what they started the last time he saw them and blow a hole in his forehead. It wouldn't kill him, but part of him would die just the same. Perhaps the most important part.

He leaned against the shed, shifting his attention back to the farmhouse. It was late. Gabriel wondered if Casen and the boys were still awake. He was weighing the consequences of knocking on the door and begging for forgiveness when someone emerged from inside.

Quinn hauled several duffle bags down the steps and tossed them in the back of Jordan's car. Seconds later, he roared down the drive in a cloud of dust and gravel.

Gabriel decided to follow.

The motel Quinn stopped at in a neighboring town was not fancy, but appeared fairly clean from the outside. Gabriel made himself invisible and watched from a few cars away as Quinn unloaded his gear into the last room on the bottom floor, far from the other guests. Shortly after, he drove to a grocery store. From the number of bags he exited with, it looked as if he planned to be away for a while. This worried Gabriel.

Now, Quinn's room was dark except for the flickering light of a television. Should he knock? What would Quinn say after all this time?

A police car crept by. The officer behind the wheel scowled, and Gabriel realized he must look like some sort of deviant hanging around the parking lot. He should have stayed invisible. Now, he had no choice. He'd have to leave or take his chances with Quinn.

Rapping softly on the door, Gabriel secretly hoped Quinn wouldn't hear and give him an excuse to leave…maybe try again tomorrow. But this was Quinn, one of the best Slayers in the Circle. He could hear a whimper in the middle of a heavy metal concert.

There was a soft curse and then the door opened a crack.

"Are you alone, Gabe, or do you have a winged posse waiting to take me out as soon as I open this door wide enough for all of them to fly in?"

Gabriel frowned. "Of course I'm alone. How did you know it was me?"

Quinn rolled his eyes. "I looked through the fish-eye lens in the door, dummy."

When Gabriel didn't answer, Quinn sighed and pointed to a small circle about eye level embedded in the door.

"And this allowed you to see outside?" Gabriel smiled. The wonders of this world never ceased to amaze him.

Quinn shook his head. "Gabe, *really*?" He pinched the bridge of his nose. "Why are you here? I should rip your damn wings off for leaving us under a jumbo pile of demons back in Tennessee – and for Jordan's death at the hands of the *Kongamato* – and for running away like a coward." Quinn gripped the doorjamb with white knuckles and Gabriel took a step back. "You know, ripping your wings off would be too merciful and I don't have time to come up with anything creative. *I* have to fix this fucking mess you left us in and right now…" He ran a jerky hand through his hair. "Right now, I'm too tired."

Quinn stumbled back into the room and slammed the door in Gabriel's face.

Jordan had *died.* She'd been killed by the *Kongamato* and he never knew.

Gabriel sat down on the curb in front of Quinn's door and put his head in his hands. Michael didn't tell him. His brother knew he would have moved Heaven and Earth to get to her – to any of his wards – if they'd been hurt.

He thought back to the last day he'd seen Casen and the boys in Tennessee and groaned. No wonder Quinn and the others had been so upset. He must have come off like a selfish bastard who couldn't have cared less about their welfare. He'd relayed the information Michael shared regarding their father and Sariel but now, thinking back, they probably thought he'd known about the demon situation all along and never told them.

His charges would never trust him again and he couldn't blame them. Gabriel had lost the only people who made him feel there was more to being an angel than just a job.

With a heavy heart, he considered his next move. Jordan still needed help. He'd go to Hell and search it level by level if he had to. He'd threaten every demon he came across.

*Might as well start now.*

Gabriel got to his feet and was stepping off the curb when the door opened behind him. He turned and faced Quinn. The dark circles under the boy's eyes and lines of fatigue made Gabriel feel even worse.

"I'm sorry, Quinn," he whispered, "for everything. There was so much I didn't know…"

"Gabe, just come inside already. It's late and my beer's getting hot."

He left the door open and Gabriel watched from the threshold as Quinn flopped onto a double bed and took a drink from a brown bottle.

"Wanna shut the door? It's colder than a witch's tit in an iron bra and I'm not heating the entire parking lot."

Gabriel shut the door and locked it. His angel eyes showed him runes and symbols Quinn had drawn on the walls and back of the door to ward the room against demons.

"Have you been with many witches?" he asked Quinn.

For a moment, the young man stared at him like he'd suggested they go skinny dipping with Michael.

"No, why?"

"I inquired because you seem to know their thermal readings. I had no idea witches' body temperatures ran cooler than non-witches, or that they favored undergarments of iron." Gabriel frowned. "I would think those would be uncomfortable."

Quinn laughed, transforming his entire face and making him appear younger. Gabriel smiled, not sure what was so funny but happy to see the boy in better spirits. He couldn't remember the last time he'd seen Quinn laugh.

"Gabe, it was just an expression! I have no idea what a witch's temperature runs, but I'm pretty sure they don't wear iron bras." Quinn wiped away tears with the back of his hand. "I don't understand how you've spent so many years around humans – especially *my* family – and still take everything so literally."

Gabriel shrugged. He tried to understand human emotions. With Jordan, it was easy to tell when she was being sarcastic. She rolled her eyes, placed a hand on her hip, or gave some sort of outward signal. Quinn was always serious, so the meanings behind his words were harder to unravel.

"Do you feel better?" he asked.

Somber once more, Quinn said, "Not really, but I have to admit it's kinda cool seeing you again, even if I am pissed at you."

Deciding the urge Quinn felt to rip his wings off had passed, Gabriel sat at a small dinette table which held a pizza box. The aroma of cheese and tomato sauce made his mouth water. Technically, he didn't need to eat or drink to survive. As long as he had his grace, he could sustain his vessel indefinitely. Still, he liked human food.

Tearing his eyes from the red and white box with the little Italian man on the front, Gabriel focused on Quinn once more.

"Why didn't Nathan and Casen come with you?"

Quinn's eyes narrowed. "How do you know they didn't?"

Gabriel *was* familiar with one human expression: Open mouth, Insert Foot. He'd mastered that one. He wanted to crawl under the table.

"Gabe?"

"I was at the farmhouse when you left."

"You were *spying* on us?"

Gabriel shook his head. "I was contemplating on whether to knock on the door."

Quinn drained the last of his beer and set the empty bottle on the bedside table. "I'll tell you why I'm alone if you tell me why you bailed on us in Tennessee."

It was a fair trade. Gabriel offered the missing pieces of the story. It was difficult, especially the part about Michael's lies. He hung his head, remembering how Quinn accused him of being nothing more than a pup at the end of his big brother's leash.

After disclosing the conversation between Michael and his Aeon, Gabriel paused to let the information sink in. Quinn got up from the bed and grabbed two bottles of water from the tiny refrigerator. He sat at the table, slid one of the bottles to Gabriel, and flipped the lid on the pizza box.

While they dined on cheesy goodness, Quinn reiterated what he'd learned. Around a mouthful of pizza he said, "So, my sister could possibly be part demon *and* part angel. Michael knew but never told you. He gave you orders to stay away from us and is sending his Amazon-in-charge after Jordan. Have I got it right so far?"

Gabriel helped himself to another slice. "Yes."

"So why are you here, *with me*?"

The pizza lodged in his throat like a lump of wax. Gabriel swallowed hard and said, "I defected from the Circle."

The words, so alien, hung from his lips. Gabriel remembered Yasen's remarks about the hierarchy and tried to quell his jangled nerves.

"You mean you've turned away from Heaven?" Quinn's voice cracked.

"No, from Michael's command." Gabriel managed a smile. "I removed my collar."

It may have been his imagination, but he thought he saw a faint gleam of approval in Quinn's stormy eyes.

"Now," Gabriel said, taking a sip of water and wishing it was the sweet tea Jordan made, "why did you leave the farm? Has something else happened?"

Quinn's story was short and to the point. "I don't trust them," he concluded, "and I don't understand why Case agreed to let Lucas summon a demon into his home."

Gabriel thought for a moment. "What Lucas Fane proposed isn't a bad idea in itself. I planned to do something similar – interrogate demons on Jordan's whereabouts." Gabriel paused. "Of course, problems could arise if Nathan and Casen were not familiar with how demons work, but they are."

"So, we just sit back and let them?"

Gabriel searched for words to allay Quinn's fears but the bottom line was, even though Casen and Nathan were knowledgeable about demons, they couldn't kill them. Only angels could end their existence. Slayers had the ability to send them back to Hell by performing an exorcism or piercing the possessed person's heart with silver. Gabriel didn't know Lucas well and had no idea how much experience the man had. If something went wrong, if the Devil's Trap was weak or not constructed properly, the demon could escape.

"Tell me how you want to handle it and I'll help any way I can," he said. "Do you think talking to Casen might help?"

Quinn pulled his pizza crust apart with his fingers and sighed. "No, it won't. When Case's mind is made up about something, there's no changing it. I told Nathan to call if they needed me and I'd come running." He looked up, eyes tired but resolute. "I can't sit by and do nothing. We have to find Jordan."

"Yes, we do, and quickly. If Jordan is a *Paladin*, she could be in danger – and not just from angels."

"*Paladin...*" Quinn appeared to roll the word around on his tongue, tasting it. "Warriors for the cause; hybrids of Light and Dark."

"What do you mean?" Gabriel asked.

"I read it in a book. Case and I found it in his study when we were researching Cambions." He shrugged. "Is that what Jordan is – a *Paladin*? What are they?"

Gabriel told Quinn about his visit with Yasen. "If such a hybrid is possible, then her condition is rare, so rare that she may be the only one." He drummed his fingers against the Formica table top. "Yasen will find more information soon."

An idea came to him. It was a long shot but was better than sitting around twiddling their thumbs. "Do you have the book you spoke of? Perhaps I can make more sense of it."

"Good thinking," Quinn said. "I'm glad I packed it. Uncle Case will be madder than a one-legged waitress working at IHOP, but he'll get over it. He told us to leave it in the safe."

Quinn got up and took a few steps toward a small dresser in the corner; a duffle bag lay on top. A knock at the door stopped him in his tracks.

He turned to Gabriel, who whispered, "Are you expecting anyone?"

Quinn pulled a gun from the waistband of his jeans. "Hell, Gabe, I wasn't expecting *you*."

From outside, an authoritative male voice said,

"Gabriel, we know you are in there. Michael has sent for you, brother. Please come peacefully."

The heart that once belonged to his vessel pumped rapidly and Gabriel lost the ability to speak, to think. Quinn, his gun trained on the door, backtracked to where he sat and tapped his shoulder. "Who is that, Gabe?"

His hands shook as he stood. "Michael sent some members of his army to fetch me. He knows I disobeyed."

Quinn regarded the gun with a pained expression and tucked it back into his jeans. "Just tell them to leave," he said. "You're an archangel. They have to listen to you, right?"

Gabriel wondered how long they had before the angels decided to enter the room. "No. They only answer to Michael. He's their leader."

"What happens if you go back?"

Gabriel knew exactly what would happen. His brother would find a way to keep him from returning to Earth. He would secretly lock him away somewhere and Yasen would be none the wiser. Michael had no right to keep him from his wards – and Quinn and his family were *still* his wards.

Squaring his shoulders, he replied, "*I'm not going back*."

Quinn nodded. "Good, that's good, Gabe. But we need a plan – now."

There was nothing for it. Gabriel knew they had

to run. If he faced down the Aeons, Quinn could get hurt in the fray.

"Let's grab your stuff. We have to leave."

"And go where?" Quinn hissed, stuffing what little he'd unpacked into one of his bags while Gabriel grabbed two more. "If they tracked you here, they can track you anywhere."

"I think I can fix that, but not here, not now."

Outside, several voices rose and fell in rapid conversation and then someone pounded on the motel door. "Gabriel," one of the Aeons called. "This is your last chance. Open the door or *we* will!"

Horrified, he watched Quinn scuttle across the room to the last bag resting on the battered dresser. Time seemed to slow down, bring everything in sharp detail. Quinn snatched the bag by its nylon straps and had covered half the distance back when the door shattered. Chunks of wood rained down like confetti, floating slowly, as if the air around them had grown as dense as water. Splinters passed like tiny, misshapen angel wings. Gabriel saw every jagged edge, each deadly point. Something grazed his face. The fish-eye lens sailed by, burrowing itself in the refrigerator door.

And then Quinn was beside him. Gabriel grasped his shoulder just as blinding, blue light filled the room.

179

## XIV Jordan

A soft tap came at the door. Jordan groaned and rolled over to look at the clock. It was a little past ten. She'd gotten about four hours of sleep. Not enough, especially after her episode with Gina.

The knock came louder. Before Jordan could call out to whoever it was to find another hobby, the door opened and Ivy breezed into the room looking fresh and lethal in black leather.

"Did you join a motorcycle gang?" Jordan asked before throwing the comforter over her head, seeking sleep she knew she wouldn't find again this day.

Ivy flipped the covers back and smiled. "I brought you coffee." She offered a chipped mug sporting the words:

*What do we want?*
*Coffee!*
*When do we want it?*
*I'll F\*\*\*ing cut you!*

Jordan laughed. "Where do you find these things?" She took a sip of the delicious brew and perked up a bit.

"I have a gift," Ivy answered, sitting on the edge of the bed. "And now you may tell me you love me."

Sitting up, careful not to spill her coffee, Jordan said, "You only get an 'I love you' if you bring octane *and* a bagel. Coffee alone only rates a 'You're an okay sister.'"

Ivy stuck out her tongue.

"Why the hell did you wake me up so early? I've only been asleep a few hours."

Her sister stretched out at the foot of the bed, ebony hair spilling around her like a fan. "Because you have that meeting in three hours and I knew you'd want time to wake up, eat, and grab a shower…and because I wanted to see if you were okay."

Most people Jordan knew would have found a more diplomatic way to bring up what happened between her and Gina or avoided the topic altogether, but not Ivy. She was straightforward with her thoughts – blunt, but caring.

She motioned for Jordan's cup of coffee and she handed it over. Ivy took a sip and waited.

"No, I'm not okay."

Her sister nodded.

"I could have lost control and killed her if you hadn't stopped me."

Ivy handed her coffee back. "And you would've had every right to do so."

Jordan snorted. "Are you telling me you would have killed her?"

"Damn straight."

"Then why did you step in?"

"Because you're not me." Ivy sat up, pulling her fingers through her hair to straighten it. "If you'd killed Gina, it would have weighed on your conscious like a hippo. You aren't built that way."

Jordan slammed her cup down on the bedside table. "I'm not weak, Ivy. I've killed demons before and slept damned well afterward."

"The situation was different and you know it. There were young kids watching." Ivy rolled her eyes. "You pretend you don't give a rat's ass what people in this house think of you, but I know the truth. You wouldn't have wanted them to see that."

Jordan didn't confirm nor deny Ivy's suspicions. Instead, she got out of bed and did a few stretches. Touching her toes, she said, "And you would've had no problem killing her in front of the kids?"

"I would have fried her crispier than a bucket of KFC's finest."

"And what makes you so different from me?"

Ivy got up and began making Jordan's bed. "Demons are like great white sharks. They're all about self-preservation."

"What in the hell do great whites have to do with

anything?"

"Listen," her sister continued, "great white sharks strike once – hard – and then sit back and wait for the animal to bleed out, until they're too weak to struggle. Demons are kind of the same way. They rarely get their hands dirty if they don't have to. Demons are known for thinking of themselves first. If Gina had threatened to kill me, it wouldn't have mattered if the Pope was watching. I would have scorched that bitch."

Jordan grabbed her coffee and headed for the bathroom she shared with Ivy and Mazie. "You're not that cruel," she called over her shoulder.

"Oh, I don't know," Ivy said following her. "I'm pretty sure the potential to be a selfish hag is hidden somewhere inside this kick-ass outfit." To prove her point, she snatched Jordan's mug of coffee off the bathroom counter and disappeared, teleporting to a safe distance.

"You couldn't hide a paperclip in those skin-tight ho-clothes!"

Somewhere deep in the house, Ivy laughed.

Wrapped in a towel after her shower, Jordan returned to her room and found her own biker-chick outfit lying on the bed, including a pair of matching combat boots and leather bomber jacket.

"Oh hell no…" she breathed.

"Yep," Ivy answered, stepping into the room once more.

"Ivy, this…" She waved her hand at the ensemble of leather, zippers, and buckles, "looks good on *you*. It isn't me. I'm the jeans and sweatshirt type."

She cringed when she pictured herself standing next to Ivy. Her sister was curvy in all the right places. She could wear a trash bag and rock it like a runway model. She, herself, was more muscular – all angles and hard planes. Ivy was Megan Fox and she was G.I. Jane. There was no comparison.

"This is the new you," Ivy explained, holding up a black lycra shirt that would hug her body like saran wrap.

Sweet Jesus and Mary, there was no way she was wearing that.

"Look, where we're going today requires a different attitude, a tougher look. You are a demon-killer, Jordan; you need to look the part. Besides, these clothes are much better for a Slayer. They offer more protection than a pair of jeans, sneakers, and a Daughtry sweatshirt.

"Don't be knocking my band." Jordan touched the supple leather of the pants, ran her hand over the high-laced boots. "Ivy, where exactly are we going?"

She shook her head. "I can't tell you. It isn't allowed." Softly, she asked, "Do you remember what

I said in your dream, after…?"

*After she killed her Guardian.*

Jordan would never forget. It was a nightmare, not a dream. Gabe's ashes had been carried away on the wind and Ivy had helped her up off the ground where she'd been lying, wanting to die, herself.

She swallowed hard, fighting back tears. "You said to never let them see weakness."

Ivy pulled her into a hug so hard she felt her bones would break. "Always remember that."

No matter how many times she did it, Jordan would never come to love teleporting. She had finally mastered the demons' (and angels') preferred way of transport, but she hated it with a passion. As soon as she could, she let go of Ivy's hand and found the closest steady object to lean on until the dizzy feeling passed – in this case, a chair…in what looked like a large, blandly-decorated waiting room.

Wooden benches, shoved against bare walls, and rows of metal chairs provided seating. At one end of the room, a plain desk and a very colorful receptionist sat in front of a bank of elevators. Jordan, Ivy, and Aamon made their way over to her.

"Are we in some sort of jail?"

Jordan studied the people occupying the seats. They appeared to be in pairs. One person was dressed like a banker in either an off-the-rack suit or plain-Jane skirt and blouse. She also noticed accessories like glasses, pocket watches, and hair parted just so or in nice, tidy buns. Their partners were dressed in rags with their hands bound in cuffs...and chains. "What the hell?"

"Exactly," Aamon said. "This is Tenura, the first level of Hell. This is where the souls of those who have sinned meet their respective demons and await judgment."

She was in Hell.

*Hell!*

"Aamon, get me out of here, now."

What was he thinking, bringing her here? She may be part demon but she definitely did not belong in Hotel Hades.

And why was there a waiting room in Hell? Where was the fire and brimstone?

On second thought, she didn't want to know. Ever.

"Jordan, it's fine. You'll be okay."

"What part of me being in Hell is okay, Aamon? What? Is it Bring Your Kids to Work day?"

"This is simply a means to an end. Those elevators are the only transportation to get us to our destination. We aren't staying."

"Where are we going?" When he didn't answer, Jordan grabbed him by the lapel of his expensive jacket. "You know, I've had enough of this cloak-

and-dagger shit. You tell me what's up or I'm teleporting home – *my home*. Have fun explaining *that* to your boss."

She wheeled around and almost ran into a demon with a bald head and earring. He grabbed her arm to steady her.

"Better watch where you're going, Cambion."

"Piss off, Mr. Clean."

Jordan stomped away and Aamon followed, leaving Ivy behind to chat with the receptionist behind the desk.

"Wait," he called.

She walked faster, weaving in and out of chairs.

"Jordan, will you wait?"

She finally stopped and sat down on an empty bench. Aamon joined her and clasped his hands together.

"I'm sorry," he began. "I should have told you more about this jaunt but I didn't want to scare you."

Jordan bit her lip to keep from screaming. "And you thought bringing me to Hell without telling me beforehand was the best way to handle the situation?" She pounded her fists on her legs. "You are such an idiot! How is it that any of your children are still alive?"

"I didn't think–"

"No, you didn't," she cut in. "You don't think, Aamon!"

He looked at his shoes while she struggled to

breathe.

"I want you to listen to me, Aamon, because I won't say this again. It doesn't matter whose genes I have floating around inside. I was groomed my entire life to hunt Evil. You might want to remember that the next time you drag me into a room full of demons."

Aamon stood up and nodded. "I understand. This is uncomfortable for you."

"You have no idea." Before he could walk away, she added, "No more games, *Father*. From now on, you'd better be straight with me or I *will* leave, angels hunting me or not. I would rather risk my life against an entire army of Halos. At least they're up front with their intentions."

She followed him to the front of the room where Ivy and the receptionist were deep in conversation. As they approached, Ivy gave her a sheepish smile, probably feeling guilty for not telling her they'd be making a pit stop in the trenches. She gestured to her friend behind the desk.

"Jordan, this is Sage."

Jordan nodded to the Goth secretary with dyed black hair, pierced lip, rice powder makeup, and deep, chocolate brown eyes. She had a dazzling smile and was beautiful in her own unique way.

"Nice to meet ya, J." She popped a piece of gum in her mouth. "Don't be too angry at Ivy-Girl. She really couldn't say anything."

Jordan replied to Sage but her eyes settled on Aamon. "No worries. It wasn't *Ivy's* responsibility to tell me."

He cleared his throat and stuffed his hands in his pockets. "Sage, is the portal ready?"

"Shouldn't be much longer. I'll let you know as soon as I get the call."

He thanked her and turned to converse with another demon.

"Portal?" Jordan asked.

Before Ivy or Sage could answer, a ruckus a few feet away caught the girls' attention. Two demons were arguing over which one was responsible for a new "lifer" who'd been dropped off. When the argument turned physical, Sage got up from behind the desk.

"Excuse me for a sec." She casually made for the two males throwing punches.

"What the hell is she doing?" Jordan watched Sage push between the two demons who were three or four times her size.

"You'll see," Ivy said.

Placing her hands on their chests, Sage yelled, "Molloch! Krampus! Take it outside!"

"Move it, bitch!" One of the demons tried to swing around her. A bolt of lightning shot from her hand, cleaving his breastbone and pitching him halfway across the room.

The other demon grabbed her by the throat.

Jordan moved to intervene but there was no need. One thrust with the heel of her hand underneath his chin caused the demon to lose his grip. When his head snapped back and he let go, Sage made good use of her own pair of impressive combat boots by pulverizing his privates, giving him an instant sex change.

She cracked her knuckles and walked back to her desk. "Those two," she gestured to the demons slowly getting to their feet, "never learn."

The one she blasted with a lightning bolt ripped his singed jacket, tie, and shirt off, displaying a split chest cavity. He looked like a walking autopsy. "You better pray to Luci I can heal this, Sage! The last thing you want is for me to have to rearrange my schedule to look for a new mark."

She smiled sweetly. "Happy hunting, Molloch."

Both demons hobbled off and normal conversation resumed throughout the room.

"I take it this happens often?" Jordan asked. "Impressive moves, by the way."

"Every damned day, and thanks. I'm more than just a pretty face."

Jordan laughed while Ivy and Sage bumped fists.

A green fire materialized inside a shallow bowl resting beside Sage's laptop. Jordan flinched, taken aback by the sudden flames. Sage focused her attention on it, becoming business-like.

"Tenura, this is Sage."

To her surprise, Jordan heard another voice come through the fire. It was feminine and cool.

"Sage, is that the tone you use when answering business calls? You sound like a truck driver."

"Of course not, Ava; I save my trucker voice especially for sluts."

Ivy stifled a laugh and Sage gave a one-finger salute to the flames.

"I would ask if you kiss your mother with that mouth but that's kind of difficult when you're technically dead."

Sage laughed. "Oh, Ava, that's rich coming from someone who has no idea who her mommy is."

Silence and then, "Tell Aamon the portal is ready." The fire went out.

Sage motioned for Aamon and said, "I really despise that Swamp Molly."

When her father joined them, Sage relayed the message about the portal and Jordan's stomach flipped. She still had no idea what the portal was and where it led to. Her palms began to sweat and she silently cursed the leather she wore. She had nothing to wipe them on.

Aamon walked to one of the elevators. Ivy gave Sage a hug, promised to call her soon, and joined him. Jordan hung back, eyes searching for the nearest exit. There didn't appear to be any.

*Shit, shit, shit!*

Sage bumped her shoulder with her own. "It's

cool."

"I doubt it."

"It's no different than teleporting." She placed a reassuring hand on Jordan's arm. "I know this whole meeting was hush-hush but Ivy would never lead you astray. You can trust her. You can trust me. We've been there and we know how it sucks."

Somehow, Jordan freed her feet from the concrete blocks holding her in place and made it to the elevator. Ivy grabbed her hand and held it, sending warm, soothing vibrations. The door slid open and Sage waved, nodding encouragement.

The inside of the elevator looked no different than any other. Aamon stepped in and Ivy half pulled-half dragged Jordan across the threshold. The door slid shut and she held her breath, waiting.

The walls, ceiling, and floor faded away and everything grew dark. Jordan squeezed Ivy's hand to make sure she was still there. Moments later she was flying through what looked like a worm hole in space. There were flashing colors of sickly yellow and orange, and a then a light that grew brighter, bigger. Jordan's stomach curled in on itself and she ground her teeth, wondering if this was what a psychedelic trip felt like.

Her feet landed in the strangest place she'd ever seen.

Surrounding her was a shaded forest full of foliage and trees. The soft, leaf-strewn ground dotted with wild plants, the invigorating scents of water, rich dirt, and growing things lent an air of Eden. Still, there was something unnatural about it. The woods were too quiet, too *perfect,* like an elaborate trap to draw in prey. Jordan felt the entire place was designed to infuse a sense of security and peace while a predator lurked just out of sight.

As if to prove her point, a blood-curdling howl stained the mock serenity, giving her goosebumps.

"Let's move," Aamon ordered.

He didn't have to tell her twice.

Thankfully, they weren't too far from a clearing. Jordan had never been so happy to see sunlight. As they burst from the trees, the ground changed from leaves and loamy soil to the gravel-covered alluvium of a desert. Craggy mountains grew like broken teeth from the silt, providing a backdrop for various cacti, desert ironwood, jumping cholla, and other vegetation. The smell from creosote bushes made her eyes water.

"Um...how did we go from a lush forest to a desert environment in the stretch of a few steps?"

"I'll explain while we walk. We aren't safe, even here, and we can't teleport on this planet."

*"Planet?"* They weren't on Earth anymore?

"Yes, we are on another planet."

"There are no planets that support life other than Earth."

Aamon skirted around a joshua tree. "None that

have been discovered, no."

The temperature was scorching. Jordan squinted as hot air blew sand across her face, stealing moisture from her body with every gust. Her tongue stuck to the roof of her mouth. Her eyes felt desiccated in their sockets.

"Why are we on a secret planet? Is your boss so important he requires a different world from everyone else?"

"Not necessarily, but what he guards does." Aamon stopped and pointed to yet another environment in the distance. This one looked tropical, like the jungles of Brazil. Jordan's mouth fell open.

"Where are we?" she asked in a hushed tone.

"Purgatory."

# XV Jordan

She was in Purgatory.

From a place where the souls of sinners go when they die to a place where those who have no souls go when they die. She'd definitely hit the fire when she jumped out of the frying pan this time. Then again, when did she not?

Jordan expected Aamon to lead them to the jungle she'd seen but instead, he turned to the right and walked slowly, eyes roaming. Maybe he was lost. It wouldn't be impossible in a place like this.

She caught up to Ivy. They were walking in an area between biomes. Here in this narrow stretch, a cool breeze blew, making the temperature felt more like late autumn. Jordan was grateful for her leather duds.

"Still mad at me?" Ivy asked. She kicked at a tuft of grass and avoided eye contact.

"No, but it would be nice to ask a question and get an answer instead of an evasion."

"I know, I'm sorry."

Aamon looked at them. "What do you want to know?"

Jordan decided to start with the simplest question first.

"Why Purgatory?"

She couldn't be sure, but she thought she saw a glimmer of relief in his eyes.

"Do you know what Purgatory is?" he asked.

Jordan nodded. "It's the place where the soulless go when they die; vampires, werewolves, almost every supernatural being or creature except angels and demons."

She said *soulless* but that was not exactly true. Some supernatural beings did have souls. The problem was that only *human* souls were allowed to traverse into Heaven and Hell. When a person contracts the vampire virus, their soul changes the second they swallow their first mouthful of human blood. The same was true for creatures like werewolves. During their first transformation from human to animal, their souls became tainted, less pure.

Perhaps out of compassion, God had decided that different didn't necessarily mean evil. He'd created Purgatory to give these non-human entities somewhere to go. After all, you can't blame the lion for killing the gazelle when it does so only to survive.

"Correct," Aamon said. "We are here because

my boss is in charge of Purgatory."

"And what? He can't leave and meet us in a normal place like an Olive Garden or something?"

He stopped outside a gate that glowed with blue light. "It's complicated."

"Isn't it always?" she mumbled.

Aamon stepped aside and Ivy took his place. She removed a small knife from her boot and made a slice across the meaty part of her palm underneath the thumb. Jordan gasped, but her sister brushed the self-mutilation off as if she did this every day. Who knew? Maybe she did.

The gate's glowing power changed from blue to white. The door wavered and disappeared. Aamon ushered them through quickly. When Jordan turned around, it was back in place, emanating blue light once more.

A stone path led to a modest Tudor home. Jordan admired the arches on the second floor and noticed the blue light that surrounded the gate enclosed the house in a sphere. Security was tight.

Aamon rang the doorbell then rocked back and forth on the balls of his feet, straightened his tie, and brushed at the sleeves of his jacket. He threw her a tentative smile, and she realized he was nervous, which did nothing to improve her own state of mind.

The door swung inward on silent hinges and an attractive woman with platinum hair, eyes colder than the Himalayas, and a scowl studied them from the threshold.

"Just when I think my day can't possibly get any worse, the universe conspires to prove me wrong."

Jordan recognized the voice. It had a nuance of a serial killer.

"Hello, Ava," Aamon schmoozed, kissing her hand. "You're looking radiant, as usual."

Ivy rolled her eyes behind his back. Jordan pretended to throw up. "You know, Aamon, you could reach her ass a lot easier if you got down on one knee." Jordan smiled sweetly up at him.

Ava raised an eyebrow. "Well, this ought to be interesting." She turned her back on them and disappeared inside.

Aamon rounded on Jordan, grabbing her arm and hissed, "Do not embarrass me."

Jordan pulled out of his grasp. "I don't have to. You're a pro at that already."

She stepped into the house without waiting for him. Behind her, Ivy chuckled.

Once inside the handsome foyer, Jordan had no idea which way to go. Ava was nowhere to be seen. A formal dining room stood to her right but it was empty. To her left was a closed door – probably a closet. Directly in front was a small hallway. She took a chance.

After passing a set of stairs, Jordan entered the living area, Ivy and Aamon on her heels. Butter-soft leather, polished woods, a grand fireplace, antique tables, and exquisite paintings made for a beautiful room, but it held no warmth. The décor looked staged, not lived in, the type of space that made her uncomfortable. Simply turning around could cause damage to something ridiculously overpriced. Jordan tiptoed to one of the couches and perched on the edge.

Not long after, Ava entered the room followed by a man so perfect he couldn't be real. Jordan's internal alarm went off even as her heart raced and butterflies swooped and fluttered in her stomach.

He was dressed casually in a plaid, button-down shirt, khakis, and Timberlands. Jordan's eyes took in a trim waist and wandered upward, lingering on a nice, broad chest. Full lips parted over perfect teeth. Smoldering eyes with full lashes and perfect brows stood out against wavy locks of dark brown hair that curled around his ears. It took a moment for Jordan to realize he was speaking to her.

"Huh?" she blurted intelligently. Dear God, she wanted to crawl under the sofa and die. Ava snickered from across the room and Jordan felt blood rush to her face.

"My name is Orias," he repeated. "You must be Jordan. Aamon has told me much about you."

His voice was as smooth as liquid gold. Jordan suddenly envisioned herself standing before him, shoulders bared, his warm hand trailing down her collarbone. She closed her eyes and resisted the urge to moan.

When the illusion faded along with the feelings of desire that piggybacked along for the ride, she reluctantly opened her eyes again. His knowing smile told Jordan that he had planted the vision in her head. Part of her felt violated and physically ill while another part wanted more, wanted him.

Ivy, seated beside her on the couch, grabbed her hand and squeezed, reminding Jordan she needed to be strong...and that Orias was a demon. She took a deep breath, threw her shoulders back, and glared at their host.

"Do that again, and it'll take a year to count the blade marks my knife will leave on your face."

Staring down Orias, she caught movement from the corner of her eye. Ava was fast, but not fast enough. Jordan rose from the couch and, without taking her eyes off the G.Q. demon, flung out her hand. With barely a nudge from her, white light arced from her palm and pushed Ava against the wall.

Aamon jumped to his feet but Orias motioned him down. Flowing around the furniture like water, he approached Ava, then turned back to Jordan and raised his own hand. She braced herself, sure the pain he would inflict would be astronomical. Blue and white light swirled around his hand like a snake before slithering to where she stood. Jordan held her breath, held her ground...

...and nothing happened.

It was hard to keep the surprise from showing on her face but she managed – just. Orias' eyes grew round and he lowered his hand. Jordan did the same, and Ava was able to move, though she didn't seem too keen to butt heads again.

"Honey, why don't you go upstairs? There's some business I need to discuss with Jordan in private." Orias caressed Ava's cheek.

"But, Father–"

*Father? Ewww.* Jordan wrinkled her nose. It should be some kind of law that demons who looked no older than twenty-five couldn't have children who looked the same age. It was gross.

"Ava, it will be fine." When she hesitated, he gave her a gentle push. "Go on."

Orias looked at Aamon. "You may leave, as well."

Her father's eyes lingered on her. Jordan saw a multitude of emotions flash in them. Suddenly, she was scared.

When Orias turned to Ivy, Jordan shook her head. "She stays or I go, too."

He nodded acquiescence.

"Ava," he called. She popped her head around the corner. Jordan wondered how long she'd been standing just out of sight. "When you go upstairs, ask your brother to join me, please."

"Why him?" she asked, pouting.

He merely pointed towards the stairs and she

stomped away.

The wait for Orias' son was uncomfortable. Orias didn't say anything, only stared at Jordan as if trying to figure out what made her tick. She could have told him he was wasting his time but didn't want to give the impression that she cared.

Her eyes drifted along the walls, admiring the beautiful paintings. They skipped from one to another and then landed on a guy. He had arrived as silently as smoke and was standing in the doorway, watching her. He smiled. It was friendly enough, and she found herself returning it before she could stop herself.

"Ah, Xander, there you are. Come, sit with us."

Xander threw Jordan for a loop by taking the seat next to her on the three-person couch even though there was an abundance of chairs and a settee he could have parked on. She glanced at Ivy, who shrugged and scooted to the end of the couch. Jordan went to follow but he placed a gentle hand on her knee.

"It's okay," Xander whispered in her ear. "Stay close, please."

She looked at his hand. It was calloused, scarred in a few places; badges of someone who hadn't lived an easy life. His arms were strong. Tendons stood out against tan skin and muscles stirred, flowing underneath the Army T-shirt he wore. By the time Jordan took in his short black hair and pure, light-blue eyes, she was on the verge of tears. For some reason, he reminded her of her brothers. Her heart ached. This guy, who didn't know her from Bob's house cat and was a demon, acted strangely protective, and for a second, she had the urge to lean against him.

Jordan nodded once and he gave her leg a squeeze before letting go. Surprisingly, she felt the absence of warmth when he removed his hand.

"Jordan, how do you like living at the cabin?"

Orias' voice startled her. She'd forgotten he was there. Viewing him now, she didn't find him as attractive as before, and was grateful.

"It's okay," she answered. "The woods are nice to walk in. It's peaceful…"

*I miss my home*, she thought. The tears threatened again and she fought them off. God, how could one guy make her so emotional? She felt as if someone had put every feeling she'd had the past three months in a blender on high speed and then poured them back into her.

Orias stretched his long legs out in front of him and crossed his ankles. Jordan couldn't figure him out. He obviously wanted something, but what?

"It must get very monotonous, not being able to go outside the boundary of the wards."

"I manage."

He smiled and Jordan felt Ivy tense up beside her. Soon…He would tell her what all this small talk was leading up to.

"How are you getting along with your new brothers and sisters?"

She was losing patience. "I like some better than others."

"So I've heard."

He stared as if waiting for something from her – an apology for what she did to Gina, perhaps? Jordan mentally rolled her eyes and hoped the chair he'd chosen was a comfortable one. He'd be waiting a long time.

Instead she said, "Can we stop with all the useless chatter? Why don't you tell me what business you need to discuss so we can go? It's getting late, I'm tired, and I'm ready to get these sweltering leather pants off before they cause a rash."

That smile again. Jordan got up from the couch and pulled Ivy with her. She had better things to do than sit with a demon while he played Doctor Phil.

"I have a job for you," he said.

Curious, she sat back down. "What kind of job?"

He crossed his arms to match his ankles. "A hunting job. I've gotten word of a rogue demon. I need her found and brought to me."

Something about this wasn't right. She didn't need Ivy's warning pinch on her arm to tell her that. "You have more demons at your disposal than a politician has brown-nosers. Why not send one of them?"

"Fair question." He tapped his temple for a

moment. "This particular demon is powerful, not to mention crafty. It would be a waste of time and resources to send someone who doesn't have a chance against her skills. *Your* powers are greater than hers, not to mention you are an experienced Slayer." He leaned forward in his chair. Jordan thought he looked like a praying mantis about to strike. "Simply put, I need the best."

*Ah, flattery.* She had to admit the appeal of leaving the cabin was immense. Maybe she could make this work to her advantage, but there was still one problem.

"What about the angels? If I leave the cabin, I'm no longer warded against them."

"Does the thought of that scare you?"

Jordan cocked her head, studying Orias. He didn't appear to be taking a jab. He seemed sincere in his question. She decided to be truthful.

"It used to." She sighed. "Being a prisoner means never seeing my family again. I can handle anything but that. Michael and I don't see eye to eye on…anything. He's an ass."

Orias clenched his jaw. His full lips pulled into a scowl and Jordan thought he was going to disagree with her. Instead, he only nodded. "And now?"

"I've realized it doesn't matter if I'm locked up in a cell in Heaven or a cabin in the Huron Mountains – a prison is a prison. The only difference is who's holding the key."

He leaned back in his chair. "I can take care of the warding issue. The question is, will you do it?"

Ivy pinched harder.

"What's in it for me?" Jordan asked. "In case you haven't heard, I'm no longer employed in the Celadon Circle. Ergo, I set my own prices."

"What is it you want?"

Now it was Jordan's turn to lean forward. "I want my own team for the job and, when I deliver your succubus with the wild hair up her keester, I want my freedom."

"How will you handle the angels without our protection? I can give you a temporary ward for the job, but they tend to become unstable with long periods of use. It's much easier to place permanent wards over a particular place, like we have at the cabin."

"I'll figure it out."

She waited – nerves raw and stomach in knots. This was her chance. All she had to do was one job and she could go home. *Home!* She didn't know what to do about the angels but she was stronger when she was with her family.

"Deal."

Jordan almost jumped off the couch and danced a jig but held her poker face. It wasn't hard, especially with Ivy's scorching gaze.

"Your team?" Orias inquired.

Of course she wanted Ivy to come, and she

probably would, even if she wanted to kill Jordan at the moment. Beside her, she felt Xander lightly touch her elbow – a small sign.

"I want my sister and Xander, if they'll both agree."

Orias' eyebrows rose. "I can certainly understand why you chose Ivy. I understand from Aamon that you two are quite close, but why my son?"

How could she explain the instant connection she felt to a guy she'd just met? Hell, she didn't understand it herself. Xander was a demon and yet, he made her feel safe. He felt like home.

"You wanted him here at this meeting for a reason. Was I wrong?"

"No. I'm just surprised you suggested he join you before I could."

She smiled. "I do have a brain. I knew Xander would be the stipulation to our deal. Why beat around the bush?"

"Why indeed."

Orias got up and walked to a wooden chest sitting on the mantle above the fireplace. Lifting the lid, he removed a round pendant on a silver chain, brought it over, and placed it in Jordan's hands.

The pendant, about the size of a quarter, was made of polished stone that appeared black in color, but changed to a greenish-blue when the light hit it a certain way. It had a circle inscribed on the surface in silver. Inside were two triangles, one inverted on top of another, with diamond shapes on both ends. Words and symbols she didn't understand decorated the outer edge and the connecting triangles within. It was beautiful.

"What's this?" she asked, running her finger over the mystical rune.

Orias sat on the coffee table in front of her. "This is the Third Pentacle of Jupiter. It will provide protection for you."

"From the angels?"

Instead of answering, Orias took the pendant and stood up. With a pianist's fingers, he opened the clasp and held the chain in front of him.

"May I?"

She nodded.

He bent and placed it around her neck. When finished, he said, "Don't take it off and don't lose it. Tuck it into your shirt if need be, especially if you get into an altercation."

He moved to a doorway on the opposite side of the room. "Tomorrow, you will spend the day acquiring any equipment you need for the hunt." He glanced at the ceiling as if turning a thought over in his mind. "You'll need a car. Shall I provide one for you or would you rather buy one yourself?"

Jordan laughed. "Sure. I'll pick some money off the *special* tree growing in the backyard and hit the nearest car dealership first thing in the morning."

Orias shook his head. "I will provide money for

anything you might need. I was not sure if you would be comfortable buying a car on your own or if you would like for me to handle the transportation."

Good point. She'd never bought anything as expensive as a car. Come to think of it, she'd never bought guns, either.

"How about I make a list of what I feel more comfortable with *you* buying and get the rest myself."

"That is doable. I'll be right back."

He left the room and Ivy shoved her, hard.

"Are you fucking crazy?" she whispered.

Jordan grinned. "Yes; I'm stir crazy from being in that cabin all the time. Tell me you aren't dying for some kind of normal life, Ivy."

She threw her hands up in the air. "Normal life? Yes, I would love one of those, Jordan. But hunting down a demon for Orias is not normal."

"It is for me."

Her sister leaned back and closed her eyes.

"You don't have to come," Jordan said. It hurt to think Ivy might bail but she couldn't fault her if she did. She hadn't forgotten the *Kongamato* or how it had thrown Ivy against a stone wall like a sack of potatoes. Hunting this demon could get dangerous.

When it came to powers, Ivy was middle of the road. The glow of her red eyes when she was in demon-mode gave away her status. There were two levels above her. Demons in those power brackets sported yellow glow or pearl-white. Lesser demons had green glow or solid black orbs. Jordan could only hope this particular baddie was in one of those categories.

"You know damn well I'm not going to let you do this alone." Ivy sat up. "I know this is important to you, but what if Orias reneges?"

"Then there will be one less demon stinking up the joint, and Orias will be *very* sorry."

"And what about him?" Ivy pointed to Xander, who'd been as quiet as a church mouse.

He placed his hand on the small of her back and, once again, she felt safe. She couldn't explain it – not here and not now.

"We'll talk about it later."

Angry, Ivy choked on the words she struggled to get past her lips, but calmed down when Jordan gave her pointed look.

Orias returned with a bulging pouch. He handed it to Jordan. "There should be enough money in there for anything you need. Make out your list; someone will be by to pick it up later. I'll have everything on it and suitable transportation delivered to the cabin tomorrow. On the front seat, you will find a report and the name of a contact."

"We won't be dealing directly with you?"

Orias motioned for them to stand and led them past the stairs into the foyer. "I'm very busy, Jordan. My contact will serve in my place. I trust him explicitly."

At the door, he said, "Xander will leave with you now. I know it is a long trip, so I arranged for a portal directly back to Tenura. From there, you can teleport to the cabin." He pointed to a spot past the gate to a swirling vortex.

"I'm sure you won't let me down."

Jordan looked into those hypnotic eyes she almost lost herself in before. Orias reminded her of someone. Later, maybe she would have time to think on it. Right now, her mind was occupied with preparations for the hunt.

"I'll get your demon. Just know you'll be next on my list if you don't keep your word."

Except for a nerve that jumped in his neck, Orias remained composed. "I'll keep that in mind."

Jordan and her new team left him standing in the doorway and made for the portal. Xander took point, eyes scanning for threats even though they were still in close proximity to the house.

"Aamon's gonna shit kittens when he hears about this," Ivy said.

"Orias is his boss. Aamon doesn't have a say. Besides, I make my own rules, Ivy. If he wants to be a part of my life, he has to accept that," Jordan said.

With a shrug, her sister entered the portal.

Jordan regarded the whirlpool of colors with trepidation, wishing there was another way back to Tenura. Wiping her sweaty palms on the front of her lycra shirt, she scanned the sky, praying for a helicopter or even a spaceship.

Xander took her hand and smiled. "Let's go together."

Relief made her shoulders sag. Grateful, Jordan nodded.

Side by side, they entered the vortex.

# XVI Quinn

**H**is head felt like a balloon on the verge of popping. The urge to spew pizza overwhelmed Quinn to the point of tears. He and Gabriel had just teleported from the hotel room and were now...

*Where the hell were they?*

Quinn's face pressed into a hard floor. It was deathly quiet. His ragged breath echoed, giving him the impression of a large room. He smelled lemon furniture polish and something else. Incense maybe?

"Are you okay?"

Gabriel's voice sounded loud in the stillness. When Quinn managed to get to his knees, the room spun.

"Ugh." He grabbed his head, closing his eyes against a merry-go-round he found himself on. "Please don't ever do that again."

He felt a hand on his shoulder and warm energy seep into his body. The dizziness passed. He let go of his head and took his first look around.

"Better?" Gabe asked.

Wiping sweat from his face with the sleeve of his T-shirt, Quinn shrugged. He didn't know what to make of the stained-glass windows, multitudes of polished pews, the altar, or the giant cross on the wall.

"Are we crucifying someone?"

Gabriel looked confused, as usual. "Why would we do that?" He shook his head and started for the back of the church. "No, we are here to find something I need, and we must hurry."

Quinn stayed where he was. Gabe didn't understand many "earthly" concepts and he guessed breaking and entering could be added to the angel's lengthy list of alien concepts.

"Hey, Gabe," he called, pulling himself onto one of the pews. "Do you own this church?"

Gabriel was on his hands and knees (a position similar to the one Quinn just relieved himself from) behind the altar.

"No," he answered. There was a squeal of what sounded like metal being bent. "I do not own any real estate."

Quinn considered explaining that not only were they committing a B and E but Gabe was also vandalizing property, then decided against it. His sister was a possible *Paladin,* they were being chased by angels who could fry him like a cheese stick, and had just *teleported*. The fact that they were in a church without permission and Gabe was tearing something apart didn't rank high on his list of things to stress over right then.

Still, he was getting antsy. This was taking too long.

"What are you doing back there?"

"Searching."

Well, duh.

"For what?"

More scuffling from behind the altar and then Gabriel stood. "For this." He held up a small box. "Hurry, Quinn. We don't have much time and I need your help. I can't do this alone."

That didn't sound ominous at all. Nevertheless, Quinn hurried to the altar. The box in Gabe's hand was definitely old, made of black wood with streaks of dull red showing through the patina. Raised insignia in what looked like gold adorned the surface, reminding Quinn of the symbols that appeared (and disappeared) on the cover of The Book.

Gabe removed the lid and set it on the altar. From its small depth, he pulled out a nail approximately six inches long with a triangular shaped head. The diameter was half an inch...and it glowed.

Quinn's eyes moved from the shining wooden nail to Gabe's impassive face and back again.

"I'm afraid to ask," he admitted.

"Hold this."

Gabriel thrust the nail into his hand and bent over to replace the box from where he had found it underneath the altar. Quinn heard the whine of bending metal again. When the box was back in place, the angel stood and removed his shirt.

"Um…" Quinn had no words.

"I need you to help me ward myself against Michael's angels."

Frowning, Quinn wondered exactly what that entailed. "If you tell me I have to anoint your body with holy water or something the answer is a resounding 'no'."

"I wish it were that simple."

Gabriel eyed the nail in Quinn's hand like one would a medieval torture device.

"Gabe…" That one word held the weight of many more but he couldn't think.

In a flat voice, his Guardian explained, "The nail is from Jesus' cross. It was blessed by Saint Jude, the patron saint of lost causes. That is why it glows."

"Gabe, I can't."

"It must be inserted between my wings. I can't reach back that far."

"Maybe we could find–"

"They'll be here soon."

"I don't think I can–"

"It will not hurt very much."

"You don't even *have* fucking wings!"

Quinn's hands shook worse than someone with palsy. He heard a *whooshing* sound he was familiar with and his heart nearly burst from his chest.

"Now, I do."

They were the most magical, awe-inspiring wonders Quinn had ever seen, stretching at least fifteen feet across. Tiny feathers no bigger than a thimble lay at the base between Gabe's shoulders, with slightly longer quills tucked between. This pattern expanded, the feathers growing in length and width. Toward the tips, they were as wide as Quinn's hand and twice as long. Though predominantly black, a spangle of color, like stars of a galaxy, rippled across like waves in the sun when Gabe raised and lowered them. Their edges held a certain gleam, mirroring the light Quinn looked for every morning in that moment just before the sun climbed above the hill.

Something inside him awoke, and Quinn was filled with hope and doubt. Hope for the future of their world, hope of a better place after they left it. And doubt that he would ever get a chance to see it. A single tear escaped to roll down his cheek.

Gabriel pulled him into a hug and he didn't fight it. It was as if the angel knew what he was feeling, how powerful it was, because he'd been there himself. After so many years of surviving with blinders on, the first time seeing the world without them was painful.

"Will you help me?" Gabriel whispered.

Quinn sniffed and pulled away. "Are you determined to do this?"

"It's the only way I know to ward myself against them."

"We don't have time to search for a different way?"

Gabriel shook his head. "We have less than twenty minutes. They're close. I feel them."

The edges of the nail dug into his hand. Slowly, Quinn opened his palm and studied the impression it left behind, wishing the lines could tell their future.

"Shit."

Gabriel nodded. "Yes. I do believe it has hit the propeller."

"The *fan*, Gabe." Quinn pinched the bridge of his nose. "The shit has hit the fan."

"Yes, that, too."

"Turn around."

Quinn moved to give Gabe and his wings room. The angel turned, bracing his hands against the altar. Quinn stared at the wings, wondering what they felt like. Were they soft like down or coarse, sharp enough around the edges to cut flesh? His hand hovered just above the plumes but he couldn't make himself touch them.

To touch an angel's wings is to make them fall.

*Where the hell did that come from?*

"Quinn?"

He snapped out of his daze. "I'm here."

"Okay; I'm ready."

*Yeah, but I'm not.*

"Press the nail in about an inch. My body will take over and pull it in the rest of the way."

"Thanks for the visual." Quinn took a deep breath. "Okay, here goes."

He located the spot between Gabriel's wings. It wasn't hard to find, as it was marked with a gold-colored cross. Carefully, he placed the point of the nail in the middle.

*Christ on a pony.*

"Just do it," Gabe said. Quinn heard him take a deep breath.

They were crucifying someone after all.

Quinn pushed the nail. And the angel wept.

Gabriel looked better and Quinn was relieved. They were camped in another hotel room – this one located in a city more populated than the one before. After the "nail incident", which Quinn never wanted to think about again, they teleported back to the shabby motel where Michael's soldiers had busted in. The place crawled with cops but the angels were gone. Quinn had the foresight to park Jordan's car around the corner of the motel when he'd returned from the store. He had registered with a fake name and I.D.

and also used the make and model of a different car. When no one was watching, they slipped around the back of the motel and left.

After a few hours of sleep, Quinn woke up with heavy, aching eyes, bad breath, and a growling stomach. Gabriel was reading The Book. He'd asked to see it after they checked into their new temporary home, before Quinn had succumbed to exhaustion.

Bright light peeked through a crack in the heavy curtains. Quinn figured it was after noon. He pushed his weary body up from the bed and sat on the edge.

Gabriel closed the book with a snap, his expression a mixture of excitement and concern. Quinn thought back to the first time he ever had sex and would bet the farm his face had looked the same way.

"We need to talk." His Guardian practically bounced in his seat while Quinn barely had the energy to raise his head.

"I know we do, Gabe, but damn, can I get a shower and some food first? It feels like my teeth have grown fur and I need some time to get my head together."

The angel's expression fell. Quinn felt bad for snapping.

"I'm sorry," Gabriel said. "Sometimes I forget about human needs."

"It's okay, I'm sorry for being an ass. I guess it's too late to warn you I'm not a morning person."

Gabriel smiled and Quinn added, "How are you feeling?"

The angel rolled his shoulders. "Much better, thank you. I don't feel the nail at all now."

"That's good. I'm glad." Quinn grabbed some clean clothes and toiletries from one of his bags and clapped Gabe on the shoulder on his way to the bathroom. "After I shower, we'll grab some food and talk while we eat. I need to call and check in with Nathan, too. Sound okay?"

"Yes. Can we get cheeseburgers?"

Quinn had yet to find anyone who could put away more food than he did, until he met Gabe. He'd cruised around until he found a Denny's. After assuring Gabe that they had cheeseburgers and fries, they went inside and managed to snag a booth in a corner, which was lucky because the place was packed.

He worked on a Grand Slam with extra hash browns while Gabe put away his second double-cheese burger platter. That impressed Quinn until he remembered Gabe was an angel. Sometimes, it was easy to forget. Other times, he wished he could.

"That book," Gabriel said around a mouthful of fries. "Where did you get it?"

Quinn took a sip of coffee and sighed appreciatively. It was amazing what food and strong coffee could do.

"I told you, I found it in Case's study."

Gabriel swallowed and drank some soda through the four straws in his glass.

"Any idea how it got there?"

"What makes you think Case or Nathan didn't buy it?"

There was no need to throw his name in. The idea of Quinn buying a book would be comical.

"Because that book can't be found in a store." Gabe pushed his plate away. It appeared his tank was full – for now. "As a matter of fact, it can't be found anywhere on Earth."

Quinn was intrigued. "What is it?"

"*The Oraculum*, also known as *The Book of Shadow and Light*."

"Can it help us?"

Gabriel frowned. "I think so. The text changes so it's hard to find the exact information we need. It will take time to learn how to control it."

Quinn sopped some egg yolk with a bit of toast and popped it in his mouth. "Damn, Gabe, you talk about the book like it's alive or something."

Gabriel's gaze drifted from the window beside them and leveled on his ward. "Exactly."

The phone rang five times and Quinn was waiting for voicemail to pick up when his brother finally answered. He sounded rushed...and pissed.

"What?!"

"Bad time to talk?

Through a hiss of static, Nathan blew out a breath. Quinn thought he heard a car door slam in the background.

"You have no idea," Nathan said.

Quinn heard the distinctive click of a shotgun as it was broke open. "Where the hell are you?"

"Nebraska."

"Who in Nebraska peed in your cornflakes?"

"Ghost."

"You're on a job? Is Case with you?" Quinn gnawed on his lip. He didn't like the thought of Nathan taking jobs on his own. Ghosts could be violent. Not to mention there were only a few ways to dispose of them. And why was Nathan back on the Winged-Ones payroll anyway?

"No, I'm not on a job." Nathan sounded a bit calmer. "This is where Lucas' demon led us to. She'd heard rumors Jordan was being held in an abandoned house in Bridgeport."

"Did you find anything?"

Nathan snorted. "Yeah, a 'condemned' sign, cobwebs, a possum, and the spirit of a grumpy 74-year-old man who died from carbon monoxide poisoning." He paused. "The ornery bastard can stay there, too. Brody's still inside. I ought to leave him – the wuss."

Nathan's mention of Quinn's twisted look-alike made him fume. If that half-wit caused his brother to get hurt he'd give him a scar to match his birthmark.

"Are you okay?"

Nathan chuckled. "Yeah, yeah, I'm fine. Don't get your panties in a bunch. Furniture started moving and the old guy threw a chair. Brody screamed and hid in a closet. After I checked all the rooms and didn't find any indication the house had been occupied since the invention of dirt, I shagged outta there and left sissy-boy. I guess he'll figure it out eventually."

"He's probably in there getting his ass kicked by the old man."

"That's a possibility."

Gabe flipped through *The Oraculum* while listening to their conversation with his super hearing. He looked up, eyebrows raised – a question to Quinn as to whether or not he'd tell Nathan the angel was with him.

"So, no sign of Jordan?" he asked.

Nathan sighed, "Nope, no sign of anyone. You know, I expected more from a high-level demon."

"How high?"

"Yellow eyes." Nathan answered. "And you know what was weird about her?"

"Do you really have time to get into that?"

"She kept asking where *you* were."

Gabe lay the book down and gave the conversation more of his attention. That worried Quinn.

"Why would she ask for me? I'm not into the

demon scene."

Quinn pictured Nathan shrugging his shoulders. "Don't know. She kept demanding to know where 'the other brother' was. Lucas finally told her you left for the night because you got mad."

"That's strange." Quinn hesitated, not sure how to bring up Gabe's reappearance. "Um, I've got some news, too."

He bit the bullet and told Nathan everything, including the name of The Book and his hope that Gabe might be able to figure it out.

"Put me on speaker," Nathan demanded.

Quinn pressed the button. "Go."

"Hey, Gabe, welcome back! So you told Michael where he could get off, huh?" Nathan chuckled.

The angel almost blushed. "In a matter of speaking. It's good to hear your voice."

Quinn asked Gabe to explain *The Oraculum*.

"My Father created the book long ago. It contains every spell, every definition, every prophecy foretold. It writes itself, which is why it changes. The book records the past, present, and future. Basically, it is the history of Heaven, Hell, and Earth."

"Holy crap," Nathan breathed. "But how did it end up in *our* house? Shouldn't a book that important be locked away somewhere?"

"It was," Gabe answered. "From what I know, Father gave it to one of his most trusted Virtues to keep safe. How it ended up in your possession is a mystery."

"Who was the Virtue He left it with?"

"I don't know. It was before my time."

They were all silent, lost in questions for which there were no answers. Finally, Nathan said, "Here comes Brody – the pansy. I'll tell Uncle Case what we've talked about when we get some time alone. This isn't something Lucas and his boys need to know."

"I agree," Gabriel said. "In the wrong hands, this book could be a means to end the world. No one other than us and your uncle can know anything about it."

Quickly, while he still had time, Quinn said, "Nate, watch your back. If you need me – call. I still have a weird feeling about Lucas and his brood, not to mention that nosy demon."

"Will do. Call me if you find out anything else."

Over the speaker, they heard the passenger door of Nathan's Camaro open and Brody yell, "Why'd you leave me? I coulda been killed!" followed by his brother's voice sounding deadly as he answered, "Get in or I'll kill you myself, Jerkoff." He ended the call.

Quinn looked around the better-than-average motel room. Gabe had sprung for a suite with a bed, sitting area, microwave, and mini-fridge, definitely one of the nicest rooms he'd ever crashed in. And yet, he really wanted to be home with his brother and uncle. He wanted to sleep in his own bed, to stop living out of duffle bags, and to work together to find Jordan. The fact that Nathan understood did little to assuage his feelings of guilt for taking off.

As if reading his mind, Gabe said, "Maybe Casen will realize he no longer needs Lucas and his demon and will make him leave."

Quinn gave a grim smile. "One can hope."

"Why did the demon inquire about your whereabouts?"

It was a question Quinn wondered about himself. Instead of answering right away, he went to the bar and poured some ground coffee – compliments of Holiday Inn – into the coffee maker. He needed caffeine.

Why *would* a demon be interested in him? Sure, he'd sent plenty of them back to their homeland. It was possible he'd tangled with this demon before. Demons who'd been on the receiving end of a Slayer weren't eager to help them afterward. The fact that Lucas had worked with this one before led Quinn to believe she had never felt the burn of silver.

When the coffee finished brewing, he placed two cups on the small table. Gabe added enough sugar and cream to make Quinn's teeth ache.

"And another thing," the angel said, stirring his coffee. "How did the demon even know about you?" He stuck the tiny, hollow stick in his cup and used it like a straw. "It's confusing. Do you think Lucas told her?"

Quinn took a sip of his coffee, sans creamer, sugar, or makeshift straw. "I'd like to think so. Lucas isn't the brightest bulb. It's not hard to picture him giving personal information to one of those bottom-dwellers and yet…I don't think he did."

"If not him, then who? How did a demon know Nathan had a brother and why would she care?"

It was a puzzle with too many missing pieces. Lucas played a part, but there was something else – something important. Quinn hoped he figured out what it was before it was too late.

# XVII Jordan

Amon was not happy. Jordan escaped to her room after an hour-long tirade that, from the sound of it, was still going strong downstairs. She grabbed a pair of sweats, one of Nathan's old T-shirts, and made for the shower before Ivy could claim it.

When she got out, her sister called, "Did you save me any hot water?"

Jordan poked her head into Ivy's room. "If I didn't it's your fault for making me wear that leather get-up and failing to mention we would be trekking through a desert in Purgatory." She stuck her tongue out and turned to leave.

"Hey, get back here!"

Jordan hesitated. She still didn't know what to say about Xander but there was no putting off the inevitable, especially when Ivy was the one waiting for answers. She needed to talk about the strange feelings she got around Orias' son. Maybe her sister could help.

"So, he makes you feel safe, like *home*." Ivy chewed on a strawberry Twizzler. "Are you sure what you're feeling isn't raging hormones? Maybe you just need to get some."

Jordan hit her with a pillow. "I'm serious!" She put her head in her hands. "I'm not saying he isn't attractive. A girl would have to be blind not to notice those soft curls and dreamy eyes. But from the moment he touched my knee, I've felt better than I have since this whole fiasco began." Jordan looked at Ivy who stared back, the candy forgotten. "It isn't lust. I felt like I knew him and always have. Am I going crazy?"

"No, I don't think you're crazy. The few times I've been around Xander, I got a strange vibe from him, too. He's different, but I don't know how."

"What *do* you know about him?" Jordan couldn't help her curiosity. At least now Ivy understood why.

She shrugged. "They found him in an orphanage when he was thirteen. No demon claimed responsibility, so Orias took him in."

"He's a Cambion?"

"Yes. It's rare for an Incubus, other than Aamon, to sire a child. It's even rarer for a baby to survive the birth, but it does happen. From information gleaned from the orphanage, Xander's mother died in childbirth. She had no family to speak of but did have a big bank account. He was made a ward of the state and they gladly took him in…along with his inheritance."

Jordan thought about her family and the way she'd been brought up. Her own mother had died while giving birth to her. She was raised to be a killer of Evil. There had been no birthday parties, vacations to the beach, or Saturday-morning cartoons, but she'd always known she was loved. How lonely life must have been for Xander. Hell, being raised by Aamon would have been better than an orphanage.

Ivy rummaged through her drawers for clean clothes and Jordan got up to leave.

"What time are we leaving to shop for supplies tomorrow?" she asked. "It won't be easy buying weapons, you know. Plus, we still have to pack."

At the door, Jordan nodded. "Orias is getting the more *sensitive* things we need. He's supposed to deliver them with the car. I guess we'll leave around ten."

"Do you trust him? Orias, I mean?" Ivy chewed her thumbnail.

It was more than a passing question. There was weight behind her words. Jordan knew her sister was keeping something from her but decided not to push the issue…for now. She was tired. Still, it irked her so she answered, "I'm not sure I trust anyone." She gave Ivy a long, hard look before walking out.

◇◇◇

"You have to take me with you!"

Jordan took another bite of vegetable soup and tried, without success, to ignore Mazie's demands. Her little sister had tracked her down and hadn't shut up since. Aamon wasn't the only one unhappy about her new job.

"If you leave me here, Gina will kill me."

Okay, that got her attention. Jordan pushed her bowl away and took a drink of water. "Mazie, she can't kill you. She doesn't have powers anymore, hon."

The youngest child in the house rolled a placemat between her slender fingers and whispered, "It doesn't take super powers to pick up a knife and run someone through with it while they're asleep."

Jordan winced. The scariest part was that it was true. Still, she couldn't take Mazie. The job was too dangerous. "I'll make sure Aamon keeps an eye on her."

"Like he did before?" Mazie shot back. "And I thought you were smart."

It broke her heart to see the desperation, to see the girl beg for her life again and know she was the one causing it. Would Gina really hurt her? Jordan hadn't seen the tramp since the night before and assumed Aamon had ordered her to stay in her room. Surely he was wiser now and would make it a priority to keep Gina in line.

"Mazie, hunting down this demon won't be easy. How can I concentrate on my job if I'm worrying about your safety? Please don't ask me to do this. It's unfair."

Her sister slammed her fist down on the table making Jordan jump. Face flushed, Mazie's eyes glowed emerald. "You know what isn't fair, Jordan? *You* burned away Gina's powers. *You* took the one thing that meant the most to her. She's at the end of her rope – do you honestly think she'll hang herself with it? Think she'll bow out and accept defeat? Gina no longer has anything left to lose and you're leaving *me* here to deal with it!" She shoved away from the table. Tears fell freely and Mazie brushed them away. "I thought you cared but you don't – not about me. All you care about is getting out of here and being with your *real* family and to hell with us, right? Well, I say to hell with you! Gina isn't the only selfish one in this house."

She stormed out and Jordan's heart ached at the sound of her sobs. They followed the girl up the stairs like sorrowful music. Jordan made herself listen to every single note.

The next morning, fat snowflakes fell gently on the mountain. They took their time, drifting on gossamer breezes, turning the cabin into a Norman Rockwell painting that clashed horribly with Jordan's mood. The snow had all of the kids talking about Christmas while Jordan was stuck in Halloween.

Ivy reported that the vehicle had been delivered. She and Xander checked it out. The slightly modified SUV had a hidden compartment where the weapons were stored. It would do.

Jordan knocked on the door to Aamon's study. She didn't want to talk to him so soon after he'd berated her for accepting a job from Orias. Nevertheless, it had to be done. Mazie's ballad had followed her into her dreams the night before, conjuring a nightmare where Gina stabbed her little sister over and over while asking, "Where's your savior now?" Jordan had awoken with a scream in her throat and gone directly to Mazie's room – not only hoping to talk to her but to assure she was okay. The girl had turned her back to Jordan, refusing to acknowledge her.

Now, doubt ate away at her like acid. Was she doing the right thing by leaving her behind?

"Come in!" Aamon barked from the other side of the door.

Great. He was still in a bad mood. Jordan took a deep breath and walked in.

Her father looked surprised to see her. He paused in his work, as if running scenarios of what she could possibly want through his head. Finally, he gestured to the chair across from his desk. After she sat, he asked, rather brusquely, "What can I do for you?"

Jordan wasted no time. "I'm worried about Mazie and need your advice."

Slowly, Aamon put his pen on the blotter, treating it like something from Tiffany's instead of Bic. "Why are you worried about Mazie?"

Jordan told him about the episode in the kitchen the night before, every single word. He pulled at the neck of his sweatshirt when she repeated his youngest daughter's remarks regarding his lack of supervision where Gina was concerned.

"I don't know if I should take her and risk her life or leave her and risk her life," she concluded.

"I see..." Aamon folded his hands on his desk.

Jordan waited for him to say he would ensure Mazie's safety and that she was out of line for suggesting he wouldn't. Instead, her father decided to leave that beaten path.

"You don't think much of me, do you?"

She chewed on her lip, wondering where he was going with his question. As was her custom, Jordan decided to be truthful and hope for the best (which she rarely got). "I don't think much of demons in general."

Aamon got up from behind his desk and walked to a small sitting area by a large picture window. He sat down on a well-worn chair and poured coffee from the service on a table beside him. Jordan wondered how many times he'd sat in that chair and stared out at the beauty of the mountains...and if he ever got tired of it.

"Do you have a minute?" He held up an extra

cup and she nodded. After he poured her coffee, she sipped it and appreciated the view. A few of the kids were playing in the snow. Brightly colored jackets mingled with the sound of laughter and snowballs. Mazie was not among them.

"I never wanted to be a demon."

Jordan turned away from the window and found her father looking at her. His eyes were soft, kind, and filled with a love she somehow knew was not for her.

"When my daughter was five, she became deathly ill. Her mother had passed away when she was two from a snake bite. Back in those days, the practice of medicine was archaic at best. The village doctor had not been able to save my wife and he would not have been able to save my daughter, either."

He took a sip from his cup. Jordan saw it tremble in his hand.

"Tatiana was…my world." He smiled. "Bouncy red curls, curious bright eyes, and the soul of someone far older than she. Everyone loved her and she loved everyone.

"When she got sick, I sat every day by her bed and watched that vitality slip away. Some days, I swore I could almost see it – her essence being carried up to the heavens. And every day, she made me swear to someday remarry and have another little girl to take her place."

Aamon looked at the floor and Jordan turned back to the window, giving him privacy to compose himself.

He wiped his eyes with a handkerchief and sniffed. "Tatiana was precious. Even though she was the one dying, her only concern was for me. She was like that – always worried about the welfare of others, even at such a young age. She would bring flowers to someone who was sad or soup to someone who was sick. She made sure to smile and speak to every person we met on our trips to the market. The entire village adored her.

"The world needed my Tatiana. I knew, if allowed, she would do wonderful things with her life. I'd heard talk of a witch who lived in Blackbird wood. People said she could make the impossible possible…for a price. I decided to see for myself."

The coffee, which had been so good going down, turned sour in Jordan's stomach. She could have walked out, spared herself the rest of his story, but felt she owed it to Aamon. She wondered if anyone else had stayed until the end. His following words gave her doubt.

"To make a long story short, I sold my soul to a demon and my daughter was cured. I got 15 years before I had to pay up and I made the most of every single day. Tatiana became a teacher, settled down with a good man, and had a child of her own." He met Jordan's eyes. "I wouldn't go back and change a thing, even though I pay for it now."

Jordan took in the posh room with its decorative wainscot and chair rail, the executive desk carved from a single piece of wood, and the handsome bookcases her brother would sell a kidney for. "It doesn't look like you have things so bad."

Aamon nodded. "One would think so."

"But you don't."

"One way or another, demons are punished for their weaknesses – whether they realize it or not."

"And what's your punishment, severe exhaustion from bed-hopping? No discounts on Viagra?" Jordan rolled her eyes.

"No." Her father's voice was deadly and she knew she'd pushed him too far. Always with the smart mouth. She never knew when to quit. Those beatings from Ira taught her nothing.

"Sorry," Jordan mumbled.

Aamon didn't react to her half-assed apology. Instead, he pushed the toe of his shoe into the carpet. Jordan was about to take her leave when he said, "My daughter's welfare was my weakness. Instead of accepting fate, I sold my soul to save her life and because of that, many more of my children have been taken from me – have paid the price."

He set down his empty cup and ran his hands through his hair. "I was willing to pay for the sin I committed thinking I'd be the only one to suffer. One moment of selfishness saved one child's life yet caused the deaths of so many others." His gaze distant, he whispered, "They die or become like me, and are taken away to live the lives my weakness condemned them to. Either way, I lose my children."

In that moment, Jordan realized Aamon did care for his kids. His weakness wasn't selfishness, not really. Maybe it was that he cared too much. Maybe he cared about her.

And she was leaving.

"You can only raise your kids to the best of your ability," Jordan said. "Make sure they know there are consequences for every action – good and bad."

He stood and smiled. "I try, but some of them are pigheaded."

"I prefer the word *tenacious*."

He held out his arms and she slowly walked into his embrace. Her father kissed the top of her head. "I won't ask you to stay because I know it would be a waste of breath, but I will ask that you and your sister be careful. I can't lose my favorite girls."

Jordan laughed into his sweatshirt. "Are we really your favorites?"

Aamon hugged her tighter. "Well, you're two of them. How's that?"

Jordan pulled away and looked up at him. God, what was she doing? He was a *demon*, one that had caused tremendous pain to her family. Aamon was the reason she was a freak of nature. But he was also her father, and needed something from her.

Acceptance? Forgiveness? Jordan wasn't sure if she could ever bring herself to *love* him, but she did understand his pain.

"If it's the best you can do, I guess I'll take it."

Tears welled up in his eyes. "Thank you." He hugged her once again. "Come back safe and don't worry; I'll watch over Mazie. I promise."

Jordan nodded, unable to talk past the lump in her throat. She didn't have the heart to tell him she wouldn't be coming back.

## XVIII Gabriel

*The Book of Shadow and Light.*

Gabriel still could not conceive how such a powerful tome had ended up in the hands of humans. He turned the pages, searching for any reference to *Paladins.* Every once in a while, a passage he was reading would change. It was aggravating to say the least. He had no idea what sorcery had been used to create the book, so he had no starting point on how to wield it.

What he did know was that there were angels and demons who would kill for it. Hidden within its ever-changing pages was the knowledge of all creation. Anyone who possessed it – and could manipulate it – would be the equivalent of a god. Gabriel couldn't help but wonder why his Father deemed such a powerful book necessary.

He got up for another cup of coffee. Strangely enough, he thought he was becoming addicted to it. Gabriel stared at the dark colored brew and thought about how vices were immoral. He shrugged and added lots of sugar and cream. If addiction to coffee was a sin, Hell wouldn't be able to hold all the people who were on their way down.

Quinn went for supplies and Gabriel stayed behind to study *The Oraculum*. He wasn't getting very far. He wished Yasen was there to take a look. If anyone would know how its magic worked, he would. Frustrated, he picked the book up again.

He decided to start at the beginning. On the first page there was a prophecy.

*There will come a day when grace shall be returned to the Watchers of the world. They will rise from their prisons and walk the Earth. They will gain followers of great importance and take their fight to the Heavens. A holy war unlike any before will commence between Good and Evil. The beginning and end will depend upon the decision of a* Paladin. *Her fall shall mark them both.*

The passage began to swirl on the page and Gabriel slapped his hand on top of the words as if he could physically stop them from changing. It didn't work. When he raised his palm from the page, the prophecy was gone and a Healing spell had taken its place.

"No!"

He frantically flipped the pages, hoping to run across the paragraph again but *The Oraculum* had decided to bury it for now. He slammed the cover shut and thought about hurling the frustrating thing out the window. They needed help.

Quinn came in shortly after, took in Gabriel's pacing and the pile of empty sugar and creamer packets – evidence of his Guardian's coffee-guzzling – and asked, "You okay?"

Gabriel continued to pace. "I'm fine." He turned the corner and headed around the couch. "Of course, I would be better if I could solve that enigma full of changing pages. I'm an archangel, for crying out loud! You'd think I could figure out a holy relic but no, all I am capable of is hiding from Michael, drinking coffee, and praying for miracles!"

He turned the corner again and headed for the coffee pot. Quinn put his hand out and stopped him.

"Gabe, how many cups have you drank today?"

The angel looked at the empty carafe, which had been full the last time he noticed it. "It would be easier to count how many pots instead."

Quinn sighed. "I think you've had enough." He led Gabriel to a chair. "Did something happen while I was out?"

"Yes! That loathsome textbook of babble revealed a prophecy that mentioned *Paladins*, but changed before I could finish it." He tossed the book to Quinn. "You take it. I'm sick of the sight of it." Gabriel sat on the edge of the bed, wishing he could hide under the covers. "I hate feeling so helpless. I hate that Jordan is missing and not even I – *an angel*

– can find her."

Quinn sat beside him, placing his hand on his shoulder. "Maybe that's your problem, Gabe."

He rubbed his eyes. "What do you mean?"

"You've never been in a situation where there wasn't a quick fix. Now, you've had several of them thrown at you all at once. You've got to stop blaming yourself for not being able to make things better with a snap of a finger. It won't always be that simple. Instead, focus on what you – what we – *can do*."

Gabriel traced the pattern on the bedspread with his finger. He couldn't remember the last time his divine powers had failed him. Unconsciously, he shook his head.

"Gabe," Quinn said. "There's more to you than a pair of wings and a halo."

Gabriel smiled, surprised but feeling better. Praise from Quinn meant more to him than it ever did coming from Michael's lips.

"But we still need help with the book. I can't get into Heaven to ask anyone. Michael will have guards stationed at every point of entry. What can we do?"

"We could call Nathan. Maybe he can make sense of it now that we know what it is. He may not be an angel but he's pretty darn close – only smarter."

Gabriel chuckled and stood. "It's worth a shot but if he can't, I'll have to try and get back into Heaven. We won't have a choice." He rummaged through the bags of groceries Quinn bought. "Oh, and ask him to bring more coffee."

Three knocks at the door, a pause, followed by two more signaled Nathan's arrival. Quinn kept the safety chain on the door and checked to make sure before letting his brother in.

Nathan had to duck to clear the doorway but once inside, he pulled Quinn into a hug. Gabriel felt this was something he should give them privacy for. He turned away but was grabbed from behind and his feet left the floor.

"Where do you think you're going?" Nathan laughed and set the angel down in order to give him a proper hug. Gabriel returned it, happy that Nathan was no longer upset with him, happy to have another member of his family back.

Nathan reached into his jacket pocket and pulled out a bag of coffee. "Here ya go, Gabe. Quinn told me you're hooked and you guys were out. Trust me. You don't want to be around him in the morning if there's no coffee. I once went to the store at the ungodly hour of 2 a.m. just so I wouldn't have to experience it again. Once was enough. I had nightmares for a week."

Quinn snatched the bag from Nathan's hand. "I'll hold onto this. If I don't, Gabe will have it all brewed and gone before sunrise."

They gathered in the small living area of the hotel room. Nathan looked around and whistled. "Dang! Why couldn't we have stayed high on the hog like this when we were on hunts?"

"Because we didn't have Gabe's money to pay for it." Quinn passed *The Oraculum* to his twin.

Nathan inspected the cover. "Gabe, tell me again what that prophecy said."

Gabriel paraphrased what he'd read. "The problem is that I don't know how to control the book."

Nathan turned to a random page and scanned it. "I couldn't find any information on *The Oraculum* or *The Book of Shadow and Light*."

"No," Gabriel replied. "You wouldn't have. Not many know about this relic."

"But," Nathan continued. "I was able to research a similar magic used to create it. It originated in Sumer."

"What's Sumer?" Quinn asked.

"A civilization in Mesopotamia. This particular magic originated from Enmeduranki – a Sumerian king who supposedly ruled for 21,000 years."

Gabriel leaned forward in his seat. "Of course! It all makes sense."

"It does?" Quinn asked. "I can't even pronounce some of the words Nathan said much less make sense of them."

"No shocker there," his brother muttered under

his breath.

Quinn flipped him off.

Gabriel listened to the twins banter back and forth. Their relationship was like an onion with many layers, each supporting the other. And at the very center was unshakable love and trust. He thought about Michael and felt a sharp pang of regret. The archangel had called him *brother* for eons but had forgotten the meaning of the word.

"So, I'm not a historian," Quinn admitted. "I have better things to do with my time. Are ya'll gonna explain this to me or keep singing the praises of virginity? I'm fairly sure it's hard to see any action when your nose is stuck in the spine of a book."

Nathan rolled his eyes. Gabriel, not quite sure what virgins had to do with anything, explained, "Enmeduranki is better known as Enoch – a Virtue and Scribe to my Father. It is more than probable that he made contributions to the book. Father sent him on several journeys."

"From my research, I learned that Enoch was "blessed with magical powers." In another book regarding the spiritual workings of Mesopotamia, one of the first rituals includes a prayer to Enmeduranki." Nathan shrugged. "I believe they're connected."

"Nathan, this conversation is about as boring as an insurance seminar. I'm not considering hara-kiri yet but I might, just for some amusement, if you don't get to the friggin' point." Quinn fidgeted in his chair like a five-year-old. "What did you learn?"

Opening *The Oraculum*, Nathan said, "I learned the simplest way to get what you want is to *ask for it*." He placed his palm on the first page of text and whispered, "Allow me to see."

The words disappeared from the paper.

Gabriel and Quinn squeezed in on either side of Nathan on the small couch. Together, they leaned over the book and waited.

When nothing happened, Quinn said, "I think you screwed it up–"

"Wait!" Gabriel interrupted. Words swirled into focus.

*Idem Opus*.

Quinn frowned. "What's that mean?"

"It's asking for identification." Nathan looked at Gabriel. "What do you think?"

The angel nodded. "I need something sharp."

"For what?" Quinn unsnapped a sheath on his belt and pulled out a wicked silver knife engraved with a pentagram. He handed it over.

Gabriel made a slice across his palm. He let a few drops of blood splatter onto the page and then healed the cut. It faded from view as quickly as his offering.

Quinn took the blade back, wiping it clean with a tissue from a box on the table. "Does anyone else feel like we just crossed over to Hogwarts?"

"It was the only way for the book to recognize

him as an angel." Nathan explained.

"Yeah," Quinn shook his head. "Sometimes, a passport just won't do. And I thought security at the airport was tight."

"Try it now, Nathan." Gabriel said. The page was no longer blank.

*Lorem Gabriel angelus Domini. Quomodo tibi serviat?*

Welcome, Gabriel, angel of the Lord. How may I be of service to you?

Nathan cleared his throat. "Show me information on *Paladins*."

The words on the page disappeared and were replaced with others. The letters had changed, though, and Quinn groaned when he saw them.

"Enochian? Really?"

"I *am* an angel," Gabriel replied. "This is our language." He pulled *The Oraculum* into his lap. "Don't worry; I'll translate it."

He read the passage aloud.

Paladins *are humans with the acquired genes of a demon and the grace of an angel. This amalgamation is rare and precarious. With regard to power, Paladins are second only to the Lord Almighty. As they harbor both Good and Evil, it can be especially difficult for Paladins to give allegiance to any single group of supernatural beings. Conflicting emotions can bring changes in personality and habits.*

"Son of a whore."

For once, Gabriel couldn't argue with Quinn's expletive. At the moment, he was at a lack for words to describe the unease that settled in his bones.

"It sounds like *Paladins* are nuclear bombs that could blow at any time." Nathan struggled up from the couch. "Other than God, she could be the most powerful being there is? What does it mean by *precarious*?" He looked from Quinn to Gabriel. "I don't like this."

"I need a beer." Quinn made a bee-line for the mini fridge.

"Ask it about the prophecy you read," Nathan requested, shaking his head at the beer his brother offered and grabbing two bottles of water instead. He handed one to Gabriel.

He would have preferred coffee, but took a sip of the cold water before turning back to the book.

"Show me the prophecy regarding the holy war to come."

Words appeared, swirled, and then Gabriel was staring at an expanded version of what he'd read before.

*There will come a day when grace shall be returned to the Watchers of the world. They will rise from their prisons and walk the Earth. They will gain followers of great importance and take their fight to the Heavens. A holy war unlike any before will commence between Good and Evil. The beginning and end will depend upon the decision of a* Paladin. *Her fall shall mark them both.*

*A* Paladin's *blood, given freely, is the key to Lucifer's cell.* The Book of Shadow and Light *is the guide. Good and Evil must work together to safeguard Earth and her people. The* Paladin's *soul must be lifted from darkness by her equal in order for her to descend. Only then can the war be ended.*

There was complete silence as Gabriel finished the passage. He had a feeling that, like him, the twins were afraid to speak – and really, what could they say? From their ashen pallor and grim expressions, both boys understood what he'd read.

A war was coming and, if Jordan was indeed a *Paladin*, her fall would signify the beginning. Her death would be the end.

# XIX Jordan

They headed south on road 550 which would eventually become Big Bay road. Jordan hoped to make it to Wausau before they had to stop for the night but that would depend on the weather, which was not cooperating. After all their careful planning the day before, buying supplies, making sure the SUV was packed, and mapping out the first leg of their trip, they had already fallen behind schedule. She mentally kicked herself every time the wind swooped down off the mountain and blinded them with heavy snowfall that was not supposed to hit until much later in the evening.

*And I still didn't get to talk to Mazie.*

Jordan, along with Aamon, Ivy, and Xander, had searched the house and surrounding wood. Her voice was still hoarse from calling her little sister's name repeatedly with no results. After three hours of Ivy's incessant complaints that Mazie was acting like a brat, would get over it, and they needed to haul ass,

Jordan had conceded defeat. With a heavy heart and guilty conscience, she'd climbed into the car – after Aamon promised to have Mazie give her a call later on.

"She's upset," he said, giving her shoulder a squeeze. "Ivy's right; she'll come around."

Jordan wasn't so sure.

Mazie hadn't uttered one word to her since the episode in the kitchen. She'd spent an hour the night before begging outside her locked bedroom door. Her pleas had gone unanswered by the headstrong girl.

*She hates me.*

A gust of wind rocked the SUV and Jordan's thoughts momentarily shifted to the weather. The storm had not abated, but wasn't any worse, either. Thank God for small miracles. With any luck, they would be out of the worst of it soon.

A quick glance showed Ivy stretched out on the backseat with earbuds in place. Eyes closed, she drummed her fingers to the music. Beside Jordan, Xander drove with the confidence of someone who faced dangerous storms almost every day, and maybe he did.

Jordan still didn't know much about him. They hadn't had many chances to talk since their return from Orias' house. Still, just being in the same room with him made her feel warm, comfortable. She'd spent some time pondering why that was. Xander was like her favorite pair of pajamas back at the farmhouse. They were soft, worn, and fit just right. Even now, she could remember how they felt against her skin. After a long day, she'd take a hot bath, slip them on, and her mind and body would sigh with relief. They were familiar.

When she looked at him, Jordan found his blue eyes glancing back. He winked before turning his gaze back to the road. She wanted to talk to him, to understand him in hopes of making sense of the bizarre feelings he evoked, but didn't know where to start.

Out of nowhere, tears welled in her eyes and she turned to the passenger-side window to hide them. Other than her brothers, Jordan's experience with casual conversation where guys were concerned was almost nil. She could hardly count Tucker, her one and only kind-of-boyfriend when she was 15.

His father owned the grocery store in town and he worked there after school and on weekends. Jordan used to drive Uncle Case's land yacht of a car to do the shopping (thank God for small towns and a sheriff who looked the other way) and Tucker followed her up and down the aisles like a lost puppy. He was cute, with hair the color of summer wheat and hazel eyes. His smile was easy, and he kept to safe subjects like books and farming when they talked. After weeks of helping her grocery shop while his father yelled for him to get back to work, Tucker managed to finagle an afternoon of horseback riding.

He arrived at the farmhouse right on time. Jordan spent all morning searching through her meager wardrobe for something nice to wear, putting on makeup only to scrub it off, and missing her mother. She had no idea what she was doing, no girlfriends to confer with – hell, she didn't even read teen magazines. Frustrated, she finally slipped on a pair of cut-off jeans, tank top, boots, and thrown her carefully styled hair into a ponytail.

The only positive was that her brothers weren't there to embarrass her and Uncle Case was busy with the cows. While Tucker backed his beautiful Appaloosa out of the trailer and got her saddled, Jordan went for Archer. They met at the gate to the fields.

To her surprise, the day started out smoothly. Jordan showed Tucker her favorite places on the farm. They talked about movies, horses – those *safe* subjects again. Later, they took a break by the pond, unsaddling the horses to let them rest and graze while they shared a thermos of iced tea, cheese crackers, and apples. In the shade of a white ash tree, Jordan received her first kiss. It was tender, sweet, and took her breath away.

On the way back to the farmhouse she felt as light and carefree as a cloud, sure that Archer's reins were the only thing keeping her from floating away. It wasn't until she got to the barn that the pressure began behind her eyes. Jordan hadn't had a vision in a few days and, with her upcoming first date, didn't give it a second thought. She was overdue.

It came on fast and she had no time to prepare. She managed to get Archer unsaddled before the vision fell upon her like a tornado and swept her away. When Jordan came to after experiencing a particularly horrifying werewolf attack on a young man, Tucker was there, shaking her, calling her name. She couldn't see him, but the tremor in his voice made her long for dark corners, somewhere safe from his curious eyes.

She told him she hit her head and passed out, but the fact that she had her eyes open the entire time, probably trembling from the vision and mewling like an injured cat, made the flimsy excuse hard to sell.

When Tucker discovered she was blind, he went into full panic mode. Ignoring Jordan's protests, he ran for Uncle Case. When she finally got her sight back, the look on Tucker's face told her there would be no more dates, no more kisses, no more following her around the grocery store. She'd seen it many times before – the shifting eyes that couldn't meet her own, the flushed skin, the painted-on smile...

He slowly backed away, claiming the need to get home and promising to call. She never heard from him again.

◇◇◇

Even now, the thought of that day left her feeling empty. It had been one of the best and worst moments of her life.

Jordan leaned her head against the cool window, watching the scenery through a curtain of white. She had thought she had it bad when she was a Seeker for the Circle. Now, she was a *Paladin* – an even worse freak. The hope for some kind of normal life was a pipe dream but still, she couldn't let it go. Just like those people who buy a weekly lottery ticket when their chances of winning are slim to none.

"Talk to me. Tell me what's wrong."

Xander's voice was like a life raft. Jordan wanted so badly to reach for it and hang on.

She sighed, turning in her seat. Even in the tarnished light of the car's interior, she could easily see his profile. Jordan wasn't so distracted that she couldn't appreciate how handsome Xander was. Though short, his dark hair had a bit of wave, hinting at soft curls if he'd let it grow longer. His nose sported a small bump on the bridge, but the quirk gave it character. A strong, clean-shaven jaw led to a pair of nicely proportioned lips – the top slightly fuller than the bottom. His chin had a slight trace of a cleft.

"How do I rank?" he asked with a smile. "Is

there hope of a girlfriend in my future or should I start making inquiries at monasteries?" His eyes, framed by long lashes, twinkled mischievously.

Jordan longed to reciprocate his teasing but knew that all too familiar path would lead to a dead end. Instead, she asked, "What makes you think something's wrong?"

His smile disappeared. "I can feel it."

Jordan nodded. "You're an empath."

"No. I can't feel anyone's emotions but yours."

"Why?"

Xander shrugged. "I was hoping you'd know. It's like I have a connection to you."

"What do you mean?" Jordan wondered if his feelings ran as deep as her own.

"I can't explain it."

"Try."

The hum of tires on pavement made a soothing backdrop for confessions and secrets. After a quick look in the rearview mirror, he said, "A piece of me I didn't even know was missing returned the day I met you. For the first time in my life I feel complete – like I finally have a purpose."

Jordan stared, not sure what to say. Xander gripped the steering wheel, white knuckles standing out sharply beneath his skin.

"What purpose?" she asked barely above a whisper.

"Maybe keeping you safe?" He flexed his

fingers. "I don't understand it anymore than you do."

Xander touched the back of her hand and she pulled her attention away from the road to look at him. "Why did you pick me for this hunt?" he asked.

Jordan's first reaction was to repeat what she told his father – Orias would have insisted he go anyway. But Xander had been honest and deserved the same. She struggled to find words that didn't make her come across like a lovesick girl with a crush. What she felt when she was near him went much deeper, and in a totally different direction, than that.

"Because you feel like home," she blurted.

Mentally kicking herself, Jordan bit her lip. As blood crept into her cheeks, making them burn, she sent up a silent prayer that Ivy wasn't listening. Though her sister knew how she felt, talking to Xander was hard enough without an audience. Besides, Ivy was comfortable around people their age. Jordan pictured her rolling her eyes in the back seat and wanted to hurl herself out the passenger door.

*There's no hope for me*, she thought.

Xander's hand covered her own. "If I had a home, I bet you'd remind me of it, too."

Resisting the urge to lace her fingers with his, Jordan pulled her hand away, reaching for her bottle of water as an excuse. She took a swig and said, "I thought you lived with Orias."

He slowed to take a sharp curve. The storm was

letting up and Jordan was glad. They might make Wausau after all.

"I wouldn't go so far as to say I *live* with Orias and Ava. I'm more like a boarder who doesn't pay rent."

"He called you his adopted son."

"Whatever. He sure as hell doesn't treat me like one. For the most part, Orias ignores me." Xander reached for her water and took a long drink. "Not that I care," he continued, handing the bottle back. "Frankly, I can't stand him – and I'd like nothing more than to wring Ava's neck. Talk about needing a straitjacket and some happy meds..." He snorted. "She's as uptight as a mosquito's ass in a nosedive."

From the back seat, Ivy burst out laughing. Soon, Jordan and Xander joined in.

After they settled down, Ivy asked, "What level Cambion are you, Xander?"

He closed his eyes. They glowed green when he opened them. Ivy nodded. He was one step above the lowest level.

That surprised Jordan. She felt certain he'd rank at least as high as Ivy.

Xander closed his eyes again. When he opened them this time, they glowed red. Again, and they glowed yellow.

Ivy gasped. "Well, that's something I haven't seen before. What powers do you have?"

At that, Xander grew quiet. Jaws clenched, he

watched the winding road.

Jordan wondered why. He probably knew everything there was to know about her from Orias, and Ivy wasn't shy when it came to discussing her demon status or anything else.

Behind her, Ivy huffed. "Oh, come on, Xander. I can't stand Orias, either. I won't be inviting him over for a sleepover so we can braid each other's hair and gossip anytime soon, so 'fess up."

He glared at Ivy so long in the rearview that Jordan reached for the "Oh, Shit Bar" above her head, sure they would run off the road. When he broke contact and looked back the way they were traveling, her heartbeat slowed to normal rhythm.

"If you can't trust us, who can you trust?" Ivy pressed on in typical fashion. "We're basically putting our lives in each other's hands by doing this job together. My sister has faith in you *and me*. She wouldn't have asked us to help otherwise. I'd never do anything to jeopardize that. I care about her too much."

Jordan reached across the seat and she and Ivy bumped fists. If she was allowed to return home when the job was done, Jordan would make it a priority to keep in touch with her half-sister. She could no longer deny she had grown to love Ivy. The fact that she was part demon had never been the issue when it came to keeping her distance.

Like a piece of agate in a rock tumbler, Jordan's

reluctance to admit her true feelings rolled around inside her head. What emerged was as lucid as clear quartz.

She was afraid – not only of getting close but of what others might think. Until then, it had never occurred to her that there was no one to worry about or impress. She was no longer in the Circle – not that it mattered. Gabe had already walked away. Uncle Case and the boys would come to understand and love her regardless.

"I'm an Invictus."

Xander's reluctant answer to Ivy's question meant nothing to Jordan. Her sister, however, looked pissed.

Scowling at the back of his head, Ivy said, "Well, isn't that enlightening."

"What?" Jordan asked.

"An Invictus has the power of persuasion," she answered, shaking her head. "No wonder Jordan invited you along for the ride."

Ivy's implication had just begun to sink in when Xander came to an abrupt stop on the side of the road. He slammed the gearshift into Park and turned in his seat.

"I did not persuade Jordan in any way."

His voice was a deep growl. The hairs on Jordan's arms stood up.

"I can't influence *feelings*, only thoughts – and my power only works on lesser demons and humans."

His eyes pleaded with her. "I swear, Jordan. I've never used my power on anyone."

Refusing to let it go, as was her custom, Ivy said, "If you've never used your power then how do you know it only works on lesser demons and humans?"

"By accident," he spat. "At the orphanage, my favorite pastime was reading comics in an old tree house that stood at the edge of the property. The activities director was a lazy sow who hated being outdoors. She always ordered us to stay inside and paint so she could stuff her face with donuts and yak on the phone."

Xander looked out the window, his faraway eyes clearly seeing a different time and place.

"One day, I pretended I had super powers. Staring at her, I thought to myself, 'You want us to go outside and play.' Seconds later, her eyes glazed over, sweat dripped off her head…I thought she was sick. Instead of spewing the half dozen donuts she'd wolfed down in front of us, she said we could go outside and play."

"That could have been a coincidence," Jordan said.

"Maybe," he conceded. "That's one of the reasons Orias wanted me with you on this job. He thinks I'm useless."

"What other powers do you have?" Ivy demanded. "I know damn well if you can change your eye color like that you're much more than an

Invictus."

He rounded on her then. "You told me to confide in you because we all need to *trust* one another, then accused me of using my power to influence Jordan." He turned in his seat, put the car in Drive, and checked the rearview before pulling back out on the road. "We'll all ice skate in Hell before I tell you anything else."

"Well, that sucks." Ivy stretched her legs and plucked her iPod off the seat beside her. "I've got money on the Raiders' game this week. It would be nice to know if they'll win." She paused, looking dejected with one earbud in place and the other swinging like a pendulum in front of her. "Then again, we'll probably all ice skate in Hell before that happens, too."

Jordan silently agreed while Xander's lips twitched in a reluctant smile.

They reached Wausau a little after 7:00 p.m. The Jefferson Street Inn never looked so good. Really. The place was fabulous as far as hotels went. Ivy insisted on putting Orias' money to good use so they got one of the most expensive suites available with a second, attached guest room.

Once inside, they all went their separate ways. Ivy headed for the coffee pot, Xander to the guest room, and Jordan, feeling a bit lost, sat on the couch. She needed a shower, some food and, most important, to make a phone call.

She made Xander stop at Wal-Mart where she bought a disposable phone. When she'd left Tennessee with Aamon and Ivy, Jordan had forgotten to retrieve her cell from Nathan's car. Afterward, Aamon had been reluctant to let her have one, stating the angels would expect her to contact her family and would trace the call. The idea of angels tracing electronic devices seemed comical and ridiculous, but Jordan held her tongue.

Now, there was no one to stop her. Ivy, of course, balked at the idea. Jordan ignored her. After three months of silence, her family felt as distant as the moon. Hearing their voices would help her reconnect.

She hoped.

Xander returned and inquired about food. Too tired to go out, they agreed to order pizza. Jordan, a steaming cup of coffee in hand, went to take a shower.

Wrapped in a fluffy robe, feeling ninety percent better thanks to good water pressure and strawberry scented shampoo, she followed the aroma of Italian spices and tomato sauce to the kitchen. In the living room, Ivy and Xander watched a *Supernatural* re-run while devouring slices of pizza. They weren't speaking, but at least they occupied the same space.

Jordan took that as a positive sign.

Finished with her supper, Ivy decided to take advantage of the whirlpool tub in the bedroom. Jordan waited until the door closed behind her, then pulled the disposable cell from the pocket of the robe. She rubbed the keys with her thumb, tracing the digits of the phone number at the farm. Her family was waiting for her, needed to hear from her. The thought of the call made her hands shake.

"I'll give you some privacy," Xander said. He took her plate, stacked it on top of his own, and carried them to the kitchen. When he walked past her to his room, she was still staring at the phone in her hand.

"You okay?"

Jordan licked her lips. "I don't know." Her voice shook. "For three months, all I've wanted is to talk to my family. It just occurred to me that they may not feel the same."

Xander sat beside her and pulled her into his arms. Jordan buried her face in his broad chest and cried. "Wha-what if th-they hate me now?" she stuttered, words muffled against his shirt. "What if they d-don't want me anymore?"

"Shh," he soothed, rubbing her back. "Call them. I'd bet my life you couldn't be farther from the truth."

"I'm – scared."

"We're all scared sometimes."

Jordan snatched some tissues from a nearby box and dried her eyes, waiting for the heat of embarrassment to color her cheeks but it never came. Crying in front of Xander, confessing her insecurities, felt no different than when she talked to Nathan.

"You won't be able to concentrate on this job until you put your mind at ease." He brushed a stray lock of hair from her face.

"I know." She took a deep breath and exhaled. "What if they're being watched? My call could put us *all* in danger."

Watching her hands shred the tissue, Xander asked, "Who would the angels expect you to call – which member of your family?"

Without hesitation, she answered, "My brother, Nathan, or my uncle."

"What about your other brother…?"

"Quinn," she supplied the name he was reaching for. Jordan massaged her temples. "Maybe, I don't know. For a long time, he and I didn't get along. We took a few steps toward repairing our relationship, but then I had to disappear. It's unlikely that the angels know that."

"Then that's who you should call. Chances are, they won't watch him as closely as the others, if they're watching at all."

Jordan had no doubt Nathan and Case were being watched. Michael knew the particulars of their family life.

"Does Quinn have a cell phone?"

She nodded.

From the bedroom, they heard Ivy moving about. Xander nodded toward his room. "Go in there to make your call. I'll sit out here and make sure she doesn't interrupt." His smile was devilish.

Jordan rolled her eyes. "No arguing."

He crossed his heart with his finger. On impulse, she leaned over and kissed his cheek. It was an innocent peck but still, she didn't want to give Xander the wrong idea.

Thankfully, he winked and shooed her away. "Be gone, woman. It's time for my show."

He flipped the channel to *Dance Moms* and Jordan chuckled. She left him to his drama and went to make her call.

In the guest room, Jordan sat on the edge of the king-size bed and pulled the phone from her pocket. She'd already activated it – nothing left to do but put in Quinn's number and press *send*.

*Please don't let this be the catalyst that brings us all down.*

Before she could change her mind, Jordan quickly dialed her brother's number and sent the call. After a brief pause, the phone began to ring.

# XX Jordan

After the fourth ring, she began to fidget. He wasn't going to answer. Jordan pressed the phone to her ear and willed Quinn to pick up at the other end.

"Hello?"

She almost cheered…until she realized it wasn't her brother's voice coming through the speaker.

"Hello? Is anyone there?"

She knew that voice – would recognize it anywhere.

*Gabe.*

Quinn *was* being watched.

Though he'd turned his back on their family, Jordan never thought her Guardian would actively participate in hunting her down. All these months, she'd almost convinced herself he didn't have a choice when he left them high and dry. Michael was top brass. He gave the orders. And yet, Gabe was manning Quinn's phone – the bastard. She wanted to scream.

"Who is it, Gabe?" a voice in the background inquired.

Without thinking, she whispered, "Quinn?"

"Jordan, is that you?" Gabe asked.

*"Jordan?!"*

The person in the background shouted and she smiled through tears.

Yes, that was her brother.

Over the line, she heard a scuffle of sorts and then Quinn was there – his voice so clear he could have been sitting next to her.

"Jordan, is that you? *Jordan!*"

She sniffed and swallowed around the lump in her throat. Still, Jordan barely recognized herself when she replied, "Yes, it's me." She paused and tried again. "Quinn, it's me."

"Oh, thank God!"

She wanted to reach through the phone and hug him. Her brother was okay. But why was Gabe there?

"It's so good to hear your voice," she said, still sniffling.

"It's good to hear yours, too. We've been worried sick. Are you okay?"

She nodded, then remembered he couldn't see her. "I'm okay. Quinn, is it safe for you to talk?"

"Yes. What about you? Tell me where you are and we'll come get you."

The prospect was tempting. She pictured herself

in a group hug, mashed between him, Nathan, and Uncle Case.

"Jordan?"

"I'm here."

It was on the tip of her tongue to tell him her location. Instead, she bit her bottom lip hard enough to draw blood. She had a job to do. Orias would hunt her down if she didn't keep her end of the bargain. There was no way she would bring that kind of danger to her family.

"Are Nathan and Uncle Case okay?" she asked, hoping Quinn wouldn't notice the change of subject.

"They are," he answered. "I'm not with them right now, but Nathan was here last night."

"Where's 'here?'" He wasn't at home?

On the other end, Quinn sighed. "It's a long story. I'm with Gabe at a motel but I swear, we're all fine."

"Why Gabe? He left us. Have you forgotten what happened in the mine?"

Quinn was quiet for a moment. "No, I didn't forget. I lost you that day, in more ways than one."

He was referring to when she died. Jordan had occasional nightmares where she was back on that rocky ledge, blood from the fatal bite delivered by the *Kongamato* rolling down her neck, dripping from the ends of her hair as it held her in its massive arms, poised for one more strike.

It never got the chance. Instead, the *Kongamato*

died, lost its grip on her, and she fell. Jordan had no idea if she died from blood loss, the broken back, or the crushed skull. Dead is dead. She supposed it didn't matter.

"It's another long story," he told her. "Do you trust me?"

"You know I do."

"Then trust Gabe."

She heard her brother gulp as he took a drink of something. Jordan longed for her coffee in the other room.

"He didn't know the whole story, Sis. Michael lied to him – is *still* lying – so Gabe left. Michael sent soldiers – it was too close for my comfort, but we managed to escape."

Was it a set-up? Maybe Gabe was playing Quinn to get to her.

"I'm going to put you on speaker phone. He wants to talk to you."

The day Gabe turned his back and left them to deal with the *Kongamatos* alone ended horribly. The creatures nearly bled Nathan and Uncle Case dry. Jordan was killed, brought back by a demon, and then forced to leave her family.

Her Guardian could have prevented it all.

*But the demons kept you safe*, a voice inside whispered.

She wanted to ignore it or argue with it, but could do neither. If not for Aamon and Ivy, she'd either be dead or Michael's prisoner.

"Jordan, can you hear me?"

Gabe sounded nervous. His voice – one she'd known her entire life – picked at her heart with sharp nails, worrying tiny pieces from the whole. Arm pressed into her midsection, Jordan rocked to and fro, desperate to ease the pain.

"Yes." She gulped, fighting back tears.

"Have the demons hurt you?"

She thought about Gina, and then quickly dismissed her. Demons were one thing, but five gallons of crazy in a two gallon bucket was altogether different.

"No, they haven't hurt me. I've been treated okay."

"Good, that's good." Gabe cleared his throat. "Jordan, I could say I'm sorry but it wouldn't be enough. I walked away from you – from my *family*. Instead of following orders, I should have followed my heart."

He paused. Jordan pictured slumped shoulders, tousled hair, and golden eyes.

"I'll give up my grace before leaving you again."

Relief washed over her as the angel inside recognized truth in his words. Though unsure about her powers, Jordan had no doubt about this.

She wanted to say something meaningful, something that would assure him they were okay, but her emotions were all over the place. Instead of an eloquent speech, what he got was, "I'm not mad anymore, Gabe. Just promise you'll look after my family and yourself. I have a feeling I'm going to need all of you soon."

"Tell us where you are and we'll come for you," he begged. "We'll get Nathan and Casen and go some place safe while we work this out."

Gabe's voice had taken on an edge that made her sit up on the bed.

"Jordan, you're in danger. Michael thinks you may be a *Paladin*. I know you aren't familiar with the word but trust me, he won't stop searching until he knows for sure, and he has an army of Aeons at his command."

Suddenly, Jordan wanted Koda. Running her fingers through his fur always helped her think. She grabbed a pillow instead.

How could she possibly explain that, as a baby in her mother's womb, she'd not only killed the angel, Sariel, but also absorbed her grace? How could she tell him she was a monster?

"Gabe, I *am* a *Paladin*."

Someone sucked in a breath. "Jordan, are you sure?" Quinn asked.

Damn. He knew something and it was bad. She could tell by the tightness in his voice.

"Yes," she said. "I'm sure of it. I…things have happened. I have powers that aren't normal for a Cambion, and sometimes my eyes glow blue instead of pearl-white."

"Don't forget about the wings." Ivy stood a few feet inside the room. Jordan frowned; sure she'd locked the door.

"Wings?" Gabe asked? "What wings?"

Eyebrows raised, Jordan asked, "Yeah, what wings?"

"Jordan, who are you talking to?" That was Quinn.

"My sister, Ivy. Do you remember her?"

"Vividly."

Ivy handed her a fresh cup of coffee. "The night you and Gina got into it, right before you burned away her powers; there was a silhouette of angel wings on the wall behind you. They slowly opened and spread out on either side of your shoulders." She shrugged as if they were discussing a suspicious mole or the possibility of Jordan having a gluten allergy instead of wings. "The shadow stayed for a few seconds and then disappeared."

"You burned away someone's powers?!" Gabe's voice cut across the line.

Jordan took a sip of coffee. Did the wings really matter? She couldn't change anything.

She thought back to that night in the hallway outside Gina's bedroom. She remembered hearing a whooshing sound and how it reminded her of Gabe. A place in the middle of her shoulders had become irritated too, but Jordan had written it off as a

279

manifestation Gina's power.

*What the fuck are you?*

Gina had asked her that right before Jordan grabbed her wrist. Now, her question made sense.

She glared at Ivy. "Why didn't you tell me?"

"I thought you knew. When you didn't react to sprouting wings, I figured it had happened before."

Jordan slumped against the headboard almost spilling her coffee. "Are you sure?"

Ivy nodded. "I know what wings look like."

"Did you get all that?" she asked Quinn and Gabe.

This just got better and better. Ivy reached over and gave her a hug before leaving the room.

*Fuck you very much, Sis.*

It wasn't Ivy's fault, though.

Jordan set her coffee on the bedside table and turned on the speaker phone. What the hell. Ivy's revelation was just one more popped seam no longer holding her together. She lay back on the pillows and waited to fall apart.

"Jordan, what do you know about *Paladins*?"

*Not enough.*

She stared at the phone, wondering what Quinn thought about all this. He was suspiciously quiet. He probably found her freakish genes repulsive. Jordan couldn't blame him.

"I know that I am part demon, angel, and human," she answered Gabe.

"There's a bit more to it than that."

"No shit, Gabe. I just found out I've got a pair of wings hidden somewhere."

"Jordan, let us come get you. We'll get this worked out."

"I can't – not yet at least. I have a job to do first."

"What job?" Quinn's voice was neutral, giving no hint of how he felt.

"I made a deal with Aamon's boss. If I hunt down a rogue succubus that's giving him grief, I get to come home, no demons attached."

"You *get* to come home? What, are they holding you hostage or something?"

Jordan shook her head. Some things never changed, including her brother's temper. "Quinn, that's how demons work. They kept me safe. I owe a payment for services rendered."

"And Aamon's okay with this?"

"Hardly. He was furious, but had no say in the matter."

Quinn switched into Slayer mode. "What level is the demon?"

Jordan thought back to the report Orias left in the SUV. There wasn't a lot to go on yet. The succubus was level "red." They were told to go to St. Paul, Minnesota. A contact would be in touch once they arrived. He provided no information on the infractions committed or powers she possessed.

"Red," Jordan replied, and braced for the lecture

she knew would come.

"I don't like it. Too many things can go wrong on a demon hunt, especially if she isn't working alone."

Jordan rolled her eyes. Quinn was a master when it came to excuses to keep her off hunts. For years, he had let her think it was because he couldn't stand the sight of her – that he blamed her for their mother's death. Now, Jordan knew he'd kept her at arm's length because he'd been afraid to lose her. Old habits were hard to break.

"Besides, you aren't experienced with demons," he added.

*Did he really just say that?*

Jordan laughed, but crumbled inside.

Her brother's voice sounded as hollow as she felt. "Oh…I forgot."

*If only I could.*

Gritting her teeth, Jordan said, "I'll be fine."

"But you're alone. We never–"

"–go on hunts alone," she finished. "And I'm not. I have Ivy…and Xander."

Quinn snorted. "Who's that? Your brother from another mother?"

"No," she answered as her heart broke. It was obvious the progress she and Quinn made in their relationship was gone. One step forward and a mountain slide back. "Xander is a Cambion, but he isn't Aamon's."

"I thought that was Aamon's job." Gabe cut in. "Demons rarely procreate without permission."

"Yeah, well, one of them must have gotten carried away. Xander spent most of his life in an orphanage. They didn't discover him until he was thirteen."

"That doesn't sound right."

"He was never claimed. Seeing as how they aren't supposed to make little demons without permission, it makes sense. The incubus responsible didn't want to get in trouble, Xander was shoved in an institution, end of story." His face flashed before her and Jordan smiled, remembering the warm feeling she got when she was around him. "He's...different – not like other Cambions."

"What do you mean?"

"It's hard to explain. We have some sort of connection."

Quinn huffed. "It's called hormones, Jordan. Don't put your trust in someone just because he has dreamy eyes and a killer smile."

"It's not like that! Whatever this is between us, it runs much deeper. He reminds me of you and Nathan. He reminds me of *home*."

Why was she even explaining this to him?

"It doesn't matter. I have my team and we'll be fine. Once I find this hothead, I'll be home free." She swallowed hard. "Unless I'm no longer wanted at home."

"What the hell does that mean? Of course you're wanted, Jordan."

Her breath caught in her chest. "Quinn, do you still love me?"

"More than anything," he said without hesitation. "Why would you ask that?"

The tears came but she barely noticed. "Because of what I am. I'm part demon and they're evil. I don't want you to think of me like that."

"Listen to me, okay? You aren't a demon or an angel. You are Jordan – my sister, and you always will be. Don't ever forget."

Her brother still loved her, at least he *said* he did. Jordan was eager to find the rogue demon and get back home. She had to make sure his feelings were true.

"I won't," she said. "Should I call Nathan and Uncle Case?"

"Not yet."

"Why?"

"They have company at the farmhouse – members of the Circle. I don't trust them. The last thing we need is for Michael to find out we've been in touch with you."

Before she could ask, he added, "Nathan and Case are fine, so don't worry. As soon as I see Nathan, I'll give him your number so he can call when there's no one to overhear. Deal?"

There was a commotion in the adjoining room.

Ivy cursed and Jordan jumped off the bed. Just as she reached the bedroom door, it opened and Xander poked his head in. "Jordan, I'm sorry to interrupt but you might wanna come in here."

"What's wrong?" Quinn asked, his voice rising to compete with Ivy's cursing. "Are you okay?"

"Yes." Jordan started for the living area. "Hang on a sec."

She passed through the doorway and then stopped so quickly Xander ran into her from behind. Ivy, scowling at the source of their problem, asked "What the hell do we do now?"

"Jordan!" Quinn yelled loud enough to alert security. "Answer me, dammit!"

She clicked off the speakerphone and brought the cell to her ear, unable to believe the mess they'd landed in. "I'm fine – we're fine, Quinn."

"What is it?"

Jordan glowered at their new visitor. The object of her disapproval hung her head, too nervous to make eye contact.

"Nothing," she answered. "My little sister just popped in for a visit. She's not supposed to be here, so I'd better go and make sure she gets back to Aamon."

A few feet away, Mazie crossed her arms and sighed.

# XXI Quinn

Quinn ended the conversation with his brother. He'd called Nathan as soon as he hung up with Jordan to tell him their sister was okay. Nathan was ecstatic, but didn't agree with his request to keep it from Uncle Case.

"He's worried sick! Why do you think he relented and allowed Lucas' demon in the house? We have to tell him."

"No, we don't," Quinn said. "Case is sure to say something to Lucas and I don't trust the man. That demon of his has led you on one wild goose chase after another." He stretched, working the tight muscles in his shoulders. "I don't like keeping this from Uncle Case, but we can't risk Jordan's safety."

Nathan had reluctantly agreed. It wouldn't bode well for any of them if Michael learned Jordan was not only a *Paladin*, but also no longer under the protection of Aamon's wards.

Quinn turned to Gabe sitting on the couch, *The*

*Oraculum* open on his lap. "Why didn't you tell her?"

The angel looked up. "Tell who what?"

Quinn grabbed a chair from the small dinette table and straddled it. "Why didn't you tell Jordan what we learned from the book? Don't you think she needs to know?"

Marking his page with his finger, Gabe shook his head. "Not right now, no."

"According to the prophecy, Jordan's going to fall – whatever the hell that means – and when she does, a massive war will begin." Quinn arched an eyebrow. "We need to prevent that, right?"

"Of course."

God, sometimes Gabe infuriated him. He hated having to spell everything out. "The best way to assure the war doesn't start is to make sure Jordan doesn't fall. How can she stop it from happening if she doesn't *know*?"

"Yes, it would be better if your sister knew the details of the prophecy. I didn't want to give her anything else to worry about right now."

And then Quinn understood. Jordan was hunting a demon. If she knew her actions could inadvertently cause a holy war, she would second guess every move she made. Hesitation could get her killed.

"We need to find out *how* she…falls. With that information, we can at least advise her on what not to do."

Gabe opened the book again. "Tell me how the

*Paladin* will fall."

Enochian language appeared and swam on the page. Seconds later, the words aligned and Gabriel read them to Quinn.

*The release of an angel's grace will incite the fall. If the act is committed in defense, there is a possibility of redemption. If the act is committed in rage, the* Paladin's *soul will be lost.*

"Wait," Quinn said. "So, an angel's death causes the fall?" He shook his head.

Why did the damn book have to talk in riddles?

Gabe's face sagged like a deflating balloon. "Yes, if Jordan takes the life."

"But angels are immortal. Demons can't kill you."

"The only way we can die is by another angel's hand." Gabe bit his lip. "And Jordan is–"

"–part angel," Quinn finished. "What does the rest of it mean?"

"If she kills an angel in defense – her own or to protect someone else – there is hope for her soul. If she kills the angel in a blind rage, Jordan will belong to Evil."

"There's too many *if's*. We need to know for sure, Gabe. This is her life we're talking about. Not to mention all this could bring a war down on our heads."

The puzzle was slowly coming together but missing key pieces still made it impossible to see the picture as a whole. For days, a nagging feeling had buzzed in the back of Quinn's mind – an irritating mosquito he kept swatting at. It would go away for a while and he'd forget, only to have it come back with a vengeance.

When Quinn's cell rang an hour later, he snatched it off the table, eager to silence Nathan's assigned ringtone. "Fly From Heaven" by Toad sounded ominous under the circumstances. Gabe practically folded in on himself. Any phone call they received now was bound to be important and, more than likely, bad news.

Quinn put the phone on speaker.

"Hey," he answered, "what's up?"

His brother's voice was easy, upbeat. "Uncle Case asked me to call. He would have, but he's busy sending Lucas and his boys on their way. He wants you and Gabe to come home."

Across the room Gabe smiled. Quinn, however, had doubts.

"What changed his mind?"

"Now, don't get mad…" Nathan began.

Quinn groaned. When his brother began a sentence that way, what followed afterward usually pissed him off.

"I told him about Jordy's call."

"Great." Sometimes, Quinn hated being right. "You did exactly what I asked you not to do."

"He had a right to know! Jordan is like a

daughter to him." Nathan's tone was condescending. "Frankly, I'm surprised you wanted to keep Case in the dark. I knew you were ticked at him, but that's low, even for you."

"Don't go there," Quinn growled. "You know damn well the only reason I wanted to keep it from him was so he wouldn't blab to Lucas. He didn't, did he?"

"Give him a little credit. Uncle Case isn't stupid."

"Really? Because I haven't forgotten why I left in the first place, Nathan."

In the background, Quinn heard the sound of typing.

"I didn't call to argue," his brother said when the clicking of keys stopped. "Are you coming home or not? I could use your help. Case still doesn't know about the prophecy. "

Though his uncle had rubbed him the wrong way, Quinn knew every decision Case made was with their best interests at heart. The details of the prophecy could very well send him over the edge. Quinn needed to be there. The only hope they had of making it through this was to stand together.

"I'll get packed," he said. "We'll be there in about an hour."

◇◇◇

Background music replaced conversation in the car. While Bob Seger advised him to turn the page, Quinn thought about the impending reunion with his uncle and Gabe watched the passing scenery.

Case accused Quinn of falling back on old ways – unable to trust others – when he'd tried to warn him of Lucas' intentions. A faint echo of pain rippled within.

*Turn the page*, Bob sang. Quinn felt he had. He wanted to begin a new story but no one could forget the old one.

When he and Gabe arrived in Dixon's Bluff, Quinn made a quick stop at the only convenience store still open to grab some beer. He called home on the land line to see if they needed anything else but didn't get an answer. That wasn't unusual. If Nathan and Case were upstairs, outside, or in the basement, it was difficult to hear it ring. Next, he called Nathan's cell. It rang several times and went to voicemail. Quinn didn't leave a message. Frowning, he called his uncle's phone. It didn't ring at all, going straight to voicemail as if he'd it turned off. It was late but not *that* late.

Something was wrong.

Quinn left the case of beer on the counter and rushed outside to the Mustang.

"What's wrong?" Gabe asked.

Quinn cranked the Mustang, revving the engine. The only other patron in the lot, Terry Simpson, who kept late hours at the small gym he owned, turned and stared. When he saw it was Quinn, the man shook his head and went back to pumping his gas. Sometimes, living in a small town had its perks. Everyone knew everyone. When he laid rubber squealing out of the parking lot, Terry didn't bat an eyelash.

Quinn quickly explained the situation.

"And the fact that they didn't answer their phones is cause for alarm?"

Quinn glanced sideways. Gabe swayed back and forth in the passenger seat as he took turns at break-neck speed. Of course, after flying with wings, riding in a speeding car was probably no big deal.

*Showoff.*

"We keep our phones near us at all times. One of them should've answered." He pulled his cell from the case attached to his belt and flipped it to Gabe. "Call them again – numbers 1 and 2 on speed dial."

The phone rang before Gabe could press a button. The screen glowed, bathing the interior of the car in a peaceful blue light. The name "Uncle C." appeared on the small display and Quinn reached for the phone when Gabe passed it back, quietly berating himself for overreacting. His relief was so great his hands shook, and Quinn swerved into the parking lot of Fred Limberg's Farmers' Market. Headlights lit up the front of the store, which was decorated with pumpkins, scarecrows, and Halloween décor. It was one of Jordan's favorite places to shop. Now, it was dark. Fred had long since rolled up the sidewalk and closed for the day.

"Hey," Quinn asked, answering the call. "Where were you when I called?"

"Tending to more important matters."

The voice did not belong to Case or Nathan. Quinn's stomach twisted into a hard knot of fear. He hit the speakerphone and said, "Lucas? Where's Case?"

Muffled shouts were followed by the meaty, smacking sound of fists on flesh. Quinn gripped the phone so tight the plastic casing cracked.

"Sorry 'bout that," Lucas drawled. He sucked on his teeth and Quinn clenched his jaws. "He's tied up at the moment."

Someone in the background laughed and hollered, "Yep, he's tied up real good!"

Quinn looked at Gabe, who nodded and teleported. Lucas' spoke again.

"Now, here's what we're gonna do. You're gonna come to the house and bring me that nifty book. Once I have it, me and my boys'll leave, real peaceful-like, and you and your family can get on with your lives."

"Why in the name of Papa Smurf's blue ass would I do that?"

Grinding his teeth, Quinn listened, helpless, as more punches were thrown amidst grunts of pain and suppressed curses.

*Hurry, Gabe. Please, hurry!*

"He's had enough, Brody," Lucas directed to his son. "We got orders not to rough 'em up too much."

"Orders from who?!" Quinn yelled. "I swear on my mother's grave, if you hurt them I'll reach down your throat and remove your fucking spleen. Wonder how long it would take for you to suck that out of your teeth?"

Lucas snorted. "You done now?"

"I'm just getting started. Wait 'til I get to my house. I'm gonna stomp a mud hole in you big enough for your sons to drown in."

"Well, in the meantime, I suggest you shut your mouth and listen. Who I get my orders from is none of your business. All you need to know is that she's one sadistic bitch who'll kill your family and enjoy a short glass of whiskey when she's done." He paused and then asked, "Do I have your attention now?"

"Yes," Quinn spat.

Where was Gabe?

"Good. I want you to drive up to the front porch, slowly exit your car with both hands in the air, and one of them better be holding that book. We'll have guns on you, so no tricks. Lay the book on the ground, turn with your back to the porch, and then get on your knees."

"I don't know, Lucas; that sounds kind of kinky to me."

"Is this a joke to you, Quinn? Guess I'll have to

show you just how serious I am."

A loud clattering noise came over the line, then a single gunshot.

"You bastard!"

Bile rose up his gullet with the force of a geyser. Quinn flung open the door to the Mustang and retched on the ground. The world outside spun in his vision.

Lucas' hee-haw laugh assaulted his ears. "That was a warning shot – the next one won't be. Get your ass to the house, Quinn. Now." The line went dead.

He couldn't wait for Gabe. Quinn snatched the keys from the ignition and went around to the trunk. Opening the secret compartment, he removed a shotgun and a Smith and Wesson 45. After a quick check to make sure both were loaded, he stuffed extra shells and bullets in the pockets of his bomber jacket.

Back on the road, he focused on *The Oraculum*. Quinn couldn't hand it over to those rednecks. In the wrong hands, the book could be as deadly as the Bubonic Plague. It was important, yes, but he wouldn't risk Nathan and Case's lives for it.

He turned away from their small business district and passed the squat building that housed the sheriff's department. There were three vehicles in the parking lot, including Wellard Briggs' old Blazer.

Though Sheriff Briggs was an ally, it never crossed Quinn's mind to stop. The tough old bird knew what they did for a living and tried to help when he could, but Quinn would never put him or his three deputies at risk. Outside help was hard to find when you hunted monsters. Theirs was a relationship carefully balanced on trust and, for the most part, need-to-know information only. Wellard had once told them if an extra gun was ever needed, they could give him a call. So far, they had managed without cashing in that favor, and wanted to keep it that way.

The driveway leading to the house came into view. Quinn shut off the headlights, turned in, and stopped. He looked around, hoping to spot a place to hide the book. He had no idea if Lucas or one of the boys was close by, watching.

He couldn't show up without the book. Nathan and Case were tied up and would be no help. Quinn had had worse odds than three on one before, but not when a family member's life hung in the balance.

He took a few cleansing breaths and put the car in gear. Just as the house came into view, Gabe reappeared in the passenger seat. Quinn yelped and slammed on the brakes.

"Shit! Wear a bell or something, Gabe."

The angel's face was bleak. "You have to get out of here."

"I know it's bad but surely we can take down three rednecks." In Quinn's opinion, Gabe more than tipped the scales in their favor.

"If it was just Lucas and his sons, then yes, but they aren't alone."

"Who's with them?"

"Illyria." Gabe cursed under his breath and Quinn sat up straighter, peering through the inky blackness toward the house. "She's Michael's first in command – a ruthless Aeon who would gladly kill Casen and Nathan just for a rush."

"Why is she here?" Quinn asked. Just what they needed, an angel who was mad as March with a penchant for thrill kills. Michael sure knew how to pick 'em.

"From what I gathered while spying, she pretended to be a demon. Michael's plan was for her to keep your family busy by sending you to chase red herrings while other members of his army looked for Jordan. She recruited Lucas and his boys to help."

It didn't make sense. As much as he detested Lucas, Quinn didn't think he would help the angels unless...

"What's in it for him?" he asked.

"Michael promised to bring his wife back."

Quinn grimaced. "Really? Angels do that?"

"It has been done in the past, but only in special circumstances."

If Lucas was promised his wife, there would be no persuading him to change his mind.

*There's a bit of darkness in everyone – makes no difference who or what you are – and desperation reveals it every time.*

Those were the words Lucas spoke the night he

called and offered his *help* to find Jordan. He'd been referring to himself.

"So, what now?" Quinn looked at Gabe, whose face was partially hidden in shadow. "I can't take off and leave Case and Nathan. If that angel is as demented as you make her sound, she might kill them."

Gabe grabbed his arm. "Listen to me. She can't get *The Oraculum*. Michael could use it to find Jordan and much more. Leave. Hide the book. I'll take care of Illyria and her hired hands. I'm protected by the ward so she won't detect my presence. I'll surprise her."

"How did she even find out about the book?"

"I don't know. That's not important right now. If she told Michael – and I'm sure she did – it is imperative that we keep it out of his hands." Gabe squeezed Quinn's arm. "I promise I won't let anything happen to our family."

The porch lights blazed to life, bathing the yard in a sickly yellow glow that didn't quite reach the car. Quinn squinted against the glare, looking for movement.

The front door opened and a woman stepped out. Lavish brown hair fell like a river down her shoulders, and a black bodysuit hugged every curve. A scabbard hung across her back, the handle of what could only be a sword peeked from the top. She stared at the car.

"Is that her?" Quinn asked, his voice barely above a whisper.

"Yes."

"I bet you could bounce a quarter on that ass."

"Why would you do that?"

If they weren't in such dire straits, Quinn would have laughed. "I just mean that she's hot...you know, nice to look at."

"Oh," Gabe said. "Yes, I suppose she is attractive but I don't see what that has to do with American currency."

There were no words.

"Go – before she gets impatient and decides to come for you. She won't wait much longer." Gabe shifted slightly. "I'm going to teleport behind Case's car. When you leave, she'll more than likely give chase. I'll intercede."

Quinn ran scenarios of *what if* through his mind, weighing the pros and cons. None of them ended well. "I can't, Gabe. If you all die, I won't be able to live with myself." He looked at the porch. The angel paced like a tiger. "I'd rather be gutted with that sword than run away and leave it all on your shoulders."

The archangel smiled. "Families depend on each other – trust each other, right?"

Quinn nodded.

"When I walked away from orders, I hoped to have a chance to prove this is where I belong. Don't take it away from me."

Illyria started down the steps. Time was up.

"Go now, Quinn! Get as far away as you can and hide that book. As soon as I take care of things here, we'll call you."

Gabe disappeared in a whoosh of invisible wings and, before the reality of what he was doing came crashing down, Quinn revved the engine and made a U-turn in the yard. Clods of dirt and grass flew into the air as the Mustang's tires chewed up the ground. In the rearview, he saw Lucas and his sons rush outside.

In the fading gleam of porch lights, the lines of hate etched into Illyria's face were unmistakable. Her eyes narrowed at the retreating car. Quinn shuddered and pressed the gas harder to the floor.

As he rounded the curve in the driveway that hid the house from view, the rearview showed two glowing figures facing off. Gabe had made his appearance. Quinn sent up a silent prayer for his family's safety, switched gears, and sped away.

He had no idea where to go.

# XXII Jordan

Jordan rubbed her weary eyes. It was late and she was dead on her feet. While she had been talking with Gabe and Quinn, Mazie had called Ivy. During their conversation, the name of the hotel had been mentioned. That was all the information their youngest sister needed to find them.

Before a call could be placed to Aamon, he called them. Ivy calmed their father while Jordan shot daggers at Mazie, who at least had the good sense to keep quiet. When she ended the call, Ivy pointed at the young girl and said, "Go home. Dad said if you are not there in five minutes, you're grounded until the next great flood."

"I'm not going back." Mazie said from her perch on the couch.

Ivy snatched the girl's X-Men book bag from the floor and dropped it in her lap. "Oh, yes you are. Gina's gone – Dad kicked her out. There's no reason you can't stay there."

"She could come back!"

Jordan sighed. "What happened?"

Mazie's brown eyes pleaded with her. "Gina threatened me. She told me I'd better watch my back – that you wouldn't be there to protect me anymore."

"Why didn't you tell Aamon?"

"He wasn't there."

Ivy tapped her foot. "He was there yesterday and today. Don't bullshit us. You had plenty of chances to tell him."

"Not to mention I tried for two days to talk to you," Jordan interjected.

Mazie's shoulders slumped. "I was mad," she whispered.

"And I was worried sick about you!" Jordan pursed her lips, breathing as hard as a bull. "You know what? I'm tired. I don't care what you do. I'm going to bed." To Ivy, she asked, "Will you call Aamon back and deal with this?" She massaged her temples. A headache was coming on strong. "I need to lie down."

Ivy frowned. "Sure, no problem. You okay?"

Jordan's faint smile transformed into a grimace as pain thumped behind her eyes. Cambions didn't get sick or experience headaches. "Yeah, I just need some rest. I haven't slept well the past couple of nights." She threw Mazie a dirty look.

Xander took over. "Go get changed. You can sleep in my bed tonight and Mazie can stay until morning. I'll crash on the couch."

Jordan wanted to argue that it wasn't fair for him to give up his bed but her head pounded in time with her heart. She nodded. "Thanks."

After changing into a long T-shirt, Jordan crawled into the comfortable bed and swaddled herself in the comforter. A soft knock came at the door. If it was Mazie, she would spank her butt. Dammit, she was exhausted.

Xander opened the door, a glass of water and some Ibuprofen in hand. "I got these at the front desk," he explained.

Jordan ripped open the packs, popped all four pills into her mouth, and washed them down with the cold water. "Did Mazie leave?" she asked.

Xander took her glass and set it on the night table. He pointed to the pillow and she lay back, allowing him to pull the covers up and arrange them just so.

"She's staying for the night. She and Ivy went to bed." Jordan sat up, but he gently pushed her back down. "We'll deal with it tomorrow. Get some rest."

Her headache flared, pulsating as if something alive wanted to burst from her skull. She gripped her head, willing it to fade.

Xander watched from the door. Jordan knew he was concerned. She was, too. She hadn't experienced any headaches since her visions stopped.

Suddenly, she didn't want to be alone. It was

irrational, she knew, but the pain in her head paired with talking to Quinn for the first time in months, the added stress of Mazie's arrival, and the upcoming hunt made her feel small, vulnerable.

"Can you stay with me for a while?"

The words left her lips before she could think and Jordan wished she could reel them back in.

"Sure."

Xander crossed back to the bed and stretched out beside her on top of the comforter. Grateful that he didn't make a big deal about her request, Jordan allowed herself to relax. After all, she just wanted some company – at least, that's what she told herself.

Xander turned the television on, but kept the volume low, and switched off the lamp. The lack of bright light along with his closeness did wonders for her headache. Jordan closed her eyes, grateful for the relief.

She had no idea when she dozed off. One minute she was listening to murmurs from the television and the next, she stood in a bedroom she didn't recognize. A four-poster bed covered in a rich, terracotta quilt was decorated with throw pillows of green and gold. An antique dressing table stood against the wall. Jordan lightly ran her fingers over bottles of different lotions, rosewater, and a silver comb and brush that sat on the crackling finish.

Two windows let in brilliant light. She pulled aside the sheer curtain and looked out. A garden filled with a multitude of flowers and trees with gorgeous, autumn leaves garnished a perfectly trimmed, green lawn. In the distance she saw a desert dotted with cacti and scrub brush. Jordan realized where she was.

Purgatory.

She raced to the door and twisted the knob. Not only was it locked, it was also wired. When her hand came in contact with the cool metal, a blue arc of electric current knocked Jordan off her feet. She landed hard on the polished hardwood floor.

Footsteps sounded in the hallway outside. She held her breath, watching through blurred eyes as the silver doorknob turned. With no hesitation, Orias stepped into the room. All thoughts of escape disappeared when Jordan's eyes met his.

He helped her to her feet and pulled her close, pressing his lips against hers. Euphoria filled Jordan, lifting her body to heights that made her swoon. Deep down, she knew it was wrong. Like scum on a pond, thoughts of disgust slowly rose to the surface and Jordan tried to pull away.

Orias' grip was iron tight. He gently used his tongue, running it over her bottom lip, sending shivers through her. Helpless, Jordan's lips parted and he deepened the kiss while his fingers sent a white-hot trail of heat down her collar bone. She moaned.

He pulled away and she could think again. Her

mind screamed for her to wake up, but Jordan's feeble protests went ignored. In one swift movement, Orias swept her up and carried her to the bed. The blankets felt like clouds beneath her and Jordan drifted, floating.

Orias loomed above her, breathing hard. He pinned her arms above her head, then brought his mouth to her neck. Inching north, he found a sensitive spot under her ear and worked it lightly with his lips and teeth, nibbling, sucking, sending fire throughout Jordan's body with every trail of his tongue. Her arousal returned with a vengeance.

His fingers deftly unbuttoned her shirt. Jordan's skin sizzled beneath his touch. Cool air raised goosebumps on her exposed flesh. She arched her back, wanting more.

He obliged.

His mouth moved slowly down, tasting every part of her. She couldn't think, only *feel*. Jordan twisted her fingers in his soft curls and then explored the contours of his strong shoulders and back. When Orias groaned, clearly enjoying her touch, her body screamed.

He hop-skipped back to her swollen lips, and they parted for him like water. Orias' fingers never stilled, lighting fires everywhere they touched. She clung to him like someone dying.

"Give this to me," he whispered.

She'd give him anything.

"I need it," his raw voice vibrated against her, causing ripples of feelings so intense Jordan couldn't breathe.

"Say you'll be mine, Jordan, only mine. Let me show you how good it can be."

His promise was too much. Her body trembled in anticipation. "Yes," she said, pushing away the unpleasant visions her mind thrust upon her. "Take it."

His eyes flashed, triumphant. Jordan shivered, her body as weak as a newborn's, powerless to stop him now.

Relishing the feel of his lips on hers, she watched through half-lidded eyes as he produced a ceremonial knife from thin air. The blade glinted, throwing flashes of light against the walls, the hilt bedecked with colored jewels.

"Are you ready?" Orias asked. There was no mistaking his hunger. He drew the tip of the blade down her neck, teasing her, and she tossed her head from side to side, wanting him so badly she ached.

There was no going back. This was where she belonged.

"Hurry," she begged, baring her neck to make it easier. She couldn't hold on much longer.

His kiss was hard, promising and demanding. Jordan rode the high.

"Close your eyes, darling." He ran the tip of the blade lightly across her exposed breast and she sighed. "Let me love you."

The knife grazed her skin and stopped at her neck. The cut was deep. Jordan gasped at the pain and opened her eyes. Orias produced a clear vial and held it against the wound. Blood, warm and sticky, streamed like red ribbons.

Jordan's vision grew fuzzy around the edges. Objects in her line of sight became dark and her heartbeat lagged. Finally, the vial was filled. Orias set it aside and then, almost lazily, licked the trail of blood on her neck before clamping his mouth over the wound. Gently, he began to suckle, stoking the dying embers of desire.

"Yes," she whispered.

Jordan closed her eyes as Orias' hands moved over her like a pianist, lighting in places she'd never been touched before. In her mind's eye, great fires burned, scorching the earth. The smell of death hung heavy in the air, mingling with smoke and ash. Demons and angels clashed. Weapons flew, creating sparks that were quickly extinguished by sweat-drenched bodies. Piles of humans, disfigured and covered in gore, lined deserted streets like trash waiting to be collected on Tuesday. Members of her family struggled with hideous creatures born of nightmares and Hell as they fought for their lives. On a distant hill, Xander and Ivy waged their own battles against a multitude of demons. Their tired voices called out, urging her to wake up. Jordan watched it all, uncaring, with Orias by her side.

"Look at what you've created."

Jordan turned to him. Her eyes shone pearl-white while his were the honest blue of sapphires. From Orias' shoulders, a pair of glorious white wings fanned the flames.

Gasping, she sat up. Something trickled down the back of her neck and Jordan wiped at it, sure her hand would come back red with blood. Flickering images from the television caused shadows to move along the walls and she flinched. Her chest heaved, desperate for cool, untainted air.

"Are you okay?"

Beside her, Xander's eyes were wide, scanning the room for threats. She wondered if something followed her out of the nightmare.

Oh, God. It hadn't been a dream, but a vision – not of something happening now, but something that *could* happen.

"Jordan?" Xander's hand brushed her leg and she swallowed a scream.

Unable to answer, she stared at her hands, wondering how she could possibly bring on the end of the world, and why.

The next morning, Jordan sat at the small breakfast table and picked at her food. Ivy and Mazie sat in silence across from her. Every once in a while, Ivy glanced at her when she thought she wasn't looking, eyebrows drawn in worry. Jordan pretended not to notice.

She replayed the night before over and over in her mind. She'd told Xander she had a nightmare. He had stayed with her the entire night, wrapping Jordan in his strong arms. His closeness eased her abraded nerves. It wasn't until the sun peeked over the mountains outside the window that she was finally able to sleep again.

The door opened and Xander came in with a large manila envelope. He placed it beside her take-out box which held a large cheese omelet and toast, then poured himself some coffee. She picked the envelope up but he placed a hand on her arm.

"Eat," he said. "News from Orias can wait until you're done."

Just hearing his name made Jordan cringe. The smell of grease and cheese was suddenly nauseating and she pushed the box away, drinking her coffee instead.

Xander shook his head and sat in the chair beside her. Jordan smiled apologetically, and then slid the envelope across the table to Ivy.

"Will you open it?" she asked her.

"I will!"

Mazie reached for the document and Ivy slapped her hand away. "Finish eating," she said, running a fingernail under the tape on the envelope. "You're going home soon."

Pouting, Mazie picked up her fork and stabbed the pancakes in front of her.

Ivy slipped a piece of paper out of the sleeve and scanned it while Jordan and Xander waited.

"Our demon has been spotted in St. Paul." Ivy fiddled with her cell, pulling up directions. "It's gonna take about three hours from here if the traffic cooperates."

"Where in St. Paul?" Jordan slid her uneaten breakfast to Xander and got up from the table. He gave her an exasperated look before digging in.

Ivy shrugged. "It says more information will come later."

Jordan nodded. She pointed at Mazie. "You, go home."

"But–"

Moving to the bedroom, she called over her shoulder. "No buts. Get your ass home now."

After a quick shower, Jordan dressed and strapped her knife to her leg. She picked up her new FN Five-Seven. It was an extraordinary gun. She tested the almost toy-like weight while admiring the accessory rail that ran underneath the barrel. Right now, it sported a flashlight/laser combo. The heavily-textured grip felt comfortable and secure in her hand. With a 30-round magazine, she wouldn't have to reload as often. With a 5.7x28mm round that could burrow through body armor; she would conserve ammunition, too. One shot usually got the job done. Of course, it wouldn't kill demons, but the silver-tipped rounds would make them stop and think.

An image of Orias sucking blood from her neck flashed in her head. Jordan's hand shook so badly she nearly dropped the gun. She sat on the edge of the bed and took deep breaths.

*Head in the game, Jordan.*

When the moment passed, she checked the safety on the Five-Seven and slid it in her shoulder holster. Her bomber jacket covered it nicely.

Back in the living room, she placed her bag by the door. Xander sat at the bar with the phone to his ear, scribbling notes as he talked. Ivy passed her on her way to the bedroom and said, "It's Orias' contact. He has more news on the demon."

Mazie sat on the couch and idly flipped through the television channels as if she had no place important to be. The girl was impossible.

"52 White Bear Avenue," Xander said, slipping the phone in his pocket. "It's a house on the outskirts of St. Paul." He gulped the last of his coffee. "I'll take our bags to the car and plug the information into the GPS."

Jordan nodded, her eyes on Mazie. "Give me ten."

Her sister stared at the T.V. as if Hugh Jackman was conducting the news on the Finance channel instead of some stiff shirt. Jordan rolled her eyes, doubting Mazie understood a word the man said about stocks and dividends. She grabbed the remote and shut it off.

"Time for you to go."

The girl finally acknowledged her presence. "You're not gonna change your mind, are you?"

"Nope."

Maize stood and smiled – the first real smile Jordan had seen from her in a while.

"Yeah, I thought so."

Shaking her head, Jordan laughed. "You are a stubborn one."

"Just like my big sis." Mazie chewed on her bottom lip. "Ivy told me when this hunt is finished you're going back to your family."

Jordan said nothing.

"I thought I was your family."

"You are."

"Then how can you leave me?"

Her voice was quiet – the words barely audible. Somehow, that made it worse. Jordan would have felt better if Mazie screamed and pitched a fit.

She sat on the couch, pulling her sister down beside her.

"You are my family – you and Ivy both. Even if I do go back to live with my uncle and brothers, it doesn't erase *us*." She waited for Mazie to look at her. Slowly, tear-filled eyes met Jordan's. "You will always be my sister. We'll still see each other, I promise."

Mazie wiped at her tears. "You don't understand. It won't be the same if you leave. Before you came to the cabin, I hated it there. No one talked to me – not even Ivy. Do you know how it feels to live in a house full of people and still, no one ever *sees* you?"

Jordan sympathized, she really did. She couldn't count how many lonely days and endless nights she'd spent at the farmhouse while her brothers and uncle Case were on hunts. Even when they were home, most of their time was spent preparing for another trip or in the fields. Still, they talked to her, argued with her, ate dinners together when time allowed. It hadn't been an ideal life but dammit, it was hers, and she wanted it back.

"I had a family, Jordan, with two parents who loved me, supported me, and it was taken away. I went to school. I had friends. I had a normal life!" Mazie's eyes smoldered with power, making her look older than her twelve years. The fire, however, died quickly. Jordan watched the familiar soft brown color return. She was once again a young girl, unsure how to find her place in this backward world that was so unstable.

Mazie squeezed her hand. "I can accept being a Cambion. I even understand why Mom and Dad didn't put up much of a fight when Aamon came for me – even a parent's love has some conditions," she said bitterly. "But I can't stand the loneliness, Jordan. I can't bear the quiet. Don't make me go back to that...please."

Jordan's mind raced, torn between wanting to keep Mazie safe and not wanting her to feel abandoned. Meanwhile, the clock was ticking. They needed to get on the road.

"How about this," she began.

Mazie groaned and flopped back on the couch.

"No, listen. I think I have the answer." Her sister raised an eyebrow and Jordan hurried on. "If you go back to the cabin and *stay there* until I finish this job, I'll come for you when I'm done."

"Come for me to do what? Say one last goodbye?"

"No, to help you pack so you can come live with me."

Her sister's face lit up like the sky after a long storm. "You mean it?"

"Yes, you pain in my ass, I mean every word." Jordan grinned to let her know she was joking, then pulled her into a hug.

"But what will your uncle and brothers say?"

"Eh, they'll learn to love you, just like I do."
Mazie pulled away, eyes shining. "Okay."

# XXIII Jordan

So, how do we play this?" Ivy asked.

She sat in the backseat with her laptop open, a poor image of the house where they'd been told to find the demon pulled up on Google maps. The good news was there was plenty of cover, and the house was fairly isolated. The bad news was that, even off the beaten path, it was still a residential area. They were thirty minutes away and had no definite plan.

"I don't want to say until we have a look around," Jordan said. "We can't rush in, guns blazing, only to find the demon has moved on and we've scarred a human family for life."

Ivy tapped on the keyboard. "According to records, the house is owned by one Clayton Shoop."

"Any family?" Xander asked.

*I hope not*, Jordan thought.

"There's nothing pertaining to immediate family but that doesn't mean he doesn't have any."

Twenty-eight minutes later, they slowly cruised by the address. The house was hidden from the street by large oaks and cedars with the thick forest of Battle Creek Regional Park to the right. On the left, a fair distance away and also surrounded by trees, stood another house.

They passed East C Street which circled to South B, a much more populated neighborhood. After that, there was nothing but densely packed woods on both sides of the road. White Bear Avenue South came to a dead end about a quarter mile past their target with barely enough room to turn the SUV around.

Nature was attempting to take back what man had stolen. Branches reached out on both sides, barely missing the car that Xander kept on the faded center line. Potholes and huge, weed-filled cracks dotted this section of pavement. There were no houses. Jordan had no idea why the road extended this far.

The SUV dipped into a particularly deep pothole and Xander swerved to the right. Gravel and crumbling asphalt pinged underneath the carriage as the tires struggled to find purchase on the eroded shoulder.

"Jesus," Ivy said. "Someone call the Department of Transportation. They must've missed this area on their scouting missions to find ways to blow taxpayers' money."

"I don't think it was missed." Xander wrestled

with the steering wheel and managed to get the car back in the center of the road. "They probably decided not to bother. With the park here, it's likely no one can erect so much as an outhouse this far down."

He stopped the car once they saw sunlight again. East C Street was ahead on their left, but not so close that they could see it or anyone could see them.

"Hand me the laptop, Ivy."

Her sister passed it over the seat and Jordan scanned the map.

"Okay, here's what I think." She pointed to the screen, marking a path with her finger. Xander and Ivy leaned in to see. "We enter the forest here and walk to the house. The woods will conceal us almost all the way to the north side." She pointed to a large copse of trees. "From this spot, we can watch the front of the house. If we move back into the forest and walk about twenty feet east, we can also see the back."

"Do we all go or does someone stay here by the car, just in case we need to make a quick escape?"

"Where are the radios?"

Ivy pulled them from the equipment bag, fully charged and set to the same channel.

"One of us needs to stay behind. All we need is for a nosy park ranger to have the car towed." Jordan looked around. "I doubt many people come this way but still, better not tempt fate."

"I'll stay," Ivy volunteered.

They piled out of the SUV and Jordan rummaged in the hidden compartment for a pair of special manacles. Made from a blend of the purest silver, titanium, and iron, they were engraved with a Devil's Trap. Once in place, they would render a demon powerless.

"We're ready," she said.

Xander took one of the radios, made sure the volume wasn't loud enough to draw attention, and clipped it to his belt. Ivy kept the other.

"If any badges come snooping or you find yourself in trouble you can't drive away from, push the alarm button three times. We'll teleport back." Jordan gave Ivy a quick hug.

She nodded. "Same goes for you. You need me, I'll flash to the front door if I have to."

Jordan smiled. "This won't take long. After we round up this heifer, we'll call Orias' contact to haul her ass back to Purgatory and we'll all go out for burgers and Starbucks."

"Hey, we're spending Orias' money. Let's make it steaks and Starbucks."

"You got it."

Jordan and Xander began walking.

*We have a plan. We have weapons and powers. I have plenty of experience hunting evil bitches. Capturing this demon will be as simple as sweet tea.*

She could taste the white-chocolate mocha from

Starbucks (and her freedom) already.

But pride always goes before a fall.

After grappling with thorn bushes, prickly vines, and a close encounter with a very inquisitive badger, they finally made it to their surveillance point. Xander walked farther down to get a look at the back yard while Jordan kept watch on the front.

The simple clapboard house wasn't much to look at. Most of the beige paint was chipped and, in some places, hung in long, peeling strips. The front porch listed to one side where a set of cinderblocks had begun to crumble. The shutters, perhaps once a burgundy color, had faded to a light pinkish-purple from the weather and sun. The yard, the part not taken over by trees, was tastefully decorated with empty beer cans, a set of bald tires, scraggy weeds, and a lone, wild rosebush that looked as if it were transplanted from some place in Hell.

"Ugly isn't it?"

In one smooth movement, Jordan drew her gun and spun around before the person finished her question. She came face to face with Mazie, who found herself looking down the barrel of the Five-Seven.

The girl threw her hands up and whispered, "Don't shoot me! Didn't your uncle teach you not to play with guns?"

Incensed, Jordan thrust her weapon back in its holster and grabbed her little sister by the collar. She yanked her farther into the woods and gave her a shake.

"I ought to whip your ass!" What in the hell are you *doing* here? I told you to go home."

"I," Mazie gulped and tried again. "I thought I could help."

Jordan turned away. Her hands itched to give the girl a few good smacks. After showing up at the hotel the night before, she shouldn't have been surprised to see Mazie again, but this was no place for a young, lower-level demon.

Footsteps sounded from the right and Jordan grabbed her sister, pushing her behind her. When Xander emerged seconds later, she let out the breath and moved aside so he could see their visitor.

He stopped and stared. Mazie wore a bright, X-Men sweatshirt, blaring pink jacket, yellow sweatpants, and Uggs. She looked like a drug-induced hallucination.

"Son of a bitch," he mumbled.

"She was just leaving." Jordan scowled at her sister. "Now."

Mazie sighed. "Fine, I'll go, but you're not gonna find any demons in there," she said, gesturing to the house.

Jordan was tired of her sister's attempts at

stalling. She'd had a few nerves left when she got up that morning and the girl had stomped on every damn one of them.

"Mazie, enough! You have no idea what's in that house. By the time I count to three, you'd better be back at the cabin. And trust me, I *will* call Aamon when I'm finished here. Disobey me again and you'll be grounded until you're old enough for Depends and Polident."

"I may not know what's in that house but I do know it isn't a demon." She puffed her chest out and smirked. "It's my power. I'm an Intuit."

Eyebrows raised, Jordan asked, "Did you say you were a twit? If so, I agree."

Xander placed his hands on her shoulders and Jordan immediately felt more composed. She took the opportunity to take a few cleansing breaths.

"An Intuit," he explained, kneading the tight muscles in her neck, "can detect what classification a being is, like demon, werewolf, vampire, and so on."

Jordan leaned back into him, wishing she was anywhere but in the woods contemplating Mazie's demonic power, worrying about keeping her safe, staking out a demon that may (or may not) be inside the house, and being bitten by chiggers.

"I'm telling you," Mazie said. "There's no demon in there." She studied the broken-down house. "But something else is."

"What?" Jordan asked before she could stop

herself.

Face pinched in concentration, the girl shook her head. "I don't know. I feel one type of presence more than the other. There's more than one being inside." She cocked her head. "If I get closer, the vibes will be stronger."

"Absolutely not."

Jordan pulled away from Xander and took Mazie's face in her hands. She gazed into her sweet eyes, reminding herself that this girl loved her. More importantly, Jordan loved Mazie. The sprite tried her patience but she only wanted to be included.

"Sweety, please go home and wait for me. I *will* come back for you, I promise."

"But I can help."

Jordan opened her mouth to protest and Mazie held up her hand. "It'll only take ten seconds to teleport to the porch and back. No noise, no danger. They won't even know I'm there."

Jordan shook her head. There was no way she was letting Mazie do this. It might only take ten seconds, but that was ten seconds she'd be away from Jordan and closer to whatever was in that house.

"It's faster than sitting out here for hours, twiddling our thumbs."

Jordan couldn't believe him. "Xander, she's twelve."

"She's a Cambion."

"She's a *twelve*-year-old Cambion."

"The demon may not even be there."

"I'll be damned if my little sister's going to be the first to find out."

Mazie's head followed their back-and-forth bickering as if watching a tennis match. When Jordan and Xander paused for a breath, she stepped in between them.

"I can do this." Her sweaty hand found Jordan's and held it tightly. "Don't you believe in me?"

Jordan pushed a stray curl out of the girl's eye and kissed her forehead. "I believe you can do anything."

"Then trust me," she begged. "Let me help."

Was Mazie trying to prove she was brave? Jordan wondered if this stemmed from Gina's dream-walking. That witch really had done a number on her. Just thinking about it made Jordan want to snap Gina's neck.

She pulled Mazie close. The young girl who loved X-Men, who was so full of life.

"I do trust you, and I know you're brave. You don't have to prove anything to me."

"But I need to prove it to myself. You understand that, right?"

Jordan did. Reluctantly, she nodded. "Are you sure?"

"Yes." Mazie squared her shoulders.

With Xander's help, she shrugged out of her loud jacket. The pants couldn't be helped, but if Mazie teleported away from the windows, hopefully no one would see her.

"Ten seconds," Jordan said firmly. "That's all you get. Do you hear me?"

"Yes."

"I mean it!"

"I know, I know, sheesh." Mazie cracked her knuckles. "Be back soon."

She disappeared and Jordan's eyes immediately went to the front porch. The girl materialized to the right of the door, well away from the windows. She pressed her back against the house and closed her eyes.

*Hurry.*

Five seconds passed. Jordan counted them off in her head.

*Hurry.*

Ten seconds. Mazie pushed away from the wall and Jordan silently thanked God. Her sister was coming back. She looked at Xander, intending to ask if he thought Mazie picked up anything. His attention was focused on the porch. Like a horror movie, Jordan saw his posture become rigid, his eyes wild.

She didn't want to turn around, didn't want to know what frightened him so. But she did. She *had* to.

The door to the house was wide open. Mazie struggled with a man in black. Another stood nearby...*with a sword.*

*What the hell?*

Xander burst from their hiding spot and ran toward the porch, Jordan on his heels. With Mazie's life on the line, it didn't occur to either of them to teleport and possibly have the element of surprise on their side.

As he ran, Xander snatched the radio from his belt, pressed the button on the side, and screamed for Ivy.

"Meet us on the porch," he yelled. "Hurry!"

Jordan pulled her gun from the holster. By the time she ran up the swayback steps, the men had dragged her sister inside the dark recess of the house, and Ivy was there.

She took in Jordan's heavy breathing and the gun in her hand. "What the fuck?"

Jordan could barely keep it together. She wanted to bust inside, peg anything in black that moved, and get Mazie back. A thin wail escaped and she fought the urge to cry.

Xander quickly explained what happened.

"And Mazie couldn't tell what was inside?"

He shook his head.

Jordan took up position to the left side of the door and listened as Ivy and Xander discussed strategy. She couldn't talk. If she so much as opened her mouth, she would lose what composure she had. But she felt something – a strange familiarity she couldn't comprehend, like something she'd tasted before but couldn't remember the name. Unfortunately, she didn't have time to explore it now. Her sister was in there. The house had gone mysteriously quiet. What were they doing?

*If they hurt her, I will kill them. I'll boil them from the inside out.*

With that thought her power surged and she welcomed it, letting it fill every part of her to the point of pain.

From inside, a voice shattered the silence. Whiney, nasally, it set her teeth on edge.

"Come inside, Jordan. Don't you know it's rude to stand on the porch?"

And with that, her rage shot through the roof. Jordan glanced at Ivy, not trusting herself to be able to tell the difference between reality and ghosts from her past.

"You've got to be fucking kidding me!" Ivy confirmed her suspicions.

At least she wasn't crazy…yet.

Taking point, Jordan opened the rusty screen door and peered inside. She couldn't see much – a small, cluttered living room with worn furniture, stacks upon stacks of moldy newspapers, empty beer cans, fast-food wrappers and containers, tons of trash, and roaches.

"Gross," Ivy whispered directly behind Jordan. "I hate anything with more than four legs."

Jordan edged around the refuse and creepy-crawlies. She wished for a jumbo-sized can of Raid and some Febreeze. Not only was the house an entomologist's wet dream, it reeked.

Behind her, bringing up the rear, Xander also held his formidable gun. He covered one side of the room while Jordan swept the other. Ivy walked with her hands at the ready. They, she claimed, were the only weapons she needed. Jordan didn't argue.

The living room was enclosed except for a narrow hall. From her vantage point, Jordan saw several doors – some open, some closed.

"What do you think?" Xander whispered. "Do we go farther in?"

The desire to run through the house in search of her sister was overwhelming but Jordan knew that was exactly what they wanted. They wouldn't hurt Mazie. She was their bargaining tool.

"No," she said, "Let them come to us."

It didn't take long. Heavy footsteps preceded the group. The hallway was so narrow they had to walk single-file.

A tall man emerged from the gloom first. He had broad shoulders, bald head, and a blank expression. His black uniform and boots resembled military fatigues.

Behind him, with Mazie held tight in hands so large they looked like they could crush rocks to powder, came a twin of the first man. He had the same bald head, clothes, build, and dead expression.

The only difference between him and the first guy was race. This one was African American.

Mazie struggled in his grasp. When she looked up and saw Jordan, she screamed, "Get out of here! Run!"

"Are you okay?" Xander asked.

"Run!" Mazie yelled. "Get Jordan out!"

"I'm not going anywhere without you." Confused, Jordan trained her gun on Baldy #2's head. "Let her go."

The first man stepped forward and Xander's gun followed him. "We will let her go if you come with us."

There was no inflection at all in his voice. The guy was disturbing in a way Jordan couldn't explain.

"How about you let her go and I won't put a hole in your forehead."

"Your weapon cannot harm us," he replied in his robot voice. "I would advise you to rethink your decision and choose more wisely."

Jordan thought about putting a bullet through his thigh just on principal. "Yeah? Well, I would advise you to shut your yap."

"Who the hell are you?" Ivy asked.

Eyes flashed electric blue. From deeper in the hallway, a familiar voice said, "They're angels."

Jordan's anger reached a new high. Ivy snarled.

Gina's high heeled boots ticked along the wooden floor. Red lips curved in a seductive smile, she sashayed to where the angel held Mazie.

"Hello again, sister." Her eyes danced. "Your kinsmen have come for you. I'm so happy I could help them out."

# XXIV Gabriel

A h. It's the pigeon that flew the coop," Illyria teased. "Michael is extremely angry with you for disobeying orders."

Gabriel never took his eyes off of the Aeon, ready to strike the second she let her guard down.

"Aren't you worried about your precious humans inside?"

She circled. He matched her step for step.

"Gabriel, be reasonable. I have Michael's blessing to do whatever it takes to retrieve *The Oraculum*. That book belongs in Heaven, not with wretched humans whose family tree runs with demon sap."

"These wretched humans, as you call them, have put their lives on the line to keep this world safe. How easily you and Michael forget everything they've done for us."

Illyria laughed. It was a throaty, almost primal sound that made his skin crawl. "I never said humans couldn't be useful. So are pack mules, but we don't entrust them with holy relics."

She repeatedly reached back to play with the handle of her sword. This quirk did not go unnoticed by Gabriel. He had to keep her distracted. Quinn needed time to hide the book and get out of her range of detection.

Though he didn't anticipate any danger for himself, Gabriel was not so foolish to believe things always go as planned. Illyria was a soldier who thrived in battle. An archangel's power was far greater than hers, but one well-placed blow with her sword would be the end of him – and his family.

"Illyria," he began, trying to appeal to her human side (if she still had one). "Please reconsider. The Baileys have done nothing wrong. They've followed every order and worked hard for the Circle which, in turn, has left Michael's army free to protect Heaven. Deep down, you know this. Why not use your skills to help me? For once, fight on the right side."

She stopped circling and turned her face to the stars. Gabriel couldn't read her expression. She looked pensive, sad, and he wondered if his words struck a chord.

"It isn't that simple."

Illyria's voice was soft and…neutral, with no trace of her chronic hostility. Gabriel could imagine it belonging to anyone. When she looked at him, he couldn't detect the soldier within. What he saw was an angel torn between doing what was right and what was easy. She was not comfortable with going against the grain – going against Michael. That feeling was all too familiar.

"Why not?" he asked, hoping there was something inside her that could be saved.

"Jordan isn't human. She's part demon. Michael ordered me to retrieve her and the book. I must follow orders." Her voice was distant. She was sliding away.

"There is more to it than that, Illyria. I overheard the conversation between you and my brother the day of our meeting. Michael has a secret, one that could be his undoing. But it's *his* secret, *his* problem, not yours. You were once known as God's Sword, striking down sinners who committed abominable acts against others – a vigilante for justice. Where is that Illyria now?"

"She almost went to Hell!" Her face twisted into a grimace. "I did the right thing once and look where it got me. If it weren't for Michael, that reaper would have carted me off to an eternity of torture – and for what? Because I enjoyed the kill? Those people got what they deserved. Michael understood. He stood up for me." She stared him down with a dangerous glint in her eyes. "You say I was a vigilante for justice, yet you've shown nothing but disgust for me. If that is truly how you feel, then where were *you* the day of my reckoning?"

"I was right where you are now, following orders and being what I thought was an obedient angel! Michael told me allegiance to God and Heaven meant compliance, so I turned away from what I truly believed. It was endless resignation – never questioning what I was told."

His chance to get through to her grew smaller by the second. It had been difficult for Gabriel to break the chains that bound him to Michael. Aeons were not only discouraged from forming opinions, they were kept in isolation, trained through relentless discipline and brainwashing to make sure they didn't. Illyria's chains were much thicker than his had been, and their reach was long.

"Loyalty to Michael isn't our job," he said. "We're supposed to protect our Father's children and the world He created for them. If we falter, we should make it right." Gabriel searched her face. "Michael tripped. I don't know how and I don't care. Instead of owning his mistake, he's hurting others, and you help cover it up." He sighed. "I did that for years. Does it make me a bad angel or a naïve one? It isn't too late, Illyria. Be better than that, better than I was."

Her laughter was shrill, full of hate and lunacy. She pointed at him.

"Oh, Gabriel, it's so easy for you. You were Michael's lapdog, his servant, his wind-up toy. Then one day, you grew a pair of wings, flew away, and turned into a motivational speaker."

Illyria dropped her smile, making him wary.

"God doesn't pull the strings where Aeons are concerned – Michael does. He is *our* father, our *savior*. We don't have options like you. As an archangel, it would be difficult to explain if you suddenly disappeared. Michael could strike down every member of his army and no one would be the wiser. We are invisible, expendable. I've seen it happen, and don't plan to become one of his statistics."

"We could tell someone – a Virtue, perhaps – and I could help keep you safe. It doesn't have to be this way, Illyria."

"Yes, it does." She pulled her sword from its sheath. Bright silver cut streaks through the night as she took a few swings, handling it like the warrior she was. "I'll stay loyal to Michael as long as he stays loyal to me. He's not the only one who can pull strings."

Maybe it was her eagerness for battle, but instead of taking to the air or teleporting, Illyria charged, her sword at the ready. Gabriel waited until she was almost upon him, then teleported to the other side of Casen's car and hid from view. Because of the ward, she was unable to detect his position. Still, he needed the element of surprise in order to avoid her blade. Hunkered beside the driver's door, he listened for her stealthy approach. There weren't many places to hide. Nathan's car, Casen's even bigger car, and a rusty

Suburban were the only options nearby. Illyria had to know Gabriel wasn't far away. Lucas would have alerted her if he'd teleported inside the house. She had the advantage, knowing he'd never leave his wards tied up and at her mercy.

There was a pop of gravel – the sound of someone measuring each step before putting their full weight down. Gabriel peered underneath the carriage and saw Illyria's boots on the other side of the car, slowly making their way around.

He saw his chance.

He teleported and materialized behind her. The sound of displaced air caused Illyria to turn. Gabriel grabbed the arm that held the sword, flooding it with raw power, hoping to make her drop the weapon.

Instead of pulling away, Illyria shoved him, using the power of her legs to knock him off balance. As soon as he hit the ground, the sound of her sword split the air. Gabriel rolled but wasn't quick enough. The blade sank into his thigh. White-hot pain seared from within as its poison spread like napalm, climbing higher, devouring him inch by inch like some sort of holocaust monster. If he didn't heal himself soon, he would die.

Illyria expected him to flee, to hide somewhere and tend his wound. Instead, Gabriel ignored the radiating pain, teleported one last time, and wrapped both arms around the angel. She screamed when he unleashed his waning energy, writhing like a worm in hot ashes, struggling to break free.

Weak, sick, Gabriel fought to hang on. The aroma of blistering skin filled his head, reminding him who the murderer was now. He wished there was another way.

Toxins raced through his body, consuming his pitiful reserves. Unable to finish the job, Gabriel was forced let go. Swaying on his feet, he watched Illyria's body fall.

Panting, Gabriel placed a shaky hand over the wound in his thigh and willed the little energy he had to heal it. His life force ebbed and flowed, sucked out of him as it disposed of the poison and then replenished as his grace recovered.

Illyria's wounds were significantly worse. Large clumps of hair had burned away. Exposed skin and tissue were charred to the point of flaking. Parts of her uniform had melted and fused with the skin.

Gabriel was disgusted with himself. If he'd been at full strength, her death would have been quick. With the wound she'd inflicted, he shouldn't have attempted at all.

He stared at her smoldering body and she returned his gaze with one good eye, the other lost somewhere in the destruction.

"Finish me," she whispered. "Let me die…a soldier's death." She pointed to the sword lying beside her.

Moments before, he could have – to save his

wards, his family. But the image of her broken body made it impossible. In her current state, the Aeon was no longer a threat, and Gabriel couldn't follow through.

When he shook his head, she laughed weakly. "And here I thought…you'd grown…a pair." She gasped between words. "I don't…deserve to die…like…this."

Turning away, he said, "Death is death, Illyria. Regardless of execution, it all ends the same."

Lucas and his boys surrendered their weapons as soon as Gabriel walked inside. He suspected they'd been watching from the living room windows. None of them were inclined to carry on the fight.

"They promised to bring my wife back. It was business, Gabriel, nothing personal against you or Casen and his family."

Unmoved, Gabriel gestured to the basement stairs. Lucas and his sons trudged slowly before him.

"I didn't know what Illyria had planned. She told us to keep Casen and the boys busy while they searched for Jordan and we just followed orders. It was her idea to truss 'em and rough 'em up – swear to God."

Nathan and Casen were bound to chairs with large zip ties. Red faced, they spewed muffled curses behind the duct tape over their mouths.

"I don't think they agree with your reasoning, Lucas." Gabriel waved his hand and the bindings disappeared.

Casen rose slowly, rubbing his chafed wrists. A good-sized lump protruded over his right eye. Nathan took a moment to shake the feeling back into his legs. Lucas watched warily from the corner where he and his boys had retreated. Gabriel braced for what was to come.

He didn't have to wait long.

Casen grabbed a shotgun and shoved the dangerous end into Lucas' gut while Nathan collared the boys. Wrapping a strong hand around each neck, he raised them a foot off the floor and then slammed their bodies to the dust-covered concrete. If they'd burst open like flour sacks, Gabriel would not have been surprised.

Doubled over, unable to speak, Lucas held up his hand. After much gasping and groaning, he looked to Gabriel. "Are you gonna sit by and watch the show or stop 'em? My sons and I are members of the Circle. It's *your* job to protect us!"

Casen pointed his gun at the man's chest. "You're not dealing with him, Lucas. You're dealing with me," he growled. "Better pay attention."

"He's right." Gabriel shook his head. "Your wife's death was no one's fault. For years, you've nursed your anger, ignored your children, and used that night to get easy assignments and a lot of money you didn't earn. It's time to let it go."

Lucas sputtered, as if choking on words that wouldn't come fast enough. "We do all the dirty work to keep this world safe! You angels cower in your Heaven, cloud-jumping, playing harps, and don't even bother to keep an eye on our families while we do!"

It amazed Gabriel how humans twisted their emotions, distorted and rebuilt them until they were unrecognizable, and then pushed them on someone else. He'd seen it first-hand. Quinn took his fear of losing the ones he loved and doctored it the same way he did classic cars. Bit by bit, he replaced all the weak and broken elements, and turned reality into something he could live with.

What Quinn – and now Lucas – failed to remember was that truth can't be destroyed or changed. Scratch away all the cosmetics, the damage still lies underneath.

Tired of the criticism, Gabriel stomped over and grabbed the man by the collar. Lucas yipped like a trapped weasel.

"You could have left the Circle. No one is required to serve." He twisted the shirt tighter. "Why don't you admit what's really bothering you – what's eating at your soul? You stayed for the money. You took easy jobs with little risk and hoarded every dollar while your wife and kids survived on welfare and bread lines. Where was the concern for your family then? The guilt is yours – *own it*."

Gabriel gave Lucas a hard shake and then let go. To Casen, the angel said, "I know you're angry, but there isn't much more you can do to him that he hasn't already done to himself." Gabriel considered his own guilt and how all of this might have been prevented if he'd been more of an angel and less of a disciple. "Sometimes, we're our own worst enemies."

Lucas herded his sons up the stairs and made a bee-line for the front door. Casen followed, with Nathan and Gabriel bringing up the rear.

"If I ever see the likes of you again I'll chain you to a stake and feed your sorry ass to the wolves!"

The sound of tires spinning on gravel as the wheezing Suburban lurched down the drive was the only reply. Gabriel listened as it faded into the distance. Shortly after, Casen came back inside, shamefaced and shuffling his feet.

"Guess I need to apologize to Quinn. Looks like he was right all along." He propped the gun up in the corner and took off his hat. "I sure wished I'd listened. Damn, I was way too hard on the kid."

"We both were." Nathan looked around the room. "Where *is* Quinn?"

"I sent him away with *The Oraculum*," Gabriel

345

said.

Casen lowered himself into a recliner with a groan. "How'd you even know what was going on?"

Gabriel relayed what happened after the grocery store pit-stop. "Now that Illyria is…no longer a threat, we can call Quinn and let him know it's safe to come back."

*For now*, he thought. He had to find a way to talk to Yasen before Michael made an appearance.

Nathan walked to the storm door and peered out. Gabriel was ashamed for him to see the mess he'd left Illyria in, the damage he'd caused…the life he'd taken. He had every right to defend himself and his wards but the death of a sister – even one as demented as Illyria – left him feeling empty, unworthy of his wings.

"Look, Gabe…" Casen began. He paused and let his eyes wander around the room.

Gabriel wondered if he was remembering what it looked like when his entire family occupied it and how empty it was now.

Casen sighed. "Nathan told me what happened between you and Michael – why you left in Tennessee. There's no hard feelings here. I appreciate you coming back and trying to help. Can't imagine that was easy for you."

With Casen's forgiveness, another link in the chain that bound him to Michael – to all the mistakes he'd made – broke. He felt lighter, more at peace, but knew he would never be completely free until he earned Jordan's mercy, as well.

"Thank you, Casen, for giving me another chance. I won't let you down."

Casen nodded. "I believe you."

To Nathan, Gabriel said, "If you'll call Quinn, I'll dispose of Illyria's remains."

His plan was to fly her to a remote place, say a prayer, and burn the body. Her soul would have departed seconds before she passed. He hoped, for her sake (and his conscience), that it was sent to Heaven. Maybe Illyria could be a better angel if she wasn't under Michael's influence.

"What remains?" Nathan asked.

Panic, like a shard of ice, pierced Gabriel's gut and spread through his vessel like winter. It couldn't be. There was no way Illyria could have healed herself. Her wounds were too extensive.

He rushed to the door, almost tearing it off the hinges when it stuck, and ran to where she'd fallen behind Casen's car. The Aeon was gone. In her place, a large, scarlet-red feather rocked to and fro in the nighttime breeze.

*Michael.*

She'd called him and he'd healed her. Only one thing would have kept her from entering the farmhouse for revenge – *The Oraculum*.

Like a good little soldier, Illyria always followed orders. She'd gone after the book.

And the book was with Quinn.

## XXV Jordan

*Angels.*

Not just any angels but soldiers from Michael's army. Jordan didn't know much about the Aeons, just bits and pieces she'd gleaned from Gabe through the years. Still, his information had been detailed enough to show her these dogs ran – hard. And now, they were here for her.

Mazie's face was the only thing that kept her grounded. She had to keep calm for her sake.

"What do you want to do?" Ivy whispered.

Without hesitation, Jordan replied softly, "Whatever it takes to keep Mazie safe."

Ivy and Xander frowned at the implication of giving herself up, but neither had a chance to object. One of the Aeons jerked Mazie's arm, making her whimper. The sound reverberated in Jordan's head and whipped her power into a frenzy.

Angels could kill demons with ease, regardless of rank or ability. Mazie was one level above a basic.

The Aeons would crush her in seconds if Jordan let her anger run free. She had to play this smart.

"You will come with us now."

The angel who held Mazie in his grasp showed no passion, no concern. That was the most unsettling trait of Michael's soldiers. If they were truly devoid of human emotions as Gabe had once told her, how could Jordan ever convince them to spare her sister?

Ivy tried a different tactic – stalling. She turned to Gina, spearing her with sharp, dangerous eyes. "How the hell did you get mixed up with the Winged Wonders here? Their yawn-inducing personalities must make it hard to find dates but surely they're not desperate enough to settle for gutter-whores just yet?"

Gina beamed. Her eyes sparkled with delight…or madness. It was always hard to tell. She circled the angels, crushing any roaches that scuttled in her way with the toes of her boots. Stopping beside Mazie, she said, "It's funny you mentioned desperation. It *does* make people do the strangest things. It can even bring mortal enemies together if there's something to be gained.

"After our dear sister left me powerless, I got to thinking about my future. Cambion souls aren't allowed in Heaven. With no way to protect myself, the only prospect I had to look forward to was an eternity in Hell as some demon's bitch."

Ivy snorted. "I have a hunch that would've happened regardless."

Gina continued in her happy sing-song voice, riding the high of the moment, Jordan guessed.

"After I left the cabin—"

"—after you were sent packing, you mean," Ivy interrupted.

"I contacted a friend of a friend—"

"You have friends?"

"—who helped me get in touch with Michael. I agreed to help locate Jordan for something in return."

"What? Laser hair removal? That'll be a huge blow to all the lonely sasquatches. Where will they find a new pin-up girl?"

Jordan had to hand it to Ivy; she never gave up.

"No, my soul in Heaven. Michael promised me a one-way ticket upstairs when I die. All I had to do in return was help his soldiers with their task. Lucky for me, I stopped by the cabin today to pick up my things and happened to be right outside Aamon's door when Mazie told him your plans." Gina looked pointedly at Jordan as she preened, crowing in triumph. "The rest was quite easy."

Mazie began to cry. Unknowingly, she'd led the angels right to them.

Jordan wracked her brain for an out – a solution. She could only think of one.

"If you'll let my sister go and swear no harm will come to my family – Cambion or human – I'll go with you."

"No!" Ivy and Mazie screamed in unison.

351

Xander grabbed Jordan around the waist and pulled her close to him. "You don't have to do this," he pleaded.

The anguish in his voice touched her and, for a moment, Jordan wondered if his feelings for her were more than platonic. It didn't matter. She'd never get the chance to find out, never understand the connection between them.

She kept her eyes trained on the Aeon and waited for his answer.

"We accept your offer and your terms. No harm will come to your families."

Swallowing hard, Jordan nodded. "May I say goodbye?" She gestured to Ivy and Xander. When the angel frowned, she added, "No tricks. I won't do anything to jeopardize their safety."

"Very well, but we will keep this one to make sure you keep your word. Once you are in our custody, we will let her go."

Jordan didn't like that arrangement but Mazie was their trump card – the only advantage they had.

"Watch them," she told Xander.

He nodded, and she turned to Ivy. Her brazen, bold sister was dry-eyed but Jordan knew they were skimming the same bitter, churning waters.

She led Ivy to a far corner of the filthy room, kicking trash and bugs out of her way. Once out of earshot, she whispered, "I'm gonna ask the angels for one more favor. After I'm gone, you'll have to finish what I can't, and promise you'll watch over Mazie. She's gonna need you."

Ivy had no trouble deciphering the cryptic message. "Don't worry; I'll be happy to finish it for you, and I'll protect Mazie – you know I will." She glanced around and hissed, "Why are you doing this? Just reduce those fairies to smut stains and let's bolt. I...I don't want to lose you. What if you get upstairs and can't break free? What the hell will I do then?"

Jordan shushed her. The angels were getting antsy and she had to hurry. She gave Ivy her phone. "After we're gone and you take care of business, call Uncle Case or my brothers. They can get word to Gabe. Hopefully, he'll know where Michael's holding me. If not, just tell them I said to look for fireworks and blazing robes."

Ivy laughed bitterly and pulled her close. "Please come back to me, Sis. I know you plan to go home when all this is over, but don't forget you have another family who loves you, too."

"Never," Jordan said. She held on, trying to express just how much she cared in that one simple act. It would never be enough. "I love you. See you soon."

Before Ivy could say more, Jordan turned away. Now wasn't the time to fall apart. She had to stay strong to face Michael.

When Ivy took Xander's place as guard, he wrapped Jordan in his arms. If she could bottle the feelings he stirred within her and bring them along, she might make it through this unscathed. She wanted to drink them in, to immerse herself so deep the thought of facing her future alone would not be so frightening.

"I can't let you do this," he mumbled into her hair. His breath, warm against her neck, caused Jordan to shiver. He held her closer.

"I have to. They have Mazie, and I swore to protect her. I can't let anything happen to her – to any of you."

She felt him nod. Xander didn't question her motives or decision – as if he had no doubt she knew what was best. Jordan looked into his eyes. "Do you think I'll ever make it back?"

He wouldn't lie to her. He knew the answer was important – could *feel* it through the special bond they had.

With no hesitation, he said, "Yes, and I'll be here waiting for you."

"Why?" she had to ask, *had to know*. "Why would you wait for me? You barely know me."

The angel holding Mazie signaled that her time was up but she couldn't leave without understanding what she was to Xander. "Hold your wings for a minute!"

"Tell me why," she pleaded.

Xander touched her cheek. "For years, I sat in that house in Purgatory, wondering what my place was in all of this. I never felt like I belonged there – belonged *anywhere*. Most of my life has been spent in confusion with no direction, no answers."

He wiped a tear from her cheek.

*When did I start crying?*

"I still don't have the answers, Jordan. All I know is when I saw you, something inside – a voice – told me I'd found my path, and it was with you."

She closed her eyes, not sure how to feel. She knew Xander was supposed to play a part in her life but she didn't know which role. If he was right, then why were they being separated?

"What if the voice was wrong?"

"It wasn't," he replied, his voice strong and sure. Ever so softly, like the caress of butterfly wings, his lips pressed against hers. It happened so fast she barely had time to register how her heart went from a comfortable canter to a full-out sprint and the swooping feeling in the pit of her stomach. When she opened her eyes, he smiled. "You're not the only one who has *dreams*. Now hurry and come back to us."

"We've given you ample time for your goodbyes," the Aeon said. "We must go."

Jordan gave Xander a look that said he'd have some explaining to do when, *if*, she saw him again and then walked to where Mazie stood with the angel.

Beside him, Gina rolled her eyes. "As if any of us wanted to watch your pitiful attempt at making out."

Ignoring her, Jordan faced her little sister. Tears still fell, but not as many as before. Mazie, it seemed, had come to terms with the way things had to be for now.

Embracing her, Jordan said, "Mind Ivy and Xander, okay? They've promised to take good care of you while I'm gone."

Mazie trembled in her arms. Jordan took the girl by the shoulders and gave them a squeeze. "Listen to me. We all have jobs to do right now. Yours is to help Ivy and Xander. If we're gonna get through this, we have to work together – be strong for one another. I need you to be strong for *me* now. Can you do that?"

Rubbing away the last of her tears, Mazie stood taller and nodded. "I'll do my best. Come back for me as soon as you can. I love you, Jordan."

When she threw her thin arms around her and held on so tight, it took everything Jordan had not to fall apart. Choking back tears, she hugged her little sister one last time and said, "I love you, too, sweet Mazie."

Ivy took charge of their sister and Jordan faced the Aeons. "I have one more request, if it isn't too much trouble."

"What is it?"

Smiling, she pointed at Gina, who suddenly looked concerned. "She stays here and pays the price for betraying her own kind, her own blood."

"What?!"

Gina approached the angel. "You can't do that. It wasn't part of the deal I made with Michael – with your *boss*!"

"And what was the deal exactly?" Jordan asked. "He only promised to save your soul, not protect you for the rest of your miserable life."

She looked to the second Aeon, the one who'd been unusually quiet the entire time they'd been in the house. Jordan suspected he hadn't conversed with them because he didn't care. He was all soldier, less human than his partner. At least, that's what she hoped.

"Did Michael give orders for Gina's protection?" she asked him.

When the angel didn't answer, Jordan got in his face, giving him no choice but to look at her. "You got what you came for. You followed orders and Michael won. What can you possibly lose by granting me this one last request?" She glanced at Mazie. "Gina has threatened that little girl's life time and time again. I'm scared for her, and now that I have to leave with you, I can't be here to watch over her! Please…"

The angel's eyes flashed blue. He looked annoyed by Jordan's proximity to him but she didn't care. Her fear of him was far less significant than the thought of what Gina might do once she was gone. Mazie would never be safe if that psychotic hag was left to her own devices under Michael's protection. Gina was vindictive, holding onto hate because she had nothing else.

"We are wasting time," the Aeon said. "Leave the Cambion; she is nothing to Michael, just a means to an end."

"No!"

Gina grabbed the other angel's arm. Fear rolled off of her in humid, noxious waves. Sweat beaded above her upper lip and forehead as her eyes darted wildly to and fro. "You can't leave me here! Take me...take me anywhere and drop me off. I swear I'll never ask for another thing. You'll never hear from me again!"

A few feet away, Ivy popped her knuckles, a grin spreading across her face like sweet molasses. Gina made a sound like an injured cat and tugged harder on the angel's arm.

"Get your filthy hands off me, demon scum!" The Aeon pushed her away.

Both angels then stood on either side of Jordan and reached for her, preparing to teleport.

"Goodbye, Gina," she said, giving a little wave. "I hope it hurts."

It all happened so quickly and yet, to Jordan, the act was painfully drawn out in slow motion. Ivy lunged for Gina and she spun away, knocking Jordan into one of her captors. While they struggled to recover their balance, Gina pulled a sword from the scabbard strapped to the Aeon's back. With a battle cry born of the monster she was, she ran straight for Ivy and Mazie.

Jordan screamed. Xander moved to intercept but wasn't close enough. She watched as terror like she'd never known crept into her muscles, paralyzing her from the neck down.

Ivy moved, and tried to drag Mazie with her. The girl was in shock. Brown eyes wide, she took in the gleaming blade, the sight of it freezing her where she stood.

Jordan watched Ivy's lips move up and down, the words lost in a rush of blood that filled her head. She was standing in the middle of a tornado. There was no wind, but Jordan's body pitched to the side. The angels' strong hands kept her upright – kept her a witness to her worst nightmare.

Ivy tugged, gaining a precious few inches, but it wasn't enough. The sword fell. Jordan's eyes followed its arc, down…down…

Mazie turned as adrenalin kicked in and she saw her impending death looming above her. With a sibilate of misplaced air, the blade tore through the fragile skin at the base of her neck, ripping through tendons, slicing muscle, and sinking into her collar bone.

The room fell silent. Even the birds and insects outside went still. Jordan couldn't breathe. Her lungs moved in and out but brought no relief. Through a white haze, she watched Mazie fall, the hideous sword jutting out at an impossible angle. Blood surged from the wound, flowing down her sister's front and back like a parted stream. Veins running underneath her delicate skin turned a blue-black color like lines on a road map, directions to the grave.

Ivy's scream was too loud, too high. It shredded the haze – that almost-comfortable cloak of Novocain Jordan had managed to wrap herself in since the blade began its decent.

"Mazie!"

Slipping in blood, Ivy shuffled to where their sister lay. Jordan watched with an odd sort of detachment as Ivy fell to her knees and the red liquid that once carried a young girl's life sloshed over hands.

"Help her!" Ivy's face was fierce as she beseeched the angels. "Help her, goddammit!"

The swordless Aeon moved forward. "We can't. Our power will not work on a Cambion. We can only heal angels and humans."

"That's not true; Gabriel used to heal Jordan when she went on hunts. She's part demon, too!"

Ivy waited on her to confirm this but Jordan couldn't speak, couldn't remind her sister that she was more than a Cambion. She could only watch and listen for the blood that oozed from Mazie's body to the floor, like water dripping from the eaves at the farmhouse when it rained.

*Pat, pat, pat.*

It was only the rain dripping off the roof.

The red rain.

*Oh, God.*

The world came rushing back as Jordan's consciousness broke the surface. The first to hit her was a tangy, coppery smell. It saturated her nose and coated the back of her throat. She leaned over and gagged. Everything came up in a steaming rush. Tears sprang to her eyes, sweat ran down her back and her knees buckled.

To her surprise, the angel holding her arm let go. Heaving, crawling, Jordan made her way through puke and blood to Ivy's side. Mazie's beautiful brown eyes were open but the life that made them shine had disappeared.

Her sister was gone.

Jordan reached over and gently closed them, then kissed Mazie's cheek. To no one in particular, she said, "I could have saved her. I could have saved her life and I...I froze. I shut down." Swallowing hard, she gathered one small, fragile hand between her own. As the puddle of blood she sat in began to congeal, Jordan rubbed the tiny fingers, willing them to grow warm again – wishing she could somehow give her life to the girl who never had a chance to live.

"There was nothing you could have done," one Aeon said, kneeling beside her. "The wound was too great. The poison infused in our weapons would have assured death, even if she had not bled out."

He spoke like a professor giving a lecture, clinical and detached. There was no sympathy, just the facts. Jordan's power, which had been strangely subdued until that moment, rose to have a look around. She welcomed the distraction it lent, especially when she saw Gina in the corner.

Xander had prevented her escape. Gina's eyes, glassy and dilated, never wavered from his. Jordan guessed he was invoking his power of persuasion.

Jordan wanted to make Gina suffer for what she'd done, but her grief over losing Mazie was too much. She couldn't think around it. Her death, and the few months that Jordan got to be a part of her life, filled her head and heart.

Someone grabbed her arm, pulling her to her feet. They stuck to the floor when she lifted them to catch her balance.

"It's time to go," the Aeon said.

Before she could absorb his words, the other angel snatched his blade from Mazie's body, jerking it upward. Jordan gasped as her baby sister dangled, suspended by the weapon. Her head lolled back and her neck popped loudly. The wound made a sucking noise as the sword slipped free. She fell like a ragdoll back to the floor.

Ivy's strangled sobs as her hands fluttered helplessly over Mazie, the lack of compassion from the Aeons, and her sister treated like a broken toy caused Jordan to lose the tiny grip she had on her sanity. It snapped like an overstretched rubber band.

Pulling her arm from the angel's grasp, Jordan turned to face them. Her eyes pulsated with energy making both Aeons stop and stare. She placed her hands on their chests, forcing power through them. Electric sparks emanated from her palms, hurling the angels across the room and into a wall. They crumpled to the floor, unconscious.

To Ivy, she said, "Go to the car, gather our weapons, and meet us back at the cabin." Jordan's fingers curled around the pendant Orias gave her. "This piece of shit doesn't work and we need to get back inside the safety of the wards."

Ivy nodded and got to her feet. With a small pop, she disappeared.

Jordan took a deep breath and went to Xander. Avoiding Gina, lest she rip her head off and waste the precious moments they had to escape, she asked him, "Are you okay?"

His pale face shone with the sweat of exertion but he managed a weak smile.

"I thought that was my line," he croaked.

Stone-faced, Jordan crossed her arms, waiting.

"I'm fine; I've got this," he said. "Do what you need to do."

What she needed was to hold him – to be held. Jordan looked down at her clothes, tacky with her sister's blood. Somehow, it seemed right that she was.

"Can you take Gina back to the cabin? I want you to help Ivy break the news to Aamon before I bring…bring Mazie home." She cut her eyes to Gina, still motionless in her trance-like state. "Make sure she's locked in a secure room. I'll deal with her later."

Xander nodded stiffly. "Please be careful, and hurry."

And then she was alone with her sister's body and two comatose angels.

Jordan looked around the room, wondering who lived there. Was the owner possessed by the rogue demon? Had the Aeons scared her off? She thought about searching the rest of the house but knew it was only an excuse to put off the inevitable. She didn't care about the demon anymore or the owner of the shack. She just didn't want to say goodbye.

Mazie's clothes were saturated in blood. It was in her hair, on her face. Jordan hated to bring her back to the cabin in such a state but it couldn't be helped. Even now, the angels stirred, mumbling. She no longer had the will to take them on. Her fury took a backseat to overwhelming loss.

Stooping, Jordan gathered her sister in her arms. Mazie's face was ashen, but she could remember when it was as warm as coffee. Her bloodless lips turned down at the corners. Jordan closed her eyes as the memory of her sister's exuberant laughter filled her head. She would never feel Mazie's arms around her neck again, never have the chance to tell her how much she meant to her.

This was her sister and she was dead.

"You told me that you loved me," Jordan whispered.

Finally, the tears came, burning tracks down her cheeks, leeching away something she would never recover.

# XXVI Jordan

**T**he porch swing rocked to and fro. Jordan sat beside Aamon with Koda at her feet. She stared at the star-filled sky and tried to clear her mind. She didn't want to think, didn't want to move. The snow had stopped falling but the night was cold. She no longer felt it. Whether from shock or her *Paladin* status, she wasn't sure.

Her clothes were stiff with blood. Long dry now, the red stains had turned rusty-brown. Aamon had asked her several times if she wanted to shower. Jordan heard him, but didn't *hear* him. After a while, he stopped asking and just sat with her, moving the swing with his legs while she drifted on thoughts she wished she could erase.

By the time she reached the cabin, word of what happened had spread throughout the house. The front room was filled with kids who spilled out on to the porch. Jordan teleported to the yard and sank to her knees. One of the children yelled for Aamon, and then she was surrounded.

Voices called out; hands shook her, pulled at her, tried to pry Mazie away. She stood on wobbly legs and screamed at the top of her lungs.

"Get back in the house, NOW!"

Electric bolts shot from her hands. She didn't hit anyone, but the five-foot circle of snow she melted was all the encouragement the kids needed. They broke rank and hightailed it back to the porch just as Aamon, Ivy, and Xander ran out the front door.

Jordan sat with her sister. Occasionally, she heard voices. They might have been speaking to her. She didn't know, didn't care.

She talked to Mazie and told her how strong she was – how brave.

"Find my mother," she whispered, pushing a curl back from the girl's face. "She'll take care of you."

She pleaded with God, begging Him to save Mazie's soul.

*Make an exception for a Cambion just this once and I'll gladly take her place in Hell when the time comes.*

The details following were blurry…

Aamon buried Mazie. Ivy had cleaned her body. They'd dressed her in her favorite X-Men shirt and used the sheets from her bed to make a shroud.

A sugar maple stood in the backyard that had the most glorious colors in the fall. Mazie called it her "Halloween tree." That was where they laid her to rest.

Through it all, Jordan sat in the swing. No one bothered her, not even Xander. He and Aamon had put Gina in a "special" room that connected to her father's study and, as far as she knew, the bitch was still there. Jordan would have to deal with her, but not yet. She concentrated on the smooth movement of the swing. After a while, she laid her head against Aamon's shoulder and fell into a deep sleep.

When Jordan woke up, she was in her bed and it was close to midnight. Someone had spread an old blanket across her comforter to keep it from getting soiled by her filthy clothes. She reeked of blood and sweat.

Still trying not to think, Jordan grabbed some clean clothes and made her way to the bathroom across the hall. She glanced at the closed door to Mazie's room and fought back tears that threatened to choke her.

Scalding water pelted her body while Jordan scrubbed blood from her hands, watching helplessly as the only part left of her sister swirled down the drain. She ended up sitting on the shower floor, praying for the pain to stop.

After she dressed, Jordan went downstairs. She found Ivy, Xander, and Aamon at the breakfast table. Ivy stood and poured her a mug of coffee. The warm brew soothed Jordan's throat and her stomach complained for something more substantial. She felt guilty, but ate the sandwich Aamon put in front of her, and then another.

No one spoke. They moved from the kitchen to the living room. Koda appeared and sat beside her on the couch. He placed his burly head in her lap and Jordan absently scratched behind his ears, trying not to think.

Ivy broke the silence. "Gina wants to talk to you."

When Jordan didn't answer she added, "She says she has important information you'll want to know."

"Is this information in exchange for her life?"

Jordan didn't recognize her own voice. It was...lifeless, just like she felt inside. The others must have noticed, as well. They regarded her with narrowed eyes.

"Well? Is it?"

Ivy nodded. "I believe she wants to make a trade, yes."

"No deal." Jordan said.

Gently, as if she might fall to pieces at the smallest amount of pressure, Xander took her hand.

"She said it has something to do with your

family."

Jordan frowned. "My family is here in this room."

From his favorite armchair, a ghost of a smile floated across Aamon's face.

Ivy cleared her throat. "That's true, but we're not your *only* family."

Jordan ran her fingers through Koda's fur. She'd forced her mind to remain blank all day and now, it was hard to assemble any thoughts at all. They took shape, forming in her mind like sand sculptures that teetered and collapsed.

There was something important about Ivy's comment.

She wanted to curl up on the couch and sleep.

Was someone talking to her?

Koda's fur was so thick and warm.

Off to the side, Aamon whispered, "She's still in shock."

"I understand, Dad, but this is important. Gina would lie like a drunken whore if it meant saving her own skin, but what if she's telling the truth? Jordan's uncle and brothers could be in danger."

"We don't know that."

To Jordan, Xander's voice sounded far away.

"Look what losing Mazie has done. Now picture her one-hundred times worse because that's what she'll be reduced to if anything happens to Casen and the boys."

Jordan felt as light as a feather. Idly, she wondered if she could float away. Just drift on currents for the rest of her life.

"Dad, we need to wake her up."

Was she asleep?

Her fingers raked through sable fur.

Someone kneeled in front of her. In her dream, Jordan managed a lazy smile. Ivy's face came into focus, then shimmered like heat waves on desert sand.

"Jordan, I'm sorry, but this may hurt."

Her tongue felt too thick. "You gonna hurth me, Ibeyy?"

"Not too much. Do you trust me?"

She smiled again and touched her sister's cheek. "Yep."

"Your family may be in danger. You've gotta shake this off and come back to us."

Ivy looked so serious. Jordan wanted to fix what bothered her. She could withstand a little pain. After all, this was just a dream.

It had all been a dream.

*Your family may be in danger*...

The thought took shape and Jordan held it with all her might only to have it unravel in her hands.

"Do what you need to do," she muttered before succumbing to the dream once more.

"Move Koda," someone said.

His warm fur was suddenly gone and Jordan

groaned as her fingers reached for him. Why were they changing her dream? She was happy with the way it was.

"Not too much, Ivy," Aamon cautioned.

Too much what?

Seconds later, a jolt of pain shot through her hand. The taste of something stannic, like tinfoil, filled her mouth, and Jordan found she couldn't swallow. Heart racing, it felt like someone was scrubbing her skin from the inside with a wire brush.

Jordan screamed.

When she opened her eyes, she found Xander, Ivy and Aamon hovering like a couple of mother demons, and Koda licking her hand. Jordan felt awake. Wide awake – and her body ached.

"What happened? What hit me?"

She tried to sit up but the effort was too taxing. She couldn't lift her arms.

"Am I paralyzed?"

*What the hell is wrong with me?!*

"Easy, Jordan, be still. I'm going to help."

Aamon's hands glowed with white light that pulsated from his chest to his arms. Poised an inch or so above her body, he moved them around, focusing mainly on her heart and her head. The pain and heaviness passed and she was able to sit up on her own.

Ivy handed her a glass of water. "I'm sorry, I had to do it."

As Jordan sipped, it all came back to her – the dream that wasn't a dream at all.

"You zapped me!"

"I didn't have a choice! You were in La-La land, and though I wish we could have let you find your own way out, we don't have the luxury of time right now." She grabbed Jordan's hand. "Shit's going down that you need to know about."

Gina sat like a queen on the steel-backed utilitarian chair in the center of the room. An iron cuff threaded with silver was wrapped around her ankle and connected to a short chain bolted to the floor. A metal table sat before her.

Regarding Jordan with a look probably saved for homeless beggars and ugly babies, she flipped a lock of golden hair, then demanded a cup of coffee and a bagel with cream cheese.

"You can fucking starve, Hag." Ivy shut the door behind them.

Seeing Gina triggered memories Jordan had struggled all day and night to repress: the glint of the sword, the *whooshing* sound as it fell, Mazie's look of fear, and sitting with her sister's lifeless body.

It all came back in a rush that squeezed the air from her lungs. Ivy and Xander had begged her to let Mazie go while Aamon's broken cries assaulted her ears. Jordan remembered thinking that his pain was almost palpable. If she'd bothered to look up, she might have seen it riding on the freezing air like some sort of black fog.

"I can't let her go," she'd explained as tears fell, plopping like salted rain to her sister's face. "That will make it real, don't you see? She needs me to hold her. I have to hold her." Jordan smoothed Mazie's bloody hair and cradled her like a baby. "I have to protect her. I can't fail again…"

But she had failed. Mazie was dead.

Her chest ached and she looked away, biting the inside of her cheek hard enough to draw blood.

"Take your time," Xander whispered, rubbing her back.

Gina expelled a heavy sigh, as if they were delaying her from a shopping trip. Facing her again, Jordan's power soared. Vision hazy and tinged with red, she balled her shaking hands into tight fists and crossed her arms.

"I want to see my father," Gina stated matter-of-factly. "If you want my cooperation, I want him here to prevent any…*accidents*." She smiled sweetly and winked.

Jordan closed her eyes and counted backward from ten. It didn't work. Raw energy whipped around inside like a cyclone. She couldn't come down. The force nearly knocked her off her feet and she grabbed Xander's arm for support.

"Aamon won't be joining us." Ivy said, placing her hands on the table, getting in Gina's face. "He's done with you, finished; you're *nothing* to him now."

"I don't believe you," Gina hissed. "I'm his favorite."

Ivy's laugh was bitter. "Not anymore. If you wanted to stay in Dad's good graces, you shouldn't have killed his little girl." Her eyes travelled around the room. "Don't you get it, Gina? This is death row and your number is up."

*No*, Jordan thought. *She doesn't get it, but she will.*

Combing her fingers through her hair, Gina flashed perfect, bleached teeth, and looked at the door, as if waiting for rescue. She was the princess of her own twisted fairy tale, and her hero waited just around the corner.

Jordan's feet carried her across the tiled floor. She grabbed Gina by the shoulder and squeezed.

"You can stop waiting for Superman – he isn't coming."

Gina's smile remained fixed but she winced from the pressure Jordan applied.

"This isn't a game!" Jordan shook her, taking pleasure in the way Gina's head flopped back and forth. "You murdered an innocent child – struck her down like some sort of annoying insect. Mazie was your sister! She did *nothing* to you." Jordan blinked, pushing tears away. She couldn't cry now. Still, her voice cracked, betraying her. "The pain she must have felt...oh God, *why*? Why make her suffer like that?"

"Did you really think I wouldn't retaliate after what you did?" Gina shot back, her face contorted, ugly. "You took something important from me, something vital. Now, we're even."

*"You took a life!"* Jordan screamed.

"So did you."

"No, no I didn't. Not yet."

The chain attached to Gina's ankle rattled as she crossed her legs and proceeded to examine her cuticles. There was no remorse, no regret for what she'd done.

Jordan had witnessed many types of monsters in her lifetime. Some killed for sustenance, others because they weren't in their right minds, and a select few took lives simply because they were ordered to. None of them compared to Gina. She killed Mazie *because she could*. Using revenge as an excuse was just an evasion. The truth was that she took pleasure in making people suffer. She was the purest form of evil.

"You are one sick bitch," Xander said, his blue eyes hard, like ice.

Gina blew him a kiss. "You may be right, handsome, but considering the fact that I'm the one with important info about a certain hillbilly family, I'd watch my mouth if I were you." She turned to Jordan. The kilowatt smile was back. "Speaking of lives, I know of three country bumpkins who don't have much time left to enjoy theirs."

"I doubt you know shit from Cheyenne, but I'll bite. What's this crucial information you have?"

"Uh-uh." Gina waggled her finger. "First, you have to agree to one condition. I don't give secrets away for free."

"I don't know why," Ivy said. "You give everything else away for free. It's a little late in the game to reach for standards, don't ya think? Hell, you probably can't pay guys to touch your *secrets* now – not without a Hazmat suit and a gallon of Purell."

"Such a clever girl." Lips pursed, Gina made a face like she'd sucked on a lemon. "Shut up and let the grownups talk." She dismissed Ivy with a wave of her hand. To Jordan, she said, "My only stipulation is that you and your flunkies keep your hands off. I leave here without a hair out of place, get it?"

"You're hardly in a position to set terms." It was Jordan's turn to smile. "Here's my counter offer; you tell me what you know and I'll make your death quick and a lot less painful than Mazie's was."

Gina blanched. "You can't do that."

"I can do anything I want; I'm not the powerless Cambion chained to the floor."

Jordan placed a finger on Gina's hand. It took a great deal of restraint, but she managed to keep the flow of energy to a trickle. Even so, it was a great incentive. Gina screamed and jerked away.

"Bitch! Stay away from me!"

"That was just a taste of what's to come unless you start talking."

Nursing her hand, she said, "If you're just going to kill me, why should I tell you anything?"

Jordan's stomach clenched. As much as she hated Gina, *she wasn't Gina*. The thought of taking her life had once been appealing. Now, she just wanted to go home.

Mazie was gone. Murdering the one responsible wouldn't bring her back, and Jordan wasn't God. She refused to allow her *Paladin* status to dictate her fate. She might be a lot of things – some good, some bad – but she would always be the one to decide which paths to take.

Xander pulled Jordan aside and Ivy joined them in the corner. "You don't have to do this," he said. "I can get the information without bloodshed."

Bottom lip trembling, Jordan closed her eyes. "Mazie…"

"…is dead," Ivy finished. "There's nothing anyone can do to change that. I know you, Jordan, and this isn't *you*. Let Xander fish the information from her demented mind and we'll blow this joint – go see your family. You need to get away from here for a while."

"But Gina shouldn't get away with this. She ended a little girl's life and couldn't care less. It's like she's not even human."

Xander shook his head. "The problem is that she

*is* human. Gina no longer has any powers. You've been so wrapped up in the supernatural world, fighting what you perceive – what you've been told – is evil, that you've lost touch with the real world." He glanced at Gina. "There are some evil SOB's in our neck of the woods, but nothing holds a candle to man."

*But Gina was twisted before she lost her powers and became human.*

Jordan grappled with her emotions. Right and Wrong were both players in a dangerous game – one she couldn't win no matter what cards she played. If she killed Gina, took it upon herself to decide her fate, she'd lose a part of herself she could never get back. If she didn't, Gina could possibly hurt someone else, and that would be her fault because she could have prevented it.

Unless...

"Come on," Jordan said. "I think I know what to do."

What she had planned was risky, but chances and wagers were all she had these days.

Gina yawned when they approached. She feigned indifference, but the veneer was cracking, the yellow color of cowardice showing underneath.

"Can you try to keep your sentimental pow-wows to a minimum? My ass is falling asleep in this chair and I'm hungry."

Ivy flipped her off while Jordan motioned to

Xander. "Do your thing," she instructed. "Make sure to get every detail."

"What are you doing?" Eyes narrow and cat-like, Gina moved as far as the chain would allow. "I'm not telling you a damn thing until Jordan agrees to my terms."

"Xander's an Invictus. We could make you spill every nasty, horrid thought in that perverted head of yours if we wanted."

Gina paled, and Jordan felt hopeful. This would work. It had to.

"Lucky for you, we don't have time for all the therapy we'd need afterward, and there isn't enough bleach in the world to scour those images from our brains, so we're only going to focus on the information you have about my family."

Struggling with the chain now, Gina screamed, "I never agreed to that!"

Ivy grabbed her shoulders and she suddenly went still. "Ain't that a bitch? Now be a good girl and give this handsome guy your undivided attention or I'll be forced to make a mess on Dad's nice shiny floor."

# XXVII Quinn

The ride back to town was the longest of his life. Even on the weed-choked back roads where farm land distanced neighbors and electric light was scarce, the night was unusually dark. Thick clouds eclipsed the moon, leaving the barest hint of ghostly shine that did nothing to cut the blackness.

The headlights of the Mustang illuminated faded white lines, flickered across the trunks of trees, and occasionally highlighted an animal before it scampered from his sight. Quinn felt like he was driving under water. It was too quiet and the weight of leaving his family behind pressed down on him like the sea. Several times he stopped the car, determined to go back and help. It wasn't that he didn't trust Gabe. Archangels probably had more juice in their little fingers than soldiers contained in their entire beings. His brother and uncle would be fine. The problem was that he wasn't one to run from a fight.

For as long as he could remember, he'd taken the biggest risks when lives were on the line. Unable to endure another loss, Quinn gladly threw himself into caves, swamps, woods, dens…wherever evil dwelled, always a few steps ahead of Nathan and Case. He did his best to make a safe passage for them to follow. To run and leave them in the middle of a dangerous situation went against his very nature. He'd spent his entire life trying to keep them alive, and because of a book, he may have pissed it all away.

*Don't think like that. They'll be fine. Gabe promised to keep them above ground.*

Though fear, with its sharp claws, clung to him, Quinn pressed harder on the gas. Soon, more light filtered through the Cimmerian world outside. Houses became more prevalent, road signs popped up, civilization appeared.

The sheriff's department beckoned. Quinn drove by the parking lot and zeroed in on a small storage building in the back lot. He circled the block and pulled in behind the pre-fabricated structure, hiding the car from prying eyes.

Sheriff Wellard Briggs used the building to store old files. He'd finally taken a step into the 21st century and purchased a few computers (along with a secretary who knew how to use them), but still preferred "old school" ways, refusing to go completely digital.

The locking mechanism on the door was a simple one and Quinn had it open within 30 seconds. He stepped across the threshold and shut the door firmly before turning on a small penlight. Bank boxes, dusty and forgotten, littered the floor, stacked in tottering piles and scattered haphazardly around the room. There was no method to the madness. The sheriff was not an orderly man – a trait that drove his wife crazy. He did have the years of the files each box contained scrawled on the lids with a black marker. Quinn chose the one labeled 1997-99.

Being careful not to disturb the thick layer of dust on the lid, he lifted the top by the edges and set it aside. A jumbled mess of file folders and loose papers, yellowed with age and smelling strongly of ink and mold, lay inside. Quinn gathered up an armful and placed them on the floor.

*Jesus, is this what I've been reduced to – breaking into a building owned by the sheriff to hide a book? I am so going to Hell.*

Glancing around like the nervous trespasser he was, Quinn listened for any noise outside. Confident he was still alone, he dried his sweaty palms on his jeans and unzipped his jacket. From its depths, he pulled out *The Oraculum*. Without hesitation, he buried the book at the bottom of the box, covering it with the original files.

After replacing the lid, Quinn made a quick inspection of the floor to assure he hadn't missed any stray papers. That's when he saw the prints left by his boots. He spent a few minutes walking around the shed, dragging and shuffling his feet. He stopped in front of several boxes, knelt down in front of them, and generally made sure his prints were everywhere. No one would be able to discern which box contained the book.

Satisfied, Quinn exited the building. He locked the door and surveyed the parking lot. There wasn't a soul in sight. With a sigh, he stepped off the low porch and around to the back – where Wellard Briggs leaned against the Mustang.

*And there goes my happy feeling.*

Knowing he was caught, Quinn joined the sheriff and took up space beside him.

"Your phone's been ringing," he drawled, the ever-present matchstick dangling from the side of his mouth.

"Did you answer it?"

Wellard scratched his chin. He was dressed in his "uniform" of faded jeans, plaid shirt, shearling coat, black cowboy hat that had seen better days, belt buckle the size of a hubcap, and worn boots. A gold star displayed on his pocket proclaimed that he was the sheriff of Juneau County. A .45 hanging from his belt made sure no one argued that fact.

"I figured it weren't none of my business."

Quinn nodded.

Wellard Briggs had served his country for two

terms in the Army fresh out of high school. At the age of 27, he'd come back to Dixon's Bluff and signed on with the Juneau sheriff's department. By the time he was 30, his hair had gone prematurely gray and he had married his high school sweetheart, Katherine "Kat" Hale. At the young age of 32, he'd been elected sheriff when his mentor and good friend, Gandy Strickland, had decided he'd rather pull steelhead out of the river than drunk kids out of smashed cars.

Now, what was left of his hair was silvery-white and cut close with a goatee to match. His wife still fussed over his love of country-fried steak with gravy and New Glarus Spotted Cow, and his hazel eyes were as keen as ever. Twenty-nine years of patrolling their small town had not dulled his senses. Nothing got past the man, which was the very reason he was privy to their odd profession.

"Do I even want to know why you were holed up in my storage barn?"

Quinn leaned his head back against the car. The night was flying by and he suddenly felt bone-tired. "I don't think so."

"You didn't come out with anything." The sheriff stuck his hands into the deep pockets of his coat.

"No."

Wellard moved the matchstick to the other side of his mouth. "I'll keep a close watch on the shed for the next couple of days…let you know if I see anyone out here that shouldn't be."

"Thanks," Quinn said, grateful for sheriffs who didn't want to know too much.

Shoving away from the car, Wellard pushed his hat back and stared long and hard at Quinn. "You okay, boy? You need some help?"

If only.

He'd like nothing more than some help right now–and the sheriff would. He'd swallow every detail Quinn fed him without so much as a burp and then climb into the passenger seat as if it was something he did every day.

Smiling at the thought of Wellard Briggs sitting in the Mustang, checking the loads in his gun with his cowboy hat settled between his knees, Quinn shook his head.

"I appreciate it, Sheriff, but it's just work. You know how it is."

Wellard heaved a sighed. "You ever need anything, you come see me, ya hear?"

"Yes, sir."

The sheriff seemed reluctant to leave. Quinn wondered just how exhausted he looked. Eventually, Wellard placed a hand on his shoulder and gave it a squeeze before turning away. As he tramped back across the parking lot, he called, "You know where to find me, boy. Be careful!"

Quinn watched until Sheriff Briggs disappeared

through the back entrance of the main building and then crawled back into the car. His phone showed one text message and three voice mails.

He checked the text message first. It was from Nathan. He smiled despite his exhaustion. True to his word, Gabe had kept his family safe – *their* family safe. He opened the text and his blood ran cold.

```
Illyria is coming for you. RUN!
Call ASAP.
```

He didn't take time to dwell on how the angel had escaped Gabe. He was parked next to the place where he hid the book and needed to put some distance between them before she showed up.

Quinn was back on the road and didn't even remember starting the engine. He drove with no specific destination in mind, and eventually found the car heading west on highway 90. His phone rang, jarring him out of the hypnotic daze he'd fallen into while staring at segments of broken white line that went on forever.

Shit. He forgot to call Nathan.

Fumbling for the phone, Quinn nearly knocked it off the passenger seat. The car swerved as he reached for it again and finally pressed the speaker button.

"Quinn?!"

"Yeah, I'm here."

"Are you okay? Where are you?"

Nathan sounded like a bottle of pop that had been shaken to the point of combustion.

"Calm down, I'm fine. I'm in the car heading west."

He heard voices in the background and then Gabe was on the line.

"Quinn, you need to abandon the car and go on foot. Stay away from areas that can easily be seen from above."

"You want me to walk? Do you know how much fun Illyria will have with that four-foot shank if she catches me without the book? You won't be able to count all the pieces she'll leave behind. Riding is safer than hoofing it."

"A car is easier to spot from the air. Leave the road and find cover. She could be following you right now."

*Comforting thought.*

"Tell me where you are and I'll come for you."

Quinn slowed the car and looked around. He'd been on autopilot since leaving the sheriff's office and it took a second to recognize his surroundings.

"I'm in Gillette, just past South Burma Avenue."

Quinn hung a left on Skyline Drive. He wanted to stay away from residential areas but there wasn't much cover to be found down this way.

"The school!" Casen yelled. "Go to the elementary school."

His uncle referred to Prairie Wind Elementary

which, if Quinn remembered correctly, boasted large parking areas and not much else. Still, it was better than nothing. Quinn knew it was nearby, but needed to get his bearings.

"Got it," he confirmed and ended the call.

Taking a quick right, he pulled the car into the empty lot of the Kum & Go gas station. This time of night it was dark and quiet. A few insects, sluggish from the cold, battered against a pitiful security light that did nothing to cut the gloom.

Quinn pulled his hands down his face in an attempt to slough away his weariness. When he opened his eyes, a flash of light reflected in the rearview mirror caught his attention.

*Lightning*?

He stepped out of the car and gazed up at the sky. Puffy clouds, backlit by the moon, lumbered across his vision like elephants. None of them threatened rain or snow, much less a storm. When the phenomenon did not reoccur, Quinn shrugged it off.

Crossing his arms against the chilly air, he turned in a slow circle. A Chevy car dealership across the way jogged his memory and Quinn knew where to go. The gas station sat at an intersection with Skyline on his left. Taking a right out of the parking lot would put him on Westover, which led right past the school.

His fingers barely brushed the metal of the car door when the sky lit up again. Quinn paused. Definitely not lightning. It was more like a pulse – a signal in three rapid successions that covered the world in blue.

As he watched, the pulse grew faster. Throbbing now, like a heartbeat, the light shredded clouds in its wake and drowned the moon. It was coming closer.

And suddenly Quinn knew.

*Illyria.*

Abandoning the car, Quinn didn't bother to grab a weapon. It was a waste of precious time. Nothing he had in the trunk would stop an angel.

He was halfway across the parking lot when he remembered his cell phone lying on the seat. Cursing, Quinn glanced over his shoulder and saw it was too late to go back for it. Blue light surrounded the exterior of the Mustang, making it glow like some extraterrestrial hotrod.

His only hope was the school, and Gabe.

He ran. When the first tendrils of cold air worked their way into his lungs, Quinn knew he wouldn't get far. He checked his watch. It was 3:07 a.m.

# XXVIII Jordan

**H**er name is Illyria."

Gina's voice was wooden, devoid of inflection. It was eerie, yet welcome at the same time. Xander explained that while under his influence she would answer any question he asked, but the replies would come from her subconscious and Gina would not be aware of what she was saying.

So far, they'd learned that an angel – Michael's first in command – had been ordered to distract Jordan's family while other soldiers looked for her. According to what Gina had overheard while negotiating the terms of her afterlife with the Archangel, there'd been a sudden change of plans. The Aeon had followed Nathan to a meeting with Quinn and Gabe regarding a holy relic – a book of great importance. Michael had immediately ordered Jordan's family be detained until it was retrieved.

"Quinn and Gabriel have the book. Illyria was told to drop everything and do whatever was necessary to get it."

"What is this book?" Xander asked.

Gina shrugged. In a stilted tone, she said, "I don't know. The name was never mentioned. Michael said it contained information on magic from all of creation and powerful spells."

"Did he say what he planned to do with it?"

"With instruction from the book, Michael believes he can obliterate all evil on Earth. No one with a drop of demon blood would be spared."

To Ivy and Jordan, Xander asked, "Is this ringing any bells for you?"

Jordan shook her head.

"I could ask Dad." Ivy looked at the door. "Maybe he knows what she's talking about."

Jordan nodded. "I have to get to my family. If this book is as important as she says, Michael will be desperate to get his hands on it. Who knows what he's capable of?"

*Would he kill for it?*

"I can hear them."

Gina was no longer under Xander's influence. With his attention diverted, the spell had broken. Face pale, eyes closed tight, she gripped the seat of the metal chair with both hands. Jordan expected her to be angry. Instead, she looked petrified.

"Hear who?" Xander asked.

"The angels." Gina's body trembled. Her breath came in short bursts. "I can hear them talking. What did you do to me?!"

"I-I didn't do anything." Xander stammered. "I don't have the power to eavesdrop on angels or transform people into two-way radios. Are you sure, Gina?"

"Fuck yes, I'm sure!" She pulled at the chain attached to her ankle. "I have to get out of here. Let me out of here now!"

Ivy stepped forward and slapped her across the face. Gina lightly touched the spot on her cheek where Ivy's handprint blazed red against her porcelain skin. "Shut your cakehole and tell us what they're saying."

"Fine!" Gina slumped and closed her eyes. "Michael is speaking to Illyria." She hesitated, cocking her head. "Illyria's in a town called Gillette. She said she used Reverberation – whatever the hell that is – to track Quinn and has his location narrowed to a square mile...there aren't many places for him to hide and she'll find him soon. Michael asked for her position...she's near an elementary school. Michael said to remember that the book is her objective, if she must use force, to keep injuries to a minimum if possible. Another angel just asked if she needs assistance and Illyria told him it wasn't necessary, that Quinn is alone...Michael told her to report back when she has the book." Gina paused, then opened her eyes. "That's it. Everything's quiet now."

Jordan leaned against the wall. Gillette was about

an hour south of Dixon's Bluff. She'd been through that town at least a hundred times and knew exactly where the elementary school was. If she teleported there, would she be able to locate Quinn before Illyria? Doubtful, but Jordan had to try.

Xander and Ivy watched her with keen eyes. "So, when do we leave?" her sister asked.

"As soon as possible." Jordan headed for the door.

"Wait! What do we do about her?" Xander motioned to Gina who, from the raised eyebrows and half-open mouth, wanted to know the same thing.

"I tell you what we're gonna do." Jordan backtracked to the table. "We're going to let Orias deal with her." Tapping her bottom lip with her finger nail, Jordan said, "Tell me, Gina, how do you think Orias would feel about one of his own using her powers on her siblings, turning on them, spying for the enemy, *killing* her sister, and making a deal with an archangel for her eternal soul?"

Gina froze, the heaving of her ample chest and an audible gulp when she swallowed the only signs that she was still in the here and now.

Jordan waited for the severity of Gina's fate to hit home…and it did.

Her face fell, as if the metaphorical screws holding it perfectly in place were loosened by a couple of turns. It wasn't a pretty sight, what fear could do to a person's physical appearance. Gina aged in a matter of seconds. Wrinkles appeared like omens, cutting furrows through her faultless ivory skin. Her cheek bones became more prominent, giving her face an emaciated appearance.

"You can't do that," Gina said, her voice cracking. "You have no idea what he'll do to me!"

"Oh, I think I do."

Jordan walked to the door. Ivy and Xander fell in beside her. Before leaving, she took one last look at the person responsible for the pain she felt. Mazie's sweet laughter echoed in her head like wind chimes and Jordan hoped she'd made the right decision where Gina's fate was concerned – hoped her little sister would be proud of her for not compromising who she was.

"The only reason I'm letting you live is because there's nothing I could do that's worse than what you've done to yourself. Death would be a blessing, Gina, and I think you know that now. You deserve every horrible punishment you've got coming."

"Jordan, wait!"

Gina's faced crumpled but it was too late for tears to move her, if they ever had a chance at all.

Ivy gently pushed her out the door and then turned back to their sister. "You can expect a delivery from 1-800-KARMA. I hope you get the biggest bouquet they have."

◇◇◇

Back in her room, Jordan changed into the black leather pants and lightweight lycra shirt Ivy gave her. She didn't bother with weapons, knowing they would be useless and could hinder any quick movements she might have to make. She laced up her black boots and ran downstairs before her mind could dwell on the fact that her brother was being stalked by an angel.

*Quinn's not dead*, she told herself. *I'd know if he was. I'd feel it.*

She met Xander and Ivy in the living room. Aamon had her sister pulled to the side and they whispered in urgent tones. Ignoring them for the moment, she turned to Xander, who looked more than a bit intense.

He had changed clothes, as well. The black military get-up made him look strong...handsome. Jordan's lips burned with the memory of the kiss they shared. Xander said his path was with her and she believed him.

When he pulled her into his arms, she didn't protest. Jordan rested her head on his chest and circled his waist with her arms, drawing him close. It didn't bother her that she'd grown so complacent, so familiar with this guy who was still, for all intent and purposes, a stranger. She was grateful to have him.

At last, Ivy joined them. Aamon reached over and kissed the top of Jordan's head. She no longer hated her father for what he'd done. He'd sold his soul to save his daughter back in a time when medicine consisted of herbs and prayers. When Jordan thought about her family, both Cambion and human, she could see herself doing the same thing to save one of their lives.

"I won't tell you not to go," Aamon said. "Just please promise to call if you need me." He sighed. "I lost one of my kids today; I couldn't bear to lose another." Pulling her and Ivy into a group hug, he murmured, "I love you girls."

"Love you, too, Dad. Don't worry, we'll be fine." Ivy kissed his cheek.

Jordan didn't know what to say. It had been a long time since a parent had shown affection toward her. Uncle Case wasn't the touchy-feely type. His hugs were few and far between.

Did she love Aamon? Jordan honestly didn't know. Part of her felt if she allowed him into her heart, showed more than cursory respect for this demon who was her real father, it would diminish Richard Bailey's memory; cheapen the risks he took to protect her. What happened so long ago was tragic. One bad decision had led to another and, in the end, no one could claim victory. Now, it was up to Jordan to decide when or if she could move on.

Standing there with Aamon, not knowing if she'd ever see him again, Jordan felt she owed him more than a casual nod.

"Dad?" she asked, hating how small she

sounded. The word floated on the air, rootless, but maybe, just maybe, one day that would change.

Ivy's head snapped to attention. Aamon sucked in a quick breath and covered his mouth with his hand, suppressing any emotion lest he ruin the moment by scaring her away.

Amused, Jordan watched her father mentally pick his way through the aftermath of the bombshell she'd dropped. His face, like some sort of fantastical creature, morphed from one visage to another – most accompanied by a grin he couldn't subdue.

Moments later, rocking on his heels, Aamon said, "Yes, hon? What is it?"

"I just wanted to say that I understand now." She licked her lips, uncomfortable with an audience. "And I'm trying – I really am."

It wasn't much, but it was more than she could have managed three months before.

Aamon touched her cheek and she placed her hand over his. "One step at a time, sweet girl, one step at a time."

Xander watched their exchange with a pained expression. Jordan wondered if he'd ever been hugged, if he'd ever had a parental figure to lean on. She doubted it.

Aamon must have been thinking along those same lines. He faced the young man who had so recently come into their lives, and then pulled him into an embrace fathers reserve for their sons.

"Forgive me for not welcoming you into our family sooner."

Xander looked about as lost as Donald Trump in a corn field. He gave Aamon an awkward pat on the back. "It's okay, you don't have to," he mumbled. "I mean, I'm not family, not really."

Aamon clapped him on the shoulder. "You have a home here if you want it, and I've always got room for another child. You don't have to be blood to be family."

# XXIX Quinn

**S**uffocating.

Quinn's lungs, constricted and burning from constant exertion, screamed for air. Legs as weak as matchsticks, he stumbled around another piece of machinery he couldn't name. His fingers trailed along the corrugated surface. Toxic snowflakes of burnt-orange rust peeled away and drifted to the floor.

The vacant factory had seen better days. It was a labyrinth of dark passages, tipped catwalks, and fetid air. The cloying scents of diesel fuel, damp concrete, and urine clung to him. It seeped into his clothes and the pores of his exposed skin. Quinn imagined how horrible the smell would be if it were August instead of October. He swallowed hard against the bile that crept up his throat.

Rounding a corner, he tripped over a nest of moldy blankets and something squeaked. A rat the size of a Chihuahua scampered from the pile. Quinn halted his labored progress until the rodent's fat, leathery tail disappeared beneath a scarred desk. He shivered. Rats were the least of his problems but he still hated them. He nudged the makeshift den with the toe of his boot and prayed no more critters were home. Quinn speculated on the number of derelicts who took refuge in the dreary, crippled building, and hoped none of them squatted there right now. To be anywhere in his general vicinity meant death.

*Death.*

It was coming for him.

The sun climbed higher in the sky to burn away the fog that lingered around the scattered buildings of this abandoned industrial park. As the wet foundations dried, their lighter color hinted at subtle purity.

Illyria was also searching for someone to purify. Quinn wondered if he'd feel clean after she scorched him from the inside out with the touch of her hand or ran him through with her sword. Maybe, once his ashes mingled with her maniacal laughter and the wind carried them ever upward toward Heaven, he would be whole again.

Vengeance and guilt, with their voracious appetites, had gnawed at his soul for years: the victims he couldn't save, the family he left behind, the sister he tormented...nothing suppressed their cravings for long.

Once Illyria took his life, perhaps their hunger

would be sated.

Unable to go any farther, Quinn's legs buckled. He crawled to a nearby wall and leaned against it. Moisture from the floor seeped into his torn jeans, adding to his misery. His lungs whistled as they sucked in air. Legs, splayed like a broken marionette, seized, and then cramped. Too tired to massage them, he clenched his jaws to keep from crying out.

In the silent, drafty room, the sound of a door shattering was akin to ringside seats at a car crash.

The angel had arrived.

It was a shame he never made it to the school. He'd tried, but no matter what direction he took, the light was there, herding him like some sort of celestial border collie.

He was only a sheep.

Quinn wondered if Gabe was still nearby. If Illyria was able to track him surely his Guardian could, too. It was a long shot but that's all he had left.

Somewhere in the dark recesses of the factory, a piece of heavy machinery scraped across the cement floor and he winced. She was getting closer, and Quinn had no strength left to run. Hell, he was too tired to crawl.

Footsteps echoed, reverberating through his mind. The angel made no effort to disguise her whereabouts and why should she? Illyria was immortal. There was nothing a simple human could do to deter her. His only saving grace was that he was the only one who knew where *The Oraculum* was. Unless she could read minds (please God, no!) Michael would never get his hands on the book he coveted. Its whereabouts would die with Quinn.

As if on cue, black boots turned the corner. His eyes travelled up shapely legs in skin-tight material, taut stomach, round breasts, long, almost delicate neck, and the face of a centerfold model. If not for the leering eyes and the wicked-sharp sword in her hand, Illyria would be the perfect picture of every guy's wet dream.

When her tongue snaked out, leaving her full, pink lips glistening, Quinn groaned and closed his eyes. "You're killing me," he mumbled.

"Not yet."

Damn, even her voice was sexy – deep and husky, like the rumble of a finely tuned engine.

When he opened his eyes again, she was kneeling in front of him. Quinn never heard her move. She was better at hunting than he was. He could appreciate that, even if he was the prey.

"I want the book," she purred, and his heart thumped a little faster. "Tell me where it is and we can both get on with our morning." She moved closer, leaning so far on her hands and knees that her nose skimmed his neck and moved up to his ear. Her warm breath mingled with the currents of chilly air, pushing against his skin. Quinn shivered even as he broke out in goose flesh.

"Tell me," she whispered.

"I can't remember," he said, breathing hard.

And for a moment there, he couldn't. It was all he could do to form a coherent sentence. Her nearness screwed with his mind, like static on a radio station. He would form a thought only to have it whisked away on a tide of gentle dissonance.

"Perhaps I can help with your memory loss."

His witty comeback was lost in translation. Her mouth inched sideways, trailing heat as she worked her way across his jaw. When they were face to face, her perfect lips hovered above his. Eyes half closed, Illyria gently pulled air into her mouth and smiled, as if tasting something sweet.

By the time her mouth met his, Quinn was groaning with need. Her lips fit perfectly with his. They moved in a synchronized dance against each other. She tasted like clover honey.

*Tell me where* The Oraculum *is.*

He could hear her in his head, gently prodding, urging. He went to break away but she climbed on his lap and dredged farther with her tongue, sliding it over his own. Suddenly, he couldn't get enough.

*Tell me*, she beckoned again.

Oh, God, she was everywhere. His mind was full of her. Illyria commanded his thoughts and actions. As this kiss deepened and she ran her hands through his hair, pulling him closer, he began to question his reason for hiding the book.

Why shouldn't he tell Illyria? It didn't belong to him. The book was a holy relic and Michael needed it far worse than they did. He could use it to save the world. No more demons to battle! No more nightmare monsters to take innocent lives. Just…peace.

*No!*

He shouted the word in his head and pushed with all his might. Unprepared for resistance, Illyria rolled off his lap but quickly sprang to her feet.

Shaking, hands balled into fists, she snarled, "You just made a big mistake. It would have been much more pleasant to do it my way."

Quinn felt more exhausted now than before she'd kissed him. Limbs heavy, every movement he made was clumsy, damn near impossible.

"Yeah, well," he said, head rolling back to rest against the wall, "I've never been one for taking the *pleasant* route. Frankly, I wouldn't know how."

"Pity, I was actually enjoying myself." Illyria paced, one perfectly manicured nail tapping against her chin. She stopped and studied him. "You aren't going to tell me where the book is, are you?"

Looking her in the eyes with all the concentration he could marshal, he replied with a definite, "No."

She sighed.

If Illyria was trying to emulate the loving seraph portrayed in picture books, she was failing miserably. All she managed was a bad photoshopped copy, a cheap imitation that didn't fool him in the slightest. Long face and drooping shoulders aside, there was a glint in her eyes she couldn't extinguish. Quinn knew that spark – had seen it many times in his own eyes reflected in dirty windows and spotted mirrors.

Illyria was closing in on her quarry and wet work was just around the corner.

The high of the hunt used to be the only reason he worked in the Circle. Unlike Nathan, Quinn didn't kill monsters because it was the right thing to do. He'd seen enough incidents in his time to know that humans could be just as evil, if not more, than the creatures he slaughtered. No, he did it for the rush, to feel *something*, to nourish the hate.

He looked at Illyria and saw the person he used to be – the person he tried so hard to forget.

Cracking her knuckles, she said, "In that case, you leave me no choice."

As smooth as a serial killer, Illyria shrugged off the façade of a benevolent angel like a cloak. What he saw underneath made Quinn rethink his decision. Maybe he should beg to resume the kiss. It would be painless and wouldn't involve blood loss.

When she bent over and touched a fingertip to his head, setting his veins on fire, Quinn knew he was right.

# XXX Jordan

Jordan was drawn to Illyria like water. Her fear of not being able to locate Quinn was unfounded. Turns out, she was more in tune with angels than she realized. Being a *Paladin* had its advantages.

She had a moment of déjà vu when she entered the old factory. Jordan followed the dark passages, trailing her hands along the cold cement walls, knowing she'd find a monster doing God only knew what to her brother at the end.

But this time, she wasn't alone.

Ivy and Xander were a few steps behind, ready to stand at her side, prepared to die with her – *for her*, if necessary. It wouldn't come to that, of course; Jordan planned to keep them far away from Illyria. Still, her odds of succeeding in the factory where she'd failed in the mine back in Tennessee went up considerably with them there.

Jordan turned a corner and gracefully tripped

over a piece of rebar. Her teeth were set on edge by ear-piercing echoes of metal clanging against concrete in a discordant refrain as it bounced across the floor. So much for the element of surprise.

She stopped the procession, face burning brighter than Rudolph's nose while Ivy snickered from behind. For someone who was supposed to be an experienced hunter, Jordan made more noise than a house demolition. She took a deep breath, intending to regroup and start again, when a scream split the rimy air. She recognized the voice, but had never heard it under such duress.

Jordan's heart plunged, and then she was running.

Footsteps slapping, the wind in her ears, Jordan didn't realize how close they were to Quinn and Illyria. She turned another corner in the maze of metal contraptions and found herself on a collision course with the angel. She only had a second to take in her brother's prone form, then dropped to her knees and rolled.

Sweeping with her left leg, Jordan's boot caught Illyria's ankle, tripping her. A blast of Ivy's power sent the Aeon careening into some shelves. Jordan placed herself between Illyria and Quinn.

He looked worse than she'd ever seen him, and that was saying a lot. Severe burns covered his head, face, and arms. The smell of charred flesh coated the back of her throat and her stomach flip-flopped. One dark blue eye was open, filled with misery but surprisingly alert. The other was fused shut.

*Oh, Quinn...*

Jordan never pictured their reunion like this.

Across from her, Illyria stood as puffed up as a peacock. She smoothed her body suit and then reclined against the wall, surveying her handiwork.

Blood boiling, Jordan was torn between ripping Illyria's throat out and healing her brother. She knew not to turn her back on the angel. The sword strapped to her back was more than a little convenient, and Jordan knew the damage it could do.

She thought about Mazie and her insides quivered. Jordan had failed her sister. How could she possibly protect Quinn from Michael's best soldier?

Sensing her distress, Ivy and Xander took their places by her side. Leaning close, Ivy gestured to Quinn. "I've got him," she whispered. "You watch the angel."

Her sister kneeled by Quinn, speaking softly while preparing to heal his wounds. A little weight lifted from Jordan's shoulders.

Xander placed a hand on her back, flooding Jordan with feelings of peace and security. "Don't let her intimidate you," he said. "Remember, you're a *Paladin*. Illyria has no idea how powerful you are. Use that advantage. Don't hold *anything* back. Understand?"

Jordan nodded, her eyes glued to the Aeon who

faked a dramatic yawn.

Soft, glowing light from Ivy's capable hands reflected off the machinery around them. She was healing Quinn's wounds.

Illyria scowled, her hair rippling in a sudden breeze. She went from Casual Friday to Manic Monday in the span of a heartbeat.

"You there, Cambion! I didn't give you permission to heal anyone."

"You there, Douchebag! Fuck off."

Ivy's tone was cool. She refused to give the angel her undivided attention.

The seraph took a step forward but Jordan blocked her way. Her sister's brazen disregard for Illyria's status instilled confidence where, a minute before, Jordan had none. Ivy had faith in her – trusted her to keep them safe. It was time Jordan believed that she *could*.

Once again, Illyria moved to intercede. Jordan grabbed her by the arm. The angel didn't appear too keen to address her directly. Was Illyria afraid or simply unconcerned?

Pinching the bridge of her nose, the Aeon said, "I'll deal with you in a moment, Ms. Bailey. Your brother and I have unfinished business. You will wait your turn."

"Your business with my brother is done."

With a thought, Jordan tapped into her power. Instinct told her to hold back, knowing how easy it was to lose control. But Xander was right. Now wasn't the time to give conscience a voice.

Pushing her inhibitions aside, Jordan opened the floodgates that harnessed her power and released every drop. Bracing for impact, she rocked on her feet as intensity tantamount to a bolt of lightning brought her to her knees. Fire licked at her veins, burning, consuming, leaving something – *someone* – else in its place.

She screamed.

"Jordan!"

The concern in Quinn's voice gave her the strength to raise her head. Through sweaty bangs, Jordan watched, helpless, as Illyria slipped around her, taking advantage of the fact that she was momentarily incapacitated. Though she struggled, Jordan couldn't move an inch until the power balanced out.

Muscles straining, she cursed herself for not invoking the full extent of her power sooner. Then again, she hadn't received an instruction manual. Knowing the side effects beforehand would have been convenient.

Illyria wiggled her finger and Ivy sailed across the room. Xander placed himself in front of Quinn and, for a second, Jordan thought she saw a hint of blue light in his eyes but then he was moving...*fast*.

Teleporting in and out of existence, Xander kept the angel on her toes. Using his combined powers and

Cambion strength, he slammed a fist into the back of her neck and disappeared, only to return and catch her off-guard again.

The place between her shoulder blades began to itch and burn, but the upside was that Jordan could move again. Slowly, she got to her feet. Across the room, Ivy did the same. Her sister hobbled like a geriatric patient but appeared to be okay.

Ten feet away, Xander and Illyria moved in a deadly dance. Illyria swung her sword like a metronome, keeping time. Beside them, Quinn, healed by Ivy's hands, bobbed and weaved like a third wheel, searching for a way to cut in and take a turn with the angel. If he got within the reach of her blade…

"Quinn, don't!"

Jordan's outburst distracted Xander. It was the opportunity Illyria waited for. The second he looked away, she thrust her sword into his shoulder. In most circumstances, the wound wouldn't be fatal, the blow too high to cause major damage. But circumstances were far from ordinary, and the weapon used could destroy in more ways than one.

Time slowed to a dribble. Ivy teleported to Xander and pulled him out of the way before Illyria could turn him into a pin cushion. Quinn's eyes blazed. It was a look Jordan knew well.

Her brother sought her out, his face full of love. Jordan saw his intentions, felt his goodbye, and called his name, knowing he wouldn't listen.

Weaponless, armed with only the hope of buying her some time, Quinn stepped in front of Illyria. The Aeon snorted and made a "come hither" gesture with her hand.

"No!"

Jordan ran. Ivy screamed her name while Xander lay unmoving beside her. Jordan gulped, choking on guilt, knowing in her heart that Xander was dying.

Illyria swung her blade and Quinn twirled out of reach, barely avoiding being ripped in two. Jordan rushed to his side. With a flick of her wrist, the angel propelled her into a rusted contraption that had probably been new when dinosaurs walked the earth.

"Tell me where the book is and I'll let you live," Illyria bartered, her sword spinning fast enough to ruffle Quinn's hair.

"Why don't you check your mama's house?" he countered, and surprised her with a roundhouse kick.

He was going to get himself killed.

Jordan teleported and grabbed Illyria in a choke hold. She pulled, hoping to give her brother an escape. Off to the side, Ivy encouraged Quinn to *move his ass*.

Power oozed from her hands and the Aeon screamed in pain.

"Quinn, go. I've got this!"

But he couldn't move. Her brother was rooted to the floor, transfixed by the scene playing out in front of him. Puffs of smoke rose from Illyria's hair. The angel howled, struggling to break free. In a last ditch effort, she reversed momentum and pushed into Jordan instead of pulling away. Both of them lost their balance and went tumbling.

Illyria landed on top, knocking the breath out of Jordan. She tried to inhale but her lungs had no room to expand, even after the angel rolled off and staggered to her feet.

Jordan struggled to her knees. Dizzy from lack of oxygen, her heart pounded in her ears while black butterflies swooped in her vision. Illyria tumbled about the room like someone punch drunk, but became more sure-footed with every step.

Once again, she made a beeline for Quinn.

Ivy appeared in a pop of displaced air and grabbed the angel's arm. From the look on her face, she was giving Illyria all she had. It wasn't enough. A mid-level Cambion was no match for a seraph. Illyria tossed her aside like a forgotten toy.

Jordan called out to Quinn but still could not breathe, couldn't get to her feet. All she managed was a choked wheeze that no one heard.

Illyria drew closer to her brother.

The Aeon's wounds were healing at a rapid rate. Jordan cursed herself for not using the full extent of her power.

*My power*, she thought. *That's it!*

Jordan called upon it, willing it to heal her.

Energy coursed through her body. Her shallow breaths became deeper. Oxygen filled her lungs. The dark butterflies faded from her sight. Renewed, Jordan jumped to her feet.

Too late.

Blinding light burst from Illyria's palms, pinning Quinn against the wall. With a cry born of war and nourished by hate, she raised the sword and buried it in his chest.

*I didn't see that.*

Jordan put up a mental wall, blocking her emotions.

Quinn was fine. That gurgling noise wasn't him taking his last breaths. Ivy's anguished screams meant nothing. Her sister was too dramatic.

Quinn was fine.

Xander was fine.

They were both *fine*, dammit!

Anguish fought with rage. The nagging itch – that deep burn between her shoulders – intensified. Unwilling to see what she couldn't face, Jordan blindly searched for the source of her turmoil.

Illyria reclined against the wall with a big grin on her face – a hunter posing with her kill. Jordan refused to look at the poor soul hanging next to her like a slab of meat. It wasn't anyone she knew.

But the pain in her heart and her trembling hands said differently. Jordan shook her head. It didn't matter. The angel started this. The demon would finish it.

Illyria patted her brother on the head.

*Don't look, it's not him.*

"My negotiations with Quinn didn't end well." The angel rolled her head from side to side. Her neck cracked and popped. "Sad, really. He had potential. Still, I'm not above giving a replay." She glanced at Ivy to make her point, and then pulled the sword from Quinn's chest. It made a sick, sucking noise as it exited, and he fell to a heap on the dirty floor.

*It's not him.*

Wiping the blood from her blade with a crumpled piece of trash, Illyria continued. "I need that book, Jordan. You will call the remaining members of your inept family and have them come here. One way or another, I will take possession of *The Oraculum*. I assume things will go much more smoothly this time."

Her cold, condescending smile reminded Jordan of a teacher she'd had in fourth grade. She wasn't surprised when, years later, a member of the Circle had been sent to hunt her down in Massachusetts for practicing bad witchcraft. With the snap of her fingers, the student of Ms. Sunday's scorn would fall ill to a three-day stomach virus. Those snaps were always accompanied by the same sick smile that never reached her eyes.

"You assumed wrong," Jordan replied.

In a whoosh and rip of fabric, wings unfurled

from her back. From the corner, she heard Ivy gasp and mumble something about how they had changed from the last time she saw them. Illyria's eyes bulged and she prayed aloud to God.

"I think," Jordan said, stretching her twelve-foot appendages, "it's Michael you should petition for help. God probably doesn't know you exist."

Though weightless, Jordan felt sure her wings were powerful. Silvery-white feathers, magnificent and glorious, were outlined in royal-blue flames. The fire kissed the edges all the way around, but never spread inward.

Illyria regarded Jordan's wings with a type of thunderstruck horror. Mouth agape, hand pressed against her chest, she whispered, "The fire represents metamorphosis." She took a few steps away, putting some distance between them. "Like a Phoenix, you're...you're changing, but into what?"

Jordan's eyes dipped to the still form on the floor – the one dressed in her brother's clothes – and the dam keeping her misery at bay exploded. Her lungs seized. The mixture of emotions, frigid and expeditious, almost swept her away.

Choking back tears, Jordan asked, "Why don't we find out?"

Illyria raised her sword. As Jordan advanced, the angel revealed her own wings. Unfurled, they were shorter, narrower, the brooding gray color of a storm cloud.

"It doesn't have to be this way," she said, moving the blade from one hand to the other.

"Yes, it does." Jordan was close enough to reach out and touch the angel. "You assured that when you killed Xander and Quinn. She paused. "It's important that you know. Your actions signed this death warrant, Illyria; not me."

The blade came down, splitting the air. Jordan smelled the venomous magic within the steel. It was sharp, astringent, like the inside of a dentist's office. It sliced through her forearm, drawing a deep gash. Before she could blink, Illyria switched hands. The next swipe split her cheek clear to the bone.

She felt no pain. Jordan chanced a look at her arm, and watched in amazement as the muscle, tendons, and skin knit back together. Even then, the irritation that came with healing was little more than a burning itch.

Illyria gasped as Ivy gave a triumphant shout.

From the corner of her eye, Jordan saw Xander, her safe haven, sit up with her sister's help. His wound had also healed. The question was, *how*?

A quick look told her Quinn had not been so lucky. There was no movement. Black lines of poison marred his visible skin, having spread from the point of impact.

She kept losing the ones she loved. It wasn't fair. Silently, Jordan cursed God for letting this happen.

*I may be a* Paladin *but dammit, I didn't ask for it!*

*I've done* nothing *to deserve this and neither did Mazie or Quinn. So God, if you aren't too busy, how about a little help here, huh? Get off your holy ass and send my brother a miracle.*

She waited a beat but nothing happened. Figures. He was probably walking streets of gold right now. He sure as hell wasn't curing cancer or punishing the wicked. God wasn't going to save Quinn.

And she was sick of it – *all* of it.

Power surged through Jordan's veins. Raw. Unmitigated. Wrenching the sword from Illyria, Jordan twisted the blade, bent it back upon itself, and flung the weapon across the room.

"Are you off your gourd? We could've used that!"

Ivy balked at the loss of a weapon that could kill angels.

"I don't need it," Jordan snarled.

Illyria's wide eyes darted around the room, pausing at the windows, doors. Before the angel could flee, Jordan charged. Illyria brought her hand up in defense. In one swift motion, Jordan caught the arm, spun in close, and wrenched it behind the angel's back. With a cry, the Aeon fell to her knees.

"Time to burn," Jordan whispered.

The echoes of Illyria's screams filled the room, shook its foundations. Plaster peppered the ground. Dust choked the air. The stench of scorched flesh filled Jordan's nostrils.

In the fire, she became the very monster she was trying to destroy.

# XXXI Quinn

Something crawled underneath his skin like worms. They tunneled outward from the point where Illyria's sword had passed through like a steel spike and spread up and down his body. Black tracer marks crept along in their wake, burning, itching. They tattooed his skin, decorating it in twisting patterns that resembled diseased vines.

Quinn was dying.

For years, the thought of burying another family member had haunted him. Unable to go through that pain again, Quinn had pushed away, tying himself in knots, bending over backward to avoid the snare.

All those reckless twists and turns. In the end, he found himself hanging from a noose he'd devised himself.

Death was inevitable. There was no escape.

Resigned, Quinn finally learned to accept what couldn't be changed. Once he stopped struggling, breathing became easier. Now, it looked like he would get his wish. Quinn would go first. Peering at his sister through heavy eyes, the thought made him smile.

Jordan looked radiant, commanding, her wings even more splendid than Gabe's. The blue fire that brushed the edges of spangling silver was awe-inspiring. Quinn realized his little sister, the one he had worried about losing, was stronger than he – not because of her *Paladin* status or extraordinary strength, but because she had endured so much and was still standing, still fighting.

Was there ever a time when she wasn't?

The sun finally broke over the horizon. One last sunrise, and it was beautiful. Even through the grimy windows, Quinn could see amazing colors flooding the pale sky, changing it into something more – something magical.

In the corner, Jordan's half sister sat with the boy's head in her lap. Watching Ivy smooth his brow, Quinn remembered the words she'd whispered to him as she healed his injuries.

"Hang in there, Quinn. Don't you dare give up!"

For a second, he'd forgotten that she was a Cambion. There had been concern in her eyes, warmth and gentleness in her touch. She had smoothed his brow, as well, and told him not to worry.

"Close your eyes and rest. I'll have you fixed up in no time."

Quinn had never closed his eyes to a demon before. May as well offer yourself to a lioness and pray she had a full stomach – there was no difference. Ivy must have sensed his mistrust. Her eyes blazed red. Like swirling smoke, he watched them slowly revert to the Delphic, stormy gray color that mesmerized as much as they unnerved him. She was an enigma that both tempted and terrified.

Ivy took a deep breath and pulled her hands away.

"Sorry; didn't mean to go all demon on you, but I have a hard time with dogmatic asswipes. So, why don't you drop the Jim Crow act? Being human doesn't make you squeaky clean, and that 'holier than thou' shit really pisses me off."

As he lay there with third-degree burns, pulled muscles, dehydration, and fatigue, all he could think about was the fact that, in so many words, she'd just called him a racist. Quinn didn't know whether to laugh or be offended. There was no comparison between minorities of the *human* race and demons.

Did he hate demons?

Yes.

If he could, he'd eradicate every damned one of them from the face of the earth. They served no purpose other than to spread pain and misery – like mosquitoes. But even as these thoughts circled Quinn's mind, he thought of Jordan.

She'd been part demon her entire life and, though they hadn't known about her genetic makeup until recently, she had always been a good person. Now that he knew she was sired by a demon, did that automatically make her evil? Up until then, it had never crossed his mind.

Like Jordan, Ivy hadn't been given a vote on her Cambion heritage. How many other demons were victims of circumstances they couldn't control?

Softly, she said, "Our sister trusts me; can't you do the same? I only want to help."

She looked pitiful and Quinn felt like an ass. With a nod, he closed his eyes.

After she healed him, Ivy helped him to his feet.

"Thank you," she murmured.

Quinn had treated her like a pariah and she was *thanking* him. Jesus.

As usual, words failed him. He had a hard time expressing himself to normals. Showing gratitude to a demon was just…wrong, on so many levels. Still, Ivy had saved his life.

He gave her an awkward pat on the back. "Ditto."

The look she gave him was nothing short of amazement, and not in a good way. It was more of a "'Who ties your shoes for you?'" expression.

◇◇◇

Darker now.

The light he lived in was going dim, and God, he was so tired. Quinn would miss his family but not the pain. Not the hunts. Not the memories. It would be a blessing to shed them and leave it all behind.

As the bags tied to his eye lids grew heavier, his body felt lighter. A sensation of floating on cold but gentle waves overtook him and Quinn wondered if it was time to let the line he'd kept a tight grip on – the one that kept him moored to the broken-down dock that was his life, his responsibilities – slip free at last.

He wanted the last sight his eyes perceived before closing forever to be that of his sister, so he slowly rolled his head to front and center…and froze.

Jordan advanced toward Illyria with murderous intent. Eyes glowing like beacons, flowing steps, shoulders back, she was out for more than a little blood and revenge. His mind, in its weakened state, tried to recall the prophecy from *The Oraculum.*

*Dammit! What had it said?*

His eyes fluttered and slammed shut. Moments before, he welcomed the darkness. Now, he had to fight it for Jordan's sake. She was going to fall.

*Fall! Something about falling…*

A memory of him, Nathan, and Gabe sitting in a nice hotel room discussing the passage darted across his mind like a fish but was too quick and slippery to grasp.

*Fuck*!

Someone screamed. It was the shrill, harrowing lament of life ending in slow torment. With the effort of a bodybuilder, Quinn opened his eyes. Illyria was on her knees before Jordan, and his sister was – sweet Jesus!

*What was she doing?*

Illyria was frozen in place, her skin alight with blinding radiance that resembled fire. The only part of her that still worked was her vocal chords and even now, the scream was losing intensity and strength. Soon, there was only the barest hint of a whimper.

The light moved across Illyria's exposed skin. What was left behind looked calcified, on the verge of crumbling. Quinn called out to Jordan, to make her stop, but the mighty roar he intended was replaced with a tiny peep that would have made a canary shake its head in shame. He tried to raise his arm to draw her attention, but his limbs were dead and useless. He wasn't going to be able to stop her from killing Illyria, from falling, from bringing on a holy war like the world had never seen.

Quinn closed his eyes. He didn't want to see the end and no longer had the strength to keep them open. The whooshing sound of wings and Gabe's voice from somewhere close had him competing with death again, but it was too late. Too late for all of them. Even so, he pushed, and the reaper paused a second time.

"Jordan, stop!"

Gabe pulled her away from the Aeon. As soon as the contact was broken, Illyria's form collapsed, flaking apart to drift into soft piles of charcoal powder on the floor.

"I'm fine," Jordan whispered. "I'm okay." Her entire body shuddered violently – the aftereffects of taking a life. Quinn had been there many times before.

And then Gabe was by his side. He placed his hands over the ghastly wound in Quinn's chest and generated soothing blue light. Within moments, the jagged hole closed and the black tracer marks began to fade, disappearing like invisible ink. Quinn's strength returned, plowing into him like a landslide, making the room spin and his heart beat in double-time.

"Don't move too quickly," Gabriel advised, helping him to sit up.

"Yeah, no problem there." Quinn took a deep breath – his first since he'd been stabbed – and clapped his Guardian on the shoulder. "Thanks, Gabe."

Jordan practically fell at Quinn's feet and sobbed. "I'm so sorry. I hesitated, I…Oh, God, you could have died because of me!"

His sister had no idea what she'd put into motion. Quinn pulled her into his arms. How was he supposed to explain that by killing an angel (one who deserved it) Jordan had started a war that could only end with her death?

Tucking a stray lock of hair behind her ear, Quinn placed a kiss on her forehead.

The simple truth was, he couldn't.

Ivy and the guy he didn't know approached with caution. Quinn guessed Gabe had something to do with their tight shoulders and halted steps. He was an angel, after all, and they had all seen firsthand what those bastards were capable of.

"You must be Ivy," his Guardian said by way of a greeting. He gave a small smile when the Cambion frowned and retreated a few steps.

"I'm not going to hurt you," Gabe continued, "but I do need to speak with you...in private." When Ivy cocked her head, uncertainty as evident as her ebony-colored hair, he said, "Please, it's important," and looked pointedly at Jordan.

Quinn watched throat muscles work under her smooth skin, and then Ivy walked to a battered table several feet away and stood stiffly, waiting.

Gabe started to follow, then stopped and looked at the boy, as if just noticing him. "Who are you?" he asked.

The handsome young man didn't appear at all nervous. He offered his hand and said, "My name is Xander. You must be Gabriel. It's a pleasure to meet you, sir."

"Really?" Quinn and Gabe answered in unison.

"What?" Xander, asked. "Did I say something wrong?"

"I think," Jordan said, sniffing, "they're surprised to hear a Cambion say that meeting an angel – especially an *archangel* – is a pleasure."

Xander smiled sheepishly. "Oh. Well, I've never felt particularly evil." He shuffled his feet. "I mean, I've never felt like I belonged in that camp…in any camp, really."

"Interesting," Gabe said. "Maybe you should join Ivy. We can use all the help we can get."

When Xander's confused eyes met Quinn's, he shook his head slightly – a cue not to question anything in front of Jordan. The young man seemed to understand.

"What's Gabe talking to them about?" Jordan asked, snuggling against Quinn's side. "And where's Uncle Case and Nathan?"

Quinn pulled her closer. God, what were they gonna do?

"I'm sure they're back at the house," he said. "Gabe promised to keep them safe. He wouldn't be here if they weren't." Mentally, Quinn sighed. "As for what they're discussing, Gabe is probably recruiting them into our little army. There's bound to be some pissed-off demons now that you're not stuck under their asses anymore, and Michael–"

"–Michael can sit and spin," she finished. "I

don't give a damn how many soldiers he sends, I'm not his property."

Quinn couldn't help but smile. "So," he said, laying his head on top of hers. "Wings, huh?"

They had disappeared to wherever wings go, but he could still see them in his mind, regal and amazing.

"I guess so," Jordan answered.

"They suit you."

And Quinn realized that they did. Jordan was exactly as Illyria described her – a sort of Phoenix, changing, becoming something more. He just prayed that whatever happened, she would remember that she would always be Jordan first.

"I love you," he said.

It felt good to be able to say that now. For so many years, Quinn had been afraid to let her know just what she meant to him. Now, he didn't have to pretend or push her away. If the prophecy was right, Jordan needed to know now more than ever how much he cared, how much they *all* cared.

"I love you, too."

Jordan kissed his cheek, and then released a bone-cracking yawn. Dark smudges framed her tired green eyes which were shot through with red lines like a road map.

Quinn took her hand, marveling over how much smaller it was.

"Let's go home."

"Home sounds good." Jordan's smile diminished the pallor of exhaustion that blanched her face.

Quinn stood up – a little dizzy but otherwise okay – and pulled her to her feet. Jordan tottered on unsteady legs.

"Am I going to have to carry you, Superwoman?"

"Ha-ha." She punched him on the arm. "Be quiet or you'll not only carry me, but make me breakfast, too."

"How about a compromise," he said. "I'll carry you for as long as you need me to…" Quinn paused to make sure she knew he was being serious. The sudden tears that sprang to her eyes told him she did. "But, we'll make Nathan fix breakfast."

Jordan hiccupped and found a smile. "Okay."

Then she grabbed her head in both hands and screamed.

# XXXII Jordan

The pain was excruciating, like someone pounding on her head with a mallet while driving a foot-long spike through it. Unable to function through the pain, Jordan swayed like a felled tree and hit the floor on her side.

*Oh, God, let me die! Please, anything – just make it stop!*

She heard yelling. Someone pulled her onto their lap – probably Quinn – and the small amount of jostling it caused made her lean over blindly and puke.

Gabe's face appeared like a mirage. His eyes were argent, gas-flame blue, his hands aglow with the power of a lighthouse. He looked terrified as he placed them upon her head.

The pain crawled down her body with the teeth and claws of a raptor. Ripping, chewing, it swallowed her inch by grievous inch.

"What's happening?!" she heard Ivy scream. Her

voice sounded far away and then much too close, as if she were hearing her through a cheap radio with sketchy reception. "You didn't say it would be like this!"

"I didn't know," Gabe answered, his face grave.

Jordan had no idea what they were talking about. She concentrated on the creeping thing causing her such agony. It moved slowly to her chest and she held her breath, waiting…waiting…

It tunneled into her heart. The organ stammered, then seized. Her toes curled and limbs went stiff as she rolled off of Quinn's lap and fought to stay conscious. The thing hollowed out a niche and, as it squirmed and pulled its way inside, her heart seemed to swell until she thought it would burst.

Time was immeasurable. Jordan didn't know how long she lay on the floor, slaving for every breath, tangled in an invisible fight she couldn't win. Eventually, the creeping thing settled down. Her heart rate returned to a normal pace, and the pain abated. She wiped at the sweat stinging her eyes and looked around. Her family leaned over her, concerned faces peering down at the condemned.

"Can you sit up?" Xander ask.

His face was chalk-white, tracks from the tears he'd shed still wet, glistening in the morning sun. Shaking hands hovered above her heart and Jordan knew he was partly responsible for stopping her pain.

"Yes, I think so."

He bent to help her and she stood on legs as wobbly as the foundation of a brothel house. Everyone surrounded her in a group hug but no one asked what happened. No one inquired about the scene she'd just reenacted from *The Exorcist*.

Jordan pulled away, taking in watery eyes and lost expressions. Ivy worked her bottom lip with her teeth. Quinn crossed and uncrossed his arms. Gabe looked up toward Heaven and mumbled under his breath – desperate tics that accompany tragic news. Xander was the only one who met her gaze without flinching.

*They didn't ask because they already know.*

With that realization came a voice. It slid into her head and melted all of her thoughts like chocolate on the tongue.

*Come to me, Jordan.*

His voice was as fluid as the delta and Jordan found herself riding waves of saccharine and silk. The others disappeared from the room and his face was the only one she saw.

*I can't*, she thought, knowing he would hear. *I have to be with my family.*

*Your family will not understand. They'll pretend to love you on the surface but there is a rift between you now – one that can never be repaired. They are Slayers at heart. Do you really believe they'll accept you now that demon blood runs in your veins?*

Jordan pushed at the veil covering her eyes and

searched for Quinn. Instead, she saw herself running through a twilight wood. Briars and scrubs tore snatches of her skin as she raced by, but she barely noticed the blood they drew. An angry wind howled overhead, shaking the oaks and pines. Their shadows danced on the straw-covered ground – gnarled fingers that reached for her in the moonlight.

Behind her, Jordan heard the deep growl of men's voices and the baying of dogs. They were getting closer. Frantic, she bulled through a stream, slipping on smooth stones and soaking her jeans. The cold water made her gasp but she pressed on, knowing that time was playing for the opposite team this night.

At the bank, she grabbed handfuls of choking weeds and attempted to pull herself up its steep, muddy side. Using her knees instead of her feet, Jordan made progress but the going was slow. Several times, the weeds broke off in her hands, causing her to slide backward and lose the ground she had just managed to gain.

And still, the dogs kept coming. When the wind paused to gather its breath, Jordan could hear the sound of scattering leaves as they ran, their cries changing in tone when the trail grew stronger. Behind them, the men on the hunt whooped and urged the hounds. They knew she was close.

The bank was too steep. She'd never make it to the top before the dogs were on her. With a groan,

Jordan slid back down to the bottom. Even at its shallowest, the icy water lapped over the top of her boots. Teeth chattering, she pushed down stream, hoping the dogs would lose her scent. She spotted a bend up ahead and knew she must get around it or risk being seen. She pushed her exhausted muscles but they had given her all they could. She slogged on anyway. What other choice did she have?

Just as she reached the bend, dogs erupted from the woods, howling for all they were worth. Risking a look back, Jordan saw them sniffing feverishly at the spot where she entered the stream. Two men ran to join them. They snapped leashes on the dogs' collars and led them up and down the bank, coaxing them like one would a confused child.

As quietly as possible, Jordan moved around the curve. She hoped to find a place where the bank's grade was passable and get back on dry land where she could move faster. When she spotted a section by the water where the soil had eroded beside a poplar tree, she thought she might have a chance. Grabbing the ridged bark with both hands, Jordan used it as an anchor to pull herself out of the stream.

She managed another fifty feet before her legs buckled. She tumbled down a slope and landed in a depression underneath a large, thorny bush. From its size and shape, Jordan guessed it to be the den of an animal. She lay there, breathing in the chilly night air laced heavily with the tang of iron and musk.

The sudden crack of a twig was her only warning before a massive hand reached in, grabbing a fistful of her shirt. Jordan twisted, reaching for something to hang on to, but the man was bigger, stronger. He jerked her from the hidey-hole, scraping her face and hands on long spines that covered the shrub.

When she was clear, Jordan's eyes travelled up, taking in well-worn boots, jeans, a plaid shirt, and shoulders that could collapse a doorway. She didn't need to see his face to know who stood over her, waiting to take her life – but she had a hard time believing it.

"Please," she begged. "Don't do this." Warm tears quickly cooled as they ran back into her matted hair. "I'm not the monster you think I am."

There was a glint of silver, but Jordan chose to concentrate on the youthful face, tousled hair, and hazel-green eyes she knew so well – the ones that always seem to be smiling, but not tonight.

The moon illuminated the deadly arc of the blade as it swung down. "I love you," she whispered right before it sank into her throat.

And Nathan's face, wrenched and marred with hate, winked once in her faltering vision like a dying star, and faded away.

*No!* Jordan shrieked in her head, shoving the vision

away. *My brother loves me. That will never happen.*

*But it will. You are different now, and they will come to see just how much. Awkwardness will lead to fear. Fear will lead to resentment. In the end, they'll kill you to save their own sanity. And then, there is the prophecy.*

What fresh hell was this? Wary, positive that she didn't want to know but had no choice, Jordan asked, *What prophecy?*

There was a pause and static filled her head. She didn't think he was going to answer. Part of her was relieved, but the feeling was short lived.

*It is written in the book – the one Michael is so desperate to get his hands on. It speaks of a* Paladin *who falls when she slays an angel. One of the greatest sins among celestial beings is for one to take the life of another. According to the prophecy, when the* Paladin *falls, it starts a holy war between angels and demons. Unfortunately, much of this war takes place on earth and humans...well, humans pay the biggest price.*

Confused, Jordan said, *But I did nothing wrong! Illyria tried to kill my brother. Surely, Heaven has rules. Angels can't just swoop down and kill innocent humans because it's more convenient than negotiating.*

*It isn't so much that you killed her, but* why. *If you acted out of self defense or to protect an innocent, the prophecy will not come to pass-*

*-I did!* Jordan said.

*But,* he went on, *if you killed her out of anger – for revenge – that is a sin. You are not allowed to play judge, jury, and executioner when it comes to an angel. When you struck her down, you thought your brother was dead.*

*Yeah, so? He was still innocent of any crime.* With a rapidly sinking heart, Jordan wondered where he was going with this.

*You can't justify killing the angel with a claim of defending an innocent when you believed the innocent was already dead.*

And there it was, her sin displayed for the entire world. She may as well be wearing one of those sandwich boards around her neck with big letters spelling out, I KILLED ILLYRIA BECAUSE I WANTED HER TO FUCKING PAY FOR WHAT SHE DID TO MY BROTHER!!! It was so obvious Stevie Wonder could see it, and the hornblowers upstairs would, too.

*What if you're lying?*

She'd give one of her kidneys, her Mustang, and every Daughtry CD she owned for him to admit he was. Somehow, she didn't think she'd have to mourn the lack of her favorite band's music or worry over the condition of her blood because one kidney may not get the job done.

*Ask your Guardian and your brother if you must, but once they confirm what I've told you, it is imperative that you come to me. You killed an angel. Michael hunted you enthusiastically before but that is nothing compared to what he'll do now. He will be ruthless. Because you are part angel, he will think he has the right to oversee your punishment. Because you are part demon,* we *will not allow it.*

*Michael will poison the minds of your human family. In turn, they will destroy your Cambion family one by one, making you watch…and then, they will kill you. The earth will burn. Many humans will die—"*

*Shut up!* Jordan screamed.

She didn't want to hear anymore. He had to be lying. She could understand her actions causing a holy war if she was some big-time demon who killed every innocent and angel she came across, but she was only a teenager – one who acted in the best interests of her family. If she hadn't killed Illyria, the angel may have gone for Ivy next. It wasn't her fault!

*Jordan, you are not to blame. Unlike angels, you understand the importance of family and the desire to keep yours safe.* He huffed and the sound bounced around in her head like a pinball. *And they call us monsters.*

*There may be a way to stop this but I will need your help. I can protect you here, and your family will be safe with Gabriel. We'll find a way to make it right.*

The world came back to her in a rush of sound and light. Quinn was shaking her arm, yelling in her face. When she made eye contact, he sucked in a deep breath and let it out slowly.

"I swear to God, Jordan, you're gonna be the death of me! I've been calling your name for the past five minutes. Are you okay?"

Instead of answering, she turned to Gabe. "Is there a prophecy about me in that book?"

Her Guardian neither confirmed nor denied her query. When she saw the tentative glance he threw around the room to everyone else, he didn't have to.

Jordan's blood turned to ice.

"There is, isn't there?" she asked. "When I killed Illyria, I…fell. I committed the ultimate sin that will start a war and you said nothing! Why didn't you tell me?!"

Her voice was loud enough to bring down what was left of the ceiling. The sheer power of it caused everyone, including Gabe, to flinch.

"I had a right to know! This is my life, dammit, but because an angel and a demon possessed my parents, everything I do now has a consequence. My one act of vengeance will be the death of countless humans and it could have been prevented if you'd just *told me the truth*!"

Anger bubbled inside her like an unwatched pot of potatoes left too long on the burner. It spilled over the sides, hissing and spitting when it touched her core. Jordan's eyes blazed pearl-white. She was in demon mode now.

Gabe held up his hands, a placating gesture that did nothing to ease her fury. "Let me explain."

"*Now* you want to explain?" she asked. "Too little too late, Gabe."

"Listen to me!" His eyes went from golden hazel to gleaming blue in a flash, irritating her more. "If you killed Illyria to protect Quinn there is nothing to worry about. It was in defense of an innocent."

She laughed at his false hope even though part of her wanted to curl up and die. She felt a shift in her psyche that was both exhilarating and frightening. Love and Hate tugged her in opposite directions, both promising her something if they won.

"I thought he was dead," she spat, hurling the words like daggers. "I wanted her to pay for what she did! There were no thoughts of protecting anyone by the time I made the decision to fry her – there was only revenge." She flung her head back and screamed up at the heavens. "Did you hear that, you bastards? I killed your precious Aeon because she deserved it!"

"Oh, God," Gabriel breathed.

Rolling her eyes, Jordan said, "Yeah, you keep praying to Him. Maybe He'll hear you one day."

Ivy stepped forward. "What about me?" she asked, addressing Gabriel. "If Jordan hadn't killed the angel, I'm sure I would've been next on her shit list. She was like a starving person with a bag of Lays chips – there's no way she was stopping at one."

Trying to ignore the pull from both ends, Jordan

said, "That might work if they considered you an innocent, Ivy, but they don't. To the angels, we're just damaged goods – vessels without souls. If Illyria had killed you, Michael probably would have given her a raise and a shiny new plaque for her wall."

"You're not helping," Quinn said with a scowl.

"By keeping all this from me, neither did you," she shot back.

The tugging grew stronger. She felt too thin, stretched to the point of snapping in two. Jordan had no idea what to do. If she stayed, she would put her entire family through hell and her head on a chopping block. If she left, if she went to *him*, the future was unknown and she wasn't comfortable with more uncertainties in her life.

*If you come to me, I will try to help stop this war. Together, we are the best chance humanity has.*

*What do you care of humanity? You're a demon.*

Suddenly, she saw him in her head. He was beautiful, perfect, like a god. Snow-white wings, blinding in their pureness, hurt her eyes as they unfolded slowly on either side of his strong shoulders. The urge to go to him was almost painful.

*Oh, Jordan, I am much more than that.*

She nodded, dazed by the vision. Inside, she felt something snap. The tug-o'-war ended in exquisite pain as a mark was placed upon her soul – *his* mark.

*To the victor go the spoils.*

When she came back to herself, Gabriel was

talking. Quinn and Ivy paid close attention to his words but Xander was staring at her. He was concerned, but there was something else, as well. The flared nostrils, downturned mouth, and clenched fists told her he *knew*...and he wasn't happy.

"Jordan, no!" he screamed.

Their special connection made it possible for Xander to feel every emotion she did. Jordan had forgotten all about it. He reached out while Quinn, Ivy, and Gabe scanned the factory for an enemy they couldn't see.

"Don't do this," Xander begged. "Fight him! You're stronger than this."

"What the fuck is going on?" Quinn asked. "Fight who?"

Jordan ignored her brother. For the moment, there was only Xander. He pleaded with her without needing to say a word, and she tried to recall why he was so important to her. The memories were hazy, as if they took place on a bright, sunny day but she was reviewing them at dusk. She felt a pang of regret. It wasn't because she was leaving him. The feelings she once had for Xander no longer had any substance. No, the regret she felt was for what she'd lost, and knowing she would probably never get it back.

"Please, Jordan," he whispered. "You can't leave me." Tears pooled in his eyes and she felt a ghost of the emotions he used to evoke in her.

"I don't have a choice."

Quinn slammed his hand down on the crippled table beside her, making dust fly into the air. "If someone doesn't tell me what the hell is going on I'm going to get my gun and shoot all of you in the leg."

Xander approached slowly and, when she didn't object or try to zap him, gently pulled her into his arms. Jordan was as pliable as a two by four but he didn't let go.

"Try to remember," he said softly. "This isn't who you are. He doesn't care about you – he doesn't care about anyone other than himself. He wants to use your power."

Wrapped in his embrace, the muddy thoughts cleared and Jordan caught a brief glimpse of *before*. Desperate, she dug and tore at the façade, clawing for purchase, but the tiny holes she managed filled back up just as quickly. It was no use. What she desired lay at the bottom of a sandpit and the walls kept crumbling.

She cried out in frustration. Time was running out and Jordan knew she only had seconds before she'd be buried again – her true feelings concealed under layers of lies and false promises. She reached up and touched Xander's face, memorized the color and shape of his eyes, focused on every blemish and line, softly kissed his lips. It was all she could take with her. Xander couldn't break the hold Orias had on her now but she knew, one day, he would.

"Save me," she managed in a strangled sob.

Xander's eyes glowed with a passionate, almost savage light – an affirmation that he understood…and she was finally able to let go.

As she faded from the room, teleporting from the people she loved, from a life she might never know again, Jordan saw Xander kiss the tips of his fingers and hold them out. He was sending his heart with her.

# XXXIII Quinn

The farmhouse was too crowded or maybe it was just him.

He was tired of strangers in business suits and polished wingtips that clashed horribly with their worn furniture and T-shirts. He was tired of waiting for information. He was tired of doing *nothing* while the fate of his sister and the world balanced on the head of a pin.

Quinn's knees bounced up and down, jostling Ivy, who sat next to him on the couch. He couldn't be still. He needed to move, to act, to escape this room filled with tension and dashed hopes.

At a slight pressure on his leg, he looked down. In a gesture totally out of character for her, Ivy reached over and gave his knee a reassuring squeeze. They'd done nothing but argue since she'd moved in a few days before. Like flint on stone, they couldn't be within ten feet of each other without causing sparks, igniting everything in their paths. Uncle Case had threatened to make both of them move into the barn if it didn't stop.

It surprised Quinn to find comfort in her touch now. The fact that they'd been sitting beside each other for almost an hour without drawing blood was a testament to just how serious things were. To occupy his mind, Quinn reflected on the events of the past week.

After Jordan disappeared from the factory, he had lost it. There was yelling, and accusations thrown, along with a few punches. The last thing he remembered was Xander's blood splattered all over his shirt. Gabe then took it upon himself to work some angel mojo and knocked Quinn out cold. He woke up in his own bed a day later.

The house had since been a flurry of demons, angels, wards, and information – some useful, some not. On a rare night when things were relatively quiet, he, Nathan, and Case converged in the study. Amidst mugs of steaming coffee and a bottle of Jameson's finest, they told Quinn what they'd learned while he visited La-La land, courtesy of their friendly neighborhood Guardian.

"Jordan's in Purgatory."

Nathan took a sip of coffee and glanced at his watch, as if their sister had simply run down to the

Quik-Stop for a gallon of milk and would be back any minute.

On the other side of the refectory table, Quinn frowned. Surely, he'd heard wrong. Maybe it was the lingering effects of the magic Gabe had used.

*Purgatory?*

He wrapped his hands around the warm mug in front of him and waited.

Casen laced his nearly empty cup with a glug of whiskey. When his uncle set the bottle down with more force than was necessary, the sound of glass against hardwood had been comparable to a gunshot in the silent room. He removed his battered Stetson and scratched his head.

"Apparently, Jordan and Xander have...or *had*...some sort of psychic connection. He could tune in to her emotions. He told Gabe that while she was zoned out in the factory, he felt an outside force invade her mind." Case fingered the brim of his hat and sighed. "When Jordan teleported, Xander had a feeling Purgatory was her destination. When Gabe asked how certain he was, the boy said, '"I should know, I used to live there."'"

Xander may have had the 4-1-1 on his old stomping ground but knew little about the "demon" who took him in. When Gabe learned of Jordan's whereabouts, he questioned Xander on his home and family.

"I don't have any family," the Cambion

shrugged. "I was taken from the orphanage by a demon and sent to Orias."

Gabe sank to the floor. "There is only one being in Purgatory who does not belong there. My father condemned Orias to the planet of Lost Souls a long time ago." He paused, a distant look in his eyes. "He is my brother. His real name is Lucifer."

Some of the pieces began to come together and formed the beginnings of a grim picture. By this time, everyone – including Aamon – knew about the prophecy. Nathan had read it so many times he could recite it by heart.

*There will come a day when grace shall be returned to the Watchers of the world. They will rise from their prisons and walk the Earth. They will gain followers of great importance and take their fight to the Heavens. A holy war unlike any before will commence between Good and Evil. The beginning and end will depend upon the decision of a* Paladin. *Her fall shall mark them both.*

*A* Paladin's *blood, given freely, is the key to Lucifer's cell.* The Book of Shadow and Light *is the guide. Many lives will be lost. Good and Evil must work together to safeguard Earth and her people. The* Paladin's *soul must be lifted from darkness by her equal in order for her to descend. Only then can the war be ended.*

"Lucifer called Jordan to his side because he needs her blood to escape prison in Purgatory. Her fall made it possible for him to compel her." Gabe had explained.

"But how did Lucifer know Jordan killed Illyria?" Ivy asked. "He's locked in a house on another planet."

"Perhaps he was connected somehow. Maybe an informer keeping tabs on your group–"

"There were no other demons around," Ivy interrupted. "I would have felt them."

Gabe sat up straight. "Did Lucifer insist on giving you any personal effects?"

Ivy shook her head, frowning at Xander's grave expression when he stepped from a shadowy corner of the room.

"Yes, he did." His voice was soft, hoarse, like rustling leaves. "Orias gave Jordan a pendant to wear. He called it the Third Pentacle of Jupiter and said it was for protection."

"That's one of the magical seals of Solomon," Gabe said. "What did it look like?" Xander recounted the specifics of the silver charm.

The angel groaned. "That isn't the Third Pentacle; it's the Fifth. It would have left Jordan open to visions, both to send and receive them. There are forty-four seals that we know of. With a few spectral alterations, any number of them could have served Lucifer, even in Purgatory."

"What exactly are these seals?" Quinn had asked.

Nathan cleared his throat and raised his hand.

"Really?" Quinn shook his head as his brother answered in textbook form.

"King Solomon possessed the power of nature and the spiritual world. Many believe he was given insight from an archangel to create the seals. Solomon used the seals in rituals. According to ancient Lore, he called upon spirits and requested their help to achieve honest and impartial goals."

Quinn rolled his eyes. "Thank you, Hermione."

"My knowledge of the seals is limited," Gabe said. "We can only hope the same of Lucifer."

Taking the words of the prophecy at face value, Gabe had insisted on bringing Aamon into the fold.

"If Lucifer rises, Good and Evil will have to work together to protect humans. We need every able-bodied being we can get, regardless of status," he'd argued when Quinn questioned the decision. In a softer tone, he continued, "I know Aamon killed your father but Ivy says he truly loves Jordan. We must put differences aside now. This war could test us in ways we never thought possible. If we are divided, *we will fail*."

It was also Gabe's brilliant idea to have Ivy and Xander close by. He couldn't be there all the time himself, and wanted someone on the premises who could teleport them away if danger came knocking.

The Cambions' impressive powers, he said, made them assets.

Quinn's eyes moved around the room and settled on Xander. The guy sat on the floor by the fireplace, absently scratching Koda behind the ears (leave it to Jordan to befriend a wild animal and bring it home). Xander didn't talk much, and spent most of his time wandering outside the farmhouse.

The day before, he'd stumbled upon Quinn working on the Charger. When Xander poked his head in the makeshift garage and saw who was inside, he quickly apologized and started to move on.

Quinn had suddenly felt sorry for him. It was obvious Xander blamed himself for Jordan's predicament. He walked around with a faraway look in his eyes, trying to reach her through their bond. So far, he had been unsuccessful. Gabe explained that Purgatory was built with isolation in mind. Special wards ensured none of the monsters that called it home could escape. It would be damned near impossible for Xander to reach her there.

"Hey," Quinn called when the guy's head disappeared around the corner of the shed. "You like cars?"

He wasn't sure what made him reach out when he hadn't given two shits for the guy since he'd been there. Maybe it was because he'd punched him in the factory. Maybe it was the desperation and loss that seemed to follow Xander around like a dark cloud. He looked out of sorts, not knowing how to fit in.

Xander shuffled back to the open doorway and focused on a spot above Quinn's shoulder. "I'm sorry," he muttered. "What did you say?"

Quinn put down his wrench and wiped his hands on an old towel. "I asked if you like cars."

"I've never had one," Xander admitted, red creeping into his face.

He eyeballed the Charger with a hungry gleam in his eyes. It was the first time Quinn had seen him show interest in anything since he'd arrived. He knew Xander had grown up in an orphanage before he'd been carted off to Purgatory. There were probably a lot of things he never had.

Quinn realized how lucky he was. He'd grown up in a house where people loved him. They weren't rich by any means but he'd never gone without. He couldn't imagine being raised by strangers, sleeping in crowded dorm rooms with no privacy, or never having enough to eat. His stomach twisted with guilt, reminding him once again what a douche he could be.

"Yours looks pretty cool, though," Xander continued. "There was a janitor at the orphanage who mopped the floors and took out trash with a copy of *Hot Rod* magazine rolled up in his back pocket. He'd leave it on the table by my bed when he finished reading it. I'd sit and look at it for hours."

Quinn motioned him inside. "My car's a hot mess right now," he said with a pang of regret.

"Can you fix it?" Xander asked.

"Yeah," Quinn replied. "I built her from the ground up. When it comes to cars, I can fix anything."

Eyes wide, Xander whistled.

Quinn smiled and waved him closer. It was hard not to like a guy who could appreciate good 'ol American steel and big engines.

Shaking off the memory, Quinn dragged his laggard mind back to the present. The living room held the semblance of a wake. Whispers circulated like sinister spirits aroused by apprehension. Uncle Case and Nathan spoke quietly in the doorway. Aamon and two other demons conversed with heavy expressions while sipping coffee by the bookcase. Every so often their eyes flashed white, and Quinn reached for his knife out of habit.

A few weeks before, Quinn had left the farmhouse because his uncle had allowed what they thought was a demon to be summoned inside a

Devil's trap in the basement. Now the fuckers roamed around freely, day and night. He would never trust them and the feeling was mutual. The Baileys' history in the Circle was legendary. Demons knew what they were capable of, and grudgingly respected them for it.

Still, demons in their house…

The sound of wings made everyone abandon their conversations and look around expectantly. Gabe popped into the room and nodded in greeting. Quinn held his breath. This was why they had gathered together. They were hoping for information, something to hang onto, to build on.

Gabe had finally been able to contact some bigwig angel he'd been in touch with by the name of Yasen. It hadn't been easy. Michael, furious over the loss of his Aeon and *The Oraculum,* had launched a massive search for his brother, Jordan, and her families – both human and demon. News of the archangel's actions travelled to the higher-ups (Gabe called them Virtues) and they'd shut Michael down. Unfortunately, this had done nothing for his disposition. Gabe had confessed to Quinn that he felt certain they'd not heard the last of the archangel.

Regardless, there was still a war to prepare for. They would deal with Michael when they crossed that bridge. Quinn hoped it wouldn't be for a while.

"Gabriel," Aamon said, grasping the angel's forearm in a show of solidarity and good faith. "Do you have any news of my daughter?"

Quinn resisted the urge to gut the demon like a fish. It chafed like a pair of wet jeans to admit it, but he could not deny the love Aamon had for his children. After learning what had happened at the factory, Quinn thought Aamon would have a heart attack (if demons could suffer from that sort of thing). He'd cursed and cried – the tears as genuine as any Quinn had ever seen – then disappeared. The demon had returned an hour later, despair hanging on him like a suit three times too large. Shoulders drooping, pain etched upon his face, he'd told them he'd tried to get into Purgatory to confront Orias/Lucifer and retrieve Jordan but the portal had been closed.

"I do have news," Gabe said. He motioned to the empty spot beside Ivy on the couch. "Please, Aamon, sit down. As far as we know, she is okay. Lucifer won't harm her – he needs her to help him fight this war."

"But he will, especially if she refuses to do his bidding!" Aamon took a deep breath. Quinn could tell he was trying to pull it together but the demon's eyes moved wildly around the room, jumping from one person to another. "You know Jordan," he said to no one in particular. "She's strong, independent. Can you imagine her reaction when Lucifer demands she give her blood, shed her morals, and help him take over the universe? He'll have to resort to violence.

She won't give him a choice."

He sank onto the couch, limp and lifeless. Quinn could imagine the demon slipping between the cushions. Ivy put her arms around her father, shushing him like one would an upset child. She had taken on the role of parent.

"You're forgetting one thing, Aamon." Nathan spoke from his place near the door. "Jordan is a *Paladin* with powers second only to God. If Lucifer pushes too hard, she'll reduce him to a crimson puddle at her feet." He turned to their uncle, who was clearly shaken by the talk of torture. Case's hat had turned into a misshapen lump of material he twisted back and forth in his hands. Nathan took it away before he could ruin it completely and then curse half the night about the loss of his most favorite object. "Let's not look for trouble where there may not be any. We have enough to deal with as it is."

When Gabe had their full attention, he pulled at his collar and took a sheet of paper from his pocket. He glanced at Xander, then cleared his throat twice. Quinn wondered why he was so nervous.

"Well, um…as you all know, Yasen has been searching diligently for any notes on *Paladins* that he might have in his possession. Today, he found something."

Gabriel unfolded the paper with clumsy hands. Dread settled in the pit of Quinn's stomach. *God, we don't need any more bad news*, he thought.

"I wrote down the information and think it would be best if I read it verbatim. These words were written by my Father." Gabe cleared his throat once more and began.

*"There cannot be Good without Evil. It is a delicate balance that must be maintained. At times, one grows greater than the other. It has become increasingly more difficult to recover that balance when it is lost. Every event in our past has led up to this moment – this incredible war.*

*"I knew Jordan would face many trials and tribulations and would need guidance. I sent for one of my most trusted angels, and Samuel did come. I requested of him the greatest sacrifice an angel can make; I asked him to fall. Samuel agreed and went to Earth. Per my instructions, he waited for a specific vessel – a woman who was corrupt, for she had lain with a demon and sold her soul for riches and fame. Samuel possessed this woman and passed his grace to her unborn child.*

*He remains on Earth, for his job is not yet finished.*

*"On the night the child was born, a demon arrived to claim the woman's soul. Her son's birth, and her death, happened within seconds of each other. Eventually, the child came to live with Evil but does not hold evil within his heart.*

*"I explained to Samuel that one day this boy will*

*come to him for answers. He will know what to say when that time comes."*

Gabe stopped reading and the room suddenly came alive again. Everyone spoke at once.

Who was the child?

What did it all mean?

Uncle Case whistled loudly and called for silence.

"Is there more, Gabe?" he asked.

The angel nodded, his eyes travelling back to the page. In a shaky voice, he concluded,

*"The child shall be known as Xander. He is the first* Paladin*, Jordan's equal, and the only one capable of saving her soul."*

And the prophecy says: *The* Paladin's *soul must be lifted from darkness by her equal in order for her to descend. Only then can the war be ended.*

Thank you for reading *Refracted* (The Celadon Circle Book Two).

If you enjoyed this book, please consider leaving a review where you bought it and also on Goodreads. (https://www.goodreads.com/).

# Acknowledgements

It takes more than an author with a keyboard and an idea to complete a book. In regards to *Refracted*, it took an entire village – and my part was made much easier by these wonderfully talented, caring individuals. I'm so blessed to have you in my corner, and honored to call you my friends. Love you bunches!

To Donna Bossert: thank you for the late-night phone chats when I couldn't find my way from point A to point B. Your insight, humor, and brilliant ideas kept me from a padded cell and fashionable jacket with buckles down the back.

To Leland Dirks: many thanks and hugs for your unyielding support and help with my work. You always believe in me, even when I don't.

To Grace Guerra: my books would be ideas and nothing more if it weren't for your encouragement and love. Thank you for being the sister I've always wished for.

To Team Refracted: I couldn't ask for better beta readers! Your patience, honesty, and enthusiasm are what kept me focused and motivated. Jeannine Verderosa, Grace Schrieffer, Donna Bossert, Grace Guerra, Courtney Rhoda, Mandy White, Sherry Molteni, Mandy Moore, Sandee Barry, and Cheryl Morton, I hope we have many more adventures together!

To the Books Untamed Posse: thank you for your love, guidance, and friendship. I'm blessed to be included in this writing circle.

To Gary Ray Anderson: words can't express how much I appreciate your support. Thank you for sharing my books with others.

To Mark Johnson: thank you for naming my antagonist. "Illyria" was perfect for a beautiful angel with murderous streak. LOL!

To Yvonne Hertzberger: I'm stubborn, I know. Thank you for your time and wisdom.

To Sean Sweeney, Rich Meyer, and Terry Simpson: I love you guys! Thanks so much for your support, humor, and big hearts.

To Silviya Yordanova: as always, thank you for the amazing cover art. You never disappoint!

To Hubby and our Children (of the corn): times will always be hard for us. Thank you for never suggesting that I go out and get a "real job." I love you to the moon and back!

And last, but *never* least on my list, to my readers: thank you for giving my books wings to fly.

Until next time ...

*Nicole*
*June, 2015*

# About the Author

Nicole Storey lives in Georgia with her amazing husband, two prodigious children, and three spoiled cats. When she isn't travelling to distant lands with potty-mouthed pixies or fighting demons, she conspires with angels to keep the world safe from Evil.

Nicole is an award-winning and Amazon bestselling author of juvenile fantasy and young adult urban fantasy books.

Nicole greatly appreciates her readers. You can connect with her at these links:
Website and Blog:
http://www.nicolestoreyauthor.com/
Facebook:
https://www.facebook.com/nicolestoreyfans
Twitter: @Nicole_Storey
https://twitter.com/Nicole_Storey
Goodreads:
https://www.goodreads.com/author/show/5155575.Nicole_Storey
Amazon: http://www.amazon.com/Nicole-Storey/e/B005J8CKPG/

**Other Books by Nicole:**

***Grimsley Hollow Series***
*The Chosen One* (Grimsley Hollow Book One)
*Eve of the Beginning* (Grimsley Hollow Book Two)
*The Search for Siren* (Grimsley Hollow Book Three)

***Celadon Circle Series***
*Blind Sight* (Celadon Circle Book One)

*The Longest Days of Night*, the fourth book in the *Grimsley Hollow* series, will be released spring/summer 2016!